"Call me crazy, but I'm actually feeling relieved now."

"Relieved? How are you relieved? Because the prank wasn't aimed at you?"

"No. Because you weren't the one who was the instigator. For a while there I thought maybe you really disliked me, or at least that you didn't want me opening the spa. I want to make sure you're sticking around this time because you see the potential in what I'm doing and not because of some misplaced sense of obligation. That stupid auction means nothing. You know that, right?"

Nick glanced over at Vivian. She was such a striking woman, with her golden hair silhouetted against the moonlight in the dark cab, that his breath snagged in his throat. He wasn't certain he was staying for *all* the right reasons...definitely not for the genuine motives Vivian was suggesting.

No—he was starting to think he was sticking around for the *wrong* reasons. He was feeling all muddled up inside his head. Confused. Part of him felt like bolting. And yet he couldn't even consider walking away.

A *Publishers Weekly* bestselling and award-winning author of over forty novels, with almost two million books in print, **Deb Kastner** enjoys writing contemporary inspirational Western stories set in small communities. Deb lives in beautiful Colorado with her husband, miscreant mutts and curious kitties. She is blessed with three adult daughters and two grandchildren. Her favorite hobby is spoiling her grandchildren, but she also enjoys reading, watching movies, listening to music (The Texas Tenors are her favorite), singing in the church choir and exploring the Rocky Mountains on horseback.

Carolyne Aarsen and her husband, Richard, live on a small ranch in northern Alberta, where they have raised four children and numerous foster children and are still raising cattle. Carolyne crafts her stories in an office with a large west-facing window, through which she can watch the changing seasons while struggling to make her words obey.

Mistletoe Daddy

Deb Kastner

&

The Cowboy's Christmas Baby

Carolyne Aarsen

LOVE INSPIRED

INSPIRATIONAL ROMANCE

LOVE INSPIRED®
INSPIRATIONAL ROMANCE

PLEASE RECYCLE · THIS PRODUCT IS RECYCLABLE

Recycling programs for this product may not exist in your area.

ISBN-13: 978-1-335-42502-7

Mistletoe Daddy and The Cowboy's Christmas Baby

Copyright © 2021 by Harlequin Books S.A.

Mistletoe Daddy
First published in 2016. This edition published in 2021.
Copyright © 2016 by Debra Kastner

The Cowboy's Christmas Baby
First published in 2016. This edition published in 2021.
Copyright © 2016 by Carolyne Aarsen

This edition published by arrangement with Harlequin Books S.A.

For questions and comments about the quality of this book, please contact us at CustomerService@Harlequin.com.

Love Inspired
22 Adelaide St. West, 40th Floor
Toronto, Ontario M5H 4E3, Canada
www.LoveInspired.com

Printed in U.S.A.

CONTENTS

MISTLETOE DADDY

Deb Kastner

For Isabella and Anthony,
who show by your innocent faith what it
really means to make loving sacrifices to the Lord.

Through Him then, let us continually offer God a
sacrifice of praise, that is, the fruit of lips
that confess His name. Do not neglect to do good
and to share what you have; God is pleased
with sacrifices of that kind.

—*Hebrews* 13:15–16

Chapter One

"Texas men are built like bricks and so good lookin', don't you think? Especially these here McKenna boys," elderly Jo Spencer crowed. The cheerful crowd gathered on the community green for the first annual Bachelors and Baskets auction clapped their agreement.

Jo swept her arm, gesturing from the top of Nick's black cowboy hat down to the toes of his boots. "Just feast your eyes on this handsome guy."

Vivian Grainger was definitely looking, though *feasting* wouldn't have been the word she would have used.

Critically assessing would be more accurate. She was trying to decide if Nick McKenna was the right man for the construction contractor job she had to fill. After all, that's what made this auction different from most of the ones she'd heard of before. The organizers weren't auctioning off *dates* with the men who had volunteered. Even the married men were auctioning themselves off for charity. Instead, the men agreed to perform some task or chore for the women who "bought" them. One of Nick's brothers, Slade, had been the first man auctioned off, and when his wife, Laney, won him, she'd announced that he'd be doing dishes and laundry for a month. In turn, the ladies offered a picnic lunch for their winning bid—hence the Bachelors and Baskets theme.

Vivian could handle her own dishes and laundry, but building construction was out of her skill set. Was Nick up for the job? She knew he was a rancher by trade, but from what she'd heard around town, he had major skills in carpentry and remodeling. Vivian needed to shave costs wherever she could but didn't want to sacrifice on quality, since her shop would be her main career focus for the rest of her working life.

"You think his brothers Slade and Jax have muscles?" Jo asked with a delighted cackle. The auction had been Jo's brainchild in the first place, a way to help raise funds for a new long-term care facility and senior center for Serendipity, so naturally she was emceeing the event. And she was clearly taking great delight in parading all these handsome men across her platform.

Jo prodded Nick's biceps with an appreciative whistle that made a dash of color rise to the poor man's face—or at least as much of his face as Vivian could see under his dark layer of scruffy whiskers. Viv's fingers itched to grab a pair of shears and a straight razor and clean him up a bit, if nothing else so she could see what she was really buying. She smothered a chuckle.

"Nick here is the biggest, brawniest of the three McKennas, and let me tell you, that's really saying something."

Indeed, it was, Viv thought with a smirk. All three McKenna brothers stood head and shoulders over most of the other men in Serendipity, and with Nick's deeply tanned, unshaven face and thick black hair long enough to brush the collar of his blue-checked Western shirt, he looked more like a mountain man than a rancher. What really made him stand out were his blue eyes, a pop of color against a background of darkness.

Not that she noticed.

Vivian flipped open her notepad and yanked out the pencil that was holding her bun together, causing a waterfall of straight bleached-blond hair to cascade down her shoulders. If a person looked close enough they might see the thinnest stripe of bright pink on a strand of hair on the right, Vivian's little gift to herself to make her stand out from her identical twin sister, Alexis. Viv had always been the wilder of the two, and even now Alexis was settled down with a husband while Vivian…

Wasn't. And she wasn't going to acknowledge the twinge in her gut whenever she thought about it, either.

She threw her head to the side to brush her hair off of her face and eyed the list she'd made in anticipation of the auction. She immediately checked off several items, just as she'd known she would. She'd narrowed down the list of potential candidates from the list of eligible bachelors that had been posted at Cup O' Jo's Café a week before the auction. Nick was currently at the top of her inventory list.

Strong?

Yes, Nick McKenna was pure, lean, unadulterated muscle. There was not an inch of flab on his whole body. She scratched through that requirement. Nick didn't even need to flex his powerful biceps for them to ripple underneath the rolled-up sleeves of his shirt.

Tall and broad-shouldered, Vivian guessed that he stood around six foot four and weighed a good 220 pounds at least. Those beefy arms of his were practically bigger than her waist—or at least, her prepregnancy midsection. At three months along, her once-tiny tummy was now starting to swell with new life.

She laid a protective hand over her abdomen. She wouldn't be able to hide her secret from the public much longer, which was exactly why she needed help to get her business up and running, and the sooner, the better. In this day and age a single mother didn't stand out as much as she once would have, but even if no one else judged her, it made a difference to her. She had betrayed everything she had once believed in, even when she knew it was wrong. She was ashamed to return to her hometown unmarried and pregnant, but with no way to provide for her baby, she'd had no other choice.

Creating a successful business, proving she could make a good life for her and her child, would hopefully show the folks she knew and loved that she meant to make her life right with God. From this point forward, there was no way to go but up.

But was Nick the right one to help her?

She'd been told he was good with a hammer. His ability to remodel was the most important qualification she required and it was the reason Nick was at the top of her list. She'd asked around town and had discovered he'd not only overseen the remodeling of his mother's house but had built from the ground up two adjacent cabins on his ranch land for himself and one of his brothers.

He knew construction and carpentry, which was just what she needed.

It was *not* one of her conditions that he be handsome…

Jo seemed to think that was the most important prerequisite in a man—any man. Vivian chuckled under her breath and tapped the eraser against her bottom lip thoughtfully as she evaluated the man standing square-shouldered on the auction block, his expression grim but confident.

No, Nick wasn't handsome. Not in the classic sense of the word, anyway. Still, Vivian had to wonder why Serendipity's single ladies weren't bidding up a storm on him right now. He wasn't Vivian's type, by any means, but if a woman liked the rugged-cowboy look— and she knew that many in Serendipity did—he fit the bill perfectly.

Granted, he could do with a haircut and a shave, which was both amusing and ironic, given the project she had in mind for him to help her build.

A beauty salon and spa. She couldn't help but smile to herself.

She knew that many of the single women in the crowd intended to bid on attractive, unattached bachelors not for help with projects, but for love's sake, or at least the possibility of it. But dating and falling in love was the farthest thing from Vivian's mind.

It didn't matter to her at all that Nick wasn't classically handsome. His attractiveness, or lack of, wasn't even on her list, and with good reason.

She wanted nothing—*nothing*—to do with men, handsome or otherwise. She'd been burned to a crisp in her last relationship. Her ex-boyfriend, Derrick, wouldn't even acknowledge that the baby she now carried was his, rejecting both her and their precious off-spring.

It was no wonder she didn't trust men as far as she could throw them. Hopefully Nick wasn't looking for a relationship through participating in the auction, because if her bid won he would be sadly disappointed if he was. Viv's thoughts were purely business oriented. That her money was going to fund a good cause—the town senior center—made her investment all the more worthwhile.

Her intention was to try and save a few dollars by not having to hire a professional contractor. Instead, she would use a skillful amateur who knew what he was doing and could get the job done as quickly and easily as possible.

"Which of you lovely young ladies out there is going to open their purses for this fine fellow?" Jo urged when no one jumped forward to bid on Nick. "Shame on you. What's taking you so long?"

Viv paused and swallowed hard, wondering if she really wanted to do this. She only knew Nick in passing—but that was enough to know he had a reputation for being as surly as the grizzly bear he resembled if you caught him in a bad mood. And based on that scowl on his face, he was in a lousy mood right now. Did she really want to inflict that on herself?

She could turn around and walk away from this auction right now and hire a professional to do the work on her salon—someone from out of town who wouldn't know or judge her—but with all the extra expenses of having a newborn, she needed to save money every way she could. She squeezed her eyes shut and raised her hand.

"Three hundred dollars." She grimaced when her voice came out high and squeaky.

She'd planned to bid low to start, expecting there to be other ladies throwing their hats into the loop. She wasn't sure what a bachelor like Nick would go for, but three hundred seemed a reasonable guess. She had five hundred dollars in her pocket and was prepared to bid higher, but she was still having second thoughts about bidding for Nick at all. Maybe she needed to rethink this and select someone less intimidating. There was something about Nick that unnerved her.

Deciding she wouldn't bid any higher, she waited for another woman to raise the stakes and let her off the hook. Surely Nick was worth more than she'd offered. Someone truly interested in him would be sure to bid more. She held her breath.

And waited.

It was so silent she could have heard a barrette drop. She slowly counted to ten, but no one else spoke up.

Which meant she was stuck with Nick, whether she wanted to be or not.

Vivian briefly considered backing out of her bid, but she didn't want to make a big production out of this. The last thing she wanted was to call extra attention to herself, and she didn't want to embarrass Nick. It wasn't his fault she was feeling wishy-washy.

She'd made her choice and, for better or for worse, she was going to stick with it. She shouldn't second-guess herself. This was a better option than hiring a professional. And while there were other men on the docket she could have bid for instead, Nick had the best credentials for what she needed, so Nick it would be.

"Are you serious?" Nick asked the crowd when no one piped up with a higher amount. He gestured with his fingers, encouraging further bids. "Somebody? Anybody?"

Clearly he expected the women in the crowd to be clamoring for his time and attention. How conceited was that? And what was so wrong with her that he wanted to get bids from anybody else? Viv didn't know whether or not she should be offended, but frankly, the way he was acting hurt her feelings. He was practically begging for anyone else besides her to bid on him.

Was she really that bad?

Then again, it could be that he was just trying to make more money for the senior center. She considered that notion for a moment and then tossed it aside, going back to her conclusion that he had a big ego to go along with that big head of his. He probably thought the ladies ought to be crawling all over themselves with the opportunity to win him in an auction.

Vivian scoffed. If that was what he was waiting for, it looked as if it was going to be a long time in coming. She almost felt sorry for him.

Almost.

"Do I hear three-fifty?" Jo asked. This time she didn't wait long for someone else to chime in, not that it seemed like anyone would. "No? Your loss, ladies, and a big win for Miss Vivian Grainger. Welcome back to town, Viv, by the way."

Vivian smiled and waved her thanks. For the welcome. Not for the win.

Jo raised her gavel.

Nick frowned.

"Going once. Going twice." The gavel swept down and landed solidly on the podium. "Sold to Vivian Grainger for three hundred dollars."

The crowd clapped politely but Vivian noticed they were more subdued than they had been with previous entries, especially when it came to the single ladies in town who Vivian had expected to be her biggest competition. Either she hadn't bid high enough or Nick had ticked off a lot of women. Another thought occurred to her. Could the lack of enthusiasm be because of *him*? Her bid wasn't any less than others had made, but she hadn't overextended, either. She could have easily been outbid, if Nick were the trophy he seemed to think he was.

She'd been in middle school when he'd attended high school. He was five years older than her, so it wasn't as if they ran in the same circles. She remembered him being popular, especially with the girls, but he'd never put much effort into his social relationships. He'd always appeared more interested in working his ranch and spending time with his family than in participating in school and community activities.

Apparently some things hadn't changed.

Viv met the gaze of her twin sister, one of the few who knew of Viv's pregnancy. Alexis twirled her hand in the air as if holding a lasso, reminding Vivian that her part in this crazy town event wasn't going to be finished when she handed over her money. Alexis, seated in front of the platform with a fishing tackle box for a cash register, was collecting the money from the winning bids, so Viv inched her way forward through the thick crowd to reach her sister.

Vivian wasn't thrilled about what was expected of her next. *Jo Spencer and her crazy ideas.* Roping the cowboy was a silly gesture concocted to amuse the crowd. Alexis handed her a rope with which she was supposed to lasso her "win."

Nick did nothing to encourage her, standing stock-still, his hands jammed into the front pockets of his blue jeans and his square, dimpled chin jaunting upward. His expression was frozen into a frown, his dark brow lowered over icy blue eyes that Vivian refused to meet.

If he was trying to intimidate her, it wasn't working, because she wasn't about to let him get under her skin. If, however, he was trying to be as immobile as a fence post to make it *easier* for her to lasso him, he was doing a very good job of it.

The problem was, Vivian didn't know how to lasso a post—or anything else, for that matter. Other than playing with a toy nylon rope with Alexis when they were children, she'd never even thrown a lasso.

The fact that Nick wasn't moving might be considerate on his part—although she had serious doubts about that, since he was practically glowering at her—but for all the good it did her, he might as well have been tearing around the stage, trying to dodge her every effort.

She glanced down at the rope in her fist and then back at Nick. The cheering crowd was getting impatient, throwing friendly taunts and barbs about pretty ladies and stubborn cowboys as they waited for her to act.

Well, there was more than one way to skin a fish. Based on what she'd observed so far, there weren't really any ground rules on the roping-the-cowboy part of the equation. She figured she could do it any way she wanted.

Intent on her actions, Viv loosened the loop on the rope and marched up to Nick with a nervous smile. He seemed even bigger up close, his blue-checked Western shirt rippling in the breeze against the black T-shirt that covered his expansive chest. His poor mother, raising three boys this size. She would hate to have seen the grocery bill when they were all under the same roof. It was a good thing he was a rancher. The man must eat an entire cow every week.

With two hands on the lasso, she reached up to ring it over his head, but even on tiptoe she couldn't quite reach high enough to flip the coil over, and his stupid hat was getting in the way.

Their eyes met and she gasped softly. Eyes the color of dark-wash blue jeans completely captured her awareness. She was so taken by his gaze that for several blinks of an eye she forgot what she was doing, forgot the clamoring crowd watching them, forgot even to breathe.

"Get along, little doggy," someone called from the anxiously waiting audience.

Laughter jolted Vivian back to life and she huffed in exasperation. Was Nick ever going to help her here? *Stubborn man.* He just stood there hulking over her, unmoving, his massive chest and broad shoulders like a brick wall in front of her and no less giving.

"Give me a break," she muttered loud enough for his ears only. "Can you not just—" She gestured for him to bow his head. A little effort on his part would be nice.

He lifted a brow and one corner of his mouth, and after a long pause, removed his black cowboy hat and crouched low enough for her to reach over the top of him.

"Moo," he said, and grinned wholeheartedly.

The crowd erupted into laughter.

He waved his hat and acknowledged the townspeople as if he hadn't just spent the last who-knows-how-long thwarting her efforts to rope him.

"Don't push it, buster." She sniffed, indignant, and arranged the lasso around his shoulders, tightening it so she could *finally* lead him off the platform. The delighted assembly whistled and applauded.

Two could play at that game. She turned to the crowd and curtsied, letting the enormous sway of her emotions go with the cool Texas breeze. It wasn't in her nature to take herself too seriously or hold a grudge for more than a moment.

Nick, on the other hand, grunted and practically jerked the rope from her hand so he could pull the lasso off himself as they exited the stage. Whatever smile he'd put on had apparently only been for the benefit of the assembly.

"Come on, Cinderella. The ball's over and the clock is about to strike midnight."

"Oh, loosen up a little bit, why don't you?" she retorted. She'd been about to end her statement by calling him Prince Charming, but the guy was as far from charming at that moment as anyone could get. He was more like the clock tower, ticking away the minutes in anticipation of ruining the fun. Or maybe one of those carriage attendants who turned back into a mouse at the end of the night.

A big, plump gray mouse with a cowboy hat, enormous pink ears too large for his head and a big black wiggly nose. She chuckled at the thought.

"What's so funny?" he demanded, tossing the rope back to Alexis as he took the steps off the platform two at a time. He threaded his fingers through his thick black hair before replacing his Stetson.

She followed him down the stairs. She imagined he wouldn't appreciate being compared to a mouse, even one in a cowboy hat, so she made a different observation out loud.

"You could use a haircut. Did you know I'm a certified cosmetologist?"

"A cosmo-*what*?" His gaze widened on her, looking as appalled as if she'd just threatened to shave his head. He yanked the rim of his hat down lower over his eyes. "No, ma'am. Not gonna happen. I don't care how much money you paid out for me back there. I'm drawing the line."

Something in the way he said it stirred a challenge in Viv's chest. He had no idea how nice he'd look if he'd give her the opportunity, and she was certain he would.

If he wanted a challenge, she would give him a challenge. She had her ways.

But she pushed the thought away. Cleaning him up wasn't her goal, now that she'd won him. He could look like a bear all he wanted as long as he helped her build her salon. But she doubted that would be any comfort to him. Based on his reaction to even the suggestion of a haircut, she had a feeling he wasn't much of a fan of beauty salons. And that meant he wasn't going to like the project she was about to lay out for him one bit.

If Vivian Grainger thought for one second she was getting anywhere near him with a pair of shears, she was sadly mistaken. Nick liked his hair just the way it was, thank you very much. And even if he did decide to get a trim, he'd see a male barber, not a ditzy, beautiful blonde with a sharp pair of scissors.

Of course the old barbershop in town had closed two years ago when Old Man Baranski kicked the bucket. No one had stepped in to take his place, and the building had eventually been used by Emerson's Hardware for their overstock. Now he had to drive for an hour just to get his hair cut—which is why he didn't bother.

One of the reasons, anyway. If he had a special lady in his life, he might care more about how he looked. But that wasn't the case right now—and it looked like it wouldn't be for a good long while.

He supposed he ought to be grateful to Vivian for bidding on him. After his last—and very public—painful breakup, most of the town's single ladies were avoiding him like the plague, as evidenced by the auction today. He supposed he wasn't really all that surprised no one else bid on him.

Vivian hadn't been back in Serendipity long enough to hear the latest rumors. She'd spent the last few years in Houston and wore Big City like a neon sign around her neck. He wasn't sure getting picked up by a woman like her was going to do his reputation any good, but it couldn't get any worse.

He'd really hoped to be bid on by some little old lady

who needed help with a few odd jobs. He'd also been more than a little concerned that an ex-girlfriend with a grudge might see this as an opportunity to repay him for real or imagined wrongs.

He was the first to admit that his record with long-term relationships was less than stellar, and he knew it was his fault. He was just really, *really* not good at making things work in the dating department.

But circumstances being what they were, he might as well see what Vivian wanted and be done with it— as long as it didn't involve cutting his hair. Who knew? Maybe he could mend some of those torn fences with his reputation if folks in town saw that he treated Vivian right.

Nick turned his attention to her, but he stood for a good five minutes while Vivian talked to her sister.

And talked. And talked.

His stomach growled, but he couldn't do anything about it. This was a Bachelors and *Baskets* auction, with the winning bidders providing a picnic lunch for the men they'd won. Lunch wasn't going to happen until Vivian led him to wherever she'd stashed her basket. He had to wait until she decided to grace him with her attention, which he guessed wasn't going to happen soon, since her mind seemed to be on Alexis, the auction and anyone in speaking distance of her.

Except for him.

Vivian gave a new meaning to the words *social butterfly*, and she definitely had the gift of gab. With the possible exception of Jo Spencer, who owned Cup O' Jo's Café and was therefore the Queen of the Gossip Hive, Nick had never seen anybody flitter around as much as Vivian. Her high, tinkling giggle reminded Nick of a fairy in a cartoon.

It was downright grating on his nerves and was practically curling the hair on his chest. Nick crossed his arms and grumbled under his breath, berating the entire chain of events that had led him to this particularly annoying set of circumstances.

She was supposed to be *feeding* him. That was the deal. She had the picnic basket.

Somewhere.

If she ever got around to acknowledging him again, he might ask where it was. He didn't mind eating alone and leaving her to her myriad conversations.

"Hey, Viv," Alexis called, nudging her sister's shoulder. When Vivian turned, Alexis gestured toward Nick. "You need to feed your man. He looks ravenous over there."

Nick bristled. While he appreciated Alexis's thoughtfulness, he was *not* Vivian's man. Not in any way, shape or form.

Except, unfortunately, that in a way he was. She'd bought him. With money. For a purpose as yet unknown to him. Unfortunately, she was very possibly expecting a date out of this. He knew perfectly well that many of the single ladies in the crowd were bidding on men for just such a reason. It was enough to make a single man shudder.

"Oh, Nick, I am so sorry," Viv apologized, laying a familiar hand on his forearm. "I completely forgot about you."

"Yeah. No kidding." His arm trembled as he fought the urge to jerk it out of her reach.

She'd *forgotten* about him? *Ouch.* He didn't want to admit it, but her words stung his ego. Even if it was Vivian Grainger. Even if he shouldn't really care whether she was thinking about him or not.

She ignored his attitude, if she even noticed it, apparently choosing to take the high road and stay cheerful instead of descending into bickering. Typical of what he knew of Vivian Grainger—her glass was always, annoyingly, half-full.

"I packed my basket with all kinds of goodies," she informed him. "Turkey and Swiss sandwiches and BLTs. Potato chips, a couple of deli salads and one of Phoebe's delicious cherry pies for dessert. I hope you like cherry."

Cherry happened to be his favorite. But as hungry as he was, he would have eaten it even if he didn't care for it.

"And I packed a special surprise."

In general, he didn't like surprises—but this one sounded like it was something to eat. His mouth watered at the possibilities.

"You'll be happy to know that everything I've packed today is legitimately store-bought," she continued, without letting him get a word in edgewise, were he inclined to do so.

Which he wasn't.

"I know the whole point of this was to serve the best of Serendipity's down-home country cooking, but trust me when I say you would definitely not want to eat *my* cooking. I can't even boil soup."

"Water," he corrected absently, wondering when, if

ever, they were going to get around to actually *eating* the food she was yammering about.

"What?" she asked, confused. She folded her arms over her stomach and swayed slightly, as if she was unsteady on her feet. Instinctively, he pressed a palm to the small of her back to support her.

"Water," he clarified. "The saying is, 'You can't boil water.'"

"Oh." She straightened her shoulders and waved him off, seeming to recover from the dizziness that had come over her moments before. "Whatever. But I do have bottled water." She paused, giggling. "To drink. Not to boil."

He was having trouble following her train of thought, if there was one. Once again he thought of a butterfly, flittering from flower to flower.

Only this particular flying insect was revved up on caffeine or something.

"And your basket is—where?" he finally asked, hoping for a straight answer but not really expecting one.

To his astonishment, she grabbed his hand and tugged him across the green.

"We're right in the middle."

Smack in the middle of the chaos. Now, why was he not surprised?

"It's not that I've never cooked before," she said earnestly, as if she thought he really wanted to know, while spreading a fuzzy purple blanket on the plush green lawn and flopping down on it. She reached into her ribbon-and-plume-decorated picnic basket, which Nick thought resembled an exotic bird, and withdrew two sandwiches. Her gaze turned distant and her lips bowed into a frown. "It's just that I'm not very good at it. Let's just say the whole experiment was a failure."

She paused and her voice made a distressed hiccupping sound. In one blink of an eye her expression filled with deep sadness. Nick's gut clenched and his natural protective male instinct started blaring five alarms.

Her response seemed a bit of an overreaction for a burned roast or whatever she'd had. What could have possibly happened to make her that upset? Had someone yelled at her? Hurt her feelings? If so, that hardly seemed fair. Cooking wasn't everyone's forte.

His instinct was to probe further, but then, just as quickly as the pain in her eyes had appeared, it was gone. She shook her head and cheerfully went on as if she'd never faltered.

"Would you like turkey and Swiss or BLT?" She punctuated the question with a laugh that wasn't really a laugh.

She held out both sandwiches to him and he gratefully accepted a turkey and Swiss, which was tightly wrapped in cellophane and marked Sam's Grocery. She unwrapped her own sandwich, shook two packets of mayonnaise and globbed it onto her BLT.

"A little sandwich with your mayo?" he teased between bites of his own meal.

She grinned. There was a lot of sunshine in that smile, so much so that it occurred to Nick that he ought to be wearing aviator shades.

"How sad the world would be without mayonnaise." The black clouds of her past had definitely lifted and her disposition could easily have rivaled Mary Poppins and her spoonful of sugar.

It was hard to keep up with her.

Her eyes glowed with excitement as she reached back into the basket. "Ready to see your surprise?"

He nodded in anticipation, hoping it was food and not tickets to the opera.

He nearly cheered when she pulled out a bucket of hot wings. He was sure he was gaping. How could she possibly have known they were his favorite? What kind of a coincidence was that? The deli counter in Sam's Grocery only carried hot wings on special occasions and they sold out fast. She would have had to put her order in early to get this batch.

"How—how did you guess?" he stammered.

She wriggled her fingers at him and spoke in a Dracula voice. "I r-r-read your mind."

"You sure did," he agreed, reaching for a hot wing. "Or my belly."

"If you want the truth, after I decided you were the guy I was going to bid on, I called your mother."

"You did *what*?" He choked on the hot wing and nearly spit it out. He didn't know if he was more shocked that she'd planned in advance to bid on him or that she'd been in contact with his mom.

"To find out what your favorite food was. I figured that was the least I could do. Alice was very helpful."

He groaned and swallowed. He could only imagine just how *helpful* his mother had been. Next thing he knew, his mom would be inviting Vivian over for dessert and toting out the baby pictures.

He felt a slight guilty twinge for thinking like that. Ever since his dad had died, it had been a struggle to get their mom to show enthusiasm about much of anything. He should be glad that Vivian's call seemed to have sparked some of that old matchmaking excitement in her. Yet that didn't make the thought of anyone pushing him and Vivian together any less off-putting. He decided to put aside his worries for now and focus on the food. Buffalo wings were too delicious to be spoiled by aggravation or dread.

"Mmm," he groaned. "Best Buffalo wings I've ever had. Bar none."

"I've never really understood that part," Vivian admitted. She'd taken a piece of chicken for herself, but took little more than a nibble before putting it back on her plate. "Buffalo don't have wings. And anyways, I don't think I'd like to eat a buffalo."

Nick barked out a laugh. Somehow taking a detour through Viv's head and picturing buffalo with wings lightened his heart more than anything else in—well, ages.

He reached for another chicken wing. While he polished off several hot wings, two sandwiches and the deli salads, Viv talked. Apparently she didn't need much feedback other than the occasional grunt or nod from him, which was a good thing, since his mouth was always full of food.

Vivian, on the other hand, hardly touched the food on her plate. She'd nibble here and there on her mayonnaise-laden sandwich and then her expression would turn a little green in the gills and she'd put it down again. He wondered if maybe she wasn't feeling well.

He was just about to ask when he stopped himself short, deciding it was none of his business. Maybe it was just his imagination and she always ate like a rabbit. She certainly had the figure for it. It would be rude of him to ask. Besides, whatever was bothering her, it wasn't affecting her soliloquy.

She told him about attending cosmetology school in Houston, how much she loved her work and the city and how her brother-in-law, Alexis's husband, Griff, had helped her finance her first salon and spa. Apparently it had been quite successful, to hear her tell it, at least until the economy tanked. Then everyone's business had taken a big hit.

"So what brought you back to Serendipity?" he asked, wiping his hands on a paper towel. Clearly she liked living in the city well enough and it sounded as if the business world was finally recovering from the economic downturn. "Or are you just visiting?"

Nick was positive he saw her blanch, and then her cheeks turned as red as the cherries in the slice of pie he was about to wolf down.

"I'm here for the long tow," she said with a sigh.

He knew what she meant.

Her blond eyebrows lowered. "I sold my spa in Houston and bought a little shop here in town." She gave a self-deprecating laugh. "I guess you could say that I'm downsizing."

"Why?"

"If you don't mind, I'd rather not talk about it."

Nick tried to catch her gaze but she wouldn't quite look at him. Here was a woman who normally couldn't *stop* talking. He'd clearly hit on a nerve. And she sounded so *sad*. It hit him right in the gut.

He rapidly backtracked out of the territory that made her uncomfortable. Anyway, he didn't want to know the specifics. It wasn't as if they were going to start hanging out together. Since he was stuck with her until he finished whatever task she had for him, he'd rather deal with the happy social butterfly, if given the choice, for as long as he had to be around her, even if her perky personality drove him half-crazy. These bipolar emotions of hers were creeping him out.

What he needed to do was focus on whatever she required of him. Clearly she had a reason for buying him, or she wouldn't have approached his mother. And he suddenly realized that whatever it was she wanted from him hadn't been addressed at all. It was the only thing she *hadn't* talked about.

It probably had something to do with the shop she'd just bought. Hopefully she was just looking for a little remodeling help or something.

He hoped. That would be safe territory. And happily, nothing to do with dating. Even if his poor mother hoped otherwise.

Sorry, Mom.

"Where is the building located where you plan to build your new spa?"

For some reason he had trouble with the word *spa* leaving his lips. One little syllable and his tongue was tripping all over it. He supposed it was because he was picturing snowy white bathrobes and massages and people laying out in the sunshine with cucumbers over their eyes.

A spa in Serendipity?

The town had one grocery store. One café. What would it do with a *spa*?

"Two doors east of Emerson's Hardware," she answered, excitement seeping into her voice. "The red building. It used to be a barbershop, but it's been vacant for a while, I think. I imagine it's going to take a little work to get it back into usable condition."

"A *little* work?" he asked, unable to smother an amused grin. Had she even seen the building since she'd bought it? "Lady, Emerson's has been using the building as extra storage space for their feed. I doubt very much they worried about keeping up with internal appearances. And you're looking to make it into some kind of fancy spa?"

"A beauty salon and spa isn't that big of a stretch from a barbershop."

Only night and day.

He snorted. It might have the plumbing and wiring setup she needed, but the interior was going to need a complete redesign—and that was *after* she cleaned out the mess that came from two years of being used as a storage facility. "It's not going to take *some* work. We're talking about a pretty major overhaul here. You're going to have to gut the whole thing out and start from scratch."

She tilted her chin up and smiled at him with a twinkle in her eye. His throat tightened. They might be as different as a tomcat and a spaniel, but he was a guy and she was an extraordinarily pretty woman, whether or not a man preferred blondes. And he'd always been partial to blondes.

"You mean *you're* going to have to gut it," she corrected, a giggle escaping from between her lips. Her impossibly blue eyes were alight with mischief. "That's why I bought you. So I guess now my spa is your…challenge." She reached over and playfully tipped his hat down over his eyes.

"And mine," she continued, as usual not letting him get a word in edgewise, "is going to be trying to work with you every day without coming after you with a pair of scissors in order to trim that thick dark bird's nest of yours."

He pushed his hat back up and grinned.

"You can try, lady. You can try."

Chapter Two

From the first second Jo had pounded the gavel and declared that Nick was sold to Viv, she'd been wondering if she had made an enormous mistake in bidding on him.

Now she was sure of it.

For one thing, Nick had stopped eating when she'd told him her plans, a chicken wing halfway to his lips. He'd actually had the nerve to gape at her like she was crazy—and then he'd practically laughed her off the community green for making the choice to buy the little barbershop. He hadn't even bothered to ask if she had good reasons for it.

Which she did.

"We can start work as soon as you're ready," she told him, hoping for sooner rather than later. "I don't know how much time you're willing to give me on this project, but I'll take whatever you offer. I'm anticipating maybe together we can do it in—what? A week? Two weeks?"

The expression that crossed his face was indescribable. The closest thing she could come up with was that he looked like he'd just swallowed a toad. His mouth moved but no words came out.

"What?" she asked, her guard rising. "Did I grow an extra eyeball on my chin?"

His lips twitched. "The expression is 'forehead.'"

She ignored him. "Do you have a problem with my— *our*—new endeavor?"

He groaned and polished off the chicken wing he'd been holding, tossing it into the bucket of empty bones. He'd eaten half the bucket when she'd first offered it to him and was now finishing it off, and that was after having eaten a full lunch and an enormous slice of pie. Hot wings as an after-dessert snack was just plain weird, as was the fact that he'd polished off almost the entire bucket of chicken literally on his own.

And he thought *she* was crazy? *Whatever.*

In contrast to Nick, she hadn't eaten much at all. Her morning sickness was catching up with her. She'd thought she was over the worst of it, but she suspected her nerves weren't helping.

"Do I—er, *we*—have problems? Where do I begin?" he asked sardonically.

"Is this too big of a challenge for you? Because if it is, tell me now. There are a few men left on the auction docket I can bid on if you think this project is more than you can handle."

He snorted. "I can handle it."

She narrowed her gaze. She'd pricked at his ego on purpose to see what he'd do. But it wasn't an idle threat. As far as she was concerned, if he was going to be a jerk to her, she'd follow through with her words and toss him out on his elbow.

She'd had just about enough of dealing with thick-headed men, and she definitely didn't need his guff. She was resourceful and could always figure out another way to renovate her spa. With or without Nick McKenna. Worst-case scenario, she would hire a general contractor. Better than putting up with Nick's less-than-stellar attitude. Talk about a glass-half-empty kind of guy.

"If you can handle the job, then what's the problem?" she jabbed.

He wiped his sleeve across his chin.

Neanderthal.

"I'm not the one with the problem, lady, because I'm not the one who picked up a piece of property that's bound to be more trouble than it's worth. Remodel it in a week? Yeah, not so much."

"You don't know that for sure." Though she had a sinking feeling that he knew more about it than she did. Was one week a totally crazy estimate? She honestly had no idea how long these things usually took.

Heat rose to her face. He must think she was a complete idiot. She wasn't—more like a wishful thinker. Her tendency toward always believing in the best-case scenario had gotten her into trouble more times than she could count, but Nick didn't need to know that.

"No. I don't." He shook his head, his brow lowering. "But I can make an educated guess. Did you buy the shop at below market price?"

Now, how had he guessed that? Alexis and Griff were the only ones who knew the details of her own private financial affairs.

"I might have," she hedged.

He chuckled. "I'll take that as a yes."

"So it's not in as good a shape as it could be. What does that matter? When it's finished, it'll be amazing. You'll see. I have an exciting vision for it."

She'd made her decision the moment she'd seen the cute little red storefront standing empty in the middle of Main Street, especially when she'd noticed that it used to be a barbershop, no less, right down to the now-cracked twirling peppermint sign. It was locked so she hadn't gone in, and the windows had been too dusty to see much more than shadows inside, but she was sure she could make it into something amazing. She didn't care that it needed work. She'd made the right decision, and now she would stand by it.

Yes, the once-red exterior paint was peeling and the sign hanging from the outside eaves was dangling by a mere thread, but that would have had to have been replaced anyway, with a bright yellow sign declaring her new spa was open for business. When she was finished remodeling, it would be the most sparkling, eye-catching property in all of Serendipity. She'd have customers lined out the door, all excited to take advantage of her many services.

For the ladies of Serendipity, the blessing of being able to pamper themselves without the hassle of a long drive to the nearest city would finally have come. Full hair services and mani/pedi's. Eventually she hoped to be able to hire a licensed masseuse so she could add massage to her list of services.

And it was *her* special blessing as well, her opportunity to prove herself, to turn her life around and make her world right again.

Her life—and her precious baby's. She needed to be able to provide for her child, but it was more than that. She wanted her son or daughter to have a mother he or she could be proud of.

"Does your vision for this building include having to gut the whole interior before you can rebuild? I'll have to take a closer look at it, but I'm guessing that's what we're going to be looking at."

Her dreams hadn't been overly realistic, she realized, but she wasn't going to admit that. Not to Nick. It was just a slight hiccup in the big scheme of things. She wasn't going to let that stop her.

"I'm not afraid of a little hard work."

He leaned back on his hands and raised an eyebrow. "You know anything about carpentry?"

She shook her head. "Well, no. Not really. But I'm sure I can measure wood and hammer a nail as well as the next woman. And I'm a fast learner. Besides, that's why I brought you in. Or *bought* you in." She giggled at her own joke.

He snorted and rolled his eyes.

"I asked around town who might know a little bit about carpentry and your name came up once or twice. That's why you were on my short list."

"Well, that explains it, then," he remarked cryptically.

"Explains what?"

He shrugged. "I was just wondering why you bid on me. Now I know. And you're right. I know how to help you out. After my dad got sick, I remodeled my mom's ranch house, where all three of us boys were raised. It gave me something positive to do with my anxiety and grief. And once I was done with that, I built cabins for Jax and me from the ground up."

"See, I was right about you. An amateur expert. Or is that an expert amateur?" Vivian smiled and breathed a sigh of relief. With the way Nick had been hedging, for a moment there she thought maybe his skills had been overrated. She really did need someone who knew what he was doing, and Nick was that man.

He didn't look convinced.

Why didn't he look convinced?

He'd just told her he'd made a bunch of stuff, some buildings from the ground up. Remodeling her shop would be a piece of pie next to that. Surely he wasn't second-guessing himself?

She stared at him a moment longer and then he shifted his gaze away from her and went foraging into the picnic basket as if it were a bottomless well of food.

He couldn't possibly still be hungry. He'd eaten— *Oh.*

The lightbulb in her brain flipped on at the very same moment she took a sucker punch to her gut. He was avoiding eye contact while he tried to think of how to phrase the bad news.

It wasn't that he *couldn't* build stuff. He just didn't want to build stuff for *her.*

He might as well have taken a baseball bat to her fragile self-esteem. With the help of a therapist she was slowly crawling out of the tortuous abyss of being engaged to a verbally and emotionally abusive man. Derrick had fooled a lot of people with his public persona. His former best friend, Griff. Alexis.

And Viv most of all.

With Derrick, she'd always believed she wasn't good enough for him. She'd tried to change to please him, to be what he wanted her to be, until she didn't even recognize the woman in the mirror. But no matter what she did or didn't do, it was never good enough for him. And when she'd discovered she was pregnant—

No. She wasn't going to go there. Not right now. Derrick wasn't the man she had to deal with right now— Nick was. He may not be the kindest or most tactful man, but she knew he was a good, decent person. He wouldn't attack her deliberately. If anything, he probably thought he was helping her by pointing out the flaws in her plan. He didn't know how much it hurt her to hear her ideas—her dreams, her hopes for the future—put down again. But no matter. If Nick didn't want to help her, he just had to say so. If he was having second thoughts about doing the work, she'd even give him the out he needed, since he hadn't made the most of the first one she'd offered.

"Just forget about it."

His head jerked up. "What did you say?"

"I said forget about it. You don't have to give me a hand with my remodel if you don't want to. I'll find someone else. Worst-case scenario I'll have to hire a contractor. No big deal."

"But the money for the auction—"

"—went to a good cause. No hard feelings."

She didn't want to be here at the auction anymore, hanging out on the community green with most of the rest of the population of Serendipity. She didn't want to sit across from Nick acting like everything was okay when it wasn't. She was tired of pretending.

She reached for the empty sandwich wrappers, stuffed them into the picnic basket and then slammed the lid closed. As closed as her heart felt right then.

She wasn't lying when she said she would make it. Somehow, some way, she would. With or without Nick McKenna's help. She shoved her hand forward, ready to shake his and be done with all of this.

Be done with him.

He frowned and stared at her palm as if it were an overgrown thornbush.

"Now, wait a minute," he said in a gentler tone of voice. Instead of shaking her hand, he laid his large palm over hers and held it. "Don't jump to conclusions. I never said I wasn't going to help you."

She sighed. "You didn't have to say it out loud. It's written all over your face, not to mention in your attitude. I know you think I'm a dumb blonde who couldn't find her way out of a plastic bag, but even I can take a hint."

He threw back his head and laughed. "Paper sack."

"What?"

He just smiled and shook his head. "I'm thick as a tree trunk sometimes. And I know exactly what my mama would say about that kind of stubbornness."

"Yeah? And what's that?" She couldn't help it. She was intrigued.

He twisted his free arm behind his back as if someone in authority were holding it there.

"She'd say," he responded with a grin, "that I need an attitude adjustment." He paused and flashed her a truly genuine smile. "And you know what, Viv?"

"What?" Despite everything, his smile lightened her mood. Maybe because he only smiled when he meant it.

"My mom would be right."

He snorted and shook his head. "And, Viv? I don't like to hear you beat yourself up. I don't think you're dumb—and you shouldn't let anyone else tell you that, either. Besides, I don't let anyone talk about me that way, and we're in this project together now." This time, he held out his hand, and she couldn't help grinning back as she gave it a shake.

Two weeks following the Saturday of the auction found Nick standing next to Vivian in front of her property. He had tied up all the loose ends that would keep him from his commitment and wanted to get started on this project as soon as possible. Construction was already beginning on the senior center and he planned to volunteer as many hours to that as he could, especially since his uncle James would soon be a resident.

Just thinking of his uncle, an eighty-eight-year-old man with late-stage dementia, was an added weight on Nick's already burdened heart.

His plate was full to overflowing, but he wouldn't allow himself to complain. Ranch work kept him plenty busy on its own, and he couldn't count on his brother Jax to lend a hand as much anymore, since Jax's miserable harpy of an ex-wife had come to town the day of the auction and abandoned month-old twin babies on his doorstep. The baby girls were adorable and an absolute blessing through and through—but that didn't stop them from being a lot of work. With the hours they kept Jax up every night, it was a struggle for him to get through his own horse training work every day, much less help with the ranching responsibilities. Slade had his family and his work at the sheriff's department to keep him busy. So that meant it all fell to Nick.

With everything going on, his stress level was off the scale. The sooner he remodeled Viv's quaint little beauty parlor, the sooner he could get out from under his obligation to her and go back to his primary concerns—his family, the ranch and the senior center.

He and Viv were both gazing up at the weathered wooden sign hanging directly over them from the eaves over the sidewalk. It was barely dangling by a thread. The thing was downright dangerous. He was surprised a good Texas wind hadn't blown it off by now.

He pulled out the pencil he'd tucked behind his ear to scribble a few notes on his clipboard. The hazardous sign was the first item on what he imagined was going to be a very long list of things to do to get this place in working order. He couldn't even imagine what the interior of the building held in store for him.

"I didn't bring a ladder," he said, his free hand resting on his tool belt. He'd known he'd eventually have to bring a truck full of heavy-duty tools to remodel this joint—from a planer to a circular saw and everything in between, but he figured evaluating the work and making a plan of action came first. "We've got to get that sign down. Today, if possible."

He still had no idea what he was getting into, but he figured he ought to at least give Vivian her money's worth in knowledge and labor. The outside of the place only needed a fresh coat of paint and it would be good to go, but he suspected that wouldn't be true of the interior.

"I noticed the sign the first day I was here. I know it's a potential hazard to people walking underneath. I can't imagine why it hasn't been removed before now."

"Nor I," Nick agreed. "You'd think the town council would be on top of something like that. They probably just overlooked it. No matter. You'll need to hang a new sign anyway. What are you going to call the place?"

Vivian propped her fists on her hips and screwed up her mouth, chewing on her bottom lip. She stared at the old sign as if it was going to give her guidance.

"To be honest, I don't know. I'm sure something will come to me once I get more of a feel for the place. It has to be exactly right."

"What did you call your spa in Houston?"

"Viv's Vitality."

"That's clever. You could use that."

She blanched and shook her head.

"No," she stated emphatically. "No. I absolutely couldn't do that. The salon in Houston is part of my old life. This has to be completely different, in every way."

He lifted his hand as if toasting her with a glass of bubbly. "Here's to new beginnings, then."

Her breath came out in an audible sigh. "Right. To new beginnings."

"Let's take a look inside and then I'll run over to Emerson's and see if they'll let me borrow a ladder."

That was one of the many benefits of small-town living. Nick had gone to school with Eddie Emerson, who would one day inherit his father's hardware shop. Since he'd known Eddie and his father all his life, he was sure it would be no problem to use one of their ladders to take down that sign.

Vivian shoved her hand into an enormously oversize pink-polka-dot handbag that sported a bow nearly as large as the bag itself. At least a good minute of fruitless searching went by before she smiled and shrugged apologetically before returning to digging. He was certain she'd forgotten the keys, but she determinedly continued to fish for them. "They're in here somewhere."

He smothered a grin. What could she possibly need to carry around with her that warranted such a big handbag?

"Ah! Here we are," she announced triumphantly, waving her keys in the air like a flag. She sorted through a large mess of keys until she came upon the one she wanted, and then approached the door.

Nick stepped around her and reached for the key.

"Here. Let me," he said, sliding it into the lock and stepping back, gesturing for her to enter first. "Welcome to your new home away from home."

He blinked hard.

His new home away from home? More like his new *nightmare*.

He'd imagined the interior would take some work—okay, a *lot* of work—but this was even worse than he'd anticipated. There was nothing salvageable that he could see. At best the paint was peeling off the walls, and that didn't count the numerous scratches and holes. Repainting wouldn't be nearly good enough. They'd need all new drywall.

The ground was covered with rotting floorboards scattered with a huge amount of old junk. Besides ancient piles of feed, there was a rusty tricycle, an old end table that appeared to be cracked through the middle, random bricks and an ugly garden gnome that stared back at him as if he were the intruder.

It would take them a week working full-time just to clear the debris, never mind prepare the inside for re-modeling. He hadn't committed to this kind of labor.

But he was all-in now. And maybe that was for the best—at least for his social standing. Vivian knew nothing of his recent dating history, so she didn't know that he was practically a pariah thanks to his vicious ex poisoning everyone against him. But Vivian had always been well liked. If he spent time with her, helping her, making sure he was seen with her, it was bound to give his reputation an upswing. It would show the rest of the town that he could be near a woman without having her run screaming in the other direction.

Or even worse, be screaming *at* him.

In public.

It wasn't that he had any romantic intentions toward Viv, but he had to start somewhere in polishing up his public image if he ever wanted to get a date again. Besides, this project wouldn't last forever. It would be a race to see whether he could finish the project before Vivian discovered the truth about him. His most recent pathetic excuse for a relationship wasn't exactly a state secret, and he was sure Viv had plenty of friends who would be anxious to tell her the whole story.

Anyway, who else would help Vivian with this disaster of a shop if not he? She wouldn't have bid on him if she had anywhere else to go, or anyone else to lean on. He suspected she hadn't had enough money to hire a proper contractor, although she hadn't said as much.

He didn't blame her for her pride. In fact, he admired her for it.

Yes, he had a cattle ranch to run, but he'd figure out some way to be there for Vivian. She was probably only now realizing how long it would take to remodel, but he'd get it done for her.

And run the ranch. And help Jax. And volunteer to help build the senior center.

First, though, he'd have to dig through all this trash.

"Oh, my," Vivian breathed from behind his left shoulder. "This is truly awful."

"You haven't been inside before today?"

Her face colored, staining her cheeks an alluring soft pink. "Honestly? No. The entire real estate transaction was done over the phone and on the internet. I haven't been back in town for more than a couple of days, and I've been busy moving myself into a cabin on Redemption Ranch. Before I knew it, the day of the auction crept up on me, and at that point, I figured we may as well take a look at it together, so we could start making plans."

"So you bought it sight unseen."

"Well, I saw the exterior, and I remembered the location from when I lived here before. The pictures the real estate agent gave me must have been from when the property was still a working barbershop. I had at least some idea of what I was getting into."

Nick personally thought she had *no* idea what she was getting into. The real estate agent who talked her into buying this property should be shot, taking advantage of Vivian that way. And the worst part was she didn't have the slightest idea that she'd been taken.

Whatever she'd paid for it, it was too much.

Vivian shook her head. "I apologize. This is all my fault. I should have come down and inspected the place before I got you involved."

Nick heard the trip in her voice and realized she must have read the expression on his face. She looked as if she were about to cry. She pressed her lips tightly together as if trying to stem the tide of her emotions, which ebbed and flowed faster than Nick could keep up with.

But he could relate to her discouragement. On the work front, he'd recently lost several head of cattle to disease. Then there was his public breakup with Brittany.

Life threw everyone curves. It was how a man—or a woman—responded to those setbacks that showed what kind of person they were.

"Well, I suppose I should call for a Dumpster to be brought in so I can start cleaning," Viv said, wiping her palms across the denim of her blue jeans. "I'll put all the trash in one corner until I can remove it. Do you want to go see about that ladder?"

Nick's gaze widened. He had to admit he'd fully expected her to turn tail and run. But she was just buckling down and pushing forward. Which either made her very brave or completely nuts. At this point he wasn't sure which.

At least there was one problem that would be quick and easy to fix. As Nick suspected, Eddie was only too happy to loan him a ladder—on behalf of Emerson's pretty new neighbor, of course. Eddie obviously saw it as an opportunity to ingratiate himself with the lady.

Nick didn't know how he felt about that, but he appreciated Eddie lending him a hand when it came to removing the signage—even if it was for ulterior motives.

By the time Nick brought the ladder back to Emerson's and returned to the shop, Vivian had managed to create quite a large pile of debris in one corner.

"Did you see this?" she exclaimed, pointing to a bent-up red tricycle with missing spokes and flat tires. "Who would leave a tricycle in an abandoned shop?" she asked, folding her arms as if she were suddenly cold. "It kind of makes me sad to think about."

"Are you making up stories in your mind about the poor little child who lost his bike?" he guessed.

Count on Vivian to be nostalgic over a rusty piece of metal.

Her eyes widened on him and then she laughed. "Yes, I suppose I am. You must think I'm a real airhead."

"No, I don't," he immediately countered, then cleared his throat.

Heat filled his chest and rose into his neck. That was exactly what he'd been thinking, and honestly, she'd done little to prove otherwise. Still, it seemed to him that she cut herself down a lot, and it gave him cause to wonder why she was so hard on herself.

"Yes, you do," Vivian scoffed. "And I suspect it's going to take some real work on my part to change your opinion of me. You have the Mr. Darcy Syndrome."

He tilted his head at her in confusion. He knew he'd heard the name somewhere, but he hadn't a clue as to where. "The what?"

"Oh, you are *so* busted. He's the hero of *Pride and Prejudice*, which you absolutely should already know.

That book was required reading for every tenth-grader at Serendipity High School since the day the school opened."

He grinned. "Are you going to tell Mrs. Keller on me? She still teaches tenth grade English, you know. I *may* have used CliffsNotes to get through. I've never been much of a reader, especially not gushy romance." He didn't mention why he didn't care for reading. His dyslexia was a well-kept secret. Only his teachers and family knew about it.

"There's a movie," Vivian suggested with a laugh. "Several of them, in fact."

"Eww. That would be worse than reading the book." Nick cringed. "You'd have to tie me down to the chair to force me to watch that frilly, girly kind of stuff."

"You have *such* a closed mind."

"Opinionated," he countered.

"Stubborn."

"Okay, we can agree on that."

"So you're stubborn and I'm a complete ditz."

Nick's gaze narrowed on her. "You keep saying stuff like that. Sweeping generalizations and insults that don't really apply to you. I don't get it. Why do you do that?"

"I don't know. You tell me. And do you really think the term *ditz* doesn't apply to me? I bought this property sight unseen and then dragged you into the mess."

Nick suspected it wasn't just moving back to Serendipity from Houston that had kept Vivian's mind busy. It sounded like she was getting over some big emotional hurdles, too. But there was no way he was bringing her past or her hurt feelings into the conversation.

"Like you said, it's Main Street. It was a reasonable

assumption to make that the property would be in workable condition when you bought it."

"Yes, but I thought I was only going to have to modify it from a barbershop to a salon and spa. I knew I'd have to paint and wallpaper but I didn't expect that I would have to fix a bunch of holes in the walls. Maybe I could just stuff bouquets of fake flowers in the holes and call it art."

She frowned but her eyes were bright and it was clear from her tone that she was making light of the circumstances.

It was more than he would have done under the same conditions. It was more than he *was* doing. He felt frustrated, angry and discouraged for her and her crazy spa idea.

But somehow, he'd fix the problem. Because he was a man, and that's what men did. His family had so many issues he was helpless to resolve: his father's death, his uncle's dementia, Jax's single parenthood. It was almost a relief to face a problem—no matter how large—that he could actually do something to fix.

Chapter Three

It took two weeks putting in every extra hour he had to get the shop cleared of clutter. Finally, Nick was able to start tearing out the old drywall. He wasn't surprised when Vivian showed up to *help*. Right on time, even though technically she had nothing to do at the shop until the construction was farther along.

Just what he needed—Viv underfoot again.

He had—wrongly, apparently—assumed that flighty Viv would quickly lose interest in the day-to-day construction part of the renovation and leave him in peace to finish off the terms of his obligation to her.

That wasn't happening. Instead, she was always hovering over his shoulder like a bumblebee, asking billions of questions about every little thing and making annoying, if innocent, suggestions on how they—meaning *he*—might be able to move things along a little faster.

She was determined to have her spa open the week before Thanksgiving. Four months was plenty of time for him to get the remodeling done, even with Viv hovering around, and even if he was only working the odd weekend. But Vivian took it all so seriously, as if the world would end if the shop didn't open as scheduled.

He wouldn't have admitted it aloud, but Vivian amused him. She was so certain all the ladies in Serendipity would be anxious to avail themselves of her services for family get-togethers and holiday parties. He didn't bother telling her that he thought if the ladies in town had managed up until now without the use of a beauty parlor, they'd probably continue to be fine without one.

Today Viv wasn't hovering quite as much as she was staring at him—or rather, *inspecting* him, assessing him. Every time his gaze met Viv's, pinpricks of premonition skittered over his skin, making the hair on the back of his neck stand on end. He couldn't shake off the feeling that she was watching him with more than just an eye toward the carpentry work he was doing.

For some inexplicable reason, she was examining *him*—and he didn't like it one bit. Whenever their gazes met, her impossibly blue eyes would sparkle and her pug little nose would twitch like a kitten's. And she had the oddest expression on her face. He couldn't help but wonder if her twin sister, Alexis, had filled her in on his very public breakup with Brittany.

He waited for her to ask, but she remained silent, which in itself was off the mark for Viv.

He turned his back, making it a point to ignore her as he focused on ripping out large chunks of the wall with a mallet and a crowbar. It felt good to be able to physically take a little bit of his anxiety out on the drywall. And while it was aggravating to have Viv hovering behind his shoulder, there was something pleasant in being around a woman, other than his mother, who didn't treat him like he had the plague.

No single woman in Serendipity wanted anything to do with him. He couldn't entirely blame them for thinking he wasn't much of a boyfriend. He'd owned up to his mistakes, both to Brittany and to God. That hadn't stopped him from getting publically humiliated at last year's New Year's Eve party.

Nick cringed as shame and humiliation burned through him. New Year's Eve the prior year had been the *night that changed everything* for him, not only socially, but emotionally and spiritually, as well.

He had been working overtime at the ranch all week, nursing sick cattle. The night before New Year's Eve, he'd barely turned in for the night when his mother called. His father had only been gone for a few months and she was having a rough time emotionally. She asked if he could come and sit with her for a while.

He'd ended up staying with her long into the night, keeping her company as she grieved through her first set of holidays without her husband, Jenson. She'd talked for a long time, sharing her memories of Christmases past.

Nick had quietly held her, but it was tough for him to listen to her stories, an extra proverbial punch in the gut, because he hadn't been there when his father passed away. He'd been too busy caring for the ranch, resenting Slade and Jax for leaving him with all the work while they took extra trips to San Antonio to be with their ailing dad.

It was a regret he carried in his heart always, so the opportunity to be available to care for his mother when she needed him seemed the very least he could do to try to make things right.

When he'd woken on the morning of New Year's Eve, he'd been bone weary, but ranch work stopped for no man and Nick had worked from before dawn until well after the sun went down.

He was supposed to be slicking up to take Brittany to Serendipity's annual New Year's Eve bash in town. He'd only slouched onto his couch for a second to take a load off his feet and catch his breath. He hadn't even been aware of closing his eyes until three hours later, when he'd awoken with a start from a deep, dreamless sleep. Somehow he'd gone from sitting up to stretched out full-length, facedown on the couch, with one long leg dangling off the end.

He remembered with alarming clarity the full moon streaming through the front window of his small cabin. It had taken him a few seconds just to figure out where he was, and another beat more before the jolt of realization hit him.

He was late to the party.

Way late.

Like missed-the-kiss-at-midnight kind of late.

He'd dressed in his Sunday go-to-meeting clothes as quick as he could and hightailed it to the party, but he knew even then he was too late to make things right. He felt terrible about letting Brittany down—*again*—but not nearly as bad as he felt when she verbally tanned his hide right in front of the entire town.

Part of the problem was that her tongue-lashing tested his pride and ego—she might have been angry with him, and rightly so, but she didn't have to air their dirty laundry in public for everyone to see. Still, once he'd simmered down, the harder blow came when he'd realized she was right.

He *had* let her down. Had neglected her. Had broken trust with her. Enough that the single women in Serendipity as a whole tended to avoid him, and every woman he'd asked for a date since that time had turned him down flat.

A man could get a complex. How was he supposed to prove that he'd learned his lesson and that he could do better if no one would give him a chance?

And *that* was the real reason he was committed to seeing Vivian's project through to completion, however silly he thought the idea of a salon and spa was on a personal level. To prove to the ladies in town—and, perhaps equally important, to *himself*—that folks could depend on him. That he was trustworthy, and not a total flake.

"How can I help?" Vivian asked, snapping him from his reverie.

"Bring me the push broom, please," he answered without turning to look at her. "It's in the back corner."

The next moment he heard a *thunk*, and then a *crumble* and then a *crash*.

What—?

He whirled to find Vivian sprawled in an inglorious heap in the middle of a pile of old drywall, shrapnel from a damaged ceiling panel snowing down on top of her. Apparently, she'd caught her foot on one of the boards, lost her balance and knocked the broom handle into the ceiling, all in the space of a few seconds.

He tethered his hammer and strode across the room,

his pulse rushing through him. Why on earth had she been standing on top of the drywall? Did she not see the danger there? Couldn't she have taken a less precarious path?

He breathed a sigh of relief when he realized she was fine, though probably a little embarrassed about her trip and fall. She crossed her arms and narrowed her eyes on him, daring him to say something.

Or worse, to laugh, which he was very close to doing, if only because she made an oddly adorable picture all sprawled out on the floor with her legs sticking out like a toddler having a tantrum. When she puckered her lips and blew dust and her bangs off of her forehead, he nearly lost it. Mirth bubbled in his chest.

He reached out both arms in a silent offer to assist her to her feet. He didn't trust himself to speak yet, afraid a chuckle would emerge.

She made an indistinguishable squeak and ignored his outstretched hands, choosing instead to roll to her knees and push to a standing position by herself, only using her palms for support.

Not such a great idea on broken drywall, which immediately cracked through.

She was vertical for about one second before she yelped and nearly crashed back to the floor.

Nick leaped forward, wrapped his arms around her and pulled her into his embrace, her head tucked under his chin and her feet dangling well off the ground as he swung her far away from the hazard. It was a good thing his reflexes had been honed by years of working with horses and cattle, or else Vivian would have landed straight onto her cute little nose.

"Put. Me. Down." Her words were muffled in the cotton of his shirt, but even so, he could tell she was irritated.

With him, apparently.

And here he'd just rescued her. He would have thought she would be grateful.

Women.

She wriggled against him and he opened his arms, relaxing his grip so suddenly that she didn't have time to respond—which served her right for her ingratitude.

He didn't set her down that hard, so he expected her to waver slightly and then right herself, but instead it appeared she was going down again. Her arms flailed in large circles and she squeaked in pain.

This time Nick ignored her protests and scooped her full up into his arms, cushioning her by cradling her against his chest. He stalked to the other side of the room, where he'd set up a metal folding chair he used for snack breaks. He pushed his lunch cooler off the seat with the side of his boot, not caring when it tipped upside down and the lid popped open. His water bottle rolled over his sandwiches, squishing them, but he had other, more important things to worry about.

Like what was really wrong with Vivian. There was more to this than just clumsiness.

He plunked her down into the chair as gently as he could, given the circumstances. She stiffened and glared at him.

Stubborn woman. Would she rather he just tossed her around like a sack of potatoes? He could have thrown her over his shoulder into a fireman's carry and have been done with it. But no. He was trying to be a gentleman here, and she wasn't helping.

Actually, she was tensed on the edge of the seat as if she were listening for the bell that would hurl her out into the boxing ring so she could take a swing at him.

Back when he was with Brittany, they'd had plenty of shouting matches. She hadn't hesitated to pick at him for every flaw and shortcoming, and he'd never been slow to defend himself...at full volume.

He straightened.

Nope. Not this time. He wasn't going to take the bait no matter how much heat was building under his collar. If they started verbally sparring, it was just a matter of time before their disagreement spread around town.

The flittering butterfly thing. It was going to be his downfall.

He couldn't afford another story circulating about his inability to treat a woman properly, even if the only thing he'd done wrong this time was to help her when she didn't want helping.

He was absolutely clueless as to what to do with her, and afraid that whatever he said or did would be the wrong thing.

"What were you thinking?" she demanded, perching one fist on her thigh and shaking a finger at him like he was an errant preschooler.

Her words startled him and he widened his gaze on her, shuffling through his previous thoughts for something that wouldn't stir the flames. "I—er—"

What had *he* done?

"You can't just go around picking people up that way, you big brute."

That was her problem?

"You would have preferred to have fallen?"

"I wasn't going to fall. I just—" she stammered as she searched for words, then harrumphed loudly and fell silent.

Nick lifted a brow and pursed his lips to contain the snicker about to emerge.

Viv wrapped her arms protectively around herself. "Okay. I'll admit I might have been a little off balance. But you were the reason I was about to take another digger in the first place. You set me down off balance on purpose."

He shrugged and grinned, neither assenting to nor denying her accusation. He *had* kind of dropped her. On purpose, although he'd had no intention of making her fall. But it served her right for not recognizing he was trying to help her.

He wouldn't have let her fall.

No—he'd gone and carried her in his arms—quite literally swept her off her feet, and then dumped her into a chair. Now he could see how *that* might come off as manhandling, to the uninitiated.

"I apologize," he said, the corners of his lips arcing downward. "In my defense, I legitimately thought you might be hurt. You were making all these funny squeaking sounds. Truth be told, I'm surprised you *weren't* injured, between the crumbling ceiling panel and that mess of old drywall."

"Well, as you can see, I am perfectly fine."

He crossed his arms and tilted his head, regarding her closely. She had snowy-white ceiling panel dusting her hair and cascading all down her shoulders, probably ruining her shirt. He wasn't sure why she chose to wear such a nice bright pink blouse when they were doing dirty work, anyway. The woman didn't know the meaning of *dress down*. But even considering all that, he had to admit that from his standpoint, which was admittedly male, she looked mighty *fine*…if you ignored the chunks of ceiling in her hair, that is.

Yet another thought he believed wise to keep to himself. He might be slow on the uptake, but his mama hadn't raised an idiot.

"Now, if you'll—" She stood, squealed in alarm and sat back down again with a thump. Murmuring in pain, she reached for her left foot.

He frowned for real this time and immediately crouched before her, gently taking her foot between his palms.

"I knew it. You *are* hurt." He felt no gratification in being right, or in saying I told you so.

"Did you sprain your ankle when you fell?"

He prodded the area tenderly, feeling for swelling and expecting another painful utterance from Vivian.

She didn't say a thing. Not even a peep. She was too busy gritting her teeth.

"I don't feel any swelling in your ankle." Maybe it wasn't so bad after all, and she'd just mildly twisted it.

"That's because it's not my ankle that hurts," she hissed, squeezing her eyes closed.

He bowed his head and looked closer, but couldn't see anything. "What, then?"

"It's my heel. It feels like I stepped on a long, rusty nail."

Nick swallowed hard. Rusty nails were nothing to

play around with, and there were plenty of long, jagged nails where she'd been standing. She'd probably have to get a tetanus shot, and he knew from experience that those things hurt for days.

He checked the bottom of Vivian's sneaker for a nail and, seeing none, tenderly unlaced her shoe.

He blamed himself for not being more careful. No matter what happened from here on out, he'd be at her side, holding her hand. He could just picture Dr. Delia plunging the needle into her arm. Vivian would be brave, of course, and not want to make a big deal out of it. And every second he was standing there he'd be feeling guilty that he hadn't taken more care with that drywall. He should have given better thought about Vivian's safety.

If she was hurt, it was all his fault. He wished he could take the pain on himself.

As gently as possible, he rolled off her sock, examined her heel and found—*nothing.* No nail mark. No puncture wound. Not even redness or a scrape.

Nothing.

"Give me my sock," she demanded, reaching for it. Nick's immediate and instinctive reaction, no doubt from growing up with a couple of pesky brothers, was to yank it out of her reach.

In hindsight, that was probably not the best idea he'd ever had. She lunged for her sock, missed and ended up sprawled on the floor—the very thing Nick had been trying to avoid for the last ten minutes.

"I said it *felt* like I had a rusty nail in my foot, not that there actually was one," she snapped crossly, in a deep, husky tone that wasn't anything like her usually high, birdlike tweet.

She must really be in pain, but she was being stubborn about it.

She rolled to a sitting position and grabbed for her sock. This time he let her have it.

"I probably just caught my heel on the edge of a board or something. The soles of these shoes are pretty thin—I'm not surprised I felt it, but as you can see, it didn't do any damage. I'll be fine."

He handed her the sneaker. "Except for the fact that you cannot walk," he pointed out helpfully.

"I'll live," she said through clenched teeth.

He'd never in his life had the misfortune of interacting with as obstinate a woman as Vivian Grainger.

"Be that as it may, you were injured on my watch and I'm taking you to see Dr. Delia."

"No, I—"

He held up his hand, staving off her flood of words. "I insist."

"But it's not necessary—"

"I think it is, and you're going to humor me. The doctor's co-pay will come out of my pocket. I sincerely hope there is nothing wrong with your foot, but I won't rest until I've heard that straight from the doctor's mouth."

Her gaze appeared to be a little bit of deer-caught-in-the-headlights, with a tiny smidge of tiger-in-a-cage added in for good measure.

What was the big deal? She was obviously in pain. Going to see the doctor was just plain sensible. It couldn't be about the money, since he'd already insisted he would pay for the visit. If there was nothing wrong with her foot, then fine, but he felt it was always better to be safe than sorry.

Strange. It almost seemed like Vivian was *afraid* to visit the doctor, even though she'd known Delia for a long time.

Was something else bothering her?

Stubborn, tenacious, bullheaded bear of a man.

Vivian wished with all her heart that she could go back to the day of the auction and bid on someone else—*anyone* else, besides this…this…mulish, dictatorial *hulk*. Someone who wouldn't constantly insist on sticking his head into her business—and now, by extension, into her baby's business.

She sighed and clasped her hands on her lap. She had to concentrate in order to keep herself from her natural maternal instinct, which was to cover her belly with the flat of her palm. That would be a dead giveaway if ever there was one. She refused to look at the giant of a man sitting next to her, whose size dwarfed Dr. Delia's small, pleasantly decorated waiting room. She was glad they were the only ones here to see the doctor.

If Vivian wasn't careful, the truth about her pregnancy was going to come out way sooner than she was ready for it to. She'd hoped, before it became public knowledge, that she'd have a chance to get her spa fixed up and her business started. Then she could at least say she was a woman who'd made mistakes but who had turned her life around rather than what she seemed like now—incapable on every level.

Oh, who was she kidding? She scoffed inwardly.

She was never going to be able to keep her secret until after the spa opened—not once she'd realized how much work the building truly needed.

She was nearly five months pregnant and with her normally slender build, it was becoming harder and harder to mask her growing middle section. There was only so much a pair of yoga pants and a billowing blouse could do for a pregnant woman.

Heat rose to her cheeks and she bowed her head in case Nick should see her distress. Would the embarrassment and humiliation never cease?

It wasn't that she didn't love her unborn child—she did, more than she ever thought it was possible to love a person.

But she was so ashamed of herself for how her little one had been conceived. Out of wedlock, and with a man who hadn't loved her. Not only had she set aside everything she believed in and denied her own moral standards, but she had set aside her relationship with God and had given in to the pressure and manipulation of a man who'd turned tail and run at the news that she was pregnant with his child.

And so she had insisted on hiding her pregnancy from the world, even though there was no possible way to continue with the ruse, especially now.

How foolish could a woman be?

She sighed inwardly. What was done was done and there was no turning back the clock. She couldn't change any of it—and she wouldn't want to, if it meant giving up the precious blessing growing inside her. She wanted this baby so much that her heart ached. She'd fallen completely and irrevocably in love with the little sweetheart the first time she'd seen the little bean with a strong, tiny heartbeat thumping on the ultrasound machine screen.

For that beautiful child's sake—and for her own—she was determined to change the vector of her life, embrace the faith she'd once denied, admit her mistakes not only to the Lord and herself, but to the community she lived in, and move on as a single mother.

It wasn't like she was the first woman ever to find herself in such a situation, and it wasn't as if she wouldn't have any help raising her baby. Alexis and Griff would always be there for her and Baby G, the nickname she'd given to her unborn baby in lieu of saying "him or her" all the time. And if family wasn't enough, she had plenty of friends and neighbors in Serendipity, especially within her church community, whom she knew she could count on to help her when she needed it.

Even Nick McKenna.

The thought sprang into her mind right out of nowhere, surprising her with its intensity. She dashed a glance at Nick from underneath her eyelashes.

Strong, steady Nick McKenna, with his back straight, his shoulders set and his large, capable hands clasped in his lap. His head was bowed as if in prayer, but his eyes were open.

He'd been by her side a lot in the last few weeks, supporting her emotionally as much as physically in the labor he was providing for the remodel. He'd brought her to the doctor when he thought she was injured, and had even offered to pay for it, not that she was going to let him.

Given the circumstances, it seemed only right that he be one of the first people to know about the baby and share in her joy. The only people she'd told so far had been her family and Dr. Delia, since she was under Delia's care.

"Nick, I—" she started, and then paused.

His head came up and his striking blue eyes met hers. He smiled softly. "Yeah?"

"I just wanted to tell you—" Vivian tried again, but at that moment Dr. Delia entered the room.

"What have we got going on here?" Delia asked with a pleasant smile and a nod in both their directions.

Heat suffused Vivian's face and she started to stammer an answer before she realized Delia was asking why she needed to see a doctor and not what might be going on between her and Nick.

Which was nothing.

Nick chuckled under his breath and Vivian wondered if he might have realized where her thoughts had gone, but aloud he said, "Vivian had a bit of a fall at her shop today. Got her foot caught up in some old drywall while we were working on the remodel."

She noticed that he didn't say anything about the broken ceiling panel raining down on her head, which had been entirely her fault. She'd been watching Nick work instead of paying attention to where she was going, and when she'd slipped on the drywall, she'd launched the broom handle straight through the ceiling.

She gasped. Come to think of it, she must look like a complete mess. She dabbed at her face with her palms and they came off covered with white powder.

She did *not* want to see herself in a mirror right now.

It was a wonder that Nick and Delia weren't laughing at her awful appearance.

But instead they were completely serious and obviously concerned for her health, although Delia was no doubt alarmed for an entirely different reason than Nick was.

"The bottom of my foot hurts," she hastened to say, to clear the situation up before things got messy.

Delia nodded, but she wasn't looking at Viv's foot. It was Vivian's belly under the doctor's careful scrutiny. Viv didn't know how Nick could *not* notice the direction of the doctor's consideration.

"Nick, do you think you can help her to the examination room?"

For a man Nick's size, he was incredibly gentle in leading her into the examination room. He hovered over her like a mother goose. He even gave her extra support to get onto the table before he returned to the waiting room.

Dr. Delia closed the door, not noticing when it caught on the door jamb and bounced back open a sliver. "I'll take a look at that foot, but since you fell, Viv, we probably ought to have a look at the baby, as well. I'm sure there's nothing wrong, but I believe we should err on the side of safety, just in case."

A deep, audible gasp sounded from the door. Nick stood gaping, clutching her handbag to his chest as if he was experiencing a heart attack.

"Baby?" Nick strode forward and took her elbow. "What baby? I thought you might need your handbag and the door was open a crack so I—a baby?"

Vivian cringed. This was not how it was supposed to

go. Sure, she'd been about to tell him the truth about her pregnancy, but she'd wanted it to be on her own terms.

Delia shot Viv a distressed look. "I'm sorry."

Viv laughed shakily. "No worries. It's not common knowledge yet, but it soon will be. It's not like I can keep Baby G a secret for much longer, anyway. The cat is officially out of the sack. It's time to share my good news with everyone."

"What baby?" Nick asked again, staring at Vivian as if she'd grown a second head. In some ways, she had—a tiny one—and a second body, as well. It had been a long day and Vivian was already feeling overwhelmed. She sputtered out a shaky laugh under her breath, mostly from nervousness.

"What is so funny about that?"

Okay, so it was a surprise to him, but he didn't have to act so shocked about it. She was a woman. Women had babies. And what difference did it make to him, anyway?

"I'm pregnant," she said in the voice she'd use when explaining something to a child. Nick was kind of acting like one.

"Since when?"

"Excuse me?" Now Viv was downright offended. What business was it of his when her baby had been conceived?

"I mean, how far along are you?" He huffed impatiently and shoved his hands in his pockets.

"Almost five months now."

He didn't appear scandalized anymore—he looked appalled and slightly horrified. His eyes were huge and brewing a midnight storm.

"You were… And you… And then…" He sputtered to a stop, tapped his cowboy hat against his thigh and threaded his fingers through his thick black hair. He gaped at her midsection. "Oh, man. I can totally see it now. I don't know how I even…"

He appeared to be holding a conversation with himself. Vivian found it a tiny bit amusing, even given the circumstances.

"I can't believe… But of course at the picnic…you were sick to your stomach. I don't know how I didn't realize that you…"

Vivian met Delia's gaze over Nick's shoulder and they exchanged a smile. Throw a baby into the mix and they'd managed to completely confuse the poor, lost male in the room.

"How could you?" Nick's voice had risen as he spoke but now it had dropped onto a cold, icy plain.

How could she get pregnant?

By trusting the wrong man, a man to whom she shouldn't have given her heart. By believing a lie. By letting her faith slide and—

"How could you come into a dangerous construction site with no thought to your safety? You could have been seriously hurt. Your baby—"

Vivian stared at him, her mouth agape. She was having trouble following the conversation, but apparently Nick's concern wasn't how she'd gotten pregnant so much as why she had shown up to help with the construction of her shop.

Well, that was an easy question to answer. Being pregnant was neither here nor there. She wasn't totally incapacitated. Women worked until their ninth month. What century did he think they were living in?

"I was taking ownership," she explained defensively. "I'm not going to leave all the work to you. It's *my* business, after all. At the end of the day, I'm the one responsible for how it turns out. It's my job to oversee the renovation."

Nick snorted and shook his head. "You can supervise from a distance. You don't have to be constantly on-site for that. You're pregnant. Very. Pregnant."

It seemed to Vivian that Nick was blurting out the obvious, and he was repeating himself. But to what end?

To insult her? To get her dander up? Because he was certainly succeeding if that was his aim.

"Yes, well, that much is true," Delia inserted, laying a calming hand on Nick's forearm and herding him toward the doorway. "Which is why I'm going to have to ask you to return to the waiting room. I need to do an ultrasound to check on Baby G. I think we might need to x-ray Viv's foot as well, just to be on the safe side on that issue. We're going to cover all our bases. Do you mind giving us some privacy, Nick?"

Vivian thought that Nick looked like he minded—very much. He paused long enough for her to fear that he'd refuse to leave the room. Thankfully, after a moment, he met her eyes. His gaze slid from there down to her belly before he huffed and puffed and charged out of the room, slamming the door behind him.

"Men, huh?" Delia said with a chuckle as she helped Vivian lie back on the examination table. "You can't live with 'em, can't shoot 'em.''

Vivian nodded in agreement. Although frankly, at

the moment, shooting Nick didn't seem an entirely unreasonable idea.

"Nick is a good one at heart, though," Delia continued. "He really seems to care for you."

Vivian felt like Delia had shocked her with a cattle prod. The last thing Vivian needed was for Delia or anyone else to get the wrong idea about her relationship with Nick—if one could even call what they had a relationship. It was a business arrangement, nothing more.

"Yeah. About that—" Vivian mumbled, but Delia didn't appear to hear her.

"Let's take a look at Baby G. We might even be able to tell if it's a boy or girl. What do you think, Viv? Do you want to know?"

Vivian sighed. There was a *lot* she wanted to know, and the sex of her baby was only one of many questions she had. She'd never been so confused in her life.

But she could get an answer to *this* question.

She took a deep breath and nodded.

Chapter Four

Despite the way Nick suddenly treated her like she was made of fine china, Vivian and Nick—mostly Nick, to Vivian's exasperation—had spent the next two weekends conquering the enormous pile of debris that was the inside of her shop. Together, they gingerly moved through her building and systematically tossed the rotting wood, broken drywall and most of the eclectic collection of abandoned storage items into a pile outside the back door.

All except the rusty tricycle.

She just couldn't let that one go. The paint was faded and flaking and some of the spokes were bent. The streamers on the handlebars had seen better days and the little bell didn't work at all. A sensible person would recognize it as the junk it was. Vivian knew she ought to toss it, but she couldn't bring herself to do so. She had no idea whether it was even possible to fix the poor, abandoned toy, but she had to try.

For her son.

She laid a hand over her swelling stomach.

Her *son*. She pictured a blond-haired, blue-eyed little boy riding on his restored tricycle, zooming around on the front concreted driveway of a quaint little cottage, pedaling as fast as he could and ringing the bell with wild abandon.

No, she wasn't going to give up on the tricycle, any more than she was going to give up on the pathetic little shop that would take more work than it was probably worth.

And now it was yet another Monday. She considered Mondays a brand-new start of another week, as yet unwritten, and another opportunity to move forward with her life.

As she approached the back entrance to her shop, she was still dwelling on happy thoughts of her baby and his little red trike and she didn't immediately comprehend that something was amiss. But when she reached to put her key in the lock, she realized the door was already open a crack, creaking softly back and forth in the breeze.

Hadn't she locked up when they'd left late Saturday afternoon?

She was fairly certain she had, though her mind had admittedly been full of myriad details regarding what was next on her miles-long to-do list. Had she been so caught up in her thoughts that she forgot to do something that was second nature to her?

Even if it was possible that she'd walked out the door without locking it behind her, she would have closed it, at least. She was one hundred percent certain about that. Who left their door wide-open when they left for the night?

Even a ditzy blonde didn't do that.

A chill rose up her spine. Had someone been in the shop when she wasn't there?

She froze, forgetting to breathe. Could she have been robbed? Had a thief broken in through the back door in order to steal from her?

She clapped a hand over her mouth and snickered at her own silliness.

A *thief*?

She must not be getting enough beauty sleep. Her imagination was running away from her. First of all, she'd be hard-pressed to find any thief within fifty miles of this town. Serendipity's police department hadn't arrested more than an occasional teenage shoplifter in years. Life in the small town was so safe that folks left their houses and cars unlocked and didn't give it a second thought.

Besides, what would anyone want to steal from this broken-down old storefront? There hadn't been anything but garbage to rob before she'd bought the place and there wasn't anything now. Nick hadn't brought in any of his heavy-duty tools yet, and as for his regular tools, he took them with him when he went home for the day. If someone *had* gone to the effort of breaking in, they were welcome to help themselves to the leftover pile of trash.

The answer struck her like lightning.

Nick must have unlocked the door.

He'd probably stopped in to take measurements or something and had forgotten to lock up behind him. She didn't work Sundays, but she knew Nick sometimes did. He was assisting her in addition to the work

on his ranch and helping out with the construction of
the senior center, so he had to squeeze in time for the
shop whenever he could. As a result, she'd given him
a key along with full run of her shop, so he could go in
and out as he pleased. She was grateful to him for taking on so much extra responsibility—far beyond what
her measly three-hundred-dollar auction bid really mer-
ited. He still teased her about the concept of opening a
spa, but it was good-natured now, and she believed it
was just part of his playful nature rather than a dig or
criticism aimed at her. And when it came to the work,
he never complained, and it looked as if he would be
staying until the completion of the remodel.

Come to think of it, she'd have to thank him when
she saw him next.

My, how he would laugh when she told him about
her encounter with the invisible, imaginary robbers.
Another strike against her in the ditzy-blonde category.
She even surprised herself sometimes. She chuckled
and swung the door open, shaking her head at her folly.

She gasped and stopped cold, a chill running down
her spine as she realized that the *nothing* she'd imagined was really *something*.

Just as quickly, the chill passed and fury flared back
up in its place, one nerve at a time all the way from the
bottoms of her feet to the top of her head. Her breath
snagged in her throat and she blinked back the sting
of angry tears.

There weren't any thieves in the building, but there
was something—two *somethings*, as a matter of fact.
And they were making a great deal of noise, not to men-

tion an enormous, smelly mess in a building that was already a walking disaster area to begin with.

Cows.

Two furry black-and-white-spotted baby cows with twitching ears and wet pink noses.

Vivian's thoughts were so clouded that seeing red wasn't just a figure of speech.

Nick.

Was this his sick idea of a joke?

Vivian wasn't laughing.

She didn't pause to consider that it might have been anyone else besides the cynical, blue-eyed cowboy. He was a cattle rancher after all, so he would have no problem getting ahold of a couple of calves. If she wasn't mistaken, that was his ranch's brand. And while he'd been very supportive of her—literally, physically supportive, hovering around her like he thought he'd be needed to prop her up or stop her from falling at any moment ever since he found out about the baby—he'd continued to tease her about her plans to open up a salon and spa in Serendipity.

She had *thought* it had graduated into gentle banter, with no real condemnation behind it anymore. But apparently she'd thought wrong.

And he had a key to the place.

A second ago, before she'd entered the building, that thought had been comforting. Now it was downright infuriating.

She ignored the stab of personal betrayal she felt. She refused to give him the power to hurt her. He didn't get to do that. She would never let a man have power over her in that way ever again.

And here she'd thought he was starting to come around, that he was warming up to her ideas. That he'd actually planned to *help* her get her business up and running. There were moments she'd even believed he was enthused by the project, or at least by the remodeling part of it.

Apparently she'd been wrong. So very wrong.

How *could* he?

How could he possibly imagine that this *prank* was funny, putting two live, dirty, stinking animals inside her shop?

Okay, so privately she had to admit the calves were a teensy bit cute, with their huge, blinking brown eyes, twitching ears and flicking tails. But the stench stung her eyes and she had to cover her nose and mouth just to breathe. She could only be thankful she'd chosen to wear a scarf today.

There were cow patties everywhere she stepped— and she wasn't wearing her riding boots. Why would she be? She hadn't expected to encounter *livestock* today.

She sighed, wondering how long the calves had been there. How could two little cows make so much of a mess? Or had Nick toted in some extra manure just for kicks? She wouldn't put it past him.

Sputtering and grumbling under her breath, she mentally listed all the ways she could calculate Nick's demise. Then she fished her cell phone out of her purse and punched in his number, her poor phone taking the brunt of her anger.

Nick was on speed dial, more's the pity. It was second on the list, right underneath Alexis. His number would be deleted as soon as he came and cleaned up his mess. She pacified herself by imagining how good it would feel to press that delete key and see his scruffy face disappear from her contacts list for good.

Just like *he'd* go away. And she wouldn't be at all sad to see him walk out the door. Or at least not much. There was still a part of her—

"Nick?" she demanded when he picked up on the first ring.

"Viv? What is it?" He managed to sound genuinely concerned, the jerk. "I can tell something's wrong by the tone of your voice."

"Ya think?"

He paused. "Meaning?"

"Meaning this isn't one bit funny." Why was he playing with her emotions? Apparently he had no idea how difficult all this was for her—even without the calves mooing in the background. Did he really think it would be funny to string her out this way?

"If I knew what you were talking about I'd probably agree with you."

"So you know nothing about the cows." It wasn't even close to a question.

"The *cows*?" Nick's query *was* an actual question. He had the nerve to sound flummoxed, as if he really *didn't* know what she was talking about.

"Mmm," she said noncommittally, deciding to let him dig his own grave.

"Viv, what cows?" Now his voice had an edge to it.

"The ones you put in my shop, of course," she said, trying to sound nonchalant about it.

There was silence on the other end of the line for a beat, then two.

"Vivian, are you in the spa building right now?" His voice was a low growl.

"Unfortunately for my sense of smell and my new sneakers, I'm afraid so."

Not that it was a spa yet. Not even close. In fact, with the stench in the room, it was about as far from anything soothing as it was possible to be.

"Stay there. I'll be right over. Better yet, go outside and wait for me. Don't worry, though. Cows are almost always docile animals. They won't hurt you."

"I'm not afraid of them hurting me," she snapped. She was at the end of her string with this man. What kind of an idiot did he think she was? "But I don't want them inside my shop. Nick, they lick their noses."

So gross.

He chuckled. "Yes, I guess they do."

"This is not a laughing matter."

He cleared his throat but she could still hear traces of amusement in his voice. "No. Of course not. Hang tight. I'll be right there."

Vivian waited impatiently for Nick to arrive, rehearsing in her mind all the things she wanted to say to him. She'd probably get flustered and not manage to say half of what she was thinking now, but she continued to fume and plan her rant anyway.

Given the enormity of the prank, she would have thought he'd be lying in wait, ready to see her immediate reaction to the animals currently lounging in her future place of business. Why had he been sitting at home waiting for the phone to ring? That was weird.

But she supposed he couldn't have known exactly when she'd finish her errands and come by the shop.

And besides, his little idea of a joke wasn't going anywhere without his assistance. He had to have known she'd have to call on him to help her get these calves out of her building.

Oh, irony of ironies.

When he arrived less than five minutes later her suspicions reinflated, ballooning to new heights. His house was at least a ten-minute drive away, assuming he drove the speed limit. So maybe he *had* been close—if not watching her, then at the very least hanging out at Cup O' Jo's gleefully waiting for her to call.

As he exited his truck, she planted her hands on her hips and glared at him. He strode forward, lifting his hat and threading his fingers through his thick black hair.

"Where are the cows, then?" he asked without preamble.

As if he didn't know.

She thumbed over her shoulder, pointing to the door of her shop. "In there."

His eyebrows rose to epic heights, as if he still didn't believe what she was telling him. As if he hadn't been the one to plant the black-and-white-spotted bovines there in the first place. He'd missed his calling, being a rancher—he was a much better actor than she'd expected.

She almost believed him.

He entered the shop with Vivian right on his heels. She didn't want to miss any of his forthcoming explanation, which she was certain had to be well rehearsed.

But what if he just laughed at her? After all, this was some kind of cruel prank, aimed at humiliating her.

He took one look at the cows and then spun around,

and ran a hand across his bearded jaw. "Well, they aren't cows."

"What? Of course they're cows. They aren't *horses*, for pity's sake," she pointed out acerbically. "I know what a cow looks like, Nick."

"No, I meant these little heifers aren't even close to being full grown."

She rolled her eyes. "Oh, that makes me feel *so* much better, then. I have two *young* cows standing around in my future spa, blinking their big eyes and chewing their cuds. And making a stinky mess with their cow patties, I might add."

"Yes, I can see that." Humor lined his voice, though she could tell he was trying to temper it.

He seriously thought this was funny. It was all she could do not to punch him in the arm, except that she'd probably end up hurting her knuckles on his mass of muscles.

Thoughtless hulk of a man.

"I don't care what you call them. I want you to get your cows out of here now. And don't bother coming back."

"*My* cows? These aren't—"

He paused, then moved forward to press a hand against the flank of the nearest heifer, right above the brand.

"I don't—that is—"

"What?" she demanded, crossing her arms and glaring at him. She couldn't *wait* to hear his lame excuse.

"I don't understand." She raised her eyebrows and waited. "You're right. These are my cattle, and this is my brand. The Circle M." He shook his head. "I don't know what to tell you, Viv. I honestly don't know what's going on right now, or how these calves got in here, but you have to believe me when I tell you I didn't do this."

Oh, she *had* to believe him, did she? If he thought that, then he didn't know her very well.

Not well at all.

Nick couldn't believe his eyes. Vivian hadn't been kidding about the live heifers in her shop, however implausible it had seemed when she'd first informed him of it.

Even worse, before she'd even spoken to him about it, she'd been certain that he was to blame. She hadn't given him the benefit of the doubt at all.

How could she even *think* he'd do something like that to her? Even if he didn't care for her, he'd never do anything so hurtful—not when he knew how much the spa meant to her, and how hard she was working to make it a reality.

And the truth was, he *did* like her. They were friends, or at least he'd thought they were. A friend wouldn't accuse another friend of this kind of prank without solid evidence, would she?

He'd thought they'd been getting along fairly well. He was committed to seeing the project through to its conclusion.

And then she'd gone and blamed him for this. She hadn't even asked—she'd assumed. That hardly seemed fair.

Resentment flared in his chest. If she didn't think he was a better man than one who'd do something this hurtful, then it would be better for both of them if she found someone else to do the rest of the labor for her remodel.

Then again…

He took a deep, cleansing breath and attempted to think the situation through rationally. Despite his innocence in the matter, he supposed Vivian had good reasons for suspecting him. The evidence did kind of add up against him.

He had a key to the shop, for one thing. And it was, after all, his brand on the heifers. There was no doubt about it—they were his cattle.

How they'd gotten there was a mystery—one he intended to solve, not only to vindicate himself, but also to find out who had accessed his herd without his permission. And, most of all, to get back into Vivian's good graces, although why he should care was beyond him.

Vivian had told him in no uncertain terms that she didn't want to see him back again, which really battered his ego. She'd shown more tact than Brittany in not yelling at him in front of the whole town, and yet the words still hurt just as badly. But then again, that was when she thought he'd pulled the sick prank.

She *still* thought he had. She'd pulled herself up on the corner of the desk he had brought in for her a few days earlier, her legs dangling and crossed at the ankles. She'd leaned her hands back on the cold metal and was eyeing him speculatively, her expression doubtful.

"You act as if you're surprised that it is *your* brand on *your* cattle," she said, narrowing her gaze on him. "Why is that?"

He shrugged defensively. "Because while I freely

admit they are my cattle, I have no idea how they got here."

"Ri-i-ght," she said, drawing out the word. "I'm sure they just wandered in here on their own. Maybe they were hanging around last evening after a night on the town and decided they'd visit my spa and get their hair done. Did you give them the key?"

"Snarky much?"

"Well, excuse me for being a little skeptical. It seems to me that all the pieces fit together to make a pretty clear picture of what happened. The evidence against you seems airtight."

"Yeah," he agreed, "except for one thing."

"And that is?"

"Me. I'd hoped you knew me better than to assume I could do anything so—"

"Stupid?"

He glared at her. "I was going to say dishonorable, but stupid works, too."

Her gaze turned from challenging to hesitant and he pressed his advantage, hoping he could convince her of his innocence, although at this point he wasn't sure if it mattered.

"Some other knucklehead put these heifers in here. Not me."

"But who? And why?"

He frowned. "That's what we've got to figure out. First, though, I'm going to clean up this mess."

She laid a hand on his arm. "*We* will clean up this mess. It's my salon, after all."

Even though Nick wasn't the one who'd pulled off the thoughtless prank, he still felt guilty about it, though he couldn't fathom why. Maybe because they were his heifers. Or maybe it was something else—something nagging at the back of his mind that he couldn't yet put his finger on. But he thought it might have something to do with the wounded look in Vivian's eyes when she'd accused him of making fun of her.

He herded the cattle out the back door and corralled them with some old crates, then retrieved the shovel and broom from the bed of his truck. He and Viv worked in uncomfortable silence, Nick shoveling and Vivian sweeping.

He imagined she was thinking the same thing he was—who was responsible for this juvenile prank? Local teenagers out on a lark? Someone with a grudge against Vivian?

He couldn't imagine the latter. Vivian might not be everyone's cup of tea but she was one of the sweetest women he'd ever met. She'd give a stranger one of her kidneys if they asked her for it. That was just the kind of person she was. Full of heart and genuine compassion.

No, it couldn't have anything to do with a personal grudge against her, or the salon. So what was it, then?

Dusk had fallen by the time they were finished. He scooped the cow patties into a pile near the back door and then transferred them into the field that bordered behind. The stench inside the building wouldn't go away anytime soon but at least Viv wouldn't be stepping on cow patties every time she turned around.

"I'll bring a trailer over here to pick up the stock," he told her, leaning against the shovel and wiping the sweat off his brow with the corner of his shirt. "And then we'll do a little bit of detective work, figure out who did this to you, and why. And how they managed to use my cattle to pull off the prank. I really apologize, Vivian."

"What? Why? You didn't do anything. I should be the one apologizing to you. I jumped all over you. I feel really bad that I blamed you without proof."

"As if the open door and my brand on the cattle weren't enough proof. Thank you for believing me, though."

She smiled at him and his stomach flipped over. He must be overtired from all the work he'd been doing. Or hungry. He refused to consider that what he was feeling could be any more than that.

"Did you want to ride with me back to my ranch?" he asked. "I can drop you by your place afterward. That way you won't have to worry about the stench of cattle following you into your car."

She glanced down at her now-dirty sneakers and frowned. "Would you mind? Alexis can drive me back here later to pick up my car."

"Not at all. It'll only take a few minutes to hitch up the trailer and I could use the company."

They talked on the way over to the Circle M, but not about the cattle or the prank. He needed time to mull what had happened over in his head and he imagined Viv felt the same. Instead, Viv chatted steadily about the floral wallpaper she was considering and the specialty massage chairs where a woman could apparently get her feet soaked and her toenails painted while the chair worked on the sore muscles in her back and neck.

That was what a spa was all about? It kind of sounded awesome.

The barbershop certainly didn't offer amenities comparable to that.

Not that he wanted his toenails painted. But a massage now and again would be nice.

They reached his ranch and he backed his truck up to his smallest trailer.

"Just hang out here for a moment while I hook 'er up," he said. "It won't take me long."

"In the dark? How can you see what you're doing?" She sounded impressed. His ego ballooned slightly, which felt good, after having it bashed so badly earlier in the day.

He chuckled. "I've had years of practice."

He hopped out of the cab and had just reached the hitch when he heard loud chortling coming from inside the barn. He turned toward the noise, frowning.

He knew that sound. He'd heard it a thousand times growing up—his youngest brother, Slade, trying to pull one over on him, get him in trouble for something he hadn't done. Slade had been forever trying to dupe him or frame him, although Nick had gotten him back far more often than Slade had been able to prank him.

Prank *him*.

Unbelievable. This had never been about Vivian at all.

He growled and strode into the barn. He was going to knock Slade's head so hard he'd see stars.

"What were you thinking?" he demanded into the darkness, even before he could see the outline of his brother. "Do you have any idea what you've done?"

Slade burst forward, laughing and slapping Nick on the back.

"Good one, huh?" he asked. "I would have loved to

see your face when you walked into that shop and saw your cattle hanging out there, big brother."

Nick grabbed the collar of Slade's shirt and gave him a shake. "It wasn't me who found the heifers, you blooming idiot. It was Vivian, and she was alone. Let's just say she was not pleased."

"Uh-oh," Slade said. "I figured you guys would be together when you discovered the stock at the shop. I didn't scare her, did I?"

"Probably. A little. Mostly you made her angry—not to mention making an absolute mess of the building. How did you get in, anyway?"

Slade grinned. "I still remember how to pick a lock. And I've got to say, that one wasn't very solid. Vivian ought to look into something a little sturdier."

"I'll let her know you think so," Nick replied, allowing sarcasm to creep into his voice. "Now, let's go. Viv is waiting in the truck and you owe her an apology."

"It was only a joke," Slade muttered, sounding just the same as he had when he'd been caught with his hand in the cookie jar as a child. Apparently getting married and becoming a father hadn't brought Slade to full maturity. Probably nothing ever would. He might be a policeman now, but goofing around was just Slade's nature. That didn't absolve him from the error of his ways, though.

"If it was a joke, it was a tasteless one," Nick felt obligated to point out. "How long have you and Laney been married now, and yet it never occurred to you that it might hurt a woman's feelings to put livestock in the shop she's working so hard to remodel?"

At least Slade had the good grace to wince and look apologetic at Nick's words.

Nick grabbed him by the elbow and half pushed, half dragged him back to the truck. He opened the passenger side door and leaned against the door frame.

"I have a dolt of a brother here who has something to say to you."

Not surprisingly, Vivian's gaze widened in surprise, especially when she saw who he was with.

"Slade? What's going on here?"

"What's going on," Nick replied before Slade could get a word in edgewise, "is that this idiot thought it would be funny to play a prank on *me* by putting my own cattle in the shop where I was working."

"A prank on *you*?" Vivian parroted, clearly stunned. "You mean this wasn't about me at all?"

"I didn't mean any harm by it," Slade said. "I thought it would be funny."

He would. Nick grunted in frustration. How was he supposed to explain the intricacies of the relationship between brothers, the masculine give-and-take? It probably wouldn't make a bit of sense to a woman, especially one as delicate as Vivian.

"It wasn't funny," Nick growled. "You hurt her feelings. Do you have any idea how she felt when she realized someone had broken into her shop and had left live cattle there?"

"They made quite a mess," Vivian admitted. "And they smell, by the way." She dropped her head into her hands and her shoulders quivered.

Nick had never felt so uncomfortable in his life. He wanted to shake Slade until his teeth rattled. Slade had been the instigator, but at the end of the day, Nick felt that he was the one responsible for making Vivian cry. He might not have been the perpetrator of the prank, but it wouldn't have happened if he hadn't been working with her.

"We're both really sorry," Nick said, and Vivian made a choking sound. "Viv? Are you all right?"

She looked up then, and there were indeed tears in her eyes, but it wasn't because she was crying. She was laughing so hard her cheeks had turned a bright pink and her breath was coming in quick, uneven hiccups.

"Doesn't your wife know that she should keep you on a leash?" she teased, shaking her finger at Slade and giving his shoulder a friendly shove.

Slade flashed his lady-killer grin. "I'm afraid I have the tendency to escape from time to time."

"And just look at what happens," Nick said.

"It's only a little mischief," Vivian insisted. "No harm done."

No harm done? After everything Vivian had been through tonight, she was being extremely gracious. They'd had to spend hours cleaning up the mess. And the lingering smell wouldn't do her any favors. Weren't pregnant women supposed to be especially sensitive to strong smells?

For all of that, he wasn't quite as ready to let his rascally brother off the hook.

"You owe her," he insisted. "We've already cleaned up after the cattle, but it still smells like livestock and probably will for quite some time. The least you can do is put some man hours in. We've got some walls and floors that need scrubbing and then new drywall needs to be put in."

To his credit, Slade grinned and nodded. "Sure, I'd be happy to help. Say the word and I'll be there. Just tell me when. And again, Vivian, I'm really sorry. I didn't mean anything by it. It was a stupid thing to do and I'm an idiot."

"Think nothing of it," she insisted. "I've forgotten it already."

Nick knew that wasn't the case. She'd be remembering the prank every time she walked into her shop and inhaled the aftereffects of livestock for a long time to come.

"I'm really sorry," Nick apologized once again when they were in the truck and headed toward Viv's cabin. "I can't believe my brother would pull such a lame prank. I thought he was smarter than that. But he's always had a habit of not thinking things all the way through."

"The truth is, I like Slade, and I'm sure Jax is a stand-up guy as well, but I wouldn't be surprised if you're the smartest of the three McKenna brothers," Vivian suggested, a smile tugging at her lips.

"Oh, there's no question about that."

A giggle escaped her. "And modest, too. I picked a real winner at the auction, didn't I?"

"If you don't count the cattle with my brand on them ending up inside your shop."

"I don't hold it against you," she assured him. "I'm not even upset with your brother, although I do wonder where his head was at—and where his wife was when he pulled the caper off. Can you imagine him trying to sneak a couple of cows into a shop on Main Street?

I guess it's a good thing he's a cop, or he might have gotten arrested."

"Maybe some time behind bars would do him good," Nick growled. "Get him to think a little bit."

"It's okay, Nick. Really."

"You have a bigger heart than I do. I'm not sure I can let this go so easily."

"As pranks go, it may have been way out there, but at the end of the day, there's no real harm done. I believe in the Golden Rule—do to others whatever you would have them do to you. I actually benefited from it in a way, because now Slade feels honor-bound to put some man hours into my salon. Call me crazy, but I'm actually relieved."

"Relieved? How are you relieved? Because the prank wasn't aimed at you?"

"No. Because you weren't the one responsible. For a moment there I thought maybe you really disliked me, or at least that you didn't want me opening the spa. I want to make sure you're sticking around this time because you see the potential in what I'm doing and not because of some misplaced sense of obligation. You've more than fulfilled any obligation from that stupid auction. You know that, right?"

He glanced over at her. She was such a striking woman, with her golden hair silhouetted against the moonlight in the dark cab, that his breath snagged in his throat. He wasn't certain he was staying for *all* the right reasons, definitely not for the genuine motives Vivian was suggesting.

No—he was starting to think he was sticking around for the *wrong* reasons. He was feeling all muddled up inside his head. Confused. Part of him felt like bolting. And yet he couldn't even consider walking away from this project—or walking away from Vivian.

"Does that mean you're going to let me stick around?" he asked, his voice deep and husky. He held his breath as he waited for the answer, then released it in a slow sigh of relief when she agreed. He still wasn't up to analyzing his feelings, but he knew for certain that right or wrong, he wanted to stay in Viv's life.

Chapter Five

Anticipating a large crowd for whatever sports television-viewing party that was currently all the rage at Cup O' Jo's, Vivian arrived early and secured her spot—*their* spots. Hers and Nick's. She'd selected a booth near the biggest large-screen TV for Nick's sake. She certainly had no interest in whatever game had everyone in town so excited.

This was the first and most likely the only time she would *ever* gather with others in town to watch—baseball, was it? She loved a party as much as the next social butterfly, but anything to do with sports...

Not her kettle of tea, by any means. At all.

But Nick had been so adamant about wanting to make it up to her for the silly stunt his brother had pulled that he'd practically begged her to come to the game with him.

She couldn't imagine why he continued to feel guilty over the cattle incident. She had assured him repeatedly that she'd put the whole thing behind her and held no ill will toward Slade—and especially not toward

Nick, who had done nothing but help her. As far as she was concerned, he was at least as much a victim in the prank as she had been. Slade had been aiming his mischief at Nick, not Vivian.

Still, Nick kept insisting on making reparation, and for some inexplicable reason, he thought hanging out together to watch a sports game of some sort qualified as making things right. He'd said something about how he knew she loved a good party.

She didn't have the heart to tell him she wouldn't know a football from that thingamajig the hockey guys hit around the ice with their sticks. She would be bored stiff and had no inclination whatsoever to even try to figure out the rules of the game. But if it meant that much to Nick for her to be there with him, she decided it wouldn't hurt her to put aside a couple of hours of her time and be a good *sport* about it.

She snorted aloud at her own unintended pun and then clapped a palm over her mouth, not wanting to be seen as the crazy lady in the corner laughing to herself.

Fortunately for her own reputation for sanity, Nick appeared in the doorway and Vivian waved him over. His eyes lit up and his grin sent a kaleidoscope of butterflies loose in her stomach.

"What's so funny?" he asked as he approached.

"Funny?"

Rats. She'd been discovered laughing at herself, and by Nick, no less.

"I, errr… N-nothing," she stammered.

He reached for the chair across the table from her and then paused. She thought it might be because he'd realized she was facing the big-screen television and he would be able to see better if he sat next to her and not across from her—not that she'd *intentionally* planned for that to happen.

Her cheeks warmed under his scrutiny.

"Is there a problem?" she asked when he didn't take his seat, either next to her *or* across from her.

"What in the world are you wearing?" he blurted out, staring at her as if she were an exotic animal at the local zoo.

Her face went from warm to burning hot and her nerves tingled with affront. Was he seriously dissing her on her fashion choices?

She'd spent extra time dressing today. She glanced down at her outfit but saw nothing amiss in what she'd chosen. A cute sports jersey—the only one she had—dark-wash blue jeans and decorative cowboy boots.

But Nick's tone wasn't complimentary in the least. He sounded horrified, and she felt terribly self-conscious. She rose one brow and tipped up her chin at him.

"A Denver Broncos jersey," he mumbled, answering his own question. He pinched his lips tightly and she thought for a moment he was angry, but then he sputtered and his blue eyes glimmered with amusement.

She still didn't see the problem, nor why he was so entertained by her choice in clothing. She would have him know *she* was one of the few women who was blessed to be able to actually *rock* the color orange.

"I guess so," she answered reluctantly. "My cousin who lives in Colorado gave it to me last Christmas. It's the only sports clothing I own so I thought it would be appropriate for the occasion."

He laughed and dropped into the seat beside her, his

arm around the back of the booth, just short of resting across her shoulders.

"Honey, I hate to be the one to break it to you, but Serendipity is located plumb in the middle of Texas. It's probably not the best idea for you to be wandering around with another state's team jersey on. You probably don't realize it, but you run the risk of being mobbed by rabid fans." A chuckle escaped him but he made a vain attempt to bite it back.

"Oh," she said, defeated at the notion that she'd somehow erred in her fashion choices. She had a reputation to maintain, after all, to look put-together at all times. She planned on opening a beauty salon and spa. She couldn't go around looking like she didn't know how to dress herself. "That bad, huh?"

He winced. "And there's more."

"More?" She was appalled by the prospect.

What had she done now?

He cleared his throat before speaking. "You, uh, have the wrong sport. You're wearing a football jersey. We're here to watch a baseball game."

"Does it matter?"

His gaze widened, and he started to nod but then stopped short.

"You know what? No. No it doesn't." His lips twitched at one corner. "At least, not to me, it doesn't. There are more…*intense* fans who might take issue with your apparel."

Viv couldn't imagine why it should matter so much. It was just for a stupid sports game, and it was only a shirt, after all. The point ought to be that she'd taken extra attention with her appearance today.

For the party. Not for Nick's sake. But if it was going to bother him…

"Should I go home and change?"

"You're not going anywhere. If someone has a problem with your jersey they'll have to go through me."

At first his statement ruffled her feathers, sounding as imperious as it did, but there was something about the thought of him looking out for her best interests that smoothed her emotional feathers back into place. He was only offering to protect her from her own fashion mistake, after all. There was some chivalry to that.

"We should probably order now before the crowd gets any bigger," she suggested. "Did you want to get an appetizer, or maybe dessert?"

He grinned and pulled her deeper into the crook of his shoulder. "Both. And whatever Chance is cooking up for the special of the day in between the two. I think I heard something about roast beef and gravy over a mound of mashed potatoes. Or if you don't want that, you can choose something different. This day is all about you, remember?"

Vivian really wasn't that hungry. It didn't help that her stomach was fluttering. She'd thought her morning sickness was finally getting better, but it appeared to be returning today in diamonds.

Jo approached their table with her pad in one hand and a pencil in the other, wearing a T-shirt that read "Here we go, Let's go, Here we go (Clap! Clap!)"

Viv couldn't help but think that was a pretty good approximation of the way she was feeling. She ordered a Caesar salad and a ginger ale just to mollify Nick. Hopefully the carbonation would settle her stomach.

He looked as if he were about to protest how little she was getting but then shook his head and turned his attention toward the café's vivacious owner. "We'll have the flowering onion appetizer with every kind of dipping sauce you've got. Give us a family-style helping of your special of the day. I think we'll wait until the seventh-inning stretch to order dessert, but be sure to swing by our table then."

"Swing by your table." Jo cackled and slapped him on the shoulder. "Good one, Nick."

She bustled off with their order and Nick turned to face Vivian. "A salad? Really? I'm treating you to dinner and all you order is a salad?"

Vivian shrugged dismissively. A salad was her standard order, and she didn't see why she should change it just because she was here with Nick, or because he was paying for it.

"I'm trying to make up for all the trouble my brother caused you," he reminded her. "You're not making this easy on me."

So…what? She was supposed to stuff herself with unnecessary carbs to make him feel better? She didn't need to be reminded that he was the only reason why she was sitting here in the wrong-colored sports jersey waiting for a baseball game to start in which she had no interest.

"I'll order a warm brownie sundae for dessert," she said, deciding that giving in to him would be easier than trying to explain her way out of it. Bye-bye, watching her diet for the baby's sake. But she couldn't see bickering over her choice of a salad. And Baby G did seem to have a preference for sweets lately. She'd been craving chocolate like crazy.

And jalapeños, but she thought Nick might not like having her add them as a side to their dessert.

She sat stiffly, watching excited townspeople funneling into the café, the volume in the room increasing exponentially with every new arrival. The folks in Serendipity loved a good party and they took their sports seriously.

Vivian generally enjoyed social gatherings. In any other situation she'd be fluttering from table to table, talking to all her friends and neighbors. But after what Nick had said, she was ultra-aware of her clothing—bright orange in a sea of white. She didn't care for the possibility of offending anyone, however unintentionally, so she stayed where she was—tucked under Nick's arm.

She was surprised to see Alexis and Griff enter the café. Her twin was no more of a sports lover than she was, or at least she hadn't been before. Vivian felt a sudden gap in her heart. She'd been away from home for far too long. Even though Serendipity was as slow moving as a rock, much had changed in the years she'd been gone.

She waved to catch Alexis's attention. Alexis smiled as she grabbed Griff's hand and guided him over to Viv and Nick's table.

"Are these seats taken?" Alexis asked, gesturing to the empty side of the booth. Alexis's curious gaze swept over both of them and she smirked, raising her eyebrows in an unspoken query. As twins, Viv and Alexis had always been able to communicate without speaking.

Vivian didn't like what Alexis was saying.

Appalled, she shook her head vigorously. She'd been so busy worrying about her fashion faux pas that she hadn't even considered the unspoken message she was sending to anyone who bothered looking. She was sitting far too close to Nick, and his arm's position was a little bit too possessive. If Alexis was getting the wrong impression, she could only imagine what the rest of her friends and neighbors were thinking. The last thing she needed right now was to be fodder for the gossip mill.

She didn't have to worry for long. Once the game began, everyone's attentions were glued to the screen. A few minutes later Jo arrived with the enormous appetizer. It was more than enough for everyone at the table and Nick invited Alexis and Griff to share.

Viv caught her sister's eye.

"Powder our noses?" she asked, just as the crowd roared in excitement over whatever boring thing was happening on the big screen.

Alexis agreed and they picked their way through the crowd to the relative quiet of the restroom. Alexis immediately grabbed Viv's elbow and twisted her around.

"You've been keeping secrets from me, girl," she accused good-naturedly. "Spill it."

"I don't have any secrets. There's nothing to spill," she assured her twin, but her voice sounded high and strained even to her own ears.

"Oh, so that's why you're sitting so close to Nick McKenna—and why he had his arm around you? Because there is nothing going on I ought to know about?"

"I wasn't—he didn't—" Vivian started to protest, but then sputtered to a stop.

"Since when are you two an item?" Alexis continued, laughing. "I seem to have missed the memo, and I'm your sister. How fair is that?"

Viv looked away and turned on the tap, splashing cold water on her face to counter the blush she knew had risen to her cheeks.

"It's a business arrangement," she assured Alexis, although one glance at her sister's reflection told her that her twin wasn't buying it for a second. "I won him in the auction, remember?"

"Which still doesn't explain why you are at Cup O' Jo's for a meal and a game. That doesn't sound like a work obligation. Actually, it sounds a lot more like a *date* to me."

"Well, it isn't." Viv yanked a couple of paper towels from the dispenser and dabbed at the water droplets on her chin. "It's a long story. His brother Slade played a prank on me the other day. For some reason, Nick felt responsible for it. He wanted to make it up to me by taking me to a party, and here we are."

"Okay. If you say so."

"And don't ask me about why we're watching a sports game, because I do not know the answer to that question."

Alexis tittered. "I wouldn't think of it."

Vivian sighed dramatically. "Moving on?"

Alexis shrugged, letting her off the hook for now, but Viv knew she hadn't heard the last of it. Her twin sister was too perceptive by far, compounded by the fact that they were identical twins who practically lived in each other's minds.

She was toast and she knew it.

"So… A business arrangement, then," Alexis prodded. "How's the remodeling going, by the way? I hardly ever see you anymore."

Vivian let out a breath, happy for the temporary reprieve and change in subject.

"Slower than I'd like. We had to gut the whole shop and start rebuilding from the ground up. Nick has been a great help to me there," she admitted grudgingly.

"Ironic, isn't it?"

"What's that?"

"That of all the men in town, grizzly ol' Nick is the one you chose to help you build your pastel, feminine spa. Talk about the opposite end of the spectrum from what your future clientele will look like."

"I should hope so. Anyway, he's good with a hammer. I can worry about finding customers later—a construction guy is what I need right now."

Alexis nodded. "So I've heard. Do you ever wonder, though, what he might look like all cleaned up? Shave and a haircut, two bits?"

"No," Viv replied without skipping a beat.

"You have to admit he's handsome, even with all that scruff."

Vivian didn't want to talk about this. She didn't even want to *think* about it.

"Imagine what you could do with a guy like that. Make him into a new man." Alexis's blue eyes glittered in the soft fluorescent lighting.

"No," Vivian said again. She didn't need a GPS to see where this was going.

"You should do it."

Viv's shoulders tightened with strain. The signs were clear. *Dangerous Curves Ahead.* "Do what?"

She didn't really want to know.

She already knew.

"Make him over."

"Yeah. So not happening. Do you think he's going to let me anywhere near him with a sharp pair of shears and a straight razor?"

"You're a clever woman. I'm sure you can figure something out."

"No."

"Come on. I dare you. Make Nick over by the end of the day of your Grand Openings and I'll do your laundry for a month. If you lose, you can do mine."

Viv *had* been bringing her wash over to Alexis's house once a week since she'd moved back to Serendipity. Her little cabin didn't come with laundry facilities. It sure would save her time if she could have Alexis do the hauling—plus the sorting and folding.

"Three months," she countered.

"Two," Alexis responded cheerfully. "Deal?"

Vivian wondered why she'd allowed Alexis to talk her into this. She sighed.

"All right, already," she reluctantly conceded, knowing Alexis wasn't going to let it go. "You win. I'll do it. But don't forget. My laundry. Two months."

Back in the shop, Nick spent the next week cleaning out all the debris left in the back of the building and framing what would eventually become Viv's office. He was exhausted almost to his breaking point, between working on Viv's renovation, doing all his ranch work and occasionally helping with the construction of the senior center, but he kept on pushing through it. He felt as if he were being drawn and quartered, being pulled in so many different directions, but it was all important. Every last bit of it.

He was determined to make the renovation area in the future salon safe for Vivian—and most especially for her baby. Viv had blatantly refused his *suggestion* that she stay at home and take care of herself and her little one until all of the construction work was completed. She absolutely nixed the idea of supervising from a distance. Whatever else the woman was, she was hands-on where her business was concerned. She wasn't afraid to get dirty, and she had such a fantastic attitude about it all—always looking for some way to make every task fun. She was enthusiastic and fully committed in everything she did.

She'd be a great mom.

But what made her a good businesswoman and a great mother was exactly the trait that was going to drive him crazy before he could get this remodel finished.

Vivian was currently located in what would be the office when he was done putting up the drywall. She was hunched over the dingy metal desk, straining to see under the dim light of a gooseneck lamp.

She was working with some spreadsheets she'd printed with her prehistoric printer. Her mouth was, thankfully, covered with the dust mask he'd convinced her to wear. There was that, at least. She'd listened to him about precisely one thing.

A small victory, to be sure, but a victory nonetheless. He'd take what he could where Viv was concerned.

He turned back to his work, measuring and cutting two-by-fours on a table saw. The saw was shooting up clouds of sawdust and he didn't want her breathing it in.

He could be just as stubborn as she was. He hoped. He absolutely refused to have her underfoot in the open construction area, where another mishap like the one that had happened a few weeks ago could occur.

Why hadn't Vivian mentioned she was pregnant when she'd first won him at auction? If he was going to be her general contractor, that seemed to him like an awfully large piece of information to exclude. Her safety was in his hands, as events had proven.

Had she been *trying* to hide her condition?

And if so…why?

The secret, if that's what it had been, was out now, and Vivian didn't seem to be minding the extra attention and support she was receiving from her friends—including him.

But that didn't stop him from feeling like an idiot now that he knew the truth. *How* had he not known? He couldn't believe he'd been so completely unobservant. Now that he knew what he was looking for, it was impossible for him not to see—the fluttery, oversize shirts, the rosy pink in her cheeks, the sparkle in her blue eyes.

Yep. She was pregnant, all right.

He was an idiot.

And now he felt more responsible than ever for making sure the renovation went off without a hitch. He still had his doubts about the probability of success for her business in Serendipity, but he would do everything he could to help it prosper, if only because he now knew she was going to be a single mom. She'd told him definitively that the father was not in the picture, so she needed to be able to make a living to support herself and her child.

He cast her a sideways glance, noting the way some of her blond hair had escaped a loose bun and was now framing her face like sunshine around a cloud. Usually her face was full of sunshine, too...but not right now.

He worried about her stress level. He couldn't see much of her face around the breathing mask she was wearing, but he noticed the worry lines across her forehead, and her body language was speaking volumes.

Her eyes were narrowed on the spreadsheets in front of her and she was mercilessly tapping the pencil she was holding. Her drooping shoulders suggested she wasn't getting as much sleep as she ought to be.

He set the wood he was working with aside, brushed the sawdust from his jeans and moved to the door frame.

"You okay?"

She dropped her pencil and looked up in surprise, her eyes wide, as if he'd startled her. Apparently she hadn't been aware of him, or the sudden silence after the persistent sound of the saw biting into the wood.

"If your eyes were laser beams that pile of papers would be ashes by now."

She pulled her mask down and smiled, but her face was creased with tired lines. She looked as wiped out as he felt. That couldn't be good for the baby.

"You've been staring at those numbers for two hours at least. Don't you think you ought to take a little break and walk around a bit? Stretch your legs? Your ledgers aren't going anywhere."

She sighed and stretched, pressing the small of her back. "You're right. I lost track of time. There's just so much to organize. I'm afraid I'm not going to be able to get it all together by the date of my grand opening."

Nick was also afraid, although he didn't share his fears with Viv. It was very clear that she hadn't realized how extensive the renovations would need to be when she'd bought the building. Whatever plans she made, he doubted she'd allocated enough time or money for this stage. Was she feeling the pinch now?

Her brother-in-law, Griff, had helped her start her business in Houston and Nick knew he was assisting her with her current business plan as well, but the responsibilities still had to weigh heavily on her shoulders. Even though Nick's first impression of Viv was that she was a bubblehead, he'd revised his opinion of her since then. She came off as warm and effervescent and possibly a little ditzy in personality, but inside her heart beat a proud woman determined to make her spa succeed on her own merit. She allowed nothing to go unnoticed and was personally involved in every single area of the remodel.

He believed that *she* thought she had the strength to do it on her own. Still, he couldn't help but think she might be over her head.

Add to that the fact that she would soon be caring for an infant and was even now dealing with the unique trials of being pregnant. Aching back. Tired feet. Morning sickness.

She needed his help. That was all there was to it.

And whether she wanted him or not, he was going to be there until the end.

He was way past wondering how he'd gotten into this mess. His big worry now was how he would ever get out of it. Vivian's problems—and by extension his own—were only just beginning. They had a long path ahead of them.

"Put that all aside for now and go enjoy a walk," he suggested to her.

"Only if you'll agree to walk with me," she said, picking up the soft pink sweater she'd hung over the back of the chair.

He stepped up and took the sweater from her hands and then helped her slip into it. He slid his palms across her shoulders to smooth the soft material and felt her muscles tighten under his fingers.

With effort, he resisted the instinctive impulse to knead the stress from her muscles, knowing she might take it the wrong way. With the sweet floral scent of her perfume wafting over his senses and making his head spin with her nearness, he was having difficulty remaining impartial himself.

"There you are, then." He cleared his throat and stepped back, reminding himself why all this was necessary.

Her baby.

"Thank you." She flashed a grateful smile at him from over her shoulder, her cheeks the same pretty shade of pink as her sweater, and his throat tightened around his breath.

Not helping.

"Er—my pleasure." The words were an automatic

response, but to his astonishment, he realized he really meant them.

Really not helping.

Fighting the urge to flee the scene entirely, he opened the door for her and gestured both directions along the clapboard sidewalk. Part of Serendipity's charm was that the buildings on Main Street still retained an old-fashioned Western flavor to their storefronts. Cup O' Jo's Café even sported a hitching post and water trough out front. Emerson's Hardware had three wooden rocking chairs under its eave, almost always occupied by three old fellows in matching bib overalls.

"Any particular destination?" he asked.

"No, not really," she replied, her voice sounding as if her thoughts were distant.

Nick examined the sidewalk each way and then turned left, determining that the clapboard that direction was in better condition. Besides, if they walked that direction they'd pass the park, where they would be able to stroll along the well-paved bike path—in full view of the community.

Couldn't hurt. He needed to remember what he was potentially getting out of this…*business* arrangement. The opportunity to redeem himself. Although thinking in those terms might actually be sabotaging his goal.

Was it selfish to want to use this to prove himself trustworthy with a woman? With Vivian?

They didn't speak as they crossed the street at the one and only stoplight in town and meandered down to the park. He tucked her arm through his elbow to offer her extra support.

He sensed something was bothering her beyond the

obvious, but he hesitated to ask what it was. What good would that do him, other than drag him deeper into the quandary of the mind that was Vivian Grainger?

Anyway, if she thought he could help with whatever was keeping her thoughts so occupied, she'd ask him, right?

After a few minutes he gestured to a park bench. As soon as she sat down, she turned toward him. Worry shadowed her eyes but she smiled nonetheless.

"It's a glorious day, isn't it?" she asked, flicking her hair over her shoulder with one hand. "I'm glad you suggested the walk."

Glorious day? Who even talked like that?

Vivian, apparently. Even when she was distracted by her problems.

"Yeah," he agreed. "It's nice."

He nodded his head in acknowledgment to a couple of female joggers, whom he recognized were old friends of Brittany's. They seemed stunned to see him sitting companionably with Vivian. He smiled at their expressions.

See? he wanted to tell them. *Not every woman in town thinks I'm a leper.*

"Well, that was rude," Vivian observed with a wry grin, her voice dripping as sour as lemon juice.

He switched his gaze from Brittany's friends to Vivian, wondering what he'd missed. He hadn't seen either of the ladies do or say something untoward. If they had, he would catch up to them and call them out on it. No one was going to be discourteous to Viv on his watch.

He hated to reveal his ignorance, but he had to ask. "What did they do?"

"What did *they* do?" Vivian's gaze widened on him and she pursed her lips. "What did *they* do? Take a good look in the mirror, buddy. Didn't your mama teach you that it's not polite to check out other women when you are currently in the company of one?"

"What? No, I—"

She arched an eyebrow.

"Vivian, honestly." He raised both hands in a gesture of truthfulness and surrender. "You've got to believe me. I promise I wasn't checking out those women, or at least not in the way you're thinking."

"No? It certainly looked that way to me. I saw where your gaze went. Not that I blame you. Brooke and Ashley are lovely women. I'm sure either one of them would be thrilled if you asked them out on a date."

He cringed. If only she knew just how wrong she was. On all counts. He wouldn't be interested in asking either one of them for a date, and they definitely wouldn't agree to go out with him if he did ask.

"Yeah, that's kind of the point." He blew out a breath, feeling his face warm under her scrutiny. "Actually, I was kind of hoping they'd notice me. Er—well, not notice *me*, so much as observe that I was sitting here with you."

"With *me*?" she exclaimed. "Okay, buster, now you've lost me completely."

"I know you may find this hard to believe, but I don't have a stellar reputation with the ladies around here," he reluctantly explained, then cringed at how egotistical he sounded. "The truth of it is, I doubt whether either one of those women would go on a date with me if I asked. Not that I want to ask," he quickly amended.

"I *do* find that hard to believe." Her gaze warmed as she looked him over. His stomach flipped. Those blue eyes were downright dangerous when they were directed at him. "I can't imagine any young lady not giving you a chance."

What was she saying? That she found him attractive? He remembered back to the day of the auction when he'd thought that dating might have been on her mind, that it might have been the reason she bid on him.

And how laughable was that? It was no wonder Brittany had felt it necessary to burst his bubble in public. His ego was so huge it could rival one of those balloons at the Macy's Thanksgiving Day Parade.

Vivian's life was full—more than full—between her coming baby and her fledgling business. She wouldn't have time for a relationship even if she wanted one, which he highly doubted. She hadn't ever mentioned the baby's father, but he didn't appear to be part of Viv's life.

He wouldn't burden her further. Instead, he turned the conversation back to himself.

"You know Brittany Evans, right?"

"Sure. Not well, though. She was two grades above me in school, as I recall. Pretty brunette. She was a cheerleader and tended to only associate with those in her…'social sphere.'"

Nick snorted. "That's a kind way of saying she was one of the leaders of a clique of snobby popular girls."

"Was she? I guess I never noticed."

No, Viv wouldn't have. Even as a teenager, she was the kind of person who was friends with everyone, from the loftiest cheerleader, the star quarterback, and the drum major of the marching band all the way to every kid in the special education classes.

Brittany, on the other hand...

What had he been thinking, dating her? She was physically attractive, but her personality had always grated on him. Why was he only now seeing how miserable their whole relationship had been?

He'd been poor boyfriend material because his heart hadn't really been in it. Brittany had had every right to trash-talk him.

"We were dating for a while," he explained ruefully. "Let's just say I didn't pay as much attention to her as she deserved, and she let me know it."

"I see." Viv paused and then shook her head. "Well, no, actually, I guess I don't see. What does all that have to do with me?"

Her words sounded suspicious and she narrowed her gaze on him.

"We had a big, very *public* breakup last New Year's Eve at the community party. Brittany basically lambasted me in front of the whole town for being an unfeeling jerk. She called me all kinds of names. She warned the single women in Serendipity—in a very loud voice—that they ought to beware." A self-deprecating laugh escaped through his pinched lips. "That was pretty much the end of my social life as I once knew it."

It was only now, as he related the story to Vivian, that he comprehended how little it mattered to him. Over the past year of forced solitude, he'd realized he was okay being alone, with just himself for company. Perhaps he was a perennial bachelor after all and not, as he'd always believed himself to be, a man who would eventually settle down with a wife and family.

Maybe he'd never had that in him at all.

"So let me get this straight," Viv said, interrupting his thoughts. "You wanted Ashley and Brooke—who are friends of Brittany's, if I'm remembering right—to notice we're together so they would get the mistaken impression that you're *dating* me? That you've moved on?"

Her eyes widened and she sniffed in astonishment. "That was what the whole point of dinner at Cup O' Jo's was about, wasn't it? To let the town know you've moved on—with me. I feel like I've suddenly been caught up in a high school drama. Grow up, Nick."

Her words hit him like a brick to the chest.

Maybe it was because she was speaking the truth.

"That's what I'm trying to do."

His first instinct was to defend himself and his actions, but instead he put all of his effort into tamping down the flare of his ego. He blew out a breath, took off his hat and scrubbed his fingers through his hair. "I know it looks and sounds bad, and I get that you're angry with me, but this was never about giving anyone the mistaken impression that we're a couple."

"No? Then what?" Her voice and expression softened. He couldn't blame her for jumping to a negative conclusion, like she had with the cattle in her shop, but this time—just like last time—she seemed willing to hear him out when he tried to explain.

"I'm trying to prove to the town—and to myself— that I'm not a total muck-up. That's what Brittany said— that no one should ever rely on me because I'd always let them down. I thought maybe if I could help you get your shop fixed up, it would show that I really can be relied on. That you were right to trust me to do the remodeling job for you. I hoped maybe you could even be my friend. But I've kind of blown it now, haven't I?"

"Yes, you have," Vivian replied with a grave frown. Then her nose started twitching and a moment later she was giggling. "Oh, Nick, you take yourself—and life in general—way too seriously. You need to loosen up."

He lowered his brow and replaced his cowboy hat. Was she making fun of him?

"I'm a typical firstborn," he snapped back. "What do you expect?"

"I know what *you* expect out of yourself. Perfection. Which none of us can really aspire to, can we? All I'm saying is you shouldn't be so hard on yourself all the time."

He raised his brow, questioning her statement. She was one to talk. He'd heard her speak negatively of herself more times than he could count.

She shook her head. They weren't going to talk about her. They never did.

"You know Serendipity," she continued, not allowing him to redirect their conversation. "Yes, folks love to gossip. And your breakup with Brittany probably was big news—until about January 2nd, when some new item of interest popped up to gain the gossips' attention. After that you and Brittany were yesterday's news and everyone moved on from there to new ground. You're probably the only one who remembers it."

"Do you think?" The relief flooding through him was palpable, sluicing over his muscles and loosening his joints and marrow until his whole body felt lighter, almost as if he were floating. He hadn't realized what a heavy weight he'd been carrying. And Vivian, with her sweet, kind words, had set him free.

"Oh, I'm sure of it. And if I'm not mistaken, Brittany has put it in the past, as well. I heard just the other day that she's engaged to Gregory Carr. Apparently it didn't take her too long to get over you, so I wouldn't beat yourself up about it."

Vivian was right. It was almost as if poor old Gregory had been waiting in the wings to snap up Brittany as soon as she was available. And clearly Brittany hadn't minded.

"You're right," Nick agreed, amazement lining his voice. He didn't know how he hadn't seen it before, but lately he seemed to have been blind about a lot of things. "And I wish the two of them well."

He was just happy it wasn't him.

"As do I," she said, chuckling at his expression. "But you do realize that in your quest to redeem yourself with the town, you *have*, however unintentionally, made it look like we are more than simple business associates."

He had. He knew he had. And it hadn't been entirely unintentional. He knew it was a bad idea. He had too many responsibilities to even consider a relationship right now. He'd only end up letting his girlfriend down, like he'd done with Brittany. And with Vivian laser-focused on starting up her business—not to mention whatever drama had happened with her baby's father—he doubted she was looking for love, either.

Yet he couldn't seem to stop himself from getting closer to her. He enjoyed being around Vivian, whether it was strolling through the park, laughing at her blaring orange Broncos jersey or even shoveling cow patties out of her shop.

Without consciously meaning to, he had set off down the very path he had promised himself he would never go down again.

He was starting to have feelings for her.

This couldn't happen. He needed to nip this in the bud. Immediately. Before he messed things up and hurt Vivian. It was only a matter of time.

"I'm thinking I'm not cut out to be a family man."

There. That should do it.

"Because of one bad relationship?" She scoffed and waved him off, though he noticed the pain that flashed through her eyes. "Don't be silly."

He snorted. "Believe me, it's been more than one. Brittany is, unfortunately for the women of Serendipity, just the last and most vocal of my long string of failures."

"You're being too hard on yourself."

"Am I?" He looked deep into her eyes, seeing warmth, enthusiasm and...*belief.* Belief in him. Confidence in the man he could become.

Trust.

If her gentle smile was anything to go by, she clearly wasn't going to let him get away with judging himself too harshly.

"Who knows?" Her blue eyes glittered with amusement. "Maybe you just haven't met the right woman yet."

Her bright smile almost convinced him that her words were true and that she believed them. But there was too much she wasn't telling him.

"Do you really believe that, or does this rule only apply to me?" he asked gently.

Her gaze dropped to her belly and she refused to look up at him.

"You've got me," she said on a sigh. "I'm really good at giving other people advice, but I'm not so good at taking my own."

"Meaning?" He reached for her hand and covered it with his.

"Does it not bother you that you're hanging around with a pregnant single woman? Do you not wonder if I'm being hypocritical, attending church as an unwed mother?"

He immediately shook his head. He didn't. He never had. Whatever Viv's story turned out to be, he had no doubt that she was a genuine woman of faith.

"Well, I am a hypocrite. Or at least, I was." She blew out a breath.

"You don't have to tell me this if you don't want to."

"No, I think I do."

He nodded for her to continue.

After a long pause, she spoke again. "I was engaged to Derrick—the father of my son. I'm ashamed to admit I allowed myself to be pulled into a verbally and emotionally abusive relationship."

His hand tightened around hers. Without knowing one more detail about this Derrick guy, Nick wanted to throttle him. That wouldn't help Vivian or her baby now, but he wished he could have protected Vivian from such a cad.

"Derrick put a lot of pressure on me to turn my back on my faith, on my morals. But I can't lay all the blame at his door. In the end it was my bad decision and wrong actions."

"You got pregnant."

"Yes." She laid a protective hand over her belly. "I knew it was wrong, what Derrick and I had done, but I truly believed it would all work out in the end. I thought we would get married, just sooner than we'd planned. But when I told Derrick about the baby, he was furious. Even though he knew perfectly well he was the only man I'd ever been with, he denied he was the father and declared he wanted nothing to do with either one of us."

Nick had a hard time believing any man could be so cruel. Any *real* man. Derrick definitely wouldn't qualify for that category.

"Has he contacted you since?"

"No. I've called him a few times, but he recently changed his phone number. I'm truly on my own."

Nick tipped her chin up so she had no choice but to meet his gaze.

"No, you're not," he whispered, his voice gravelly. "You're not alone."

Chapter Six

_"U_ncle Nick! Uncle Nick!"

Vivian laughed as young Brody, Slade's adopted four-year-old son, launched himself into Nick's arms. In Brody's exuberance, he overshot his mark and nearly barreled into Vivian.

Her pulse jumped up and she placed a protective hand over her middle. It was only Nick's quick reflexes that kept her from being wrestled right off the park bench.

Nick leaned in to catch Brody, swinging him into the air and wiggling him until he giggled in delight. The black-and-white-spotted ball the boy had been holding dropped to the ground, unnoticed.

"Look where you're going, little dude," Nick said, setting the boy on his feet again. "You nearly knocked over this pretty young lady here."

Vivian's heart skipped a beat. Did he really think she was pretty? Did that mean he didn't see her as damaged or flawed, even after all she'd just told him?

"It's nothing," she assured them.

"Yes, it is," Nick contended. "In the McKenna family little men learn to be courteous to ladies. And that includes not knocking them off of park benches. Especially not women about to have a baby. We have to be extra respectful of them."

Vivian had a sudden vision of being cradled in Nick's arms the day she'd fallen over the drywall. He'd been so afraid she'd hurt herself. At the time all she could remember was feeling annoyed, but now the memory came along with sensory details, things she'd missed the first time.

The gentleness and worry lining his deep, rich voice. The scent of leather and spice that was uniquely Nick. The rippling of the muscles in his arms and chest. The way he carried her as if she weighed no more than a feather, even though her body had thickened with her unborn child.

"Brody, you have to treat girls with respect. You have to be nice to them."

Brody made a face and reached for his ball. Evidently he wasn't a big fan of girls yet.

"What do you say you apologize to Miss Vivian?" Nick gently took the boy's shoulders and turned him toward her.

Little Brody's head hung. He looked adorably contrite. "Sorry I almost hit you," he muttered almost too quietly to hear.

"You are quite forgiven, sweetheart. No hard feelings, okay?" She reached out a hand to the boy and they shook on it.

Nick stole the ball from Brody's grip. He hefted the

ball back to Brody and grinned at Viv. "Do you mind if I play with my nephew for a few?"

"No, not at all. Take your time. After spending the whole morning with a mask over my face, I'm enjoying the fresh air. Have fun playing with your basketball."

Brody crowed with laughter.

"It's a soccer ball," Nick corrected, one corner of his lips tugging up.

"You kick the ball, not bounce it," Brody informed her in a solemn tone of voice.

"I apologize for my mistake," Viv said with equal seriousness. "I'm a complete newbie where sports are concerned. I promise I will remember that fact for the next time I observe soccer."

Nick winked at her and lobbed the ball out onto the green grass. Both Nick and Brody chased after it, hooting and hollering as they kicked it back and forth to each other.

Vivian waved to Laney, who was sitting under a shelter chatting with a group of women and then turned her attention back to the boys. She thought the game itself was as boring as watching oil dry. Kicking the ball back and forth, back and forth, with no end in sight. But she enjoyed watching Nick interact with his nephew.

Nick's expression, usually so serious, relaxed, the hard ridges and lines of stress diminishing. Rich laughter bubbled from his chest as he feigned right, then left, and then let little Brody steal the ball away from him—all without letting the boy know that Nick was giving rather than taking.

She loved watching how Nick subtly raised the child's confidence as he taught him how to move the ball—

dribble…apparently the word was *dribble*—across the grass using only the insides of his feet.

Considering the fact that they'd both admonished her that soccer was all about *kicking* the ball, it seemed to her that they spent an awful lot of time bouncing the ball off of other body parts—in particular, their heads.

At one point, Nick even picked the ball off the ground and tossed it repeatedly at Brody so the boy could practice popping the ball into the air with his forehead.

What kind of barbarity was that? What was he trying to do? Give the poor little dude brain damage?

Men. And little men. It was easy for Vivian to believe they might well be an entirely different species. Would it be the same way with her son? How could she ever hope to keep up with Baby G if she didn't understand the way he ticked?

If it was anybody but Nick, she would have worried about Brody getting hurt, but his affection for his nephew was obvious in Nick's every move, head-bonking notwithstanding. His encouragement was visibly raising the boy's confidence level in addition to his skill on the playing field.

And he thought he wasn't cut out to be a family man? Anyone with eyes in their head could see how good he was with children. How could he not see that in himself?

Nick smiled and waved at her, and for the first time in her life, she wished she'd paid more attention to sports when she was in school so she could join Nick and Brody in their play. She'd attended a few games in high school, but she had always been too busy talking with her friends to pay any attention to what was happening on the field. And she'd hated phys ed.

Who would teach her son how to dribble a soccer ball, or even pop it off his forehead, though the thought made her cringe? She certainly wouldn't be the one to do it.

Here she was, in a park full of happy, joy-filled adults and children, and she felt the most completely and utterly alone she'd ever been. Her baby's future, his care and his happiness, all depended on her. She had no partner in life with whom to share both the blessings and the burdens of parenthood.

It was she and she alone.

How could she possibly teach her son all the things he'd need to know to grow into adulthood? How could she be both mother and father to him? She didn't even know the difference between a basketball and a soccer ball, much less how to play the games. It was a silly thing, she knew, but at the moment it felt totally overwhelming.

She was long past being angry that Derrick had abandoned her, but she still couldn't comprehend how he could possibly refuse to be a father to his own son, or even to acknowledge paternity.

Deep down, Viv knew that it was the best thing for both her and her child. What kind of father would Derrick have made anyway, moving in and out of their son's life? He wouldn't have given the baby any stability or security.

Not to mention, Derrick hadn't treated her well, and she doubted he would have been any better with their baby. It was by God's grace that she had gotten out of that toxic relationship and returned to Serendipity where she belonged. She couldn't bear the thought of her precious baby exposed to that kind of abuse. But even though in her heart she knew it would have been detrimental to have had Derrick in their lives, it still didn't seem fair that her child had to grow up in a single-parent household—especially hers.

She felt so completely inadequate for the task. A child deserved to grow up with a mother and a father.

In a perfect world.

She didn't realize Nick and Brody had stopped kicking the ball around until Nick suddenly dropped onto the bench beside her, his breath coming in short, shallow gasps. Sweat slicked his forehead and he used the bottom of his T-shirt to dab it away.

"Brody, you need to take it easy on your poor uncle Nick," Nick said, grabbing the boy around the shoulders and tickling his belly. "I'm too old to keep up with you."

Nick met Viv's gaze and raised his eyebrows, clearly expecting a laugh. She really should be laughing.

Nick, an out-of-shape old man?

Laughable.

She managed to wrestle up a smile but couldn't summon the mirth to go with it, even when Nick lagged his tongue out to the side and panted like a pooch.

"You goof," she said, playfully shoving his shoulder. She appreciated what he was doing to get her out of her funk, even if it wasn't working.

He narrowed his gaze on her and then reached out and gently caressed the line of her jaw. A million tiny electrical currents accompanied the slow path of his fingertips.

"You usually think so." He leaned forward until his lips were mere centimeters from her ear. His warm breath fanned her cheeks, sending a shiver of awareness down her spine.

"What's wrong?" he whispered.

"It's nothing." She nodded toward Brody.

"Right. Hey, dude, you'd better go check in with your mom." He waved at Laney as Brody darted across the park to return to her side.

With Brody safe with Laney, Nick turned his full attention on Vivian. "Are you feeling all right? Is your morning sickness bothering you?"

Did she look nauseated? If she did, it was all Derrick's fault. Just the thought of him was now enough to turn her stomach. But she was tired of thinking about him. He was no longer a part of her life and she didn't want to waste any more brain cells or emotional energy wondering about him.

She placed a palm over her belly. She'd been feeling tiny little butterfly flutters for a couple of weeks now, but this time she felt definite movement under her hand.

She gasped.

Nick's brow lowered. "Should I call 9-1-1?"

After all of the conflicting emotions she'd experienced over the past hour, the thought of Nick calling 9-1-1 because he thought she might be experiencing morning sickness was too much for her.

She didn't know whether to laugh or cry, so she did both. She chuckled and hiccupped simultaneously and then tears of joy sprang to her eyes.

All of her anxiety dissipated. Her problems appeared

minute compared to the magnitude of the joy of feeling new life moving within her.

She wasn't alone. She carried Baby G under her heart. Soon she would be holding her precious newborn in her arms. There was nothing but God's blessing in that.

And she had Nick hovering anxiously over her, looking as if he was about ready to jump out of his skin. It warmed her heart to see him act that way. Even though he had no vested interest in them, he was overtly protective of her and her baby.

"I just felt him move," she explained, her voice cracking with emotion.

Nick's large blue eyes filled with wonder.

"I've been feeling flutters for a couple of weeks now, but this is the first time I've felt a good, solid kick."

Nick chuckled. "Baby G probably wanted to join Brody and me in our soccer game."

"That must be it," she agreed, joining in his laughter. "I guess I'd better start learning the rules of the game.

"Oh!" She reached for Nick's hand and placed it on the side of her swollen belly. "There he is again. Can you feel him? I think it's his heel."

As if in answer to her question, the baby moved again. Vivian thought he might have done a full backflip this time, the little show-off.

Nick's smile couldn't have been any wider and his gaze shone with delight. "I did. I felt him move. It's amazing. What a blessing you've got there."

Her hand tightened over his and she swallowed hard against the tumult of emotions welling inside her.

Now that he'd gotten their attention, Baby G appeared to be doing gymnastics.

Nick chortled. "I think he's showing off for his uncle Nick."

Uncle Nick?

Her heart skipped and then charged into beating double-time.

Maybe her son *would* have a solid, trustworthy male role model in his life, after all. She'd assumed once the spa was finished, her association with Nick would end.

She was exhilarated to hear that she was wrong.

And if Nick intended to be involved with her baby—what did that mean for the two of them?

She was afraid to even begin to consider the implications, but they nonetheless nestled someplace deep in her heart.

She offered up a silent prayer. She wasn't alone.

Though a manager had been hired in October and residents had been trickling in for weeks, Thanksgiving Day marked the official grand opening of Serendipity's senior center. It seemed only right to celebrate such a momentous occasion on the day set aside for giving thanks.

Nick finished a family meal with his mother, Jax—along with his new fiancée, Faith, and his adorable, twin baby girls—and Slade and Laney with Brody. After a relaxed dinner filled with good food and great fellowship, Nick and his mother headed out to watch the town council cut the red ribbon and invite the public to see the results of their generosity at the auction.

As with the rest of his family, Nick was anxious to see how his uncle James was settling in to his new home.

But along with this successful grand opening, Nick was mulling over other plans, ones that had gone awry, not at all as hoped or expected. Despite the fact that he'd spent every spare minute at Viv's shop, they hadn't been able to open the doors to the salon and spa in time for the holidays the way she'd planned.

Vivian hadn't said anything—she always kept her chin up and her attitude positive—but he knew the burden of stress she was shouldering, and it had to be overwhelming.

She was the bravest, most stalwart woman he'd ever known, but he worried about her, and he was concerned about the baby. Once the town had found out about her condition, his mother had encouraged him to watch over Vivian, informing him that undue stress could send a woman into premature labor. Nick wasn't sure how he could help, other than to do what he was already doing—taking care of as many details regarding the spa as possible and surreptitiously trying to make sure she took care of herself.

He felt woefully inadequate. But what else was he supposed to do? Though she denied it, he knew it was more than just her business affairs that were bothering her. Ever since that day in the park, she'd been more withdrawn and introspective.

Something was different. Something had changed. He hoped it had nothing to do with this Derrick fellow, but he couldn't be sure.

Unless she chose to open up to him and talk about her problems, he was powerless to help her.

He'd told her the truth about what had happened between him and Brittany and had come clean about the agenda he'd created after Vivian won him in the auction.

Had those confessions led to Viv having second thoughts about working with him? He wouldn't be surprised. Why should she trust him, a man who had consistently proven himself untrustworthy? His past was catching up with him, rushing in on him, coloring his future.

Lord, make me a new man.

It was more than just changing his behavior. Change had to come from his heart. And, he acknowledged, as he watched old Frank Spencer, Jo's husband and the president of the town council, cut the ribbon to the senior center, only God could transform a man's heart and make the old man new again.

Nick prayed the Lord would bless him, that he would find the much longed-for peace, and that he could somehow then pass it on to Vivian and her baby.

He tucked his mother's hand into the crook of his arm as the crowd jostled their way into the new center. The facility was set up into two wings—one side for active seniors who needed little more than an occasional check-in, while the other side was a long-term care ward which provided around-the-clock care for folks like Uncle James. At the hub of the two wards was the main office, the cafeteria and a large common area with two television sets and a variety of reading material and board games.

As they entered the center, Nick kept a discreet eye out for Vivian, but he didn't see her anywhere, although her twin sister, Alexis, was hosting the bake sale.

"Do you want to go and see if we can find Uncle James?" Nick asked his mother.

Alice patted his shoulder. "You go on ahead, dear. I'll catch up with you in a minute."

A group of Alice's friends from church were waving her over. His mom didn't get out as much socially as she'd used to before Nick's dad had died, but helping Jax with his twin babies had put a bit of a spring back into her step—as had the announcement of Jax's engagement to Faith, who Alice doted on. Nick was glad to see she'd begun embracing life again and reconnecting with her friends.

Sometimes, like now, being a large man in a tight space with a lot of people was more of a detriment than a help, and it took him a while to make his way through the crowd to the corridor leading to the long-term care ward.

He wasn't sure what kind of condition he'd find Uncle James in today. Some days the man was entirely lucid. On other days, he had no idea who Nick was, and even on occasion became frightened or aggressive in Nick's presence.

His own father had been the same way near the end. Nick had never been entirely comfortable with Jenson's illness, and deep down he wondered if that was part of the reason he hadn't been there when his dad passed. Had he used the ranch to avoid emotions he'd rather not confront?

Nick wasn't the same man now. He was committed to making regular visits to his uncle James, whether or not the man was aware he was there.

He was looking for his uncle's apartment when he

suddenly heard a soft, high tinkle of laughter coming from a nearby room. The sound reminded him of a fairy.

He knew that laugh.

He peeked into the room where he'd heard Viv's laughter and stopped short, his breath catching in his throat.

She was sitting between two old ladies, and the three of them were chatting and giggling like schoolgirls. Nick didn't think either of the women knew who Viv was—maybe they didn't even know who they were, themselves. They both had dementia's blank-eyed stare, and yet Vivian had them fully engaged as she painted their fingernails a glistening bright red.

Vivian didn't look the least bit uncomfortable with the old women. Nick knew that in their minds, Vivian might be a long-lost daughter or granddaughter, or an old friend rather than just a kind stranger, but they were clearly enjoying her ministrations.

As Viv stretched the small of her back, she glanced up and met Nick's gaze as he stood in the doorway. She extended her hand and her sunny smile to him.

"Well, don't just stand there, Nick. Come on in and let me introduce you to these two lovely ladies. This is Opal," she said, gesturing to the woman on the right. "And this is Marjorie. They share this suite."

Nick grinned and tipped his hat to the ladies. "Nice to meet you both."

"Nick here is doing all the carpentry on the beauty salon I've been telling you about. He's doing a lovely job. I'm so pleased with the outcome."

Pride swelled in Nick's chest. He usually had women yelling at him, not praising him. It felt mighty fine.

Her kind words made him want to earn Vivian's respect even more.

"Are you all related?" he asked.

"They're sisters," Viv answered. "But I'm no relation to them. I'm just floating around here today offering my services to all of the residents. Primping hair and painting fingernails and toenails for the ladies. Shaves and haircuts for any of the guys who want it."

She gave him a once-over that made his nerves tingle. He didn't like the look in her eye, nor the fact that she had shears and a razor in her apron.

"Your husband is a real looker." Marjorie gestured toward Nick.

"Yes, but he's unkempt," Opal added frankly. "You really should do something about that hair, Viv."

"Oh, I'm not—" Nick started to say, but Vivian cut him off with the briefest shake of her head.

She was right, of course. The women would probably just get confused if he tried to explain that he and Viv weren't married. The old folks saw what they wanted to see.

"I know, right?" she said instead. "He won't let me anywhere near him with a pair of scissors. I'm going to keep trying, though."

Gathering her supplies, she kissed each of the ladies on the cheek and reached for Nick's elbow, guiding him out of the room.

He stopped just outside the door.

"They thought we were—"

"I know," she said, smothering a chuckle. "Can you imagine?"

Their eyes met and held, and for one moment, as he

lost himself in the impossibly deep blue pools of her eyes, Nick *could* imagine. His pulse jolted to life and his gaze dropped to her lips.

She laughed nervously and turned away from him, gesturing to a room across the hallway.

"Were you looking for your uncle? I believe that's his apartment over there."

It took Nick a beat to regroup. He glanced at the door number and nodded. "Yep. That's him."

"Does he need his hair cut, do you think?"

"I doubt it. He usually keeps his hair shaved into a buzz cut."

She produced a pair of shears from her apron pocket and waved them at him in mock menace.

"How about you? What do you say, Nick? Are you ready for a haircut and a nice close shave?"

He belted out a laugh and held both hands up in protest. "You stay away from me with those things."

"Spoilsport." She pouted playfully, her full lips arcing downward. "Just think of what good advertising you would be for my salon."

He shook his head. "No, ma'am. Your beauty salon doesn't need my kind of advertising. That would be catastrophic—especially since it isn't even open yet."

A shadow crossed her gaze and he wanted to kick himself.

Way to go, McKenna. Remind her of all the hurdles they still had to jump over to get her spa up and running.

He reached for her free hand—the one without a sharp instrument in it.

"It'll happen, Vivian," he promised. "Maybe not on

our original timetable, but your spa *will* open, and it will be successful. Wait and see. Remember, it's all in God's hands, sweetheart."

"I know," she said through tight lips.

She didn't sound like she believed him. It was discouraging, his Vivian losing faith.

His Vivian? Now, where had that come from?

"Nick? Is that you?" Uncle James appeared in the doorway in a battered brown bathrobe and mismatched house shoes. "I thought it was your voice I heard."

"Hello, Mr. McKenna," Vivian said brightly, all traces of her own worries instantly erased as she addressed the man. "Are you settling in okay?"

James stared at her, suddenly confused. "Who are you?"

Vivian's smile didn't waver. "My name's Vivian."

"Viv's a friend of mine, Uncle James."

James seemed to dismiss her, his gaze fixed back on Nick. "Are you here to take me home?"

Nick swallowed hard. How could he explain to his uncle that this *was* home?

He looked to Vivian for guidance. She was way better at dealing with people than he was. She flashed him an encouraging smile.

"Do you have any treats in that minifridge of yours?" she asked, diverting his uncle's thoughts. "Nick hasn't eaten in at least an hour. I'm sure he's famished."

She glanced back at Nick and winked, her lips twitching with mirth.

He nodded, acknowledging both her sense of humor and his thanks.

"Come on, Uncle James," he said, gently turning

his uncle by the shoulders and leading him back into the room.

"I'll stop by the cafeteria and see what they've got for you," Viv volunteered. "But then I've got to get back to the other residents. There are a lot of ladies waiting to get their hair done."

He watched her walk away, marveling at her ability to give of herself to others even when she was struggling through issues in her own life.

Not every woman had such a large and loving heart.

But then again, not every woman was Vivian Grainger.

Chapter Seven

Three weeks before Christmas, with the holiday season in full swing, Vivian found herself busier than ever. Now in her third trimester, she felt like someone had strapped a giant watermelon onto her body, but thankfully the morning sickness was long behind her and her energy level was at its peak.

Baby G was more active with every day that passed, although he was growing so big he had a lot less room to move within her. She was a little short on sleep because her son apparently believed her rest time was his playtime. Sometimes it felt like he was using her ribs as monkey bars, but she gloried in every movement. She couldn't wait to meet her sweet little one face-to-face and hold him in her arms.

Not long now. Her due date was only a few weeks away, about a week into the New Year.

In the meantime, she had plenty to keep her mind and hands occupied. She volunteered at the senior center twice a week, keeping the residents happily curled and manicured.

Once she'd passed Thanksgiving, she'd accepted both rationally and emotionally the fact that it was going to take her longer than she'd originally hoped and anticipated to open the spa.

Deciding on a new grand-opening date had been problematic, since she had to take into account that Baby G was soon to make his debut into the world. It would be difficult, but not impossible. She would open her salon, have her baby and take a two-week maternity leave before returning to work.

As for the building itself, things were finally falling into place. The electrical system was correctly rewired, the plumbing issues were fixed, and the inspector would make final rounds with Nick on Wednesday.

All new styling chairs had been installed, as had the massage chairs for pedicures. She had a massage table for use with guests looking for a deep tissue massage.

A beautiful walnut desk and file cabinet now graced her office. She'd hired her staff, two young ladies with recently obtained cosmetology and massage licenses who were excited to begin their careers at Viv's salon. She was glad she could hire locally and contribute to Serendipity's economy.

And she'd finally settled on a name for her new business.

Tranquility.

A name that she hoped she could live up to, that she could really offer her clientele. Maybe she'd even eventually find some of that peace for herself.

She prayed she'd be able to have the salon open for at least a week or two before her baby came. She wanted to be there to make sure the grand opening went off as designed and everything in the salon was working smoothly. Still, to be on the safe side, she'd taken the time to create a contingency plan and was confident the two girls could hold down the fort until she could get back to work after the baby was born.

It wasn't ideal by any means, but with Nick's help with the remodel and the young cosmetologists ready to take over when the baby was born, it could be done.

It had to be. She couldn't afford to wait much longer before the salon started bringing in revenue.

Today, though, she would put her apprehensions about the opening of Tranquility aside.

The senior center was throwing its highly anticipated, first annual Christmas party. Decorations, food and fellowship, brought from the townsfolk's hearts to the beloved elderly population in their care.

Christmas was by far Vivian's favorite time of year, when everyone's attention turned toward the infant Jesus, when hearts and minds were filled with an attitude of joy and giving. Peace on earth, goodwill toward man. Evergreen trees and lights on all the houses. Candles lit in the darkened sanctuary of the church for the midnight service. The children's pageant, which was always adorable and often amusing.

It warmed her heart to think that in just a few years, her son would take part in the pageant—playing the part of a sheep or a donkey, perhaps. He would be the cutest kid in the pageant, whatever his role—and he would have the proudest mama.

She laughed at herself as she entered the senior center facility, her arms laden with rolls of sparkling garland in several colors, with which she would help decorate for the festivities. She was definitely getting ahead of herself. Her son needed to be born before he could participate in the nativity play.

Alexis, Griff, Jo Spencer and a half a dozen others were gathered in the commons area, digging through bins overflowing with glittering ball ornaments, tinsel and strings of colorful lights that had been donated to the senior center. An enormous Virginia pine tree was set up in the middle of the room, waiting to be trimmed.

"Late, as usual," Alexis teased as Vivian dumped her armful of garland next to the other decorations.

"Better late than later," she quipped back, knowing even as she said the words that her maxim wasn't quite right.

Thankfully, Nick wasn't there to correct her, and everyone else just let it go. The saying, whatever it was, could apply to her salon as well as her habitual lateness, a personal trait she had tried but failed to amend over the years.

"I see you haven't had any success cleaning Nick up. Are you ready to do *my* laundry for two months?"

"I'm not out of time yet. The salon's official grand opening isn't until next week."

"I prefer liquid fabric softener in the washing machine as opposed to the dryer sheets you use."

Vivian made a face at her twin, knowing it was entirely possible that she *would* be doing double duty on laundry soon. Up until now Nick hadn't budged on the whole haircut-and-a-shave thing. She doubted she was going to get him to change his mind in the next week.

"Okay, folks," Jo said, taking charge as usual. "We need a game plan here. The tree needs trimming. Griff and Alexis, why don't you take care of that task. I need a few of you to *deck the halls* with garland, tinsel and evergreen wreaths."

She paused and tapped her chin. "Now, we need a little bit of a North Pole flavor in that corner over there. We'll have to to get creative and make a sleigh with the trimmings we have here in the bins, but we've got a reindeer, thanks to Nick McKenna. Vivian, why don't you and Nick work on that together."

"But Nick is—"

"Even later than you are, for once," Nick said from behind her left shoulder.

Startled by his voice, her heart leaped into her throat. She placed a hand on her pounding chest to even her breathing.

"Your bad habits are rubbing off on me," he teased.

"I beg your pardon," she said, whirling on him, only to nearly crash into the life-size, one-dimensional wooden cutout of a reindeer.

"I've got Dasher," he informed her, moving the reindeer up and down to simulate flying. "Dancer, Prancer and the rest of the lot couldn't make it today."

"Did you carve that? It's pretty intricate. I've got to say, I'm impressed."

Nick nodded. "I drew the pattern myself."

He was clearly pleased with her praise. She thought his chest might have ballooned a bit and he was standing a good inch taller.

"What are we going to do for a sleigh?" Viv asked as they sifted through the decorations in the bins, looking for ideas to create the North Pole.

"What about this?" Nick asked, holding up a large

tablecloth, which was a bright red trimmed with green around the edges. "We can push a couple of folding chairs together and drape this over them."

Vivian caught his enthusiasm. "We can use some gold garland for the reins. And here's a bag of fake snow. It'll be a mess to clean up but it'll definitely give us the ambiance we're looking for. Oh—and we can wrap red ribbon around that concrete pole over there to make it look like a giant candy cane."

Nick chuckled. "The North Pole. Nice."

For the next half hour Vivian and Nick built the scene in the corner of the commons. Nick set up his reindeer and wrapped the pole in red ribbon, while Vivian worked on the sleigh and spread glistening fake snow across the floor around their display.

"We should see if we can find a couple of large, empty boxes," Vivian suggested as they stood back and examined the scene they'd created. "I've got an extra roll of wrapping paper in my car."

"I like that idea. We can stack the fake presents next to the sleigh."

Their gazes met and Vivian smiled up at him. "Now all we need is Santa."

Nick shifted his gaze away from her to where Alexis was trimming the tree. "It looks like your sister is about finished."

"The tree is beautiful. I love the twinkling lights. They bring such peace to my heart."

"Hey, Nick, can I get your help over here?" Alexis asked, waving him over.

"Sure. The tree looks great, by the way. What do you need me to do?"

"Put the angel on. I'm not tall enough to reach the top of the tree and Jo shanghaied Griff into helping decorate the cafeteria."

"Not a problem," he said, picking up the angel—a sweet, smiling figure robed in white with gold trim. But then, with a wink and a smile, he immediately turned to Vivian and placed the angel in her hands.

That made less than no sense. If Alexis couldn't reach the top of the tree, then Vivian would fare no better. They were identical twins, after all.

"Up we go," Nick said, hoisting her into the air before she even knew what he was going to do.

"Nick, you can't—" she started to protest, but then realized it would do no good. He could, apparently, and he did. He'd quite literally swept her off her feet on more than one occasion.

Of course, now she was over eight months pregnant, so it was a little bit awkward.

"Are you going to make me stand here holding you all day or are you going to put the angel on the top of the tree?" Nick asked.

She put the angel on the top of the tree.

"There, now," he said, gently setting her back on her feet and holding her waist firmly until he was certain she was stable. "My family has an old Christmas tradition. Prettiest girl gets to top the tree."

Vivian rolled her eyes and pointed out the obvious weakness in his statement. "You have two brothers."

He grinned. "Okay, you got me. Our tradition is that the youngest member of the family tops the tree. It was Brody this year, since Jax's twins aren't quite old enough to grasp the concept of Christmas. Or trees. Still, all things being even, I like my idea better."

"You do realize that my identical twin is standing right here next to me."

"So I'm surrounded by two beautiful women. It's a really tough situation for a guy to be in, but I'll try to bear it. And I'm standing firm on what I said. The prettiest girl got to top the tree."

Vivian's face grew warm. Alexis was beaming at her, clearly not at all offended by Nick's declaration. Her eyes were glittering with amusement.

Nick looked like the cat who caught the parakeet.

"Besides," Nick added, "technically, the youngest person did top the tree. You had Baby G's help, didn't you?"

She couldn't help but laugh.

"Festivities are about to begin, people," Jo declared, clapping her hands to get everyone's attention. "Let's get these bins put away so we can all join the *p-a-r-t-y.* Party!"

What a card Jo was, parading around in her green T-shirt that proclaimed Elfette and her matching green hat that contrasted with the brassy red curls of her hair.

Vivian grabbed one of the bins and followed the others to the storage closet, where they neatly stacked everything away out of sight. She'd thought Nick was right behind her, but when she turned to speak to him about wrapping some empty boxes, she discovered he wasn't there. Strange. Maybe he'd been held back in the commons area for some reason.

She decided she'd have to see to the fake presents herself. She found a couple of empty boxes in the storage closet and made a quick detour to her car, where she wrapped them in foiled paper.

By the time she returned to the commons area, it was filled with senior residents and their families, along with a smattering of nurses. She looked around for Nick but he was nowhere to be seen.

She also didn't see his uncle. Maybe Nick had gone to fetch James and accompany him to the party.

She stacked the presents next to the sleigh and then made her way over to the punch bowl. She sipped at a cup of hot apple cider, content for the moment just to watch folks interacting with each other. The nurses that had relocated to the area to accompany some of the frailer residents moving in from surrounding towns were welcomed like family. The folks in Serendipity were like that.

Vivian's heart warmed. She felt blessed to live here, to be back home again where she belonged. Whatever happened in the future, she had this.

What more could a woman want?

She didn't want to answer that. Not today.

She set her empty mug on a nearby tray and was just about to start mingling when Jo caught her by the elbow and shoved a black point-and-click camera into her hand.

"We're about to start, dear. Would you mind taking pictures?"

Start?

Vivian thought the party had started a while ago. Was Jo talking about something else? But what else was there?

The buzz of conversation dissipated as everyone

turned their attention to the corner where Vivian and Nick had set up their display.

She couldn't really see what was happening through the crowd of people, and from this vantage point, she definitely wouldn't be able to take any pictures of whatever was going on.

She was making her way through the crowd and had just reached the beribboned North Pole when she heard Nick's deep, rich voice, loud and clear.

"Ho, ho, ho. Merry Christmas!"

Nick caught one glimpse of Vivian's startled face and knew it had been worth whatever discomfort he was feeling from wearing this thick, itchy red suit. He didn't have much time to enjoy her reaction before she raised the camera she'd been holding and the flash went off, temporarily blinding him.

He should have expected that. It was actually his camera that Nick had given Jo, telling her to pass it on to Vivian. It wasn't so much that he wanted to be able to see a picture of himself in the Santa getup as it was making sure Viv was there when he made his entrance.

He knew she'd be amused by the prospect, probably even more than his brothers, but he had to admit he kind of liked it when she teased him.

How he had been talked into playing this role in the first place he would never understand. He was the last man on the planet anyone would expect to dress up as Santa Claus. Yet one day when Nick was visiting his uncle, the center's facility manager approached him and told him Jo had suggested asking him if he'd mind playing Old Saint Nick for the seniors at the center.

Mind?

Of course he minded. He might have the right name, but that was the only thing he had in common with the jolly old elf.

Christmas spirit wasn't exactly his forte.

But then he'd thought about Vivian, who regularly and selflessly offered her services to the residents of the care center. He knew the elderly here would revel in a visit from Santa.

And so he had said yes.

Everyone's eyes were turned on him, making his skin prickle. The red suit was itchy, the pillow he'd stuffed down the front of his coat kept shifting awkwardly and when he went to sit down on the makeshift sleigh, the chairs beneath him shifted apart and the reindeer he'd spent countless hours constructing nearly capsized.

Carefully adjusting his weight so his "sleigh" would remain stable and he wouldn't slip between the chairs, he set down his pack filled with gifts for the residents and wondered what he was supposed to do next. He hadn't been given a script, and it wasn't like the elderly were going to come sit on his lap and tell him what they wanted for Christmas.

Were they?

The thought made him chuckle, which he quickly masked as the loud, hearty laugh of the character he was supposed to be playing.

Deciding there was no reason to linger any longer than strictly necessary, it appeared the obvious thing to do would be to pass out the gifts. He was anxious to wrap this up and get out of the torturous Santa suit.

Anything he could do to move things along would be a blessing.

He reached for the bag, but before he could pull out the first gift, he was stopped by his brother Jax, who slid one of his infant girls—Nick's niece—into Nick's arm and a family-sized black leather Bible, its pages gilded with gold trim, into the other hand.

Nick raised his white-powdered brow. "What, exactly, am I supposed to do with these?" he whispered raggedly.

Jax scoffed and shook his head. "I should think that would be obvious. I have the Bible bookmarked to the second chapter of Luke. Read the gospel story about the nativity of our Lord. And Violet here," Jax said with a grin, "is your special effects team. Don't worry. She's my mellow baby."

"I can't read aloud to a crowd of people." Nick was panicking and almost started to hyperventilate. He'd always been a poor reader and struggled with dyslexia. He would never be able to do a Bible story justice, especially one as holy as the birth of Christ.

Jax clapped his shoulder. "I believe in you, bro."

"Let me help you with this." Nick was so focused on trying to drag a breath through his closed throat that he hadn't even noticed Vivian approaching.

She took the Bible from him and relief rippled through his tense muscles. With her outgoing personality, he was sure Vivian excelled in front of crowds. He was certain she would do a bang-up job reading the Christmas story.

She opened the Holy Scriptures and removed the

ribbon bookmark, and then promptly handed it back to Nick with a sunny smile.

"There you are. I figured the Bible would be difficult to open, seeing as you have a baby in your other arm."

"Opening the Bible wasn't my big concern," he muttered, but she was already crouched before him, watching him intently, waiting for him to start reading.

Way to force the issue. Folks had settled down in chairs or on the floor and the room was filled with silent expectation. Even baby Violet appeared to be staring up at Nick in anticipation of the story.

Santa suit. Seniors. Bible. Baby.

He couldn't get out of it now.

He cleared his throat and concentrated on the words before him.

"In those days a decree went out from Caesar Augustus…"

The first few sentences were a little rough, but then he fell into his role and got caught up in the story. He must have heard it a hundred times over the years, but it never grew old, remembering the story of God coming to earth as Man. Nick all gussied up as Santa Claus as he read the story represented it in a whole new way. Kind of choked him up.

"That was beautiful," Vivian breathed when the last word was spoken.

"Indeed," said Jo, who added applause for his efforts to her comment. "Well done!" The rest of the crowd joined in the applause.

He nodded, acknowledging the residents and their families. With a tender touch, Jax gently transferred Violet back into his own arms. Nick winked at his brother.

Jax had certainly taken to fatherhood well, especially considering the fact that his twins had been literally dumped on his doorstep five months ago.

"Good job, bro," Jax said. "I'm proud of you."

"Back at ya," Nick said, refusing to acknowledge the swell in his chest. He wasn't usually so emotional.

"Are we ready for some gift giving?" Jo announced in a voice loud enough to penetrate the room.

Nick handed the Bible to Vivian and she set it aside.

"I'm as ready as a man can be," he whispered, for Viv's ears only. "I am so itching to get out of this ridiculous suit."

She giggled and patted the pillow on his stomach. "I think you look cute."

Cute?

Heat flooded to his face. It was a good thing Santa Claus was supposed to have rosy cheeks, because he knew his were flaming.

Without him having to ask, Vivian positioned herself next to the sack of gifts and handed carefully wrapped gifts to him one at a time, allowing him to have the fun of passing them out to the seniors.

"That's a lot of wrapping," he commented to Viv as he pressed a package into an old woman's hands.

"You're telling me," Vivian said with a laugh. "It took Alexis and me an entire day to get them all done."

"You and Alexis wrapped *all* these gifts?"

She sniffed. "Don't sound so surprised. I am capable of wrapping Christmas presents, you know."

"I didn't mean it that way. I just meant that it's incredible that you put that much effort into it."

She smiled softly. "It's worth it. Look at all these happy faces."

And there were. The seniors were reveling in their visit from Santa and the small gifts each of them had been given.

When a nurse helped Uncle James approach the sleigh to receive his gift, Nick got a little choked up at how frail the old man had become. James hadn't recognized Nick the last couple of times he'd visited, but now he looked Nick right in the eye, his gaze sparkling with recognition.

"You are Saint Nick," he said with a solemn nod.

Nick reached for his uncle's feeble hands. "It's Santa to my friends."

When all of the gifts had been given out, Nick posed for a few pictures, all taken by his helper elf Vivian.

He was relieved when she took his hand and announced that Santa had other places he needed to visit. He smiled and waved and *ho, ho, ho'd* until he was completely clear of the commons room, and then he blew out a big breath that made his snowy-white beard lift right off his chin. His shoulders sagged with relief.

He was thoroughly exhausted, not only physically but mentally and emotionally, as well. Playing one of the world's most recognized characters took a lot out of a guy.

Vivian turned and beamed up at him. "You were absolutely wonderful out there."

"Please don't ever let me agree to do anything like that again," he begged, scratching at a particularly itchy spot on his right shoulder. "I'm more of a behind-the-scenes kind of guy."

"Well, I think it was nice that you did it, especially because I know it wasn't easy for you. It was a true loving sacrifice, and I don't think you'll ever know how many people you touched today."

"Really?"

She nodded fervently. "Really. I know I personally got a little teary-eyed when you read the nativity story."

He scoffed softly, not knowing what to do with the compliment. "Flakes of that fake snow probably got in your eyes."

"I'm serious," she countered. "And what's more, I think you deserve a reward for all your hard work."

"A reward?" he echoed.

She just smiled and pointed up.

He tilted his head.

Mistletoe.

They were standing directly under a sprig of mistletoe. Had she maneuvered him here on purpose?

Before he could react, she reached up on tiptoe and brushed a soft kiss across his white-bearded cheek.

"Oh," she murmured, clapping a hand over her mouth. "I—I can't believe I did that."

Without another word, she darted off down the hall and then ducked back into the commons area. She knew he couldn't follow her there. Not while he was still dressed in the silly red suit. Clearly she didn't want to be alone with him.

And yet, she'd just kissed him.

He covered his cheek, as if trying to imprint the feel of her lips against his skin. Even if her lips had technically never touched his skin.

Was she sorry she'd kissed him?

He wasn't.

He wanted to kiss her again, a real, lips-on-lips kiss this time.

He mentally poked at the tentative feeling. He'd failed so many times before in his attempts at a relationship. He didn't want to make the same mistakes with Vivian.

He couldn't. It wasn't only his heart he had to consider—or even Vivian's. It was her baby's.

If he were to become invested in Vivian's life—and that was a big *if*—he had to do it right, and he had to mean it. Or not do it at all.

But first he needed to get out of this itchy Santa suit and find the woman.

Chapter Eight

What had she been thinking?

Kissing Nick?

She was an idiot. She'd always been impulsive, giving in to whatever felt right at the moment, but this one took the whole cookie.

That kiss was going to change the entire tenor of their working relationship and the timing couldn't have been worse. With the salon's grand opening less than a week away, she needed to be at a hundred and ten percent, and that wasn't going to happen if she was constantly daydreaming about mistletoe every time she saw Nick's face.

And worse, she had no idea what *he* was thinking. They'd met with the building inspector yesterday and Nick wouldn't even make eye contact with her. After more than an hour of avoiding her gaze and keeping his full attention on the inspector, he'd left without speaking a word to Viv.

Thankfully, the building had checked out. Finally,

it seemed like everything careerwise was starting to come together.

Tranquility.

Not that she knew anything about that anymore. She hadn't had a serene moment since the second she'd moved back to Serendipity.

She wondered how Nick would like the name. She hadn't shared it with him yet. She was fairly certain he was still iffy about her beauty salon being successful in a town as small as Serendipity, but at least he'd stopped voicing his qualms out loud.

At the moment, she needed his help more than ever. It was time to let everyone know the date of her grand opening, and that meant posting flyers all over town, talking to other local business owners—especially Jo Spencer, whom Vivian counted on to be a walking, talking commercial for her spa. Viv needed to spread the good news any way she could. She'd just expected Nick to be by her side.

Except Nick hadn't shown up since the building inspection and she wasn't keen on having to be the one to reach out to him.

She was quite finished humiliating herself, thank you very much. She was afraid to find out what he thought of her now.

She didn't even know what to think of her actions. Maybe it was nothing. Maybe she just had a thing for men in Santa suits.

No. That wasn't it. She could avoid the truth all she wanted and tell herself any number of fibs, but she'd kissed him because he'd opened up his heart and she'd liked what she'd seen.

A man who purposely tried to stay out of the public eye set his personal fears and doubts aside for the elderly residents of the senior center. He'd showed them the dignity and respect they deserved and he had made them feel special. He'd brought them joy and Christmas spirit.

So she'd gotten caught up in the moment and had been carried away by a stray sprig of mistletoe. Who could blame her?

She'd just have to let it go and hope Nick would do the same.

In the meantime, there were flyers to hang up all over town, and if Nick wasn't here to help her then she'd have to do it all by herself.

She started stapling her advertisements to every telephone pole on Main Street. When she got to the end of one side of the town, she crossed the street and moved back toward where she'd started. Afterward she planned to talk to all the neighborhood business owners. Hopefully she'd be able to talk a few into hanging her flyer in their windows or on their community bulletin boards.

Last, she would hit the park, the church and the high school. She had the notion that there were more than a few teenage girls who would want to avail themselves of her services, to get their hair and nails done for a Christmas party or for Serendipity's annual New Year's Eve bash.

Finished with all of the telephone poles, she said hello to the three old men killing time in front of Emerson's Hardware and then ducked into the store.

"Hey, Eddie," she said, greeting the young man behind the counter. "I just wanted you to know that the grand opening of my beauty salon and spa is this week-end." She pressed a flyer into his hand. "I'm calling it Tranquility. Can I count on your support?"

He chuckled. "I've already heard about your grand opening from Nick." He scratched his buzz-cut hair. "I don't think I'll be needing any of the services you offer. Sorry I can't be of more help to you."

Vivian scrunched her brow in confusion. "Nick has already been by here?"

"Yeah. He came by earlier this morning. He made it sound like he was hitting all the businesses in the area. Trying to strong-arm people into coming for opening day, I think." Eddie chuckled.

Nick had already been by? Her heart started warming until the rest of Eddie's words sank in. What was Nick doing? Forcing people to agree to attend her grand opening?

She couldn't even imagine why he thought it was a good idea to compel people to become customers. Surely that would backfire and make folks not want to attend at all.

How could he not know that?

She felt a twinge on her lower back. The baby must be moving about more than normal. She sighed quietly and rubbed the spot with her fingers.

"You're welcome to put up a flyer on our community bulletin board if you'd like."

Vivian offered her thanks, pinned up her advertisement and moved on to the next shop. As she visited business after business, it became apparent that Nick was definitely ahead of her. Everywhere she went, Nick had already been. And it sounded as if he was using the same strong-arm tactics with everyone. At this rate she wouldn't have a single customer who wanted to be there of her own accord.

Maybe that was why the clipboard she'd brought along to sign folks up for services on the day of her grand opening remained empty. Everyone she spoke to seemed to have a reason why they couldn't commit.

Her grand opening was officially going to be a disaster. From the looks of it, she would be standing in an empty beauty parlor on opening day with nothing to do but twiddle her pinkies, while outside people would pass by and gawk at her pathetic little excuse for a spa.

Maybe Nick had been right all along. Maybe Serendipity *didn't* need what she had to offer.

Had she put all of her time, effort and money into her business for nothing?

By the end of the day, she was bone weary and completely discouraged. And as if that wasn't enough, Baby G was evidently trying out for some kind of Olympic tournament. Vivian had been having cramps and spasms all day.

She ended up back at her shop, intending to drop off her empty clipboard and what was left of her flyers and call it a night. Instead, not even bothering to turn on the lights to the building, she slumped into one of her styling chairs, leaned her head back and closed her eyes.

She didn't even hear Nick enter the building until he spoke, causing her to leap halfway out of her chair. She felt like a cartoon cat with its claws stuck in the ceiling and its fur ruffled in fright.

"I see you've got your flyers tacked up all over

town." Nick sat in the styling chair next to hers and spun it around with his boots.

She covered her face with her hands. "Don't. Just don't, okay?"

"Don't what?"

"Don't say, 'I told you so.'"

"Okay. I won't. But I'm curious—what did I tell you that I'm not supposed to say I told you about?"

She slid her palms down her cheeks and met Nick's gaze. "Not one. Not one single solitary person signed up to get services on the day of my grand opening. Or any other day, for that matter."

"Hmm." Nick didn't look surprised. Why would he? He'd been calling the salon a failure from day one. Nothing that happened now would be any great shock to him.

"Well, you can sign my mom up for a haircut or something. Jo Spencer, too, I would imagine. And don't forget about Alexis. She's your twin. She has to be there."

Peachy.

While she was grateful for their support, that was three women out of a whole town—one of whom, as Nick had said, would feel she had to be there because she was Vivian's sister. And while Serendipity was small, the fact remained that over half its residents were women—women who were going elsewhere for their salon services.

"Maybe I should just call the whole thing off."

"Why would you do that?"

"Uh—because no one is coming."

No paying customers, at any rate.

"You don't know that."

"Empty clipboard, Nick."

His brow lowered. "This isn't like you. Where's the sunny personality, the-glass-is-always-half-full woman that I'm used to seeing?"

"Right now, I'm feeling partly cloudy with a good chance of showers." She sniffled. She had no intention of crying, not in front of Nick, but despite her best efforts to the contrary, the showers were coming hard and fast.

"Hey." He stood and reached for her hands, drawing her to her feet and into his embrace. He held her tightly, protectively, with one arm around her shoulders and the other spanning her waist—almost as if he were embracing her son, as well.

She breathed deeply of his warm leather and spice scent. She burrowed her head against his chest, reveling in the rumble of his breath and the steady beat of his heart.

She could forget everything when she was in his arms, even her own doubts. She felt safe there. Sheltered. As if nothing bad could touch her, or her baby.

A sound emerged from Nick's throat, somewhere between a growl and a groan. He slid his hand into the hair at the nape of her neck and tilted her head so she had no choice but to look up at him. Even in the meager light, she could see that his gaze had turned dark, the deep blue of the midnight sky.

Vivian couldn't move, or breath, and she couldn't look away from the longing, the silent plea brewing in his eyes.

She should turn away. This—whatever was happening between them now—could be nothing more than chemistry. Hadn't he been the one reminding her over and over of the ways he'd failed in his past relationships? Hadn't he said that he wasn't capable of giving his heart away?

But even so…it had been so long since she'd been held in a man's arms, and she'd never experienced anything quite like the emotions tumbling through her now.

Despite Nick's size, his embrace was extraordinarily gentle, the work-roughened hands he used to frame her face tender. Under her palms, she could feel his shoulder muscles quivering with tension and instinctively knew he was holding himself back, struggling for self-control. He knew her past and was clearly being sensitive to it.

With an unspoken question radiating from his gaze, he gave her more than enough time to react, to pull away, but she could no sooner change what was happening between them than she could stop the world from spinning on its axis.

She would probably regret it. In some ways, she already did. And yet—

She slid her hands from his shoulders down to his biceps and tipped up her chin.

His gaze dropped to her mouth. She trembled as he lowered his head and brushed his lips over hers. His beard was prickly, not anything like the cotton-soft, snowy-white beard he'd been wearing at the senior center, but his lips were gentle as he tentatively explored hers.

She didn't know how she'd come to this point with Nick. They were opposites in every conceivable way. She was an optimist. He was the world's worst pessimist, always considering the bad before the good. She was the owner of a soon-to-open beauty salon and spa. Nick looked like a mountain man.

But as he bent his head and deepened the kiss, none of it seemed to matter. Not their clashes in personality, or their arguments, or even their trust issues.

Tomorrow was soon enough to sort out her emotions. Tonight she needed the comfort Nick was offering her. Being held in his strong arms quickened her pulse. Warmth welled in her chest and spilled out to every corner of her being.

She'd been fighting her feelings for Nick ever since the first day back at the auction. She'd been fighting her fear of being hurt, of heartbreak.

And it wasn't an empty or unreasonable fear—she might get hurt again.

But for tonight, she was going to believe the best about Nick, that his fear of commitment could be overcome, that they could make a relationship work.

Maybe she'd been wrong all along.

Maybe Nick did care.

At first, Nick had taken a dispirited and disheartened Vivian into his arms with no more than the overwhelming need to comfort and protect her, but somewhere along the way, his entire world had shifted.

Maybe it was the sweet, full softness of her lips. Or maybe it was the spring-flower scent of her perfume, or the electricity pulsing across his nerves as her fingers trailed across his biceps. Maybe it was the moment he'd lost himself in the liquid blue warmth of her gaze before he'd kissed her.

But whatever the reason, what had started out as one friend comforting another had quickly sparked into a life of its own, and instead of dousing the flame, he'd stoked it into a raging bonfire that was quickly growing out of control.

It wasn't just the chemistry between them, the way his heart expanded with warmth when Vivian was in his arms.

No—it was so much more than that. He wanted to protect her from the trials she was facing, wipe away her tears, lift her up so she could enjoy the success she'd worked so hard for, the triumph she so richly deserved.

He wanted her to trust him—and he wanted to be worthy of that trust. Was it possible that she could ever trust him with her heart, and maybe even, eventually, with her child?

But how could she, when he couldn't even trust himself? He couldn't ask that of her. It wasn't right—not for her, not for her soon-to-be-born son and not even for himself.

With every day that he spent with Vivian, his heart grew nearer and nearer to hers. The risk of hurting her scared him more than the unlikely possibility of a reward.

The best thing for him to do—the right thing for all concerned—would be for him to step away from this kiss, this project and Vivian's life.

He'd get her through her grand opening and then that was it.

"Vivian," he murmured, his voice thick with emotion as he drew her away from him.

Her cheeks splashed with pink as her eyelids slowly fluttered open.

Oh, but she was beautiful.

Nick wasn't sure he could stand the pain that contracted like a sharp claw around his chest at the thought of not having her in his life anymore.

She smiled up at him. A sound emerged from her throat that sounded like a contented purr.

"I—you—" he stammered, dropping his arms and backing away from her.

Nick threaded his fingers through the thick length of his hair. He could see his reflection in the mirror behind Vivian. He looked like a wild man, and it wasn't just his tousled hair and the dark shadow of his beard.

It was the sheer panic in his eyes.

He swiveled on the heels of his boots, not wanting Vivian to see the truth of his feelings in his telltale gaze. Not now, when she was already under so much stress. Putting anything more on her shoulders couldn't be good for her or for the baby.

He'd allowed his emotions to get the better of him and he was ashamed that he'd led her on, to a place he had no right to go. Somehow, he'd have to make it right, let her down as gently and as painlessly as possible.

She deserved better than what he could offer.

"Nick?"

The hair on the back of his neck stood on end. The way she said his name—

He whirled around to find Vivian clutching the edge of the counter with one hand and her other over her expanded middle. She was half-doubled over and her expression was a mixture of fear and pain.

Instantly, Nick was by her side, one arm around her waist and the other supporting her elbow.

"What's wrong? Is it the baby?"

Vivian nodded and gulped in a sharp breath of air. "I think—"

She cut off her sentence midthought as her brow lowered and she pinched her lips.

Something was wrong. Vivian wasn't due for a few weeks yet. He couldn't remember exactly what she'd said, but he was positive her due date was after the first of the year.

"Should I call 9-1-1?"

She grabbed his wrist. "No. Call Dr. Delia."

"My truck is parked out back. I'll take you straight to the doctor's office and call Delia on the way."

He'd expected her to argue with him as she had the day she'd twisted her ankle in the shop. She'd been so adorably stubborn about it, completely refusing to admit she'd even been in pain, much less that she needed to go see the doctor.

It was frighteningly telling that she merely gritted her teeth and nodded her acquiescence to his suggestion this time. She must really think something was wrong if she wasn't putting up a fight over this.

Continuing to support her at the small of her back and with a hand on her elbow, he gently propelled her toward the back door and then out to his truck, locking the door to the shop behind him.

Three times on the short way out, they had to stop while a wave of pain racked through Vivian's body.

Was this normal? Contractions coming so suddenly, so hard and fast, with very little relief between them?

Nick was no expert by any means of the word, but he'd always thought that the portrayal of labor and delivery in movies and television shows was unrealistic— sudden, sharp labor followed by a baby born within what appeared to be mere minutes.

He seemed to recall, through the few experiences he'd had around pregnant women, that labor tended to be long and intensive, some lasting for days before the baby was born.

That's not what was happening here. It was more like the movies. Her labor wasn't slow or gradual at all.

Did that mean Vivian's baby was going to be born momentarily? What if he couldn't get her to the doctor's office fast enough?

Panic enveloped him as he opened the passenger side of his truck and scooped Vivian into his arms, gently depositing her into the seat and buckling her seat belt for her.

She didn't speak, not even to protest him hovering over her which, for a chatterbox like Vivian, worried Nick more than anything. She didn't make a sound, other than an occasional soft groan. Not only did she not protest the way he was taking over the situation, but it appeared she was barely aware of what was going on at all. It was as if she'd completely withdrawn into herself. The only thing she seemed to be aware of was the rapidity and strength of her contractions.

Nick slid behind the wheel and revved the engine. His every impulse was to gun the accelerator to equal the race of his pulse, but getting in an accident or being pulled over for speeding by one of Serendipity's finest would only delay their arrival at the doctor's office.

As he drove, he pulled up the doctor's emergency number on the truck's console. Delia's phone rang several times before she answered. With each consecutive unanswered ring, the noose around Nick's heart grew tighter and tighter.

At length she answered, the sound of a dozen people talking and laughing in the background. He felt bad about interrupting a family gathering or party, but his concern for Vivian came first.

"Delia? It's Nick. I'm sorry to bother you at home," Nick said, wondering if his voice sounded as rattled to Delia's ears as it did to his own.

"It's no problem. That's what I'm here for. What's up, Nick?" she asked cheerfully.

"It's Vivian. I'm pretty sure she's in labor right now. I thought maybe I should be taking her to the hospital, but she insisted on seeing you instead. And as fast as this seems to be going, right now I'm not sure she would make it to the hospital before delivering if I tried to get her there."

"Hold on a second." There was a pause while it sounded as if Delia was rummaging around a drawer, probably for a pen and paper.

"How far apart are her contractions right now?"

How far apart? What did that mean? It seemed to him that Vivian wasn't getting any kind of break in contractions at all.

"I'm…not sure? They seem really close together to me."

"Has her water broken?"

Nick nearly slammed on the brakes as his stomach

lurched. He was *so* not the right person to be taking care of Vivian in this emergency situation.

Delia chuckled. "It's okay, Nick. Put Viv on the line for me."

"I'm here," Vivian said, her voice low and husky. "Nick's got his truck console on speakerphone."

"Okay, great."

Nick appreciated Delia's calm, collected and reassuring tone. "About how far apart are your contractions, hon?"

"I haven't timed them," she said through a tight jaw. "They are coming pretty quickly, some right on top of each other. Maybe a minute or two apart, otherwise. I'm frightened that there's something wrong with the baby."

"Let's not borrow trouble. I do think, given the circumstances, that it would be best for you to meet me at my office, rather than trying to drive straight to the hospital."

"We're already there," Nick said, cutting the engine in front of the doctor's office.

"Great. I'll be there in five."

Nick turned to assess Vivian. Her head was tipped back against the seat and her eyes were closed. But she looked as far from relaxed as it was possible to get. She groaned and rubbed at a spot on her stomach.

"Should I be reminding you to breathe or something?" Nick had never felt as helpless as he did at that moment, seeing Vivian's pale face in the moonlight, crumpled with anguish. If he could, he would take that pain away from her in an instant and bear it himself. As it was, he was totally and completely useless.

Less than useless. Even thinking about the various elements of childbirth made him queasy and light-headed. He felt itchy all over, as if he were breaking out in hives. His next call was to Alexis, but unfortunately, she and Griff were out of town. He'd have to deal on his own.

He breathed a sigh of relief when he caught sight of Delia's headlights as she parked on the opposite side of the street. He had every confidence that Delia would be able to take things from here and, as an added benefit, she was married to one of the town's paramedics, should it become necessary to transport Vivian and her baby to the hospital.

Please, Lord, don't let it be necessary.

Nick helped Vivian out of the truck and Delia stepped to the other side of her, so they both supported her as they entered the doctor's office. Delia led them straight to the examination room.

"First things first," Delia said in a no-nonsense voice as Nick helped Vivian lay back on the paper-covered medical bed. Delia lightly ran her hands across Vivian's belly and then measured it with a tape. "You're just the right size for thirty-six weeks and four days, so baby is growing just fine. Ideally, we'd like to keep him cooking for another week at least, but if he's ready to make his debut then no worries. Let's get you hooked up to the fetal monitor and find out what this little mister is up to."

Nick cleared his throat. "Should I leave?"

Vivian clenched his hand in hers. "No. Please don't."

Nick pressed his lips into a tight line to avoid showing all the emotions flooding through him. He met Delia's gaze and raised his eyebrows.

Delia smiled in reassurance. Evidently he wasn't as good at hiding his emotions as he'd thought he was.

"It's fine for you to stay right now. In a few minutes I'll have to send you out for a bit, but let's get Vivian comfortable first."

Vivian sighed in relief until another contraction racked through her. Her manicured fingernails dug into Nick's palm but he didn't mind the pain. It gave him something to focus on other than fearing for Vivian and the baby.

"First of all," Delia said, addressing Vivian but with a glance at Nick, "I want to reassure you that I have delivered dozens of babies right here in Serendipity. And you're far enough along that we should be okay without any special equipment beyond what we've got. So just in case it should become necessary and this little guy doesn't want to wait to be born, we can handle it."

Maybe *Delia* could handle it. But that didn't mean it would be as simple as she was making it sound. Nick could tell she was leaving stuff out—probably a lot of stuff. It unnerved him even further.

"Can you give her something for the pain?"

"We have options," Delia started, but Vivian yanked on Nick's arm and shook her head vigorously.

"No drugs. They would affect my son. I'm doing this naturally."

Nick's gaze flashed to Delia but she merely shrugged.

"We can absolutely handle this exactly the way you'd like, Vivian. Let's figure out how much time we have and then, if we've got enough of a window, we should avail ourselves of my husband's services to get you to the hospital. You've had a completely normal pregnancy, so I don't anticipate any problems with the birth, but at this point the little guy is three and a half weeks early and his lungs might need a little bit of help at first."

The doctor said it so offhandedly it sounded as if it were no real worry, but if it was possible, Vivian's face went a shade paler. Nick's own gut took a hit. Was the doctor saying Viv's baby wouldn't be able to breathe if he was born here in Serendipity tonight?

Delia placed her hand on Vivian's shoulder. "We won't make any decisions until we have a better idea of what's going on tonight, okay, Viv?"

Vivian nodded and then gasped and held her breath as another contraction rocked her.

"Don't forget to breathe through it," Delia reminded her as she attached a fetal monitor to Viv's stomach. "Did you take a prenatal class to teach you how to breathe through your contractions?"

Viv needed to take a class to learn how to *breathe* a certain way? Wow. There really was a lot Nick didn't know about childbirth—and he was absolutely certain he did not want to learn about it just now.

He was forgetting to breathe himself and was starting to feel a little light-headed, but there was no way he was going to budge from Viv's side. Not as long as she needed him there.

"Is Alexis your birthing coach?" Delia asked.

What was a birthing coach? Nick pictured Alexis with a whistle around her neck shouting plays out of a book but he knew that couldn't be quite right.

"Yes, but she and Griff are out of town for the weekend."

"I see. Is there someone else you could call? I'll be

there for the birth, of course, either here or at the hospital, but it's comforting to have someone else by your side to offer you support."

"I could call my mom," Nick suggested. "I'm sure she'd be thrilled to help out."

There was an ulterior motive for Nick's suggestion. If his mom was there, that would give him a good excuse to be there as well—even if it meant driving all the way out to the hospital. If he chauffeured his mom around, he would be there when Vivian's son was born.

And he really wanted to be there when Vivian's son was born.

"That's a good idea," Delia said. "What do you think, Viv? Would you like Nick to call Alice for you?"

Vivian nodded and chuckled through her pain. "I suspect Alice will be able to help Nick, too. He looks a little green around the gills."

Nick made a face at her but by that time she was deep in the midst of another contraction and had once again retreated inside herself.

"I'll just step out and call my mom," he said.

"Good. That will give me the opportunity to examine Vivian. I'll let you know when you can return to the room."

Nick breathed a sigh of relief when the door closed behind him and he was alone in the waiting room. He removed his hat and scrubbed a hand through his hair.

How had everything gone so wrong so quickly? It was only days before the official grand opening of Tranquility—the name he'd seen on the flyers she'd made—and weeks before Baby G was supposed to be born. And now suddenly Vivian had started labor.

Had he somehow caused her premature labor?

He'd seen the stress and discouragement in her gaze when he'd met her back at the salon earlier that evening. She'd been convinced her grand opening was going to be a complete and utter failure. Which was an unfortunate and unexpected byproduct of a plan he'd worked up.

If only she knew. The complete opposite was true. The whole town was coming out for Vivian's big day. He'd worked hard to make sure it happened. He'd hoped to give her a nice surprise with his efforts.

Instead, Vivian was lying in the room next to him strapped to a fetal monitor and very likely soon to give birth to her premature son.

He fished his cell phone out of his pocket and speed-dialed his mother, who answered on the first ring.

"What's wrong, Nick?" she asked in lieu of "hello."

He hadn't expected that, and her question completely threw him off his game. "What makes you think something is wrong?"

"Because you never call me unless you need something." She couched the accusation in a loving laugh. "So what is it this time? You don't know how to boil artichokes? You just turned your white T-shirts pink?"

"It's Vivian," he said, tossing his hat onto an end table and slumping into the nearest chair. "I'm pretty sure she's in labor right now. And I think it's all my fault."

Chapter Nine

To Vivian's relief, her contractions had slowed and become irregular, not to mention far less painful.

"Everything looks fine," Delia assured her. "False alarm this time. They are called Braxton Hicks contractions. Your body is practicing for the main event. Your baby will probably be born right on schedule."

"*Practice* contractions? I am going to hate to see what the real contractions feel like."

On one side of her, Nick squeezed her hand. On the other, Alice patted her shoulder reassuringly.

"We women have toughed it out and delivered babies since the beginning of time," Alice reminded her. "I know it seems impossible to imagine right now, but no matter how bad the labor pains are, once they put your sweet little baby boy in your arms, you'll know he was worth every last contraction."

"But that won't be for a few weeks yet," Delia assured her with a smile.

"And the funniest thing of all is that the good Lord gives us selective memories," Alice continued. "Even the memory of the pain will be mostly forgotten. And it's a good thing, too, or Nick would have been an only child."

Vivian glanced at Nick, expecting him to laugh and come back with a quip about the hassle of being raised with Jax and Slade, but to her surprise, he was frowning, his brow lowered over stormy blue eyes.

"Could these—what did you call them? 'Fake contractions?' Could they have been brought on by stress?"

Delia's gaze widened. "Possibly, but it's highly unlikely. Braxton Hicks are just a woman's body preparing for the real thing. And as Vivian here can tell you, sometimes they can feel quite real and be every bit as painful as a true contraction, but they're not really a sign that anything is wrong. Sometimes it's nothing. Sometimes the baby is slightly out of position and the mom's body is making some last-minute adjustments."

"I imagine she has been under a lot of stress," Alice murmured. "What with the grand opening of her beauty salon right around the corner. Have you been working yourself too hard, sweetheart?"

Vivian opened her mouth to speak but Nick beat her to the punch bowl.

"Yes, she has. She spent all day today on her feet, plastering advertisements all over town. I doubt she even took time to sit down and eat lunch."

Vivian bristled. Of course she'd eaten. She'd gotten a corn dog to go from Jo's Café, along with a bag of sour cream and onion potato chips. Her eating habits didn't even remotely resemble her prepregnancy fare, but then, little did, these days.

"Vivian, I'd like you to stay another half hour or so just to make sure we're clear of all contractions. And then I want you to take it easy. I know you've got your grand opening coming up, but try to rest if you can and stay off your feet as much as possible."

Delia removed the straps of the fetal monitor, but when Vivian tried to sit up, Delia laid a restraining hand on her shoulder.

"Keep resting for me for a little while longer, will you, hon?"

Vivian took a deep breath and then sighed. She would rather have gone home to her own house and not have everyone fretting over her, but she supposed it was good that they cared.

Alice had even offered to attend the actual birth, being an extra support person along with Alexis. Vivian had gratefully accepted. It felt nice to have a mother figure by her side, especially since her own mother had passed away from cancer when Viv and Alexis were only six years old.

"I guess I'll be on my way, then," Alice said, kissing Vivian's cheek. "But you make sure to have Nick program my cell phone number on your speed dial. Feel free to call me day or night, and it doesn't have to be because you are in labor. I'm always happy to talk."

"Thank you. Really, Alice, I can't tell you how much your support means to me."

Alice patted her arm. "I know, dear. I know. As of this moment you can consider the whole McKenna clan as family, can't she, Nick?"

Nick made a choking sound. Even through the scruff on his cheeks she could see the heat rising to his face. Alice's words had probably embarrassed him, poor man. Even so, they were welcome to Vivian's ears.

Nick cleared his throat. "I'll walk you out to your car, Mama. And, Delia—if I could speak to you for a moment?" He nodded his head toward the waiting room.

Vivian laid with her hands clasped around her middle, staring at the ceiling. Her silly baby had apparently gone to sleep, now that the excitement was over.

It felt like quite a bit of time had passed, and Delia and Nick still hadn't returned. What was taking them so long? Were they still in the waiting room? Would they mind if she came out there, too? Viv hadn't had a single contraction in over an hour, and she badly needed to use the facilities, which were located off of the waiting room.

Finally, half out of curiosity as to where Delia and Nick had disappeared to, and half because the baby was now awake and was currently using her bladder as a trampoline, Viv rolled off the narrow bed and opened the door to the waiting room.

To her surprise, Alice hadn't left yet. She appeared to be deep in a hushed conversation with Nick and Delia.

Vivian didn't know whether it was the tone of their voices or maybe their postures, but something made her freeze in the doorway without making her presence known.

"So then, you want me to be there a little before ten o'clock?" Alice asked, clearly confirming something Nick had said earlier.

Nick nodded. "I told Vivian I'd signed you up for a haircut so she'll be expecting you. The official opening time is at ten, so any time around there should be fine."

Vivian cringed. They were talking about her—and her hopeless grand opening. Of course it would be fine if

Alice arrived just as the door opened. It wasn't as if there was going to be a huge line waiting for Viv's services.

"And what about me?" Delia asked. "Did you want me there a little before ten, as well?"

Nick shook his head. "No, you don't have to come—"

Vivian gasped and clapped a hand over her mouth. She ducked back into the examination room, all thoughts of leaving for home or using the facilities instantly evaporating.

She suddenly felt as if all the air had left the room. She was shaking so hard her teeth were chattering.

Nick was actually telling people *not* to come to her opening instead of urging them to come? Why would he do that?

She slipped back onto the exam bed and turned toward the back wall, curling into a ball. If only she could disappear from here and not have to face Nick—or anyone in Serendipity—ever again. She was just so, so tired and disheartened.

"Vivian?" Nick's deep voice came from behind her. A moment later she felt his large, warm hand on her shoulder.

Why did he have to be so gentle? Tears pricked Vivian's eyes.

"Are you all right?" he asked, having the gall to sound genuinely concerned.

Vivian knew she was trembling under his touch but she couldn't seem to help herself. She'd never been so angry in her life—not even when she'd discovered the cattle lounging inside her shop.

She'd been angry with Nick then, too, and had immediately blamed him for the whole incident. And then she'd had to ask for forgiveness because he hadn't been at fault.

But this time there could be no doubt. It would be hard for her to misinterpret Nick's words to Delia.

No. You don't need to come.

"I thought I might have heard you a minute ago but I must have been mistaken," Nick said.

Vivian didn't trust her voice to answer.

"Delia says you can go home whenever you'd like, but I'm not in a rush if you still want to rest for a while. Take all the time you need."

He sounded so sweet. So gentle.

So sincere.

How could he act this way when her world was about to break into tiny, irreparable pieces? Is that why he'd asked about stress bringing on labor? Because he already knew how the grand opening would turn out?

Little did he know—and neither had she, until this moment—that the worst part wasn't that her business had been set up for failure.

It was that Nick had concurred.

She'd *trusted* him. With her business, her friendship and even, perhaps, eventually with her heart. She'd been starting to feel like her emotions were healing, that she might be able to fall in love again and that this time that love might last forever.

She'd thought Nick was different. Certainly her feelings for him were unlike any she had experienced before.

How could she have been so wrong?

Nick really had his work cut out for him. Vivian had managed to staple advertisements to every single telephone pole in Serendipity, and that was to say nothing of all the community bulletin boards and shop windows. She was nothing if not thorough.

There couldn't possibly be a single resident in Serendipity who didn't know about Tranquility's grand opening, and that meant trouble for Nick.

Folks around here would welcome any excuse for a party, and they especially liked it when they were able to help their neighbors at the same time. That's why the Bachelors and Baskets auction had been such a success, and the opening of the senior center, as well.

Now, with Tranquility's grand opening…

How was he supposed to put that kind of fire out? It was the day before the grand opening and he'd heard the buzz about town. He could only hope Vivian hadn't.

He'd tried to stay a step ahead of her and make sure everyone was hush-hush about his surprise for the event, but even one person letting the cat out of the bag would be one person too many, and enough to ruin all his plans.

He tried to open the back door to the salon, but it was locked. He was surprised Viv wasn't here yet—putting all of the finishing touches on the place, giving the floor one last mop, shining the mirrors until they sparkled, arranging the stock of premium products that had only arrived yesterday.

For the past week, Viv had been busy training her two new protégés, Nicole and Lauren. She'd barely spoken a word to Nick. In fact, if he didn't know any better, he might have thought she was purposely avoiding him.

He put his key into the lock and flipped on the lights as he entered the building. It looked perfect—just as

perfect as his plan would be…he hoped. There had been a moment that night in Delia's office when he'd been certain his plan had been uncovered. In hindsight, it hadn't been such a great idea, discussing his strategies for the grand opening with his mom and Delia when Vivian was potentially within hearing range.

He'd been concentrating so hard on the mechanics of getting the right people to show up at the right times that it hadn't even occurred to him that Vivian might walk into the waiting room and ruin the surprise altogether.

At one point he'd heard what he thought was a gasp and his heart had leaped into his throat, but when he'd whirled around, expecting to see Vivian, he'd found the examination room door closed. And when he'd returned to the exam room, Viv was still lying on the bed, so all was well.

He was grateful he'd just imagined it. Talk about a way to take all the fun out of the secret.

Still, Vivian was acting odd around him—and when she finally arrived, it only got worse. He told himself that she had too much on her mind—preparing for the grand opening and for Baby G's imminent arrival.

She barely spoke to him, and when she did, it was to order him about, telling him to do this or that. Gone was the sweet, sensitive Viv with a ready smile and a tinkling fairy laugh. In her place was a frowning woman with drooping shoulders and black circles under her eyes.

It was clear she wasn't following Delia's suggestion to rest more and put her feet up.

"Are you getting enough sleep at night?" he asked

her, cornering her as she stocked new product onto the front shelves. She shrugged rather than answered.

He grabbed an armful of red shampoo bottles with long, pointed nozzles and started placing and facing them next to the shelf where Vivian was working.

He tried again. "Are you overexerting yourself? The doctor said you shouldn't be pushing too hard. You need to think about the baby."

"I'm fine," Vivian snapped, scowling at him. "And I *am* thinking about the baby. Why do you think I'm working so hard to get my business up and running?" She pulled the bottom corner of her full lower lip between her teeth. "Don't nag me. Who made you the sleep police?"

"I'm just concerned. You know what Dr. Delia said."

His initial reaction was to snap back at her. But that was just one of the many ways he had learned and grown through his relationship with Vivian. He now tried to give more thought to his words and his attitude before he spoke. He tried to consider the other person's feelings first, and tried to discern what God would want him to say or do. Right now Vivian was clearly testy because she was stressed about the grand opening. She still deserved gentle treatment and compassion, even if she wasn't in the right state of mind to show those qualities herself.

And hadn't Vivian been the one to teach him the old adage that you could catch more flies with honey than with vinegar?

Although knowing Vivian the phrase would come out something like catching more hummingbirds with honey or flies with jelly in that delightful way she had of mixing her metaphors.

In any case, the good old Golden Rule applied. Do to others whatever you would have them do to you.

And if he felt half as physically and emotionally wiped out as Vivian looked he wouldn't want someone pushing his buttons, intentionally or not.

Vivian made a hissing sound through her teeth. "Yes, yes, I know. I'm sorry. I didn't mean to harp at you. It's just that I can't finish all the last-minute details of the grand opening if I'm lying on my couch with my feet propped up."

"Okay." He wanted to tell her she could always ask for his help…but he knew it wouldn't do any good to argue with her when her will—and her jaw—was set. "But at least tell me what I can do to make things easier on you."

Vivian had been facing a row of premium conditioners, but suddenly her hand jerked away and four bottles fell clattering off the shelves.

He immediately reached down to retrieve the bottles, knowing how difficult it was for her to pick things off the floor in her current expanded condition.

As soon as he straightened up, she wrenched the conditioners from his grasp. "I think you've already done enough."

He felt as if there was an entirely different conversation going on between them, in a silent language that he had no idea how to translate.

What did she mean? They'd been working together on this project since day one, when she'd bid on him at the auction. And now all of the sudden he'd *done enough*?

What was that supposed to mean? He certainly didn't have a clue. And it was difficult not to get his back up when she continued to talk in riddles.

"We'll be good to go if we work together on this." He was frustrated beyond belief but he focused all his energy on keeping his tone mild.

She just stared at him as if he'd suddenly sprouted a pair of horns.

Or maybe that look meant she wanted him to disappear.

Well, he could do that, he supposed, and make one more pass around the neighborhood, reminding everyone when they should arrive for the grand opening.

"Okay," he concluded.

"Okay?" He thought he saw a flash of distress cross her gaze before irritation replaced it.

She wanted him to leave, but she didn't really want him to go? He wasn't about to try to solve that particular female quandary.

"Okay, I'll leave, if that's what you want," he clarified. "But not until we've taped the butcher paper over the front windows. That's a two-person job and I don't want you climbing any ladders."

She opened her mouth to protest and then promptly closed it again. He was right and they both knew it, so there was no use in her arguing with him.

The butcher paper had been his idea, and one of his brighter ones, he thought. It was ostensibly to hide the interior of the finished salon from prying eyes until it was revealed during the official grand opening, but really it was a way for him to mask what would be happening on the street outside the shop.

"I don't know why we're bothering," Viv said as Nick used packing tape to secure the butcher paper to the top of the window. "Anyone who wanted to could already have looked in the window for the past few weeks and seen all the new fixtures." She shook her head. "Not that anyone would want to see the inside of a beauty salon."

He wanted to argue with her, or shake some sense into that stubborn blond head of hers. Didn't she realize what an amazing job she'd done? She'd made the beauty parlor as beautiful as she was.

This pessimism was so not the Vivian he knew and... *liked.* It was as if someone had switched off the light inside her.

This whole idea of his wasn't working out the way he had planned it at *all.* Or rather, it *was* working, but he hadn't planned it very well or considered all the contingencies he might encounter.

She just had to last until tomorrow.

So did he. Because right now, seeing her downcast face, he was an inch away from blurting out the whole truth himself.

But at this point he might as well keep his mouth shut and let things unfurl as they would. She was kicking him out of the salon early, anyway. The next time he saw her, he would be able to make everything in her world right again. Her downcast features would turn to delight and happiness.

Whether or not she ever forgave him for his subterfuge and the unnecessary pain he'd caused her was another thing entirely. After everything was out in the open, she still might never want to speak to him again.

And even if everything went off without a hitch, even if Vivian was as shocked and delighted as he hoped she would be, and even if the sequence of events erased the strain between them, their relationship would still never be the same again.

Because after tomorrow, he'd have no real reason to seek Vivian out anymore. He'd be of no use to her. More than that, he wasn't good enough for her and her baby. Sure, they might remain friends on some level and exchange pleasantries at church or social events, but it wouldn't be the same. He wouldn't be seeing her every day and working together with her, and that thought gripped painfully at his chest.

Her sunshine had finally started to seep into his cold heart. What would happen to him when the clouds returned?

No doubt about it. There were dark days ahead. But he would take comfort in the fact that Vivian, at least, would be basking in the balmy glow of happiness and success, with her thriving business and her healthy baby boy.

Seeing Vivian happy, even from a distance, would have to be enough for him. She and her son deserved the very best that life could offer them, and, as he'd once again proven by this botched-up grand opening scheme, he was not it.

And he never would be.

Chapter Ten

Vivian took extra care in her appearance, gussying up in her most fashionable dress and styling her hair for the special opening-day event. She didn't know why, considering she was entirely convinced no one would attend her grand opening—well, except those who had been coerced into being there. Her sister, Jo Spencer and Alice, since Nick had signed her up to get her hair done.

Even if she was dressing only for the few people who would take the time out to visit her, she wanted to look her very best. She had very little pride left, but if she was going to fail, she would go out looking her best.

As she curled her hair into soft waves, she thought about what she was going to do next. All of her plans since the moment she'd returned to Serendipity had re-volved around remodeling the beauty salon and plan-ning for her grand opening.

But if the salon failed, then what was next for her and her son?

She hated to have to think about letting Nicole and Lauren go so soon after hiring them. What a disappointment that would be. But if she didn't have the work for them, she wouldn't have money to pay them, and for their sakes, it would be better for them to pursue their careers elsewhere. They deserved more than the measly tips they would receive in a town too small to really warrant a salon and spa.

She was convinced now more than ever that Nick had been right all along.

She met her own gaze in the mirror. "That's enough of that negative thinking," she admonished her reflection. "Chin up, smile on your face. Even if it's just a few loyal friends, they still deserve your best efforts."

She'd been through what she'd thought were impossible circumstances before, when she'd discovered she was pregnant and Derrick had abandoned her. She'd survived, and she would walk through fire to the other side this time, as well.

In any event, she had the birth of her precious baby to look forward to. She couldn't wait to meet her son and hold him in her arms.

And it wasn't as if she would starve. She was one of the blessed ones, and she thanked God for it. She had family, and they wouldn't let her down. Alexis and Griff would support her for as long as she needed to get back on her presently pregnancy-swollen feet.

And rise, she would—although she would be doing two months of Alexis's laundry in addition to her own. Her soon-to-be new arrival would create even more laundry for her.

The thought made her chuckle.

"See?" she told the mirror. "There's humor to be

found in any situation if you look hard enough, no matter how grim it might appear on the outside."

Her chuckle turned into full-blown laughter. She wasn't usually in the habit of speaking out loud to herself in the mirror.

She pulled her hair back and tied it up with a soft lavender-colored ribbon.

There, then. She'd done her best. There was no use putting off the inevitable.

She drove down Main Street on her way to the salon. Serendipity wasn't a busy town in general, but today it was even quieter than usual. Quite vacant, actually, especially for a Saturday. Even the three old men in the bib overalls who were usually a firm fixture on their rocking chairs in front of Emerson's Hardware were noticeably absent.

It figured. She wouldn't even be able to use her status as a local oddity to draw in foot traffic today.

She pulled her car around to the back alley where the shopkeepers tended to park. Nick's truck was already behind the salon but there was no sign of him.

Not surprisingly, the back door was unlocked. Nick was sitting in one of the styling chairs. His head was back, his eyes closed, and his hands were clasped across his muscular chest. His black cowboy hat was tipped low over his brow and his breath was coming slow and even, as if he was napping.

He looked completely relaxed. If he wasn't asleep then he was close to it.

It figured. Well, she was glad *someone* wasn't stressed out about the way this day was going to play out.

"Didn't get enough sleep last night?" she remarked wryly.

He tipped his hat back with his fingers and grinned broadly, his blue eyes clear and sparkling.

"On the contrary," he said. "I slept like a baby, and then I was up with the dawn, well rested and raring to go. I was feeling antsy, so I decided to come on by the shop early. I rearranged the stock room and labeled all the shelves so it will be easier for you to find specific products when you need them. Alphabetical order. That seemed to be the most logical way to go."

"You did *what*?"

He held up his hands as if to stave off the dressing down he'd clearly realized she was just about to give him.

"Before you start squawking, at least take a look at it. If you don't like how I've stocked everything I'll re-arrange things however you want."

"The stock room is the least of my concerns," she said, looking around the salon. She tossed a glance over her shoulder. "And I don't squawk."

"We did good, didn't we?" He came up behind her, near enough to touch her. She could feel his breath fanning her cheek, but he kept his arms at his sides.

It *was* good. She was proud of how the remodel had turned out, with its relaxing lavender-painted walls and glistening gray-tiled floor. Soft instrumental music piped through the room, adding to the feeling of—

Tranquility.

"Where did all the flowers come from?" she asked, just now noticing the vibrant bouquets of fresh flowers in vases at every styling station.

"Oh, that's nothing. I thought the scent of fresh flowers would make the salon distinctly—I mean, well—" He stammered to a halt and lifted his hat, threading his fingers through his thick hair.

"Distinctly—?" she probed.

"Your, uh, perfume reminds me of spring flowers," he blurted out. "I wanted Tranquility to smell like you."

Her eyes widened and warmth bloomed in her heart. That had to have been the sweetest thing anyone had ever done for her, bar none. She didn't even know what to say.

"That was…very thoughtful of you."

He'd gone to all the trouble of buying fresh flowers because they reminded him of her? It was nearly an hour's drive to a floral shop, which was the only place a man could get so many bouquets at once.

She would almost have thought he was rooting for the grand opening to be a success, if she hadn't heard words from his own mouth to the contrary.

Nothing made any sense right now.

Nick glanced at his watch. "Only half an hour to go. Are you getting excited?"

"I'm not sure it's hitting me yet," she said honestly. "It doesn't feel real."

She was counting the minutes, but not the way Nick was probably imagining.

Nicole and Lauren arrived, bubbling over with excitement and chattering up a storm. It was bad enough that Viv was anticipating her own crash and burn without bringing the girls into it. That was the real shame.

"Oh, to have the energy of youth," she murmured,

stretching and rubbing the small of her back. "I feel like I'm over the mountain."

Nick burst into hearty laughter. "You're hardly over the *hill*, Viv."

"Well, I feel like it right now."

Nick's gaze narrowed on her, assessing her. "You're still carrying too much weight on your shoulders. I told you that you should rest more."

She crinkled her nose at him. Resting more was simply not in her vocabulary. Not now.

"Did anyone ever tell you that you're stubborn?" Nick asked rhetorically.

She shrugged. "It might have been mentioned once or twice over the years."

"Well, I, for one, admire that trait in a woman."

What? That wasn't what she'd expected him to say. She'd thought he was gearing up to insult her.

He made a sweeping motion with his arm. "It takes real guts and determination to take an old, run-down shop and turn it into this. It's incredible."

"Yeah, Viv, it looks amazing," Nicole said.

"Beautiful," Lauren agreed.

Nicole was scheduled to work the mani/pedis while Lauren was doing facials. Today, Vivian was supposed to be the one doing haircuts and perms on the clientele.

Supposed to be being the key words.

"It doesn't matter how nice it looks without guests around to enjoy it."

"Then I guess it's time to let your new customers see what all this fuss is about." Nick walked to the front window and grasped the edges of the butcher paper.

"Are you ready?" he asked, glancing backward and flashing Vivian a toothy grin.

Despite knowing there was probably hardly anyone outside and no reason to hope for better, Viv inhaled deeply and held the air in her lungs. A sense of giddy anticipation filled her chest.

"Drumroll please." He ripped off the paper in one smooth motion. "And… Tranquility is officially open for business. Vivian, will you do the honor of flipping the sign on the door from Closed to Open?"

She let out her breath in an audible *whoosh*.

Instead of the three or four people she had expected, Main Street was packed, lining both sides of the street for as far as Viv could see. Some of the ladies from the altar guild at church had set up a table and were selling baked goods. It looked like a party.

Her party.

"What?" she breathed, her heart welling at this unexpected outpouring of love, kindness and support from her friends and neighbors. It looked as if the whole town had turned out for the grand opening.

Nick chuckled. "I doubt if you're going to be able to cram all these guests into one day. I'd hazard a guess and say you've probably got a good month of work ahead of you, and that doesn't count repeat customers, of which I'm sure you'll have plenty. I wouldn't be surprised if you are thoroughly booked when you get back from your maternity leave."

Vivian could hardly believe what she was seeing, but Nick was right. Tears of happiness and gratitude poured down her cheeks.

"I can hardly believe my eyes!" With a squeal of delight, she launched herself into Nick's arms and hugged him tightly. He laughed and swung her around.

She could have kissed the man. In fact, she might just.

"Surprised, darlin'?"

Surprised didn't even begin to cover it. Alexis, Jo and Alice each had a clipboard and were making their way through the crowds of the people she'd spoken to as she'd canvassed all the neighborhoods. She even spotted Eddie Emerson, joking around with a group of his friends.

Never in her wildest dreams could she have imagined that so many people would turn out to support her, to make Tranquility a success.

The expression on Nick's face was one of sheer pleasure and appreciation. He was relishing the moment as much as she was. When their gazes met, she could see pride there, too. But she was confused. Hadn't Nick been against her plans? She'd heard him tell Delia not to come to the grand opening. Delia apparently hadn't listened to him, because she and her husband, Zach, were hanging out at the front of the line, chatting with some friends.

Nothing made sense anymore.

"I suppose we'd better get busy," Nick said.

"We?" It sounded as if he was taking mutual ownership in Tranquility. She supposed in many ways the small shop was as much his as it was hers. The majority of the remodeling had been done by his hands. But she couldn't even fathom the change that had come over him. Did he really want the salon to be a success, after all?

"That's right," Nick affirmed. "I'm going to be running the cash register today—oh, and manning the phone. I imagine it will be ringing off the hook before long. That way you three lovely ladies can focus on beautifying Serendipity."

Vivian was certain she was gaping, especially when Nick flashed her another one of his heart-stopping grins.

In one smooth move, he tossed his hat on the hat rack in the front corner and opened the door. The first folks in line were clamoring to get in. Jo and Alice barked out orders like a couple of kindergarten teachers rounding up children after recess.

Vivian expected Nick to step away from the door once he had opened it. He'd said he was going to man the cash register and the phone.

Instead, he was blocking the entrance completely, his large, muscular frame filling the doorway.

Leaning a shoulder against the door frame, he raised his brows as if he was waiting for something.

"Nick?" she asked, once again confused by his actions.

"Where do you want me?"

Was this a trick question?

"Behind the cash register?"

"Well, sure, I'm going to man the register for you for most of the day. But not yet. I'm going to be the first one in line to get—" His throat clogged and he had to stop and clear it. "I'm going…" he said again, in a steadier voice "…to get a haircut."

Vivian gasped. The girls giggled. Nick lowered his brow and marched determinedly to the nearest styling chair and sat down with a little more force than was strictly necessary, sending the chair spinning.

Could it be that she was not going to have to do two months of Alexis's laundry, after all? She wanted to crow in exaltation.

His fingers were clenched to the arms of the styling chair and his jaw was taut with strain. If Vivian didn't already know better, she would have thought the man was getting ready for a dental procedure, staring up at a novocaine syringe and a whirring drill.

Maybe a little nitrous oxide would help take the edge off the poor man's agony, for he was clearly in excruciating pain.

The very thought of having to use laughing gas to get Nick through a haircut sent her into a spasm of giggles. She covered her face to mask her amusement.

"That's a sight we won't see too often," Jo said, entering the salon and tossing her fully filled-out clipboard onto the front desk next to the register. She was wearing one of the homemade T-shirts she was known for. This one proclaimed It's a GRAND Day!

"I'll say," Vivian agreed.

"Maybe we should take a picture of him and frame it so we can hang it on the wall at the café."

That nearly sent Vivian into another fit of laughter. She was seriously struggling to regain her composure, but she couldn't help an occasional little snort from escaping her lips.

Nick cleared his throat—loudly.

"If you ladies are finished having fun at my expense, I would appreciate getting this over with. I would like my hair cut now, please. I'm sure the people waiting in line behind me are anxious to have their turn to be tortured."

Vivian wrapped a cape around Nick and laid her hands on his shoulders. "Would you like me to give you a shampoo and conditioning treatment? It's free with a haircut today."

She literally felt him cringe.

"Okay, then," she said, knowing better than to push for too much. Reaching for the spray bottle, she misted his hair with water. "What would you like done today? A little off the top?"

It took him a moment to answer. "I have no idea. Whatever. Just please don't cut my ears off."

"I think I can promise that won't happen," she said with a laugh. "Do you want a shave, as well?"

He frowned and tilted his chin from side to side, examining his reflection. "I guess."

She picked up her comb and shears and met his gaze in the mirror. "You know this doesn't hurt, right?"

He huffed and crossed his arms underneath the cape. "Speak for yourself."

She combed through Nick's thick hair and pulled the first section between her fingers. Her shears were posed for the first snip, but something stopped her.

Here she was, one clip away from having two months of laundry done for her—so why was she hesitating?

Nick seemed willing—if grudgingly so. But even though he was making no move to get away, she knew he'd probably rather be pretty much anywhere else in the world right now. Yet he was here, making the sacrifice.

The town gossip mill would definitely be ruminating over this day for a long time to come—which Vivian knew was the whole point. The transformation of Nick McKenna was nothing to take lightly.

And when everyone saw the way her styling techniques made a new man of him, a man who could step off the pages of a fashion magazine, the line outside her door would never cease.

Her business would be an overwhelming success.

One snip and she'd be on her way.

Nick desperately tried to look as if none of this bothered him, but given the fact that all of the women in the room were laughing at him, he figured he'd pretty much failed at his attempt to remain cool and collected.

This was silly. It was just hair. And it wasn't as if he *never* visited the barbershop—just maybe not as often as other guys did.

What he didn't like was getting all frou-froued up with most of the town watching like he was some kind of sideshow act. Who knew how many people were gawking at him from outside the store window?

Which was the whole point, but that felt irrelevant at the moment. He was *trying* to make a spectacle of himself, get everyone's attention so he could prove Vivian's talent was worth her weight in gold.

What better way than to let her turn him from a beast into—*ugh*. What *was* she going to turn him into? He didn't even want to think about it.

Maybe it would be less painful if he just closed his eyes.

Vivian ran her fingers through his hair. He couldn't

hear the snip of scissors, and yet he imagined lengths of it were floating down to cover the shining gray-tiled floor.

Viv was unusually quiet, though. Whenever he visited the barbershop, he'd always found it almost obnoxiously loud, full of men shouting and laughing and jibbing each other.

He supposed he'd thought a beauty salon would be even noisier, given that women liked to gab so much.

But it was strangely silent in the room. Was it supposed to be this way? Maybe the spa would live up to its name, after all.

Curious, he opened his eyes. Vivian's gaze wasn't on his hair. She was staring at his reflection in the mirror, her comb and shears still poised for action.

Suddenly, she dropped her arms and slid the instruments of torture into the pockets of her apron.

He lowered his brow. "What?"

She merely smiled. "You're done."

"What?" He looked in the mirror, confounded. What was the woman talking about? He couldn't see any difference at all. And when he glanced at the floor, it gleamed back up at him, free from all traces of hair.

"You haven't done anything yet."

"Exactly."

"But I thought—"

"You have no idea how difficult this is for me." She groaned. "Just so you know, I'll be washing Alexis's laundry for two solid months because of this."

"Now you've really lost me."

Viv sighed dramatically. "I *may* have mentioned to Alexis that I could get you cleaned up by the end of the day of the grand opening and that if I did, she would do my laundry for two months."

"Cleaned up," he repeated. His gaze widened. "And then if you didn't, you have to do two months of *Alexis's* laundry."

"Something like that."

He pressed his lips together to keep from laughing, but in the end he had no choice but to give in to it.

"You certainly like a challenge, don't you?"

"It makes life interesting."

Challenges certainly *did* make things interesting, and Nick had never known a challenge quite like Vivian Grainger.

"So let me get this straight. Alexis will have to do your laundry if you manage to make me look like a dull lawyer instead of a rowdy rancher?"

"Well, I hope it wouldn't be as bad as all that." She stepped back and folded her arms over her rounded belly.

"If that's what you need to do then I don't mind," he said.

He felt like he was a specimen under a biologist's microscope.

"No, I don't think so," she said at last. "You're good to go."

Nick spun his chair around. "Come on, Vivian. You have the opportunity here to get back at me for all the grief I've caused you—not to mention getting free laundry service for two months. How can you pass up on that?"

He'd been thinking of Slade and the calves when he'd spoken and thought she would be laughing at the reference, but instead, a moment of anguish flickered in her eyes. She masked it quickly, but not fast enough. He knew her too well.

"What's wrong?"

She looked as if she was about to say something—something serious—but then she apparently thought better of it. She smiled and gestured to the waiting line.

"If we're through here, you're holding up my business."

He stared at her for a moment, completely baffled, but then he nodded. "Right. I belong behind the cash register."

The rest of the day went by in a whirl of familiar faces, names, cash transactions and credit card swipes. Nick was new to the appointment software but it didn't take him long to pick it up. And thanks to Jo, Alexis and his mom, he and Vivian would have to work after-hours entering all the appointments folks had signed up for on the clipboards. The calendar went out for at least two months, and that was without repeat customers.

Nick couldn't have been more pleased with the overwhelming success of Tranquility's grand opening. Vivian beamed with delight when lines of people filed through to congratulate her on her new business and wish her well.

The altar guild made a killing on baked goods. A win-win, as far as Nick was concerned. They kept the ravenous hoard filled with sweets while the church's donation box was filled with stacks of dollar bills.

The grand opening celebration was supposed to go from ten in the morning until five o'clock at night, but it was well after six before they were finally able to turn the door sign from Open to Closed.

Vivian immediately dismissed Nicole and Lauren, thanking them for all their hard work and sharing with them excitement at the future of Tranquility.

As if there had ever been any question about it.

Nick couldn't believe he'd ever given Vivian such a hard time about her plan, especially in the beginning. Of course Serendipity needed a beauty salon. Everyone needed their hair cut now and again, and why shouldn't the ladies of Serendipity pamper themselves with a manicure or a facial?

Vivian had been right and he had been wrong, and he was man enough to admit it. More than that—he was happy to admit it.

"Unbelievable," Vivian said, slumping happily but tiredly into one of the styling chairs. "I honestly thought my grand opening was going to be a complete disaster."

"I was afraid you might be worried about that, although scaring you wasn't intentional on my part. I didn't realize when I started all this that my actions would cause equal and opposite reactions."

"Chemistry?"

"Physics." He shrugged. "I excelled in the sciences in high school, but when it comes to real life, my little experiment started bubbling over and I didn't know how to keep it from exploding."

"I heard you talking to Delia and your mom about the grand opening the night we were at the doctor's office."

"I thought I heard you come into the waiting room that night, but when I turned around, the examination room door was closed, and when I looked in on you,

you were resting quietly. I decided I must have been mistaken."

"I didn't want you to know I'd heard what you said. You really hurt my feelings."

"No, wait. If you heard me talking to my mom and Delia, then you would have known about the big surprise I had planned for your grand opening."

Her brow lowered and he thought she might have winced. "That's not what I heard."

He was trying to follow the gist of the conversation, but somewhere along the way he'd become completely lost. He backtracked to the last place he had seen tracks, where he had any idea what they were talking about.

"Vivian, what exactly do you think you heard me say that night?"

"I believe your exact words to Delia were, 'You don't need to come.' I don't think that's open to more than one interpretation."

He chuckled. So that was what this was about. He'd started to think he'd dug himself in so deep that he'd never get out, but *this* he could handle.

"It might have changed your interpretation if you had stayed around long enough to hear the entire sentence."

"What does that mean?"

She shifted in her chair, looking as if she was unable to find a comfortable way to sit. Nick imagined it probably would be difficult for her to get comfortable while carrying around an almost full-grown baby inside her. She was getting bigger every day, but not in a bad way.

"What it means is that you didn't hear what I really said to Delia, which was that she didn't need to come *at the same time as my mom did*. I was afraid if too many people came early to the event, they'd start making too much noise and you'd figure out what was happening. I didn't want you to know how big of a crowd awaited you until I pulled the butcher paper down from the windows. That was supposed to be the surprise."

Tears filled her eyes.

"So the reason you were canvassing the neighborhood ahead of me was in order to plan this...surprise party."

"Guilty as charged, although I never meant for you to get hurt in the process."

"Unbelievable."

"I know. I'm sorry."

"No, it's not that. I'm the one who should be apologizing to you. Once again, I automatically jumped to the wrong conclusion about you, and I should have known better. I'm so ashamed of myself for being so distrusting. You deserved better from me. You have repeatedly shown me that I can depend on you, and what do I go and do? Leap to all the wrong conclusions. Again."

She reached for his hand. "I should have trusted you, Nick, and I'm sorry I didn't."

His chest warmed, expanding until he thought it might burst, and his heart leaped into his throat.

She trusted him?

"Thank you," he said, his voice gravelly. "You'll never know how much those words mean to me."

She smiled softly. "Oh, I think I do."

They were silent for a moment, each lost in their own thoughts. Vivian shifted in her chair several times before attempting to stand.

Even that movement was complicated. She braced

both hands on the arms of the chair and strained to achieve the forward momentum she would need to roll out of the chair, but to no avail.

He stood and reached out his hands to her, giving her the leverage she needed to rise.

She groaned and then made a deep, eerie moaning sound that echoed throughout the salon.

"I feel like a beached whale," she explained when he looked at her funny.

"That was supposed to be a beached whale?" He chuckled. "You sounded more like a mummy."

"I suppose that's apropos," she said, joining in his laughter. "Since I'm going to be one of those soon, too."

He rolled his eyes.

She paced slowly back and forth across the room, stopping from time to time to stretch and rub the small of her back. Nick suspected she'd overdone it today, and she had definitely been on her feet too much.

"We have an impressive list of new clientele to enter into the appointment database," Nick told her. "I don't know about you, but I'm too exhausted to tackle that project tonight."

She fought back a yawn and nodded. The dark circles under her eyes told Nick more than any words she could say.

"It's nothing that can't wait," he assured her. "But if today was anything to go by, I think you may have to consider hiring an assistant to make appointments, man the cash register and answer the phone."

She leaned against a counter and smiled weakly. "It's incredible, isn't it? The outpouring of love and support the community gave me?"

"I'm not surprised."

"I can't believe I need to consider hiring another employee. When I woke up this morning I thought I was going to have to let Nicole and Lauren go."

"Well, you can put all those worries to rest. Your biggest problem now is counting your piles of cash. And then put some of that money toward bringing in an assistant to take some of the work off your shoulders. Now that the grand opening is over, I expect you to follow Dr. Delia's orders and put your feet up more often."

"Bossy much?"

"My brothers probably thought so when we were growing up together."

Their gazes met and held. Nick felt as if all the oxygen had left the room. She was so beautiful.

"But this isn't me trying to be dictatorial," he continued. "It's me worrying about you and Baby G."

She broke eye contact with him, staring out through the front glass into the darkness beyond.

"I'll be all right. It's not your job to worry about me, Nick."

A lance pierced his heart. What did she think? That after all of these months working together, he could just set his feelings aside and walk away from her? Didn't she realize how much he cared for her?

"I really appreciate all the help you've given me," she continued, "both in remodeling my salon and everything you did to make my grand opening a success."

She still wasn't looking at him, and her words sounded very much like a brush-off.

It was happening again.

"I was glad to do it."

What else could he say? His emotions were in turmoil.

"It'll be kind of weird not having you around here, but I know you must be anxious to return your full attention to your ranch."

That was the truth. He'd been neglecting his ranch in favor of helping Vivian.

Now he was going to have all the time in the world to ride the range and care for his cattle.

And think.

Alone.

That one word held a lot of impact.

Not so long ago he was comfortable being by himself, didn't see the need to seek out others for company. And then he'd been bought at auction by a vivacious woman who'd showed him that there was so much joy to be had in opening himself up to the world. It wasn't going to be so easy this time to hibernate on his ranch and keep his head stuck in the sand.

"I guess we'll still see each other at church." His voice broke on the last word.

Her gaze returned to his. Large droplets of tears illuminated her impossibly blue eyes, making them into infinitely deep wells. He could happily lose himself in that gaze for the rest of his life.

Was she feeling the shock of their future separation as much as he was?

Was there another way?

"Vivian," he began, not sure how to ask the question that was burning inside him. He desperately needed an answer, but was almost afraid to hear what she might say.

He reached for her, but she stiffened in his arms.

Had he been reading the signals all wrong? Seen what he wanted to see in her gaze, heard the longing he was feeling in her voice rather than truly noticing what she was trying to convey?

"Viv, I—" he started again.

Vivian trembled and grasped at the material on the front of his shirt.

"I've been trying to ignore this all day," she said in a ragged whisper. "I thought maybe if I didn't acknowledge it, it would go away."

A chill skittered up Nick's spine. Was she speaking of her feelings for him? Had she, like he had, come to the place where she could no longer deny her emotions?

He framed her face with his palms, allowing his joy to run free, wanting her to see the love in his eyes.

But her gaze didn't mirror his.

Her expression was tight with pain and her eyes full of agony.

"Nick," she said on a groan. "I think I'm in labor." She puffed out a breath. "For real this time."

Chapter Eleven

As excited as Vivian was to meet her son and hold him in her arms at last, getting to that point ended up being a lot more time-consuming and complex than she'd anticipated.

All through the day of the grand opening, she had been experiencing twinges and minor cramps, but they were nothing compared to the Braxton Hicks episode she'd had earlier, and so, in the excitement of the day, she'd ignored them.

But what had started out feeling like a dull backache had progressed through the day until, by the time the last guest had exited and she'd changed the sign on the door to Closed, the contractions had become quite regular and she could no longer ignore them. They started at about fourteen minutes apart and then gradually grew closer together.

Nick had immediately panicked when she'd informed him that she was in real labor, insisting that she sit down and rest while he made the necessary phone calls.

Even as distraught as he appeared, Vivian was glad

to have Nick with her. He was a take-charge kind of man, and for all that she teased him about it, his ability to put plans into motion was very handy.

He'd called Dr. Delia first and had Vivian talk through all her symptoms and everything she was feeling. These contractions were different. Deeper and more regular. Delia assured her that first labors were usually quite long, but because Serendipity was so far from the nearest hospital, Delia told Nick to take Vivian there immediately, promising that she would meet them there.

Nick called Alexis and Alice and told them the news, and then tenderly supported Vivian as they made their way out to his truck. His attention and hovering was adorable. She couldn't bring herself to let him know that she was perfectly capable of walking on her own, and that in the space between her contractions, she really wasn't in a lot of pain.

So instead, she let him fuss over her and enjoyed the extra attention. He drove to Alice's house first and they exchanged Nick's truck for Alice's more comfortable sedan.

As they drove to pick up Alexis, Alice took the wheel, while Nick sat in the backseat with Vivian, holding her hand and talking her through her contractions. In between, he cradled her in his arms and whispered encouragement to her.

At his mother's urging, Nick used the stopwatch feature on his cell phone to time the length of her contractions and how far apart they were.

At first, Vivian had picked up on the anticipation and adrenaline of the moment, but it wasn't long before the pain started to wear on her. She was already bone weary from a long day and she couldn't seem to find any position that was comfortable to sit in for any length of time.

And then there was her underlying fear—she wasn't yet thirty-eight weeks along, which was technically the earliest date to be considered a full-term birth.

By the time they got to the hospital, Vivian barely knew what was happening, other than what was going on within her own body.

Nick tried to pull into the emergency parking lot, but Alexis assured him that Vivian would be better cared for if they used the hospital's main entrance and went directly up to the maternity ward.

Nick found a wheelchair just inside the main door and gently settled Vivian into it, wrapping her in his warm sheepskin jean jacket. The jacket smelled like him, all leather and spice, and the familiar scent helped to calm her.

From there it was all a blur. Triage, being hooked up to a fetal monitor when she really wanted to move around. She missed Nick's presence when he was herded off to the waiting room, but Alice and Alexis were right by her side, holding her hands and reassuring her that all was well.

After several hours of labor, in which Baby G wasn't making the progress Delia would have liked—Vivian, too, for that matter—Viv was convinced to get an epidural. She'd simply been too tired to continue the fight without assistance.

After the epidural had been administered and Vivian was able to relax, her labor sped up again, and before long she heard the blessed sound of her son's first cry.

Georgie, as it turned out, wanted to greet the world sunny-side up, which Delia said was probably the cause of her severe Braxton Hicks contractions as well as why her labor had taken so long.

Nick visited the moment he was able. His eyes were glowing with amazement when Vivian passed little Georgie to him. The baby looked so tiny in Nick's huge hands, and yet Vivian knew there was no safer place her son could be.

"Hey, there, Georgie," Nick crooned in the high voice men used with babies.

He grinned at Vivian. "He looks just like you. Blond hair. Clear blue eyes. Cute little wrinkled nose."

Vivian smiled, her heart full to overflowing.

"Is Georgie a family name?"

She shook her head and laughed. "No. But I'd been calling him Baby G for so long that it only seemed right that I gave him a name that started with the letter *G*."

"I like it."

Vivian didn't know why Nick's opinion mattered so much, but it did.

"He came out full-sized and healthy, but the little brat was sunny-side up," Vivian told him.

"What does that mean?"

"Most babies are born facedown. The first anyone saw of Georgie was his smiling face."

"That's proof positive that he's your son." Nick gently placed the baby back into Viv's arms.

"Yes, but it made my labor longer and more complicated."

"Is it true what my mom said? That you forget all about the pain after the baby is born?"

She snorted. "Well, I don't know about that, but I do know that having Georgie was worth any amount of pain."

"When are they cutting you loose from this joint?"

"Tomorrow morning."

"Good. My mom will be here to take you home, okay? I've got some things to do and Alexis says she needs to get a head start on your laundry."

"But I didn't win the dare."

"She saw me cave. She said that was good enough for her."

Vivian chuckled. She didn't want to admit that she'd hoped Nick would be the one bringing her home. After everything that had happened, she just wanted to be with him.

Back at the salon there had been a moment when she'd thought she glimpsed the same emotions she felt in his eyes, but she must have been mistaken if he was so quick to leave her and Georgie's sides.

She tucked her heartache aside as she spent the rest of the day learning how to care for a newborn baby. She'd been worried that she might not be a natural mother and was surprised and relieved at how easily changing and feeding Georgie was for her.

As promised, Alice arrived first thing the next morning to await Vivian's release from the hospital. Alice had become more and more of a mother figure to Vivian and she didn't know what she was going to do when she was no longer involved with the McKennas. They really had become like family to her.

Alice slowed her sedan as she entered the long driveway of Alexis and Griff's ranch property. Vivian was currently staying in a small cabin on the outskirts of the ranch, at least until she could make other arrangements—which, happily, she would soon be able to do, since the salon was taking off so well.

"Are you ready to introduce baby Georgie to his new home?" Alice asked, her voice lined with excitement.

"Oh, yes. And to show him off around town."

Alice turned the curve just past Alexis's main ranch house and Vivian caught the first glimpse of her own little cottage.

She gasped in shock. Multicolored helium balloons were bobbing everywhere, along with an enormous blue banner with baby footprints and the words Welcome Home, Vivian and Georgie.

Tears filled Vivian's eyes as she saw all the people waiting on the lawn for her. Not only were Alexis and Griff there, but all three of the McKenna brothers, their significant others and their children.

Nick stood on the walk in front of the cabin, an enormous bouquet of red roses in his hand.

As soon as Alice pulled to a stop, Nick strode forward and opened the car door, gesturing to the scene before her.

"Welcome home, fair princess and little prince. Your family awaits."

Nick's eyes were alight with joy as he handed Vivian the flowers and unbuckled the baby from his car seat.

Family?

Yes, this very much felt to Viv like a family scene, and for the first time, she released all the fear and tension she had that she alone would not be enough for her son.

She didn't need to be worried, for Georgie would be surrounded with love and care.

"Thank you all," she whispered, her voice cracking. "This is so far beyond anything I could ever have imagined."

"That's not all," Nick said, taking her shoulder and turning her toward where Slade and Jax stood shoulder to shoulder.

When they backed away from each other, Vivian saw what they had been hiding behind them.

The little red tricycle, all repaired and cleaned and gleaming in the sunlight. The spokes had been straightened and the streamers on the handlebars had been replaced, as had the little bell. It had a fresh coat of red paint and the chrome had been polished.

Vivian exclaimed in delight. "Oh, Nick. How did you know?"

He chuckled. "You didn't think I noticed that you kept taking the trike out of the junk pile? After a while I got the hint."

She put her free arm around his waist and hugged him tight.

He cleared his throat. "You might want to look a little closer."

Intrigued, she turned her gaze back to the tricycle and realized it wasn't just the silver spokes, polished chrome and bright red paint that was catching the sunlight.

There, on the seat, was an open black velvet box. Inside was a beautiful diamond solitaire.

She clapped a hand over her mouth and her tears fell freely.

Nick reached for the box and knelt before her.

"I wanted our families to be here to share in our joy," he said, smiling up at her. "Little Georgie will always have plenty of family to dote on him."

Vivian knew Nick was making her a promise.

She nodded, trying to breathe, trying to swallow, but her head was spinning and nothing seemed to be working.

"Vivian Grainger," Nick said, holding Georgie in one arm and extending the ring in his other. "I love you. And I think I've loved Georgie even before we formally met. Will you do me the very great honor of becoming my wife?"

She couldn't see through her tears and she couldn't speak, but she nodded and put out her left hand.

When Nick slid the ring on her finger, it was as if every fear, every concern, vanished like mist in the morning sun.

He stood and embraced her. "I want you to know that you and Georgie will always be safe, protected and cared for, as long as I'm around. You've both stolen my heart."

"Oh, Nick." She reached her hand up and brushed her palm over the sweet, scratchy beard that was Nick McKenna. "I love you, too. I have for a long time, I think. You've already given me so much. I can only hope I can make you happy for the rest of our lives together."

"You already have," he said huskily, and brought his lips down on hers.

Their families hooted and applauded but Vivian was too wrapped up in Nick—and their future together—to really notice.

When she hadn't even been looking, love had crept up on her, and finally her heart was experiencing what she'd been searching for all along.

Tranquility.

Epilogue

Christmas Eve had always been one of Nick's favorite times of the year. He always enjoyed the children's nativity pageant and the midnight candlelight service at the church.

This year, however, topped anything he could ever have imagined. He couldn't believe all the blessings he'd received.

He had thought he was meant to be alone. Now he had a beautiful fiancée and her bouncing baby boy to make his life complete.

And tonight was special in another way. Nick's heart beat in anticipation as he sat with his family in the darkened church with nothing more than the glow of candles for light.

The choir started the hymn, slowly and reverently.

Silent night. Holy night.

Nick joined in, his baritone mixing with the other voices. He smiled at his mother. Her heart was healing. Although she still grieved for her departed husband, she had started living her life again.

There was a soft gasp and Nick turned to the back of the sanctuary, where Vivian was slowly walking up the aisle. Soon, she would be walking up this very same aisle to tie her life to his, but tonight she had another important role to play.

She was dressed in a blue robe with a white mantle, and in her arms she carried a swaddled, sleeping Georgie.

When she reached the front of the church, she laid Georgie in the life-size manger and knelt next to him, softly joining in with the others to sing the rest of the hymn.

Nick was so proud he wanted to burst. His heart swelled so much he thought he might not be able to endure the sweet tenderness.

Georgie's very first Christmas pageant, and he had landed the prime role.

Baby Jesus.

* * * * *

THE COWBOY'S
CHRISTMAS BABY

Carolyne Aarsen

To my sisters, Yolanda and Laverne.
Thanks for keeping me grounded.
And to my brother-in-law Jan, who bid on
the opportunity to be a part of this book.

In repentance and rest is your salvation.
In quietness and trust is your strength.
—*Isaiah* 30:15

Chapter One

It looked comfortably the same.

Erin McCauley parked her car in front of the Grill and Chill on the main street of the town of Saddlebank and turned off her car, her ears ringing in the sudden silence.

Though she had arranged to meet her sisters, Lauren and Jodie, at the ranch, she'd thought of stopping at the café to grab a soda because she was parched.

Her thirst was only part of her reason for her detour.

The other was that each mile she clocked northward from California to Montana increased the shame of the last ten months digging its unwelcome claws deeper with every roll of her car's tires. Now that she was so close she had to fight the urge to turn her car around and drive back south.

So she used the excuse of a pit stop to delay the inevitable surprise and questions.

I should have told them, she thought, her mind ticking back to a time when she was a more innocent girl walking down these very streets. *I should have told*

Lauren and Jodie everything that was happening in my life.

They would know soon enough, she reflected, stretching her hands out, making a face at her chipped nail polish. She eased her stiff and sore body out of the car and looked around the town with a sense of nostalgia.

The same brick buildings lined the street but the trees in front of them had grown taller and many of the flags flapping from their standards looked new. A bench and a couple of tables stood on a sidewalk in front of the Grill and Chill, but otherwise it was still the town of her early childhood.

A cool wind sifted down the street, tossing some stray papers and tugging a few leaves off the trees. It was mid-September. The kids were back in school and soon the leaves would be changing color.

I'm almost home.

The words settled into a soul in need of the solidity of this place. A soul disillusioned by life and by people. A soul that had grown tougher the past year.

The door of the Grill and Chill opened and a tall, lean figure stepped out, dropped a cowboy hat on his head and painstakingly worked his way down the three steps leading to the sidewalk. He moved with a pronounced limp, though he didn't look that old. His plaid shirt was sprinkled with sawdust. A leather belt and a large rodeo competition buckle cinched frayed, faded blue jeans that ended on scuffed cowboy boots with worn-down heels.

He was the real deal, Erin thought, mentally comparing him to the fake cowboys she'd seen advertised on billboards on her drive up here from San Francisco.

When he lifted his head sea-green eyes met hers and her world spun backward.

The face looking back at her was hardened by time, grown leaner over the years. Stubble shaded a strong jaw and his eyes were fanned by wrinkles from spending time outside. But Dean Moore still held that air of heedlessness. The tilt of his head, the angle of his battered cowboy hat showed her he still looked at the world like it was his for the taking.

Then he smiled, his eyes lit up and his features were transformed.

The old curl of attraction that she had always fought when she was around him gripped her heart. Her mouth, if it was possible, became even drier.

He walked toward her, his smile growing. "Hey, there. What are you doing here?"

Erin stared at him, surprised at his casual question. But to her consternation, even after all these years and all that had happened to her, he could still lift her heart rate. "I'm headed home," she managed.

"Vic said you were too busy to come to town. I thought you were getting ready for a visit from your uptight sister, if you'll pardon the little joke."

And then realization dawned.

He thought she was Lauren. Her twin sister. And she knew the exact moment he realized this himself.

His mouth shifted, his eyes narrowed and he visibly withdrew.

Crazy that this bothered her. Dean was so far in the past he may as well have been a character in the fairy stories she had once loved reading and drawing pictures of.

"My apologies. I thought you were—"

"Lauren," she finished for him. "Sorry. I'm Erin. The uptight sister."

He frowned as he assimilated this information, his hands slipping into the back pocket of his worn blue jeans. "Jodie and Lauren said you were coming this evening." He didn't even have the grace to look ashamed of himself.

"I'm early. Heavy foot."

He was silent a beat, as if still absorbing the reality of her presence. "So. How've you been?"

She wanted to make some glib remark about what he'd said about her character but didn't have the energy so she simply went with "Fine. I'm fine."

"Right." He gave her a tight smile, visibly retreating.

She shouldn't be too surprised at his reaction or what he'd said about her. Every time he'd asked her out the summers she spent on her father's ranch, she'd turned him down. He was a rough-living young man who rode hard, drank hard and played hard.

And yet, there had always been something about him that appealed. Some measure of self-confidence and brash self-awareness she knew she lacked.

In spite of the attraction she'd felt, her practical self had told her that Dean Moore was not the kind of man a good Christian girl wanted in her life.

And now?

She was hardly the sweet, innocent girl who'd left Saddlebank all those years back. Hardly walking with her Lord like she used to. She'd turned away from God nine months ago. When she'd found out she would be a single mother.

"So, you headed to the ranch?" Dean asked.

"Eventually. I thought I'd make a quick stop at the Grill and Chill." Her mouth was even drier than before. Some soda or tea and a few moments to settle her nerves before seeing her sisters was just what she needed.

"Okay. Well, I'll see you around."

She held his gaze a beat longer, surprised at the twinge of attraction he still created. The usual battle of her head and heart, she thought. Drawn to the wrong kind of person.

Then a muffled cry from the car pulled her attention away from him and to her baby still tucked in her carrier in the backseat.

Erin opened the door and took a second to inhale the sweet scent of baby powder and Caitlin's shampoo. With a gentle finger she stroked her baby's tender cheek, still amazed at the rush of love this tiny infant could pull from her. Six weeks ago she'd come into Erin's life and since then regardless of the exhaustion and confusion that dragged at her every day, Caitlin had been a bright spot in a life that had, of late, had some dark and hard valleys.

Erin grabbed the muslin blanket from beside her and laid it over top so her baby wouldn't be exposed to the wind or the sun, then gently pulled the seat free, tucking her arm under the handle and straightening.

Dean still stood there, frowning as if still trying to absorb the reality of her situation. His puzzlement grew as he glanced from the car seat hanging on her arm to her ringless left hand.

Yes, I am a single mother, she wanted to say, *and no, this was not in my long-term plan when I left here that summer. After turning you down yet again.*

Their gazes locked for a few heartbeats more as if acknowledging a shared past.

As she closed the door of the car he touched the brim of his hat in a surprisingly courtly gesture, then turned and left, his steps uneven, his one leg hitching with every movement.

She guessed this was from his rodeo accident almost a year back. Lauren had alluded to it in the texts they had exchanged the past few months.

Sadness winged through her. How much had changed for both of them since that summer, all those years ago.

She took a few steps almost getting bowled over by a young woman.

"Hey, Dean, wait up," the woman called and while Erin watched she ran up to him, tucking her arm in his. She was slender, tall, her brown hair shining in the sunlight, her trim figure enhanced by a snug tank top and denim pants. "You coming to the dance on Friday night? I was hoping you'd save a waltz for me." She slid a red-painted fingernail down his arm. Her head tipped to one side as she obviously flirted with him.

Erin recognized Kelly Sands, a girl a few years younger than both of them, daughter of a local, wealthy rancher. She remembered Kelly as a somewhat spoiled girl who loved a good time more than she loved the consequences of it.

"I doubt I'll be going to any dance," Erin heard Dean say, his voice gruff.

"Oh, c'mon. It will be fun. We can hang out. Like old times."

Then for some reason Dean glanced back at her and Erin saw herself through his eyes.

Hair pulled up in a sloppy bun. T-shirt with a ketchup stain from when she held Caitlin while trying to wolf down a hot dog. Yoga pants worn for comfort and ease of movement and flip-flops for the same reason.

Yeah. Not so much to compare to.

Then just as Erin was about to step into the café Kelly turned to see where Dean was looking. She frowned her puzzlement and then suddenly her smile grew brighter. "Hey, Erin. Wow. I haven't seen you in ages."

"It's been a few years," Erin admitted, her pride stung that while Kelly, who barely knew her, could see the difference between her and Lauren and Dean couldn't.

"And look at you. With a baby." Kelly let go of Dean's arm and scurried over, lifting the cloth covering the car seat. "Oh, my goodness. She's adorable." Kelly looked up at her. "I'm guessing from the pink sleeper she's a girl."

"Yes. She is."

"I didn't know you were married," Kelly continued, covering Caitlin again and, as Dean had, looking at her left hand.

Erin didn't want to blush or feel a recurrence of the shame that she struggled to deal with.

So she looked Kelly straight in the eye. "I'm not."

The girl released a surprised laugh, as if she didn't believe her. "Really? You of all people?"

Erin wasn't going to dignify that with a response so

she simply kept her chin up, figuratively and literally, and held Kelly's gaze, saying nothing.

"I guess people really do change," Kelly said. Then with a dismissive shrug of her shoulder she walked back to Dean. "And I'll see you on Saturday," she told him, her hand lingering on his arm.

Erin pulled her gaze away, wondering why she cared who Dean hung out with. But as she looked over at the door of the Grill and Chill, Dean's reaction lingered, as did Kelly's comment.

If she went inside she would probably meet someone she knew. And face more of what she'd just dealt with.

She couldn't handle more censure, puzzled glances and assumptions.

So in spite of the thirst parching her throat, she put Caitlin back in the car.

Then she headed home.

"Just drop me off at home," Dean said as Vic turned off Main Street, heading toward the highway and the Rocking M. "I don't feel like coming with you to Lauren's place."

"Home is twenty miles out of the way." Vic shot his brother a questioning glance. "And I promised Lauren I'd get these groceries to her as soon as possible. I guess Erin is supposed to be arriving late this afternoon."

Actually, she would be there sooner.

But Dean wasn't going to mention that to Vic. He was still absorbing the shock seeing Erin had given him. He still didn't know how he had mistaken her for Lauren.

Though they were twins, Lauren's eyes were gray;

Erin's a soft blue. Lauren's hair was blonder, Erin's held a tinge of copper. And Erin had always had a quiet aloofness that he'd viewed as a constant challenge.

Seeing her again so easily erased the years since they were last together. One look into those blue eyes and once again he was the brash young man who was willing to take another chance at rejection from Erin McCauley. Once again he felt the sting of her steady refusals.

And then she'd pulled the car seat out of the back of the car and he felt as if his world had spun in another direction.

He hadn't known she had a baby. Or that she was married, though she wasn't wearing a ring. Neither Lauren nor Jodie mentioned a husband.

When he'd taken a closer look at her, he'd seen the hollowness of her cheeks, a dullness to her eyes. When she'd told Kelly she wasn't married his world took another tumble.

Erin McCauley was always the unobtainable. Elusive. He had always known she was too good for him. And now, here she was. A single mother.

"I want to get working on that toolshed I promised Mom I'd finish," he said, wishing he could forget about Erin, frustrated at the effect she had on him. "And I'm tired."

He hoped his brother would accept his excuse and drive out of his way to bring Dean home but he doubted it. Vic was still in that glazed-eye stage of romance and would take advantage of any chance to see his fiancée.

"Tired and sullen from the sounds of things," Vic said with a laugh. "I'm sure Mom won't care if you're a day late on the shed. Besides, you didn't have to come to town with me today. I wouldn't have minded if you checked the cows in the higher pasture."

"They were okay when you rode up there last week. I doubt much has changed."

"We've always checked them regularly," Vic said but Dean ignored the comment. He had accepted Vic's invitation to go to town precisely because he felt grumpy and guilty about not checking the cows. But he had hoped Vic wouldn't nag him about not riding.

Dean hadn't been on a horse since that bad toss off a saddle bronc that had shattered his leg and put his dreams of a rodeo career on hold. Vic had been at him to continue his therapy, to cowboy up and get back on the horse.

But Dean wasn't about to admit to his brother why he didn't do either.

"I know we do, but I was busy. That's why I want to get working on that shed for Mom." He knew he was wasting his argument but couldn't give up without one last push. He really didn't want to see Erin again. Especially not after he'd made that stupid joke about Lauren's "uptight" sister.

"Then the shed is two days late instead of one." Vic shrugged, turning onto the highway heading toward the Circle M ranch where Lauren and Jodie were waiting for their sister.

If they did a quick drop-off he and Vic could be on their way home before Erin arrived. When he'd met her it looked as if she was headed into the Grill and Chill so there was a possibility.

But Vic was whistling some vague country song,

which meant his brother was happy about seeing his fiancée again. Which meant Dean would have to watch Lauren and Vic give each other those stupid, secret smiles. And the occasional kiss.

He was happy for his brother. Truly.

But ever since his girlfriend Tiffany broke up with him, less than twenty minutes before the ride he'd injured himself on, Dean had struggled with a combination of anger and betrayal.

Being dumped just before a ride that could have put him on the road to a major title was bad enough. Finding out that she was leaving him for his brother, whom she'd had a secret crush on the whole time they were dating only added insult to the actual injury he'd been dealt.

The fact that Vic and Tiffany hadn't gotten together after the accident helped, but knowing his girlfriend preferred his brother over him still stung.

And now Erin was in back town. Erin who seemed to prefer anyone to him.

Every summer since their parents' divorce, Erin had come from Knoxville to Saddlebank to stay with her father. And every summer, from the time they were both fifteen, he'd asked her out. And every time she'd turned him down. Thankfully his ego was more intact then. He kept thinking that his dogged persistence would do the trick, but when she told him the last time he asked her that she didn't approve of his lifestyle and didn't approve of him, he got the message.

He knew sweet Erin McCauley was above his paygrade and that she frowned upon his ever-increasing rowdiness, but at that time in his life obstacles had just seemed like challenges he could overcome. And Erin, with her gentle smile and kind nature, was exactly that kind of challenge. One that he'd lost.

He'd had girlfriends since then but deep down he always compared them to her.

His gold standard.

And now?

Pain twinged through his leg and he shifted it, grimacing as he did. Now he had even less to offer her or any other woman. A crippled ex-bronc rider trying to figure out what he was going to do with his life.

"So what does Jan have you working on these days?" Vic asked, pulling him from the melancholy memories.

"We're finishing up a hay shed for the Bannisters and there's a big job coming up in Mercy I'm hoping to get in on."

"You still enjoy the work?"

"It's work," Dean said carefully knowing that his brother was fishing. Again. Feeling him out about coming in as a partner on the ranch. That had always been the plan when Vic made a deal with Keith McCauley to lease his ranch. Then came the accident that changed so much for Dean. Now he wasn't sure what he wanted anymore or where he fit. Rodeo was off the table and he didn't know how much of an asset he could be to Vic.

If he couldn't ride a horse.

"Once Erin comes back Lauren and Jodie can make a final decision about the Circle M. And I was hoping you would make one, too," Vic returned.

"I thought their dad said in his will that only two of them had to stay two months." When Keith McCauley died his will stipulated that two of the girls had to stay two months on the ranch in order for all three to inherit.

"Lauren and Jodie both fulfilled the conditions of their dad's will, that's true, but I think they just want to talk it over with Erin. Out of courtesy." Vic waited a beat, then shot him a glance. "And once that's done, we need to make a decision about you coming in with me as a partner."

"I know. I need some time." Dean shifted in his seat again, stifling his frustration as he watched the fields flowing past.

"You've had time. This was the plan," Vic continued, his voice holding an edge of anger. "We talked about it before I approached Keith McCauley to lease the ranch from him, and now that it's pretty much a go I want to expand the herd. But I can't do that if I can't get a commitment from you."

Dean knew he was stalling and understood his brother's exasperation. Ranching together had been their plan for the past ten years. When he'd dated Tiffany he'd imagined his life with her in the little house on one corner of the Circle M Ranch, tucked up against the river.

He had been working for Jan Peter for a couple of years as a carpenter and had already planned the renos he was going to do on the house after he and Tiffany got married.

But those dreams had been busted in two decisive moments. When Tiffany broke up with him and when he smashed his leg half an hour later.

"Lauren and I are getting married soon," Vic continued. "I need to know where we're at. If I need to bring in another partner or if you're still part of this."

"I know and I appreciate that you've been willing to wait," Dean said, staring ahead at the road flowing past rolling fields toward the mountains cradling the valley. "But I'm not sure where I belong anymore."

"What do you mean? You belong here. You're a rancher. It's your legacy and it's in your blood."

Dean released a humorless laugh. "And what kind of rancher can't ride a horse?"

Vic looked back at the road, his one hand tapping his thigh as if restraining his impatience. "You just need to try again."

Dean's mind ticked back to the last time he tried to get on a horse. Vic had come upon him trying to mount up. He wanted to help and they'd had a fight. Dean had wanted to try on his own and his brother didn't think he could. Trouble was, Vic was right. And though he had come across all tough and independent, truth was he was scared spitless and secretly thankful for the chance to walk away.

"And lots of ranchers don't ride horses," Vic continued. "They use their trucks or quads—"

"You can't take a quad up into the high pasture or the back country. We both know that," he said, his voice hard. "Ranchers in this country ride horses. Simple as that."

And Vic's silence told Dean that his brother knew he was right.

"You'll ride again" was all Vic said.

Dean wished he had his sibling's optimism. Because right about now, he felt as if both Vic and his boss, Jan, were merely helping him out. Giving the poor cripple a hand up.

He wasn't used to that. He was used to being independent and doing things on his own. Like he had up until the accident.

And now they were going to see his brother's fiancée and the girl he'd once cared for. And he was coming as half a man.

Chapter Two

This was it.

Erin slowed as she headed down the driveway and made the final turn. She saw the house situated on the hill, overlooking the fields and the mountains beyond, and felt the land wrap itself around her heart and stake its claim.

She wanted to stop and take it in.

But Caitlin had been fussing ever since her aborted stop in Saddlebank and Erin never had gotten that drink.

She headed toward the house, parking beside a couple of smaller cars. She didn't recognize one but guessed it was Jodie's from the stickers on the windows and the beads hanging from the rearview mirror. The other one she knew to be Lauren's. Plus, in spite of the dust on the road, it gleamed in the afternoon sun. Lauren always liked things orderly and tidy.

Caitlin was screaming by the time she shut the engine off. Erin jumped out, quickly unclipping her car seat, grabbing the diaper bag.

The door of the house burst open as she headed up the walk and Jodie and Lauren spilled out, arms wide, calling out her name.

And then stopped dead in their tracks staring at the car seat she lugged up the walk, Caitlin now howling her protest from within.

"Hey, guys. Can you take her? I'm parched." Erin unceremoniously thrust the car seat toward Lauren, gave Jodie a quick smile and rushed into the house, not even bothering to look behind her. She knew she was being a coward but she really was dying of thirst.

And she needed a moment.

She ran to the bathroom, turned the tap on and gulped down a glass of water. Then another. As she lowered the cup she caught her reflection in the mirror. Hollow cheeks, sallow complexion and hair that looked like she had been attacked by an angry squirrel. Of course Dean would have to see her like that.

And why do you care?

She cared because even though Dean was eminently unsuitable and definitely not her type, he'd always held an undeniable appeal. He represented a part of her that sometimes yearned to be cool. Accepted. Independent.

Well, you're not, she told herself, finger-combing her hair and with quick, practiced movements, tying it up in a loose topknot.

Sam liked it when she wore it down. And since she'd broken up with him, she'd deliberately started wearing it up.

Besides, that way Caitlin couldn't grab it.

A faint wail resounded from the living room and then the sound of her sisters hushing her baby.

She held the edges of the counter, dizziness washing over her. She blamed it on a combination of not eating for the past twelve hours and the nerves holding her in a steady grip all the way home.

She splashed some water on her heated cheeks, patted them dry, sucked in a long breath and left to face her sisters.

As she walked around the corner she felt a sense of coming home. To her left was her father's office, to her right the kitchen where she and her sisters had spent a lot of time cooking and baking and trying out recipes. Things they were never allowed to do at their grandmother's house back in Knoxville where they lived ten months of the year.

The living room lay ahead with its soaring ceilings and large windows that let in so much light. The huge stone fireplace dominated the one wall but no fire burned in it now.

Jodie sat on the loveseat cradling Caitlin in her outstretched arms. Lauren sat beside her, Caitlin's tiny fingers clutching hers.

"You are just the sweetest little thing," Jodie continued, bending over to nuzzle her cheeks.

Erin's heart softened at the sight of her sisters so obviously in love with her baby.

And the one thought threading through her mind was, *We're not alone anymore*.

Lauren sensed her presence and looked behind her, her smile stiffening as Erin came nearer. But then she stood and walked around the couch, her arms open wide.

Erin stepped directly into her twin sister's embrace,

fighting down the surprising and unwelcome tears as Lauren hugged her. Hard. Tight.

"Oh, sweetie. What has been happening in your life?" Lauren murmured.

Erin simply clung to her sister unable to find the words.

She was the first to pull away scrubbing at her cheeks, thankful that she hadn't bothered to put on any makeup.

"Sorry. I just…" She looked at her sister and gave her a watery smile. "I missed you."

Lauren cupped her face in her hands and brushed a gentle kiss over her forehead. "Missed you, too, Rinny."

The pet name was almost her undoing again.

But then Jodie stood, shifting Caitlin in her arms, grabbing Erin in a one-armed hug. "Hey, sis," she said, pressing her cheek against hers. "Love this little girl."

Erin pulled in a shaky breath and struggled to keep her composure. All the way up here she'd been nervous and afraid of what she would see in her sisters' eyes. But now that she had arrived and her sisters had met Caitlin, she felt a loosening of the tension gripping her the past few months.

"I love her, too," she whispered, stroking her daughter's cheek.

They were all quiet for the space of a few heartbeats, each connected by this precious baby.

"So…" Lauren let the word drag out and Erin knew the moment of reckoning had arrived.

Then a door slammed and a male voice boomed into the quiet, "Grocery delivery," and Erin felt a temporary reprieve.

She turned to see Vic walking into the room, half a dozen plastic bags slung from his hands. He was as tall as Dean, his hair lighter with a bit of curl, his features softer and a brightness to his eyes that Dean didn't have.

He dropped the bags on the counter, then looked over the girls. He did a double take as he saw Erin, then released a huge grin.

"So you finally made it," Vic said, walking over to her. "Your coming was all Lauren and Jodie have been talking about the past week."

Then Vic surprised her by pulling Erin close in a quick embrace. "Welcome back to the ranch," he said, resting his hands on her shoulder. Then he turned to Lauren and brushed a quick kiss over her cheek. "And good to see you, my dear."

"And you brought the groceries." Lauren gave him a quick hug. "Well done."

Vic placed a hand over his chest. "You know me. I have a servant heart."

Erin watched their casual give-and-take, thankfulness welling up at the sight. Lauren had had her own struggles, as well. Being left at the altar by a man she'd given so much of her life to had soured her on men. To see her so relaxed with Vic gave Erin a glimmer of hope for happy endings.

At least for her sisters. Herself, not so much.

Then Vic noticed Caitlin in Jodie's arms. "Well, well. Is there something I missed?" Vic joked, grinning at Jodie. "Something you want to tell me?"

His comment was meant in fun but shame flickered through Erin.

"Don't tell Finn." Jodie gave Vic a wink and then shot Erin a meaningful glance.

"She's my daughter," Erin said, the words echoing in the house. The same house that often held the condemning voice of their father, reminding the girls to behave. *Be good.*

And I was. I was always good, Erin told herself, clenching her hands, fighting down the disgrace she'd struggled with ever since she saw that plus sign on the home pregnancy kit.

Vic's puzzled stare just underlined her own shame. Then the porch door closed again, echoing in the silence that followed and Dean came into the room.

Don't see the man for twelve years and then twice in one day. Just her luck.

Dean's shadowed gaze ticked from her to her sisters as he set a couple of grocery bags on the counter, then the baby Jodie still held, then finally back to Erin. He gave her a quick nod. "Hey, again," he said, taking off his hat and dropping it beside the bags. "Didn't think you'd beat us here."

"I changed my mind about going to the Grill and Chill," she said.

His smile tightened and she wondered if he had hoped to arrive and leave before she came.

"So. You have a baby," Vic said, stating the obvious.

Erin took her from her sister, cradling her close. "I do. She's six weeks old and her name is Caitlin."

She didn't have to look at her sisters to read the questions that hovered ever since she'd thrust her daughter into their arms. She had been in and out of touch for the past half year and hadn't even come to their father's funeral. She had been on bed rest and couldn't travel.

But every time she picked up her phone to tell Jodie and Lauren, every time she wrote up a text to explain why, she'd gone with inane details instead. The truth would take hours and pages.

Plus she just couldn't deal with the inevitable questions about the circumstances and the baby's father.

"Do you guys want some coffee?" Jodie asked, her voice artificially bright.

"I'm good."

"Sure. That'd be nice."

Dean and Vic spoke at the same time then looked at each other. "We can stay for a while," Vic said, tilting his brother a questioning look.

Dean shook his head and Erin guessed he was about as comfortable around her as she was around him.

You'd think all those years would have eased the awkwardness, Erin thought, rocking Caitlin. It was as if she and Dean were back in those unwieldy high school years when emotions were heightened and judgments abounded.

But now, it felt as if the roles were reversed. She didn't know where Dean was at in his life, but she wasn't the girl she once was. The girl who thought herself too good for Dean Moore.

"I think we should let the sisters spend some time together," Dean said. "We should go."

Vic looked like he didn't want to agree.

"And I'm sure Lauren and Jodie want to get to know their niece," Dean added.

His voice held an odd tone and she shot a quick

glance his way to figure out what he meant. But he wasn't looking at her.

She didn't know why that bothered her. It was like she wasn't there.

"Okay. We'll push off then," Vic said, giving Lauren another brief kiss. "I'll call you tonight."

Lauren's soft smile for Vic gave Erin a tinge of jealousy. She was happy for her sister. Happy her life had come to this good place. But it was hard not to wonder what her own future looked like.

Just before Dean left, his eyes drifted to Erin once more and for a heartbeat their gazes held.

She wasn't sure what to read into his enigmatic expression.

Didn't matter, she thought, cradling her head over Caitlin. She had other priorities and another focus.

Dean Moore's opinion of her wouldn't affect her at all.

"I should change Caitlin," Erin muttered, looking around for the diaper bag, as the guys left.

"Here's what you want," Lauren said, bending over and picking up the bag from where it lay beside Caitlin's car seat.

"I'll be right back," Erin said, once again retreating to the washroom. She didn't linger, however, and made quick work of changing her daughter's wet diaper. Caitlin's eyes were drawn to the lights above the sink and as she kicked her bare legs Erin felt again that wave of love. This tiny baby was so amazing.

"Love you so much," she whispered as she picked her fragile body up and held her close.

Lauren was pouring water into the coffeemaker when she came back and Jodie was putting together a plate of snacks. Cheese and crackers and cookies.

Her favorite white chocolate macadamia nut, from what Erin could see.

"Just go sit down," Lauren said, turning on the coffeemaker and then setting out some mugs.

Erin walked into the living room and dropped into the nearest couch, finally giving in to the weariness that had fuzzed her brains and dragged at her limbs. She leaned back into the chair as she cradled her now-quiet daughter in her arms, letting herself absorb the familiarity of this place. She knew Lauren and especially Jodie had resented coming here those summers of their youth, after their parents' divorce, but she'd always enjoyed it in spite of their taciturn father.

"You look tired," Jodie said as she brought the plate to the living room.

"I am. Been driving most of today. It's a good thing Caitlin was so well behaved for most of the trip."

She glanced around the room, then frowned as she noticed an empty space in one corner of the living area. "Did you sell your piano?"

"No. We moved it to Finn's place. A tuner was in Saddlebank to work on the church's piano so we thought we would take the opportunity to move and tune mine while he was around." Jodie sat down beside Erin, her hand reaching to touch Caitlin, now swathed in her linen blanket. "She's so perfect," she breathed, her finger trailing over her tender cheek.

Erin's throat tightened up. The words she had rehearsed all the way here now seemed pointless and superficial in the face of her sister's acceptance. Then Lauren sat down across from her, her hands clasped between her knees, her blond hair hanging loose around her classical features.

"You look amazing," she said to Lauren. "I think being engaged agrees with you. Congratulations, by the way. I'm happy for you. For both of you." Erin turned to Jodie, encompassing her younger sister in her congratulations as well. "I never thought a free spirit like you would end up marrying a sheriff."

Jodie released a light laugh. "Me, neither. Though Finn isn't a sheriff like Dad was. He's a deputy, but he's quitting in a year. Hoping to focus on horse training, which is his first love. I don't know if you remember him. He stayed with the Moores when his mother took off on him."

"Vaguely." Erin hadn't gotten too involved with many of the people in Saddlebank. When she was here, she had spent a lot of her time on the ranch walking in the hills, or riding. The ten months they lived in Knoxville, where their mother moved them after her parents' divorce, were always a dissonant time for her. While her sisters loved being in Knoxville, and disliked being on the ranch the two months a year they were sent here by their grandmother after their mom died, she was the opposite. Though their grandmother tried, Erin knew it must have been difficult for her to raise three grandchildren. Erin, of all the children, seemed to sense the tension more keenly than her sisters did.

So when they were shipped off to the ranch to be with their father, who reluctantly took them in, Erin found a peace that eluded her sisters. She would faithfully do the chores assigned to them by their father before he went off to his job as sheriff of Saddlebank County, then literally head to the hills with her sketchbook. She loved her time alone with her thoughts.

And her God.

She stopped reminiscing, turning to Lauren again. "Speaking of the Moores, I certainly didn't think a cowboy like Vic was your type, either. You always were so businesslike. So proper and—"

"Stick in the mud." Lauren laughed as she brushed her hair back from her face, gold hoops swinging from her ears. "You can say it. I was."

"That's not what I wanted to say," Erin objected. "I meant, you were always so focused and so self-disciplined."

"Qualities I get to apply to running Aunt Laura's flower shop right in Saddlebank now that she's retiring."

"I'm glad to hear you're taking it over," Erin said. "I have such good memories of that place."

"Her home and store was a sanctuary for us," Lauren said with a gentle sigh. "And we needed that from time to time. Though I think Jodie and I managed to find some peace the past few months. Since Dad died."

Erin felt it again. The tug of unmet expectations. The sorrow she'd felt when she heard her father had died and she couldn't come to the funeral.

"I'm so sorry I didn't come," she said, struggling once again with her shame. "I do want to visit his grave when we have a chance."

"We'll go there. On Sunday."

Which meant she was expected to attend church.

However she wasn't getting into that now. They had other things to discuss.

"He also wrote us each a letter when he found out he was dying," Jodie said, laying her hand on Erin's shoulder. "There's one for you, too. I found them in the house when I was cleaning up."

Erin looked down at Caitlin, wondering what their straightlaced, overly strict father would have said about his first grandchild. Born out of wedlock.

And more.

"I'd like to read it. But later." She had to get through this first hurdle—trying to find a way to explain to her sisters what had happened to her.

"Yes. Later," Jodie agreed.

A beat of silence followed and Erin knew that while they had much to catch up on, her baby was, for lack of a better metaphor, the elephant in the room that could no longer be ignored.

"So, this is Caitlin, like I said before," she began, pleased her voice came out so steady. "She's six weeks old. I was on bed rest for two months before her birth. That's why I didn't come to Dad's funeral. I cut back on my graphic design work so I could focus on her." The words came out stilted. Cold. As if she related the events of someone else's life. "She was a Caesarean birth, which meant another few weeks of rest and taking it easy."

And another few weeks of putting off what she knew she had to have done many months earlier, when she discovered she was pregnant.

Tell her sisters.

It wasn't until she knew they weren't selling the

ranch that she finally dared to return. Finally thought she might have a place to create a home for herself and her daughter.

And she knew exactly where that would happen.

"Oh, honey. You should have told us," Lauren said, hitting her directly in the guilt zone.

"I didn't know how to tell you I got pregnant." Erin cuddled Caitlin closer, fighting to maintain her composure, frustrated at the sorrow that threatened. She didn't want to feel sorry for herself. She had made her own choices and was living with the consequences. She didn't want Caitlin to even sense she might have regretted having her. "I didn't know where Jodie was living," she continued, swallowing down her tears. "You were dealing with the aftermath of Harvey leaving you days before your wedding. I knew how devastating that was for you so I didn't think you needed my troubles. I was trying to handle this on my own."

No one said anything as the grandfather clock ticked off the seconds, then boomed the hour.

"And now you're here." Jodie put her hand on Erin's shoulder. "I'm glad you came."

"I am, too." Erin gave her sister a careful smile. "Once I found out you girls weren't selling the ranch I felt like I had a place to come back to."

"It is your home," Lauren said. "Though, in our defense when we talked about selling it you said you didn't care either way."

"If you sold it, I would have figured something else out. But knowing this place was available to me. That I had a share in it…" She let the sentence trail off.

"You felt like you had a home," Jodie finished for her.

Erin nodded. "I know you girls didn't always like coming here over the summer, but for me it was comfortable."

"You and your long forays into melancholy," Lauren teased.

Erin laughed, thankful for the gentle return to lightness and comfort.

"And I'm going to ask the other awkward question," Jodie said, her hand still resting on Erin's shoulder. "Is Caitlin's father involved?"

Erin bit her lip trying to find the right way to tell them. "We aren't together anymore."

"Is he supporting you in any way?"

Was that a faintly chiding tone in Jodie's voice or was she being especially sensitive?

"He is not interested," she said firmly. "And I don't want to have anything more to do with him. It's...what we had...is over."

She was skating on the very edge of vague but her response and her vehemence seemed to satisfy her sisters. She simply couldn't deal with the past. She wanted to move forward into the new place she had found herself.

Caitlin stirred in her arms and Erin held her closer, as if protecting her. Too easily she recalled the look on Sam's face when she'd given him the news. She'd thought he would be happy. Thought he would finally make a decision about their relationship.

Instead the fury on his face and the check he wrote out to her to pay for an abortion had cut her to the core. And when she found out he was married already, her world tilted so far over she didn't think she would ever find her footing. She'd walked away and never contacted him again.

Now she was here and ready to look ahead and leave the past behind her.

"Well, you have us," Lauren said, leaning forward. "And you have a share in the ranch. Vic and I discussed the situation and he'll be talking to his banker about buying your third of the ranch out to give you some cash."

Erin knew she was entitled to a portion of the ranch and had already planned what she wanted. "The only thing I want is the Fletcher house. I want that to be my home."

"But, honey, you can stay here. In this house," Lauren said, sounding hurt.

"No. You and Vic will be living here. I don't want to be in the way."

Lauren didn't reply, which confirmed Erin's guess.

"We can figure out what the house and a few acres of it are worth and I'll take that as my share of the ranch." Erin looked down at Caitlin as a slow peace sifted over the chaos that had rocked her life for the past half year. "I just want a place of my own. A place I can be alone."

"That's fine and we can deal with the other details later on," Lauren agreed. "But the house you want to move into will need work."

"So I'll do it."

"You're a graphics designer, not a carpenter."

"I know a few things about building." Erin chuckled at her sister's incredulous look. "I learned a lot rehabbing the house my roommates and I lived in."

"Well, yes. You said that in some of your texts," Jodie agreed. "But—"

"You just can't imagine that your daydreaming sister can concentrate long enough to handle a skill saw. You should see some of the work I've done."

They hadn't of course. Jodie was running around, trying to find herself, playing piano in bars and looking for some kind of peace. Lauren was following her ex-fiancé Harvey around, looking for some kind of commitment.

All the while Erin had been looking for a home. A place to settle down and a man to settle down with. When she bought the house with her friends and started dating Sam she thought she'd found at least both.

She stopped her thoughts from heading down that dead-end road.

"At any rate, we should to talk to Jan Peter about this," Lauren insisted. "The local carpenter."

"Let me see the house first," Erin said. "I know moving in with you is the more practical option but I've been living on top of three roommates for the past year. If it'll work for me to live there while the work is going on, I don't mind."

"But what about Caitlin? Should you move her into the house?"

"We'll look at it first, then I'll decide for sure. But at this stage Caitlin tends to be oblivious to what's going on. Sleeps like a baby," she joked.

Erin didn't miss the sidelong glances Jodie and Lauren shared. Spacey Erin, making inappropriate jokes.

"I'll talk to Vic and Dean about it," Lauren said. "We could see what they say."

Erin knew staying in this house with Lauren was her best option but she couldn't shake the need for some quiet. For a place to put down some roots.

"Another thing, I'll need to get internet service up and running," she said. "I want to get working as soon as possible."

"Do you have work?"

Erin looked away from responsible Lauren to her younger sister Jodie who probably better understood that life could be erratic at times. That plans get messed up.

"I've just started up again." She glanced down at her daughter. "I had… Caitlin and a few other things to deal with. But I've got a few bites on some feelers I put out."

"I'm sure you'll be back at it in no time." Jodie gave her a one-armed hug and leaned closer to Caitlin, cupping her tiny shoulder with one hand. "And now you've got help."

Erin felt tears threaten at the thought that she wasn't on her own anymore. But she wasn't going to let herself get pulled into the pity vortex. She had made her own choices. Made her own bed.

Now she had to lie in it.

Chapter Three

"So it looks like the basic structure is sound." Jan Peter looked around the inside of the house, pushing against a wall between the dining and living room. "The bearing walls are solid and if you're not knocking any of them out, we won't need to look at supporting beams."

Jan was a tall man with friendly eyes, graying mustache and a quiet air that hid the savvy businessman he really was. Dean followed him around, his uneven footsteps echoing in the empty space. He had to force himself to concentrate on what Jan was saying and not to look too hard at Erin who stood beside her sister in the living room, her baby cradled in her arms.

He would have preferred not to see her so soon after their first meeting, but his truck was still at Alan Brady's mechanic shop and wouldn't be ready until tomorrow, so Jan had picked him up today. Then, as they drove, he'd told Dean he had to stop at a job right on the way. It wasn't until they pulled into the yard that he discovered they were looking at the same house he had spun his own dreams around. When he and Tiffany were dating they would stop at this house, peek in the windows and plan.

Instead he was listening to his boss talking with Erin and Lauren about what they needed to do to make the house ready for the winter, and struggling with mixed feelings at her presence.

Today she wore blue jeans. Her hair looked tidier. She looked less weary and far more attractive.

"I just want to know if I can move in right away," Erin was asking.

"If we're not doing any interior work you can, but it'll be noisy," Jan said, turning back to Dean. "So what do you think we'll need to do? I know you've talked about fixing up this place yourself."

Dean was pleased that Jan asked his opinion. "The shingles on the roof are good but the siding should be redone," he said, remembering the changes he and Tiffany had talked about. "I'd replace the living room window—the seal is busted and it's all fogged up. Same with the one in the spare room upstairs."

"Spare room?" Jan slanted him a questioning look. "Which one is that?"

When he and Tiffany were making plans they had given each of the rooms a name. Master bedroom, first kid's room, second kid's room and spare room. But he wasn't about to admit that much in front of Erin.

"The smallest one," he said, hoping he sounded more nonchalant than he felt. "To your right when you go up the stairs."

"Did you live here?" Jan asked.

"No. I just been here before," Dean said, catching Erin's confusion as well in his peripheral vision.

He wasn't about to satisfy it, either. Bad enough that she got to see him in all his crippled splendor, she definitely didn't need to hear about losing his dreams when Tiffany jilted him.

In favor of his brother.

"I think you're right about the work it needs." Jan turned to Erin. "The renos Dean suggested are the ones we have to do to get the house ready for winter. We'll pick a warm day to replace the windows. You won't be cold, but you might be fighting flies that day." Jan grinned at Erin but she was looking around, a peculiar smile on her face, as if the idea of living here held infinite appeal.

Dean knew how she felt. He was thirty-three and still living at home. That definitely hadn't been in his ten-year plan. When his brother started renting the ranch from Keith he had hoped to get this place subdivided. This house had been his goal.

"So I could live here? Right away?" Erin asked.

Jan shrugged, brushing off the dust he'd gathered while inspecting the attic. "You could move in this afternoon if you want. Like I said, you'll have to put up with a few inconveniences when we do the windows."

"That's good news."

Jan turned to Dean. "I'm putting you on this job. If you need help I might be able to spare a guy here and there but for the most part I think you can do this on your own."

"I thought I would be helping on that new barn you're building by Mercy." He didn't want to work on this house. He didn't want Erin to see him making his slow and methodical way up and down a ladder or scaffolding.

And the fact that it bothered him, well, that bothered him, too. He wasn't supposed to care what people thought of him. He was Dean Moore. A tough-as-leather cowboy and, even more, a saddle bronc rider.

One-time bronc rider, his thoughts taunted him.

"Isn't there someone else who can do this work?"

Erin's question caught Dean off guard, though he shouldn't have been surprised. Clearly she didn't think he could do the job, either.

"Dean's capable," Jan said. The faint narrowing of Jan's eyes encouraged Dean though it would take a lot more than a bit of restrained anger on the part of his boss to balance out Erin's lack of confidence.

"I wasn't thinking of that," Erin said, lifting one hand, clearly flustered. "It's just… I thought…" She waved off her comments. "I'm sure Dean is more than able to do the work."

"Good. I think so, too, otherwise I wouldn't have put him on the job."

"Look, if this is going to be a problem, let me work on that job in Mercy," Dean said.

Jan slowly shook his head, gnawing at one corner of his mouth, a sure sign he had something he didn't really want to say. "Sorry, I just hired on a new guy and he's married and got a couple of kids. He needs the hours. Besides, this is close by and I won't have to charge out traveling time for you." Jan gave him a careful smile, as if hoping that would placate him. "And this way you can start whenever you want. Work your own hours."

It all sounded so reasonable, but his boss's comments still bothered him. And he was trying hard not to read subtext in his reasoning. Working his own hours meant flexibility for the rehab he was supposed to be doing and for the days he wasn't well because the pain took over.

"Of course," he said. "I get it."

Then his eyes slid sideways to where Erin stood. She was looking at him and he didn't imagine the pity on her face.

Anger surged through him. Anger with his circumstances and that Erin had to be a witness to this moment.

He wasn't good enough. Simple as that. Just a washed-up bronc rider who couldn't even get on a horse.

Erin hadn't wanted anything to do with him all those years ago. He was convinced she certainly wouldn't want anything to do with him now.

"Be it ever so humble." Lauren turned off the vacuum cleaner and looked around the living room with a half smile. They had been busy in Erin's new house most of yesterday and today, cleaning and moving furniture in.

"It looks homey," Erin said, pushing a brown leather recliner into the corner beside the rust-colored couch Lauren had just finished cleaning. A wooden table replete with scuff marks and coffee rings sat in front if it. Mismatched end tables flanked the couch, each holding different lamps. A love seat in a pink plaid sat across from the couch. They had come out of a storage shed on Vic's mom's place. The rest came from the second-hand store in Saddlebank.

Two wooden chairs and three folding chairs were tucked under the oval wooden table in the dining room.

A metal watering can holding daisies and lilies sat on the table. That particular touch of whimsy was courtesy of Jodie, who had shown up only briefly, full of apologies. She and Finn had a last-minute meeting with Abby Bannister to scout out some wedding photo locations.

It didn't matter to Erin that Jodie couldn't be here. She would see her again. That much she could count on now that she was back at the ranch.

"It's perfect," Erin said, folding her arms as she glanced around the room. Her home.

Her own.

And the best part was the cast-iron wood stove taking up the far corner of the living room. She already could imagine being curled up on the couch, reading a book, Caitlin in her arms, the lights low as a fire crackled in the stove.

"And you're sure about this?" Lauren was asking as she plumped the pillows they had found at the bargain store in Mercy. "You're sure about living here on your own?"

"Believe it or not, I am," Erin said. "You have no idea what a treat it will be for me to have my own office."

"Vic said the internet people might be coming tomorrow so it will be a day or two before you're connected again."

"That's okay. I'll need a couple of days to get myself organized."

"Will you be able to keep busy? Out here?"

Erin chuckled at the skepticism in her sister's voice. "I actually just got a call this morning from a previous client in Colorado. He wants me to do a series of static and interactive graphics for his website and some promotional material he will be putting out. It won't be for a month or so but in the meantime I've got a few feelers out on some other work."

Lauren shot her a puzzled look. "Still can't believe all that coloring and sketching you used to do has translated into a job."

"The degree in graphics design probably helped, too."

"Of course." Lauren gave her a smile, then dropped the pillows on the couch. "So this is the last of it. I'm really glad we managed to find a crib for Caitlin, as well. At least she won't have to sleep in an apple box."

"Or a bottom drawer of a dresser like Granny always said Mom did," Erin said with a laugh.

Lauren released a gentle sigh, glancing down at the engagement ring on her finger then over at Erin. "I've been thinking about Mom lately, what with so many changes in our lives. Jodie getting married, me engaged. And now you with the first—" She stopped there as if not sure what to say.

"The first grandchild," Erin finished for her. "I've been thinking about Mom, too. And Dad. I know I've said it already, but I'm sorry I missed the funeral."

Lauren gave her sister a quick hug. "You had your reasons. Did you read Dad's letter to you?"

"I haven't had a chance. Caitlin was fussy most of last night."

"You should have woken me or Jodie up," Lauren chided, giving her shoulders a gentle shake. "Either of us would gladly have held her."

Erin felt a surprising hitch to her heart. The six weeks she'd spent at the house with her roommates after Caitlin was born had been fraught with tension. Though her friends were helpful and for the most part considerate, she still overheard muted grumbling about short nights and interrupted sleep. She wasn't accustomed to having help offered.

"Sorry. I didn't think—"

"That Jodie or I would want to hold our own niece?" Lauren shook her head. "Honey, you're with family. You're allowed to have expectations."

Which was probably part of her problem with Sam, Erin figured. She didn't dare have expectations. Each time she brought up their future he would gently tell her she shouldn't pressure him. They would talk later.

Then later came and here she was.

"Speaking of," Lauren said, tilting her head, "I think I hear something."

Erin heard a squawk from the room she'd claimed as her bedroom and was about to go get Caitlin when Lauren stopped her.

"I'll do this. You just sit down."

Then she hurried off.

But Erin wasn't about to sit down. Not with the bags of stuff they had purchased sitting on counters. She was eager to put it away. To get her kitchen cleaned up and organized.

Just then Dean came into the house carrying a box holding her laptop and router and Erin was distracted by a more important task.

"Here. Let me," she said.

"I got this." He shot her an annoyed glance.

"I don't mind helping," she said, reaching out to take the box from him.

As she did her hands brushed his and they both pulled back at the same time. Which made the box tilt precariously.

Dean shifted and took a sudden step left. In the process he fell against the recliner, which teetered as Dean struggled to regain his footing.

Erin made another grab for the box, but Dean caught his balance, grimacing as he did.

"Are you okay?" she asked, concerned at his quick intake of breath.

"I'm fine. Leave me alone."

"I'm sorry. It's just that's my laptop in that box. I need it for my work and I didn't want—"

"Didn't want it to fall?" Dean gave her a sardonic look and handed her the box. "Here. Take it if you think I'll drop it."

She wanted to protest, realizing she had overreacted. She wanted to explain that the laptop was new. That she still owed money on it. That she needed it for her job. A job she now needed more than ever since she had Caitlin depending on her and she had medical bills to pay.

But that would have taken too many words and too much exposing of her life to someone she preferred to keep in her past.

Then she looked up at him and was dismayed to see him staring at her as he still clung to the box. They stood there, old memories braiding through the moment. How intense he could be the times he asked her out. How her foolish heart had beat just a little faster each time he did. How her practical mind told her to say no.

Then he gave the box a tiny shove, returning it to

her. But as she took it, she felt as if he was also pushing her away.

She shook her head as she set it on the kitchen table, suddenly disoriented. It bothered her that a simple touch of Dean's hands created such a strong reaction in her.

Then Lauren came out of the room holding Caitlin and reality settled her faintly beating heart.

She had a daughter to take care of. She had responsibilities. Her reaction to Dean was just a hearkening back to old memories. With all that had happened to her in the past, she knew she was stronger than that.

She had to be.

The next morning, Dean parked his truck and shot a quick glance at his watch. 7:45. He couldn't see any movement inside the house. Maybe he had come too early?

Not that it mattered anymore. The growl of the diesel engine coming on the yard would have woken Erin up.

The house was tucked into a copse of trees and as he got out of the truck the wind picked up, rustling through the leaves of the aspen. They were already showing a tinge of orange and yellow amongst the green. Fall was on the way, but thankfully today was warmer.

He walked to the back of his truck and opened the tailgate. The ladder he needed to unload was long and unwieldy and he would have to do some creative lifting to get it to the house.

As he manhandled it out of the truck, he felt a strong twinge in his leg followed by one of regret. Jan had offered to come by and help him get everything ready, but after Erin expressed her doubts about his ability he wanted to prove he could do it himself.

The end of the ladder came off the truck and crashed to the ground. Next step was getting it to the house.

"Do you a need a hand?"

Dean's heart jumped and he spun around, almost unbalancing himself in the process.

Erin walked toward him, her baby tucked in some kind of carrier strapped to her front.

She wore a long sweater that flowed as she walked. Her hair was tied up in a loose bun-looking thing emphasizing her narrow features. And once again he wondered what had happened to her the past few years to put that edge in her voice, that hardness in her eyes, the hollows in her cheeks. Wondered if it had anything to do with the baby she carried.

"I'm okay," he said, lifting his chin as if challenging her to help him. "I do this for a living."

"I'll let you get to your work. But let me know if you need a hand."

He just nodded, glancing from her face to the baby bundled against her chest. "I doubt you'll be able to help much."

"Excuse me," she huffed, sounding insulted. "I know how to handle a hammer and nails. I've done home renovations before."

Her snippy tone was a shock. "So tell me, Miss Home Renovations, why is it okay for you to question my abilities but not okay for me to question yours?"

She looked taken aback. "What do you mean?"

So now she was going to play dumb. Tiffany had excelled at that. Throwing back his suspicions about her faithfulness by going on the defensive and lobbing out questions.

He wanted to make it easy for both of them and drop it. But if he was working here for the next week or so, he needed to face her doubts head-on. "Tuesday, when Jan and I were here, you asked if there was someone else who could do the work. Like you didn't think I was capable."

She blushed, which did two things. Confirmed his suspicions and made him even angrier.

"I may not be able to ride a bucking bronc, but I can fix your siding and replace your windows," he said, wishing he could keep the anger out of his voice. Seeing his ex-girlfriend's pitying look just before she dumped him had been a tough pill to swallow. Going through the slow and painful steps of rehab even more so. But to have this girl whom he once admired and dreamed of dating treat him like less of a man was like a slap. "It might take me longer than usual and if that's a worry, I'll tell Jan to adjust your bill," he snapped. "Call it a disability discount."

Erin took a step back, looking as if he had hit her and he regretted being so defensive.

"I'm sorry" was all she said. Then she turned and strode back to the house, her sweater flaring behind her in her hurry to get away from him.

He blew out a sigh as she closed the door, shaking his head at his stupid outburst. *Way to go, Moore,* he chided himself. Way to treat the customer.

She was probably in the house, calling Jan up and telling him she didn't want this crazy man on her yard anymore.

He sucked in a breath and picked up one end of the ladder, pulling it away from the truck. Then he started toward the house, his steps deliberate as he dragged the thing behind him.

He hoped she didn't look out the window at this point to see just how disabled he really was. He knew it shouldn't matter to him what she thought.

But it did. Far too much.

As he lifted the ladder against the house, moving slowly and carefully, he struggled with his own doubts.

He would finish up here today and then he would phone Jan and tell him he had to find someone else.

No way was he going to work for someone who didn't think he could do the job.

Especially not Erin McCauley.

Chapter Four

Erin drizzled the glaze on the bundt cake she had made, then stood back to admire her handiwork.

Too much? Not enough?

What kind of cake did you bake for the man in front of whom you'd made a complete fool of yourself? What kind of cake said "I'm sorry" the best?

This morning, after her run-in with Dean, she had packed up Caitlin and made a quick trip to town to talk to the people at Dis-Connected about getting her internet up and running. From there she'd headed to the grocery store to pick up a few things she was missing, as well as supplies to bake this cake.

But now that it was done she was having second thoughts. Should have just gone with cookies. Or muffins.

She tossed the bowl with the remainder of the icing into the sink. Seriously, how indecisive could she be? Had Sam done this to her? Stolen her identity and her confidence?

The answer to that would be a resounding yes if she

were honest with herself. But she didn't want to admit he'd had that much influence in her life. Lauren had always accused her of being a people pleaser. Her life with Sam was the epitome of that personality trait.

She could hear Dean clattering around outside, going up and down the ladder. She didn't know what he was doing out there, only that she wasn't going out to watch. After his outburst she doubted he would appreciate spectators.

Well, the cake was done and it was a quarter to twelve. He would be quitting for lunch soon. Perfect time to bring it out to him.

She glanced at the clock again just as her phone rang. It was Jodie.

"Hey, sweetie," Jodie trilled, "I'm about five minutes away. Can I stop in?"

"Of course. You're always welcome here."

"I kind of figured, but I don't want to intrude."

Jodie's words gave her a tick of sorrow. In her shame and retreat from her sisters had she come across as so unapproachable?

"Will Caitlin be awake?" Jodie asked.

"She's sleeping now, but I'm sure she'll be up soon." Thankfully Caitlin had settled in last night. It was as if she too sensed they had arrived at their final destination.

This morning Erin had gone for a walk around the property and down the road, just to get a sense of the place. To let herself enjoy the space, the quiet and the simple fact that this belonged to her and only her.

Then she'd made a fool of herself in front of Dean.

"Then if it's okay, I'm coming over," Jodie said.

"That would be great."

This way she could put off the agony of indecision over the cake she had just made and, instead, catch up with Jodie. She wanted to talk about the wedding and settle back into her sister's life. The easier sister's life.

Though she and Lauren were twins, she always felt like the younger sister around her. She knew Lauren loved her, but the dismayed expression on Lauren's face when she'd arrived with Caitlin showed Erin how disappointed her twin was.

Whereas Jodie's reaction had been one of joy.

Erin set the cake aside, quickly washed up the dishes she had used, tidying with a sense of anticipation. She shot a glance around the house. Everything was in order.

Outside she could hear thumps and the occasional screech of nails. She was very curious as to what he was doing, but her embarrassment over how he had misinterpreted their last interaction kept her inside the house, uselessly tidying. Then she heard a muffled squawk from the bedroom and she rushed to pick up her daughter. Just as she came out of the room she heard a vehicle pull up.

And as Jodie came up the cracked and uneven sidewalk, carrying a bouquet of flowers, Erin's throat thickened and tears welled up in her eyes.

She opened the door and Jodie hurried toward her, arms wide.

"Hey, sis," Erin managed as Jodie grabbed her in a careful hug.

Jodie held her close, Caitlin snuggled between them as tears spilled.

"Oh, honey," Jodie murmured, rocking her back and forth. "It's been a long road for you, I think."

Erin sniffed, annoyed at how easily she cried in front of her sister, yet thankful for someone whom she felt comfortable enough around to do exactly that.

Jodie pulled back and smoothed Erin's tears away with the balls of her thumbs, her expression sympathetic. "You're home, you know."

"I know. I think that's why I'm feeling so weepy."

"And you just had a baby."

"That, too," Erin said with a tremulous laugh.

"So, you take these and I'll take her," Jodie said, handing Erin the flowers while she carefully removed Caitlin from Erin's arms, cradling her as they walked into the house.

Jodie sat down on the couch and bent over her niece, inhaling slowly. "Oh, my goodness. She smells so sweet." She rubbed her nose over Caitlin's tiny one. "And you are such an amazing gift. You are, you know," she cooed to Caitlin. "You are a perfect little gift to our family. We're so blessed to have you."

Erin felt the bonds of guilt and shame that had held her soul loosen at Jodie's simple, accepting words.

"By the way, Lauren and Aunt Laura both say hi, hence the flowers," Jodie said indicating the bouquet Erin was cutting the ends off of. "They both wanted to come, but they both have to work whereas self-employed me can take time off and have you and Caitlin all to myself," she said, her head tilting slightly as she heard the sound of hammering. "So I noticed Dean's here already?"

"Yeah. He came this morning," Erin said, removing

the fake flowers Jodie had brought yesterday from the metal watering can and filling it with water. "And now I've got this apology cake cooling on the counter that I don't know what to do with."

"Apology cake? Never heard of that recipe," Jodie said, frowning her puzzlement.

"Well, it's about a cup of my-big-mouth, mixed in with three tablespoons of wounded pride and a soup-çon of McCauley."

"Oooooh, that cake," Jodie said with a knowing nod of her head. "I should have baked a few of those in my life. That and Humble Pie." Then she shot her a questioning glance. "So I'm guessing the cake is for Dean?"

"Oh, yeah."

"What did you say to him?"

Erin set the flowers in the pot and put it back on the table, avoiding her sister's gaze. "I kind of made it sound like he wasn't capable of fixing my house. At least I think he took it that way."

"Oh, dear."

"It wasn't that I thought he couldn't do it," she said, fiddling with the flowers, arranging them just so. "It's just, well, I'm not comfortable being around him and my mouth got away on me."

"Honey, that's my line, not yours."

"I know. I was feeling weird."

Weird and ashamed. She had always been the good girl. The one who turned down Dean's many requests for dates because he was too rough and rowdy for her. Now she was the one who wasn't "suitable." She was the one who had messed up her life.

"Anyhow, I felt bad so I thought I would bake him a cake," Erin continued.

"I should go get him so we can eat it. He's probably not had lunch yet." She shot her sister a questioning glance as she stood. "If that's okay with you?"

"I guess." Dean would be working here so she figured she might as well try to smooth things over between them as soon as possible.

Jodie walked to the door still carrying her baby.

"I'll take Caitlin, though," Erin said, holding out her arms for her daughter.

"I'll be careful."

Erin held Jodie's puzzled gaze for a beat, surprised at the flutter of panic that seeing Jodie walk away with her daughter created in her. "I know. It's just... I haven't had anyone else taking care of her since she was born. Besides, she needs her diaper changed."

Jodie seemed to understand and handed Caitlin over to Erin, but as she did she held Erin's eyes. "Are you okay?"

"I'm fine," she said, disappointed at how breathless she sounded, glancing down at Caitlin. "I'm just fine."

"Okay, I'll be inside shortly."

Then Jodie disappeared around the side of the house.

Erin took a steadying breath, her heart finally slowing down. What was wrong with her? Why the panic attack? This was her sister, not some random stranger.

Hormones. That's what she was blaming it on, she reasoned, cuddling Caitlin closer as she walked toward her bedroom.

A few moments later she had Caitlin's diaper changed and her baby lay swaddled up in a bouncy chair Lauren had rustled up from some of the cousins. Caitlin stared, cross-eyed, at the little stuffed animals hanging from the bar straddling the chair, her mouth a perfect little O.

As Erin held her daughter's tiny fingers, wrapped tightly around her own, her heart pinched.

Would it ever get old? she thought, marveling at the delicacy of her fingernails, the delicate swath of her thick eyelashes.

"You didn't get those from me," she murmured, brushing her finger over her baby's cheek. Unbidden thoughts of Caitlin's father entered her mind and behind that came the ever-present shame and guilt. "I didn't know," she whispered to her baby. "I just didn't know."

"I'm too busy to stop," Dean grumbled, yanking on a piece of the siding and tossing it to the side to join the pile already there.

"You have to eat lunch some time," Jodie said, looking up at him perched up on the ladder, her hands planted on her hips.

Dean ignored both her and the grumbling of his stomach at the thought of lunch. He was hungry, but he wasn't about to get down the ladder in front of Jodie. He inserted his claw hammer under the next nail.

"I packed a lunch" was all he said. "I'll eat it when it works."

"Then come and eat it with us," she said, slipping a wayward strand of hair behind her ear. "Erin made a cake. She called it an apology cake. Not sure what that meant, but I think she feels bad about something she did or said to you."

Dean couldn't help the flush warming his neck. Erin's doubts about his ability had fueled most of the work he'd done this morning. Had made him push himself harder than he probably should have.

But the fact that she felt sorry tweaked his ego just enough. That and the fact that his leg was on fire and he really could use a break.

"Give me about five minutes and I'll come inside."

"You got 'er," Jodie said with a quick salute. He waited until she was around the corner of the house before he worked his awkward way to the ground, fighting his frustration at each halting step.

His physiotherapist had warned him that it would take time and to be careful. Not that he'd spent that much time with Mike the past couple of months. Mike had called Dean a few times, but Dean had ignored the calls. Every time he went it was like he was reminded again of how useless he was and he hated asking Jan for time off work to make the appointments.

Dean stopped at the bottom of the ladder. He massaged his aching leg, stretching it out, still debating the wisdom of going into the house. Then he heard Jodie calling him and he knew he couldn't put it off any longer.

With a sigh he brushed the sawdust and dirt off his shirt and pants and walked through the overgrown grass to his truck. He grabbed the thermos of coffee he'd made this morning and grimaced at the sight of the plastic grocery bag holding his lunch. A couple of peanut butter sandwiches and some homemade cookies. He'd had a few good-natured battles over this with his mother when he started working for Jan. She'd wanted to make his lunch, accusing him of not packing nutritious food.

Well, she was right. But there was no way, on top of still living at home, that he was letting him mom pack his lunch, too. That was too many shades of pathetic.

He took his time going down the uneven sidewalk on his way to the house from the truck. His legs were still shaky from the exertion of going up and down the ladder and the last thing he needed was a stumble. He'd have to call Jan tonight and ask if he could get some scaffolding instead. The siding would be more work than he thought.

He paused just inside the door of Erin's house, his eyes adjusting from the bright light outside.

Erin stood with her back to him, stirring something on the stove. Soup, he guessed from the mouth-watering smell.

"There you are. I thought you were ducking out on us," Jodie called out, carrying some bowls to the table.

"No. Just getting my lunch," he said as he toed his boots off.

Jodie gave a pointed look at the plastic bag he carried. "That's what you're eating?"

"Proudly homemade," he said, waving it aloft, grinning at her. He'd spent enough time with Jodie over the past few months that he felt at ease with her.

Then Erin turned and her eyes grazed over him as she brought the pot to the table.

He wished it didn't bother him. Wished he could be as casual around her as he was around Jodie.

He glanced around as he set his bag on the table. He couldn't see Caitlin and figured she was sleeping.

"So, this is nice," Jodie said, grinning from him to

Erin like they were all one happy family. "Like old times."

Dean wasn't precisely sure which old times Jodie referred to, but from her overly bright smile he sensed she was trying hard to make everyone comfortable.

"Where do you want me to sit?" Dean asked.

"By that sad little lunch you packed and may as well save for your dog, Lucky," Jodie returned, grabbing a bowl and filling it up. "We have real food. I brought bread from the bakery and soup from the Grill and Chill. George was right ticked when I asked him if it was fresh. Got all grumpy Gus on me. Honestly, not sure what Brooke sees in him."

"Are they dating now?" Erin asked, finally speaking up, but looking at Jodie as she asked about the couple who had been off and on as long as Dean knew them.

"That's the rumor. There have been a few George and Brooke sightings ever since the concert this spring. I have stopped holding my breath when it comes to that relationship. But then, who knows how the heart works. I never thought I would end up with Finn or Lauren with Vic."

While she chattered away Erin brought a plate of sandwiches to the table. They looked ten times better than the flattened and misshapen ones resting in the bag beside the bowl of soup Jodie had given him.

"I think we can start," Jodie said as she sat down directly across the table from Dean leaving Erin to sit either on his left or his right.

"Shall we pray?" Jodie asked brightly, holding her hand out to Erin who took it and, in what Dean could only assume was an automatic gesture, held her other hand out to him.

As soon as she realized what she had done, she blushed and snatched her hand back.

"What, you don't want to hold Dean's hand?" Jodie teased, as if trying to eradicate the sudden awkwardness. "He doesn't bite."

"Are you going to pray?" Erin asked, her voice holding a slight edge completely at odds with the girl Dean once knew.

"Sure. Sorry." Jodie flashed her and Dean a smile, then bowed her head. "Thank You, Lord, for this food. For the blessing of family. Be with Erin and Caitlin as they make their new home here. Thank you that they are back here with us. Bless our work this afternoon. Amen."

Dean murmured an automatic amen which netted him a puzzled glance from Erin.

He knew how it looked to her. He'd always been the wild and crazy one laughing at her for going to church, mocking her faith even while part of him admired her quiet fortitude.

Well, people changed, as Kelly had so eloquently stated the other day on Main Street. And he found himself wanting to apologize for all the times he'd teased her about being a Bible thumper.

But not here and not now.

"So, how are things looking on the house?" Jodie asked, as if determined to make conversation.

"It's going to need more work than we initially thought." Dean blew on his soup and gave Erin an apologetic look. "So it's going to cost more than you might have figured on."

"That's okay," she said. "This is going to be our home. I want it to be sound."

"The ranch will cover the costs anyhow," Jodie assured him. "So don't worry about that."

"In that case…" He flashed Jodie a grin, trying not to let the tension around the table get to him.

"Let's not get carried away," she warned.

"So, no addition with a brick fireplace and stained-glass windows?"

"This is a house, not a church."

"According to my mom, God is as much present in a family gathering as a church one."

Dean laughed and once again he caught a puzzled look from Erin.

Okay, so maybe he was laying it on a bit thick, chatting with Jodie like he wasn't totally aware of Erin sitting beside him shooting him covert glances with those slate-blue eyes of hers. Acting like he and Jodie were best buddies when they'd just gotten to know each other better the past couple of months.

"How did Caitlin sleep last night?" Jodie asked Erin, drawing her sister into the conversation.

"Good. I think she was still tired from the drive on Monday." Erin stirred her soup and gave Jodie a tight smile. "It was a long trip."

Dean heard a note of sorrow in her voice, wondering precisely what caused it.

"You drove all the way up from San Francisco?" he asked.

She nodded, shooting him a quick glance.

"So what were you doing there?" As if he didn't know exactly what had kept her occupied all these years. Because somehow in spite of Tiffany, in spite of all the girls between then and now, she always hung, like a painting, in the back of his mind. Elusive and mysterious.

"Working as a graphic designer."

He wanted to ask her more and fill in the gaps between the last time he saw her and now. Wanted to know what had put those shadows under the eyes of the sweet, innocent girl who had turned him down one last time with a sad smile. A girl who'd told him he had to turn his life around.

Well, he had. Just too late for her, he guessed.

Chapter Five

"Thanks for the cake. It was delicious," Dean said, making a move to push his chair away from the table. "But I should get to work."

Erin wondered if she should tell him the story behind the cake. But sitting beside him at the table made her far too aware of him and apologizing would only exacerbate that. When Jodie had offered to pray and he had neither mocked nor teased her, she felt as if the earth had shifted beneath her.

He used to laugh at her faith. Call her Thumper, as in Bible thumper. But now, it seemed, the tables had truly turned.

"Do you need a hand?" she asked as she got up.

His angry frown told her that the apology cake hadn't taught her enough of a lesson.

"Like I said, I know how to handle a hammer," she retorted, determined to fight the self-conscious feelings he created in her. "I don't want to just sit around while you're working."

"It's okay," he said, seemingly placated by her response. "I've just got the one ladder. I'm going to call Jan to come with a scaffold tomorrow."

"You shouldn't be working so soon after having a baby, anyway," Jodie warned Erin. "Especially after a Caesarean."

"It's been almost two months," Erin said. "I won't be able to do any of my other work until I get the internet connection up and running. I need to do something."

The two months of bed rest and the exhaustion that claimed her after Caitlin's birth had been difficult enough to endure. She wanted to stay busy. To keep thoughts of the future at bay and the fear that could clutch her at times.

But you're home now.

"I'll let you know if I need a hand," Dean said, his tone brusque as he grabbed the bag holding his lunch.

Erin guessed he wouldn't, but didn't bother challenging him. She'd find something else to keep herself busy. Something she could do inside the house.

"Thanks again for lunch. It was good." He held up his bag. "Good thing I made this myself. My mom might be insulted if I fed this to my dog."

"I just hope Lucky isn't insulted," Jodie retorted. "Of course he's still a pup and thinks everything you do and everything you give him is amazing."

Erin was surprised at her flush of jealousy at the easy give-and-take between Jodie and Dean. At one time Jodie wasn't so accepting of him. She and Lauren had consistently warned her against him, as if she needed reminding of his unsuitability.

Now Jodie and Dean chatted away like brother and

sister and for some reason it bothered her. She felt like she was on the outside looking in.

But just before he left his eyes caught hers and once again she felt it. That dangerous thrum Dean could always create in her.

Trouble was, while she'd resisted it then because he was unsuitable, she resisted it now for an entirely different reason.

The door closed behind him and Erin felt like she could breathe again.

"Cake was really good," Jodie said as she helped her clean up. "But you forgot to tell Dean why you made it."

"It seemed redundant" was all she said.

"It could have helped things along." Jodie put the bowls in the sink and started filling it with water. "He'll be working here for a few weeks. It would help if he knew you were okay with him being here."

Unfortunately she wasn't.

"He's had a tough go." Jodie turned to Erin, still holding the soap bottle. "And while I know we were kind of down on him when he was younger, he's not the same guy he used to be. The accident really changed him. So did him getting dropped by Tiffany."

Erin needed to deflect and dodge right about now. The last thing she needed was to hear Dean's praises sung. The irony of their situation wasn't lost on her. Instead she grasped at what Jodie had said.

"Dean was dating Tiffany Elders?" Tiffany was the kind of girl Erin used to be marginally jealous of. Pretty, confident and comfortable chatting up any guy she met.

"For a while. But she broke up with Dean just before

his accident, hoping to get together with Vic again. She broke his heart."

"Vic's?"

"No. Dean's."

Erin wasn't sure why the thought of Dean nursing a broken heart over someone like Tiffany bothered her. "Sounds like a soap opera," she said picking up a dish towel to dry the dishes Jodie was washing up. "First one brother, then the other."

"I guess. But Dean's better off without her and Vic feels the same way. She was just trouble bouncing from one guy to the other. Last I heard she was in Colorado dating some married guy." Jodie shook her head as condemnation and guilt curled in Erin's stomach.

"I think I hear Caitlin," she murmured dropping her dish towel and hurrying to the bedroom. She closed the door behind her and leaned against it. As she did a far-too-familiar prayer rose up.

Forgive me, Lord.

She fought down the habitual pain and humiliation, wondering if she could ever feel like her life was on the right track.

But she was home now and had a chance at a new start.

She walked over to her daughter's crib, her heart melting at the sight of Caitlin's perfect features, her chubby little fingers curled up, her hand resting beside her head. A wave of love washed over her, so intense and overpowering it nearly toppled her. But, always behind that, came the slithering feeling that she didn't deserve this baby or her love.

"I'm sorry," she whispered, stroking Caitlin's head,

fighting down unwelcome tears. "I do love you and I will take care of you to the best of my ability."

She bent over and brushed a kiss over her tender skin, cupped her head in her hand. Caitlin sighed, shook her head, then drifted back into sleep.

As Erin straightened she saw Dean walking slowly back to the house from his truck. Instead of going around the other side, he walked directly toward her window. He looked up and their eyes held. Then he gave her a curt nod and moved on.

"Everything okay?" she heard Jodie call out.

Erin gave her daughter one more kiss, then returned to the kitchen and her sister's company.

"We're fine," she said.

They finished doing the dishes and Jodie stayed a while longer before she left. That afternoon the internet company finally came and installed her wireless network and Erin was able to connect with her clients.

Her inbox tinged for about fifteen minutes as she scrolled through her email, deleting offers from graphics sites she subscribed to and various other businesses, and skimmed through a couple of letters from her former roommates checking to see how she was doing. She shifted them into another mailbox to reply to later.

Then her heart jumped as she saw an all-too-familiar name crop up in her inbox. Sam Sibley.

She immediately sent it to trash, emptied it and then blocked him. She didn't want to read anything he had to say. They were done.

The rest of the day was spent working on her latest project, but the entire time Sam's deleted email hovered in the dark recesses of her mind.

Consequently she ended up working late into the night knowing she wouldn't be able to sleep anyway.

Someone was trying to get in the house.

Someone was trying to get Caitlin, and Erin couldn't get to her. She was outside and Caitlin was in the house. Crying.

Sam was in the bedroom. Sam was here to take her baby.

Erin panicked, yanking at the door to the bedroom, but it was stuck. Caitlin's cries grew louder. More desperate as Erin struggled to get to her daughter. It was as if her legs were tied together and she was swimming against an invisible current that pulled her back.

Her heart thundered in her chest as she fought against the implacable force. She had to get Caitlin. Sam was taking her away.

"Erin. Erin." Someone was calling her name through her daughter's cries.

She couldn't see who it was.

"Erin. Wake up."

The voice pierced the gloom surrounding her and she surged upward and into bright, blinding light.

She glanced around the unfamiliar room. Where was her baby? Where was she?

Living room. On the couch. She scrambled to her feet, blinking away the sleep that fogged her vision and just about fell over as her legs gave way.

But then an arm caught her and held her up.

"Hey. Erin. Are you okay?"

The voice was familiar and Erin struggled to get her mind to catch up, to wake up.

Slowly she became conscious of where she was. What was happening?

Dean stood beside her, holding her up. His eyes were focused on her and he was frowning. She held his gaze, trying to figure out what was going on. Then her eyes shifted and her heart jumped.

Caitlin was cradled in his other arm and she wasn't crying anymore.

Erin sucked in a breath, fighting to catch her balance, too aware of the fact that she leaned against Dean, his arm around her warm and strong.

She tried to pull away, but he wouldn't let her.

"I'll take her," she said.

"Just sit down and I'll give her to you. You're still half asleep." Erin struggled to fight him off, but she was still disoriented and couldn't get her bearings.

"My baby," she called out, reaching out for Caitlin.

"I'll give her to you just as soon as you're sitting down."

She obeyed and true to his word as soon as she was back down on the couch, he nestled Caitlin in her arms. Erin pulled her close, her panicked heart finally slowing down. But as soon as she relaxed she became aware that Dean still had his hand on her shoulder. For a moment she felt a sense of protection. Of being watched over.

But slowly reality intruded and she pulled herself back.

"I'm sorry," Dean said, straightening. "I heard her crying and she wouldn't stop and I thought maybe something happened to you. So I came in and she was alone in the crib."

Erin's heart slowed, but behind the receding fear

came the crash of guilt as she held her daughter close. How could she have been so irresponsible? What if it wasn't Dean who had come in?

She took a breath, willed her racing heart to slow as she stared down at Caitlin, as if to make sure she was really lying quietly, now in her arms.

"I'm sorry. I was just worried about you," Dean continued. "Are you okay?"

She nodded, then finally dared to look up at him. "Yeah. I'm fine. I guess I fell asleep here."

His eyes on her looked kind. Caring. And again she felt an unwelcome flutter of attraction.

"That happens. I'm sure you're still tired from the trip up here. And, well, having a baby, I guess."

He sounded so considerate. His voice didn't hold the usual mocking tone she was so used to hearing. Her heart twisted as she thought of how their lives had diverged. At how his old appeal now morphed to attraction. At how he seemed to have become a different person.

"Sorry you had to get her," Erin mumbled, looking back down at Caitlin.

"It's okay. I didn't think she would settle for me."

"She's a good baby."

"Probably takes after her mom." His words were quiet, but they held a faint question in them. As if wondering if Caitlin's father had anything to do with her personality.

But Erin wasn't going down that road. She dragged one hand through the tangle of her hair, suddenly aware of how ragged she must look. Wearing the sloppy, comfy clothes she had put on last night after Dean left for the day. Her hair listing to starboard from the rough bun she had twisted her hair into.

An unwelcome memory of Kelly slipped into her mind. Trim. Slim and cute.

"So, are you going to be okay?" Dean asked.

"I'll be fine."

Suddenly she wanted him gone. She felt an unreasoning need to rush into the bathroom. Shower, clean up and put on decent clothes. Some makeup. Let him see her not as a disheveled mommy but an attractive woman. Why had she fallen asleep here?

She remembered working on her laptop. Putting together an ad proposal for a company. She glanced beside her, then the other side.

"What's the matter?" Dean asked.

"My laptop. I can't find it."

"Is this it?" Dean bent over and picked up her computer from the floor. But as he straightened he lost his balance. He shifted, tried to correct himself, but then fell sideways.

Against the table.

He cried out in pain and Erin jumped to her feet, still holding Caitlin. She caught him by the arm, much as he had done for her just a few moments ago, trying to pull him upright.

He was heavy, his arm like a band of steel under her hand. She didn't know if she would be able to get him balanced.

As soon as he regained his footing, he shook her arm off, his eyes narrowed, his jaw set in a hard line.

"I'm fine," he growled. "I didn't need your help."

She snatched her hand back, her head coming up, angry herself.

"Just doing for you what you did for me," she snapped, then she hitched her baggy pants up, drew Caitlin close and strode past him to the bathroom.

Dean knew he'd been a jerk just now. Erin was simply trying to help him just as he'd helped her. But it bugged him to look so helpless in front of her.

Dean watched her march away from him, with Caitlin in her arms. Frustration gripped him as he hobbled out of the room, thankful Erin wouldn't be able to see his painful and humiliating retreat. He wished he could have stridden from the room as confidently as she had. Made a better exit than limping along like some old man, grabbing onto chairs as he rode out the burning agony in his leg.

He slowly came outside, then leaned against the house, giving himself some time to recover.

Cowboy up.

The cliché of rodeo riders everywhere echoed in his brain.

Well, he didn't know if he had to cowboy up. He wasn't a real cowboy anymore.

He heard the sound of a vehicle coming down the driveway so he stepped away from the house. He waited as Jan's truck, emblazoned with the sign "JP Construction," pulled up and stopped.

It was Jan and Leonard with the scaffolding. Dean made his way over, masking the throbbing in his leg. Wouldn't do for his boss to see how badly he was managing.

"Hey, thought we'd drop this off before we head over to Mercy," Jan said as he swung out of the cab. "Which side of the house do you want this on?"

"North side," Dean said. "It seems to be the worst so I was starting there."

"Sure thing." Jan got out, Leonard joining him. The young man wore his usual canvas bib overalls, his long hair anchored with a ball cap. Leonard was a good kid. Hard worker.

Dean shouldn't have been surprised that Jan was taking him to work on the job at Mercy and leaving him here.

Leonard went to unload and Dean, knowing he couldn't do much to help them, hobbled back to where he was working to take the ladder down, gritting his teeth the entire time.

He cleaned up around the site while Jan and Leonard made quick work of setting up the scaffolding. He gathered up the debris he had created, bringing it to the pile he had started away from the house. Once he was done he could get Jan or one of his crew to help him haul it all away.

By the time he got back, the throbbing in his leg had thankfully settled to a dull ache. He looked up at the siding that had to be removed and the work that lay ahead, planning his week.

Is this really what you see yourself doing the rest of your life?

The thought created a flicker of panic. He had fallen into the carpentry work to fill time while his brother Vic was making plans with Keith McCauley. Plans put on hold when Lauren and Jodie had talked about selling the ranch.

But now that was settled and Vic was talking about expanding, making a place for Dean.

While part of him was excited at the thought, he couldn't ignore the fact that he hadn't been on a horse since the accident.

As he had said to his brother, what kind of rancher can't ride a horse?

But was carpentry really in his future?

"You got a lot done already," Jan said as he clambered down from the top of the scaffolding. "From the looks of it you'll be done this side by tomorrow."

His boss's simple compliment helped to assuage the feelings of uselessness swamping him.

"I think so."

"The windows will be coming in on Tuesday so we'll bring them Wednesday and help you install them." Jan rested his hands on his hips, looking the house over. "You figure the rest of the windows are okay?"

"They're a standard size so even if they did need replacing down the road we won't have to change the openings."

"This is a cool spot for a house," Leonard was saying as he joined Jan and Dean. "I think I could live here."

Dean had thought the same at one time. A memory of him and Tiffany walking around this house making dreams slipped through his thoughts, but as quickly as it came he dismissed it. She was history and while he had managed to forget her, her legacy still stuck with him. The look of pity on her face when she saw him lying in the hospital bed was one he'd never forget.

"It's a great house," he said. "Worth fixing up."

The door of the house opened and Dean felt an uptick of his heart as Erin came around the side. Her hair was pulled up into a loose ponytail and she had changed into other baggy pants topped with a large sweater. Even in casual clothes and no makeup, she still looked amazing.

"Good morning, Jan," she said, avoiding Dean's gaze.

"Things are coming along well on your house," Jan said, giving her a gentle smile. "Dean's doing a great job."

"I'm sure he is," Erin said, still not looking at him.

"I was just telling him we'll be putting the windows in on Wednesday. The forecast is for decent weather, but you might want to go to your sister's place with your baby that day. The house will get kind of chilly while we're working."

"Good to know. Thanks." She gave him a quick bob of her head. Then she turned to Leonard, holding her hand out. "Hi. I'm Erin."

"I'm Leonard. Dryden. Leonard Dryden that is."

Dean would have been blind not to notice the blush creeping up Leonard's neck, or the way he stared at Erin. Not that he blamed him, but he was surprised at how jealous he felt.

"Sorry. I should have introduced you," Jan said. "Leonard's family moved here a couple of years ago. He's been working for me since. Erin just moved here. She's Lauren McCauley's sister."

"I kind of figured," Leonard said, his hands resting on his hips, his head tilted to one side as if to examine her more closely. "You look exactly like her."

"She should," Dean put in. "They're twins." He wanted to blame the faintly acerbic tone in his voice on the fact that Leonard was the one chosen to work on the job in Mercy.

Instead of the fact that he was more annoyed at the way Leonard was looking at Erin.

"Really? You're that old?" Leonard's shock and the way he pulled his head back expressed his total disbelief.

"Thanks, I think," Erin said with a light smile.

"I mean, you look really pretty and all, but Lauren seems way older than you."

"Again, thanks." Erin's smile had deepened, softening her features, lighting up her eyes.

And the jealousy Dean felt in Leonard's presence only grew.

He had never been on the receiving end of a full-blown smile from Erin McCauley. The only smiles he got from her were either faintly mocking or faint, period.

"So, you single?" Leonard asked.

"Down, boy," Jan shot his helper a frown. "Let's talk about the windows. Unless you guys want to keep doing this?"

"No. Please let's talk about the windows." Erin turned back to Jan, remnants of her smile remaining.

"Like I said, I would recommend being gone that day," Jan said. "It's not supposed to be real warm and I don't think your baby would appreciate getting chilled."

"You got a baby? No way." Leonard's skeptical tone erased the last of Erin's humor. She nodded, slipping him a quick, sidelong glance.

"Yes. I have a little girl."

"Whoa. That's heavy duty."

He didn't actually take a step back, but Dean easily saw the retreat both in his expression and in his body language.

And it made him want to reprimand the kid. Especially when he saw the sorrow that clouded Erin's smile. He doubted she felt more than passing amusement initially, with Leonard and his puppy-dog admiration, but his sudden withdrawal must have been hard to take.

"She's really cute," Dean put in, feeling a need to defend her. "I even got to hold her this morning."

Finally Erin glanced his way, her expression holding a hint of thanks.

"How did you swing that?" Jan asked glancing from Erin to Dean, curiosity in his voice and eyes.

Dean wasn't sure how to answer that. Not without embarrassing Erin again.

"She even quieted down when I held her" was all he said, hoping the vague answer would keep more questions from Jan at bay.

Erin ducked her head and Dean guessed she was still embarrassed over what had happened this morning.

He felt bad that he had barged into the house, but hearing her baby crying for about ten minutes after he had arrived and not knowing how long she'd been before that, he'd figured he better check. Make sure nothing had happened to Erin. He hadn't seen her when he stepped into the house and had gone straight to Caitlin's room to find her squalling, her face red, her little hands bunched into fists, waving around.

He'd picked her up, bounced her, and had gone looking for Erin when she wasn't in the bedroom.

He'd found her lying on the couch and had panicked, thinking something had happened. He'd given her a shake while the baby slowly settled in his arms.

Thankfully she'd just been asleep. But the look of sheer terror on her face when she saw him holding Caitlin wasn't one he'd soon forget.

"Well, aren't you the fortunate one," Jan said, a meaning tone in his voice, his smirk telling Dean that he read the situation differently.

"I was just helping out," he protested, then caught himself from saying more.

"Of course you were," Jan said. "Which was why I knew you were the best man for this job."

Dean knew there were other factors at play, but he wasn't going there now.

"Anyhow, we should push on," Jan said, pulling his phone out of his pocket as it dinged and glancing at the screen. "And looks like I'm needed at the other site." He frowned, biting his lip, and Dean wondered what was going on.

Jan shoved the phone in his pocket and glanced from Erin to Dean. "So you'll be ready for the windows on Wednesday?" Jan asked.

"That should work." To get there would mean working tomorrow, a Saturday, but that didn't matter. Not like he had lots of other things going on in his life.

Jan waved goodbye and then they were walking back to the truck.

As soon as they drove away, Dean turned to get back to work. But was stopped by Erin's light touch on his arm.

"I never did say thanks," she said, her voice quiet, her eyes not meeting his. "For picking Caitlin up and settling her down this morning."

Dean wasn't sure what to say. If he were entirely honest with himself, that moment when Caitlin stopped crying, when her cries faded and she lay, for those few seconds pliant in his arms, he had felt a surprising tenderness.

And a flash of yearning.

"It was okay. I didn't mind," he said.

"I felt bad that I seemed abrupt with you."

He released a humorless laugh. "If anyone was abrupt it was me with you. I shouldn't have been such a jerk when I stumbled. You were just trying to help."

"I'm sorry—"

"No. Don't apologize for that. I'm the one that's sorry."

Their words hung between them. Two people trying to find their way through this awkward moment.

"Anyhow, thanks for getting Caitlin. That was really sweet of you." Erin peeked up at him through some loose strands of hair that had fallen away from her ponytail.

He had an unreasoning desire to reach out and tuck those strands behind her ear.

"You're welcome," he said, giving her a careful smile.

Their eyes held and in spite of everything Dean's heart rate jacked up. So did his breathing. Her lips parted like she was about to say something and the urge to curl her hair behind her ear was replaced by the urge to kiss her.

He shook the feeling off and turned away from her before he gave in to the impulse.

In another time and in another place he might have tried.

But he wasn't that guy anymore.

And she was never that girl.

Chapter Six

And so, Erin, I need to say that I'm sorry. I wasn't the father I should have been. I wish I could do it over, but I can't. In my own way I loved you. Please, remember that at least.

Erin finished the letter from her father and laid it down, sorrow threading through her as she looked around the ranch house that had been her childhood home.

When her sisters called yesterday morning, asking if she wanted to come to the ranch on Saturday for some sister bonding time, she had readily agreed. Dean was coming to work on the house again and for some reason, she wasn't sure she wanted to see him.

So she had come here yesterday. The three of them had taken Caitlin for a long walk around the ranch, had laughed, cried and shared stories, catching up on each other's lives. When Erin made a move to go home Jodie and Lauren had demurred, stating that Lauren had found a secondhand crib and put it in one of the rooms downstairs and fixed up her old room for her to sleep in.

She had agreed, but last night as she lay in her old bed in her old room, she had felt the same sorrow and regret her father now talked about in his letter. Her father's words resonated through her, bringing up memories and emotions.

While her sisters had resented their time here, she'd loved it. And guessed her father sensed that, too. They would talk about the ranch together, the few times they connected face-to-face. Sometimes she rode with him to move the cows.

Though he was a taciturn man, there was the occasional time he had told her she was a good girl.

For her father, that was high praise.

She looked down at the letter again, re-reading her father's apologies and struggled once again with a sense of shame. She certainly wasn't the innocent girl he was writing to and she wondered what he would think of her now.

And behind that, why she hadn't come more often to visit? She had all kinds of excuses for staying away and now, after reading her father's much-belated expressions of regret, they seemed facile. Lame.

She felt she should pray and ask God for forgiveness.

But she shook the feeling off. The same contrition that kept her from praying had kept her from attending church with her sisters this morning.

Then, before she could delve too deeply into her dark thoughts, the door of the ranch house burst open and Jodie and Lauren's laughter filled the eerie silence.

She got up from the couch, still holding Caitlin, and walked toward the porch just as her sisters came around the corner.

"Hey, you," Jodie said. "How was your morning?" She gave her sister a quick hug, then stroked Caitlin's cheek with one finger. "And how's our baby girl?"

"We're both fine," Erin said. "How was church?"

"Pastor Dykstra had a good sermon and the music was great. Too bad you couldn't come."

Wouldn't come was more like it, but Erin wasn't about to admit that.

There was no way she, who once was such a strong proponent of morals and standards, could show up with a baby in her arms and no man at her side. Besides, she and God hadn't spent much time together the past while. It would seem hypocritical.

"Can you give me my niece?" Jodie asked, holding her hands out to her sister. "I need my Caitlin fix." Erin grinned as she carefully transferred Caitlin, still bundled up in a pink muslin blanket, to her sister. Caitlin's head twisted back and forth, her mouth opened and then she sank back into the sleep that had claimed her ever since Erin had fed her this morning. Jodie nuzzled her as she walked over to the couch.

"Did Aunt Laura play piano during the church service?" she asked Lauren as the latter plugged the kettle in, then came over and gave Erin a quick hug.

"No. They've got a new singing group at church. Jodie plays with them once in a while." Lauren's hand rested on Erin's shoulder as she held her gaze. "Did you have a chance to read your letter from Dad? What did you think?"

Erin wasn't sure how to articulate her emotions. "It was good to hear he regretted some of the things he did."

"Dad mellowed a lot before he died." Jodie looked up from nuzzling Caitlin's cheeks. "He even apologized to me. For everything."

"I'm glad for you," Erin said.

Jodie and her father had had a complicated relationship. Jodie bore the brunt of his occasional bad moods the summers they'd spent with him after their mother died. Lauren and their father had a more practical, though distant, relationship. For some reason he and Erin got along. Mostly, she suspected, because she always did as she was told.

Caitlin started fussing and Erin took her from Jodie. "I think she needs to be changed. She fell asleep after I fed her last."

She snagged her diaper bag and walked through the kitchen, past her father's office to the bathroom at the end of the hallway.

Erin took the changing pad from her diaper bag, laid it down on the counter and laid Caitlin on it, smiling as her daughter's little hands batted the air. Her tiny mouth was pursed and her eyes were fixed on the light above the sink. Erin made quick work of removing the wet diaper.

While she worked she could hear the low murmur of her sisters talking and then heard her name mentioned.

"—just wish she could spend more time on herself," she heard Lauren say. "It's like she let herself go."

Erin stopped dead in her tracks at her sister's words, glancing down at the yoga pants and loose T-shirt she wore.

"Cut her some slack," Jodie protested. "She's a mom and probably dressing for comfort more than looks."

But while she guessed Jodie was sticking up for her, the comment made Erin feel worse.

She pulled back, returning to the bathroom to give her sisters a chance to finish their conversation.

But that was a mistake because when she stepped back in she caught her reflection in the mirror. No makeup, hair slightly askew from where Caitlin had grabbed it while she was burping her. The T-shirt was an older one and, at one time, she thought it attractive. It had an asymmetrical style with ruching caught by large wooden buttons down the side.

But now, with her sisters' words in her ears, she saw the missing button, the stain that never washed out. She saw the loose pants with their drawstring waist.

Is this what Dean saw?

She felt a shiver of revulsion, her mind racing back to the memory of Kelly and her snug jeans, cute T-shirt and perfect hair and makeup.

Erin knew it shouldn't matter what she looked like, but that her own sisters would mention it made her wonder what Dean saw when he glanced her way.

And why do you care?

She wasn't sure why. But she did.

Monday afternoon Erin parked her car in front of Brooke Dillon's hair salon, Cut and Run, and bit her lip.

"What do you think, baby girl?" she asked Caitlin, who was tucked away in her car seat in the back. "Am I being vain?"

Lauren's words from Sunday still echoed in her brain and while she knew she was taking them too much to heart, they still bothered her. This morning when Dean had arrived she waited until she knew he was working, then slipped out for her walk feeling suddenly self-conscious. And then she'd decided to go to town. Get her hair done.

But now that she was actually here, second thoughts assailed her.

Who are you trying to impress?

And as that last question slouched into her mind it was followed by a picture of Dean.

She pushed the car door open and got out, burying her changing feelings. It was just a cut and color. Something she'd needed for a while. Besides, it would be a great pick-me-up. A symbol of her new start here in Saddlebank.

As she stepped into the hair salon, Caitlin's car seat hooked on her arm the aroma of expensive shampoo blended with the pungent scent of hair dye and hair spray washed over her. Their Aunt Laura had taken them here once in a while to get their hair done and the smells brought back happier times in her life.

A woman with purple-and-pink-streaked hair looked up from the chest-high reception desk, the ring in her lip bobbing as she gave Erin a welcoming smile. "Welcome to Cut and Run. What can we do for you today?"

"I'd like a color and cut." She glanced around the full salon and realized how foolish her request was. Every chair was full and a few ladies sat in the reception area flipping through magazines.

The girl tapped her fingers on her cheek as she looked at the book. "I'm not sure we can get you in. Let me talk to Brooke." She left, and as the women with the magazines glanced her way, then at Caitlin, she felt a sudden need to retreat. One of the women was Kelly's mother. The other Erin recognized as one of the youth group leaders she had worked with a couple of summers all those years ago.

She was just about to turn to leave when someone called her name.

"Erin?"

Then Brooke herself came around the desk toward her. She wore a black silk blouse and a black skirt. Her blond hair was pulled back in an artful swirl of curls held by a glittering clip, and delicate silver chains hung from her ears. She looked elegant and beautiful and Erin felt even dowdier. The Brooke she remembered from her visits to Saddlebank had been less put-together. More casual. Looks like the roles were reversed now.

"I heard you were back in town," Brooke said, smiling at her. "Keira told me at church yesterday."

Of course. Erin should have known how quickly word got around a place like Saddlebank.

"How is Keira?" Erin asked.

"Great. She and Tanner are married. They have a little boy."

"Oh, that's great." Erin and Keira and Lauren used to hang out the summers they were back in Saddlebank. And though they had lost touch, she did know that Keira and Tanner had been dating and then broke up. She never knew the reason why. So she was glad to hear they were together again.

"And this must be Caitlin." Brooke leaned closer, her features softening as she touched Caitlin's cheek. "She's so precious." Brooke smiled, but then her smile seemed to shift and to hold a touch of sympathy as she straightened. "Your sisters seem crazy about her and I can see why."

Erin just nodded, far too aware of her washed-out shirt and loose-fitting blue jeans she thought would be suitable for a trip to town.

"I heard you wanted a color and cut?" Brooke asked, suddenly all business.

"It's okay. I can see you're too busy. I'll come back," she said, taking a step back to the door, her escape route.

Brooke waved off her objections. "Nonsense. I have time. Just come with me."

Miss Purple and Pink Hair frowned at her. "But I thought—"

"I have time," Brooke said, her voice firm. "Call Heather and reschedule. I know she won't mind."

"I don't want to cause any trouble," Erin objected. "Like I said, I can come back."

But Brooke was already walking away from her and the receptionist was already phoning so she followed along.

"So, your little girl going to be okay while we work?" Brooke asked as she pulled a cape off the chair and motioned for Erin to sit down.

"She's been fed and changed—"

"Oh, look at the adorable baby." An older woman who was sitting at one of the hair dryers flanking the wall got up and scurried over, her hair tucked into various bits of foil, a cape covering her clothes. She crouched down in front of the car seat, her hand stroking Caitlin's cheek. Then she looked up and Erin recognized Paige Argall, the town's librarian. "Hello, Erin," she said, her smile deepening as she got up. Then she gave Erin a quick hug. She pulled back, her hands on Erin's shoulders. "Welcome back to Saddlebank."

The warmth in her tone created a thickening in Erin's throat.

"Thanks."

"Is my niece here?" A voice called out and then Aunt Laura bustled into the salon. Short, plump, her graying hair cut in a shoulder-length bob, Aunt Laura, with her smiles and good humor, was the exact opposite of her brother, Keith McCauley, Erin's father.

She hadn't had a chance to see her aunt yet and when Aunt Laura's arms slipped around her and pulled her close the tears that threatened came again. Erin let them flow for only a moment, then struggled to pull herself together.

"Oh, honey," Aunt Laura said, bracketing Erin's face with her plump, work-roughened hands. "What a long road you've been on to get back home."

Which just about set her off again.

"But have you seen her baby?" Mrs. Argall, still crouched down beside Caitlin, asked, unbuckling her. Then she looked up at Erin. "Can I take her out?"

"Only if you let me hold her, too," Aunt Laura insisted before Erin could say anything.

"We should get at the hair." Brooke pointed to the still empty chair and with a flush, Erin hurriedly sat down, hoping Caitlin would behave herself.

"You didn't need to cancel the other appointment."

"Heather won't mind," Brooke said.

"Oh, absolutely not," Paige added, cuddling Caitlin in her arms as she walked back to the dryer. "My daughter-in-law will do anything for a relative." Aunt

Laura sat down beside her and they were joined by a young girl who was sweeping up.

"So what are we doing today?" Brooke asked as she fastened the cape around Erin's shoulders.

"I'm not sure exactly," Erin said, making a face at her reflection in the mirror. Her hair hung limp and boring around her face as Brooke pulled it free from the ponytail tie.

Brooke lifted and fluffed, angling her head this way and that, the diamond on her ring finger flashing in the lights from the salon. "We can go with lighter streaks on the top, darker on the bottom. To give the hair some definition. I wouldn't cut too much off, though."

Erin just nodded as Brooke made suggestions. She had no preference, only that something be done. She wanted a break from her past. A reason to feel better about herself.

Or so you can look good for Dean.

She pushed the thought aside, but it lingered as Brooke folded foils in her hair and painted color on them, bringing her up to date on all things Saddlebank. Erin found out that Heather was expecting, as was her sister-in-law Abby, who was married to Lee, Keira and Heather's brother. Allison Bamford, George Bamford's sister and Brooke's future sister-in-law, was going back to college. Alan Brady had expanded his mechanic business and an outsider had bought the grocery store.

But while she chatted, Erin gave her only half her attention. The other half was on Caitlin who was being cooed and oohed and aahed over by most everyone who was in the salon.

Seeing her daughter being passed around made Erin

feel ashamed that she had stayed away from church, thinking people would judge her.

There hadn't been any condemnation in anyone's voice. No hint of reproach.

Only abundant acceptance and love.

And once again Erin had the feeling that moving back here had been the best thing she could have done for herself.

Dean carefully made his way down the scaffolding and when he got to the ground he stood back, a feeling of satisfaction washing over him. He had managed to finish off the siding as far down as he could reach.

And it looked great.

He heard the sound of a car arriving and he couldn't stop the silly lift of his heart.

Erin was home.

He wasn't going to go and check, but when her car door closed and he heard her walking to the house, he stopped piling up the scraps of siding he had dropped. Would she come and see what he'd done? Then the door of the house opened and his heart did that stupid jump again, but her footsteps returned to her car. This was repeated a few times until curiosity overcame his good sense.

When he came around the house, the hood of the trunk was up and all he could see of Erin was her feet.

"What's up?" he asked, hoping he sounded like he was simply making casual conversation. Not being snoopy.

Erin squealed her surprise, then slammed the trunk of the car shut.

And Dean could only stare.

Her hair was shinier, shorter and sort of sassy-looking. And she wore snug blue jeans and a pale pink, loose sweater over a white tank top. Gold hoops swung from her ears.

"Wow," he said, disappointed at how breathless the sight of her looking so different made him feel. "You look…amazing."

Her cheeks flushed and she ducked her head in a self-conscious gesture.

"I thought I should get something done to my hair and then I met up with Aunt Laura and we went shopping. I got some new clothes that I decided to wear right away."

"Well, you look great." Too late he realized how that might sound. "I mean, not that you didn't look great before."

"I looked like a college student cramming for finals," she said.

"You looked casual. Comfortable."

She grinned at that. "Thanks for that, but I think I like amazing better."

He wasn't sure what to say so he focused his attention on the boards of floor samples she had stacked against the car. "What are you planning?"

"I thought the inside of the house could use some work, too," she said, heaving the samples up by the handles. He hobbled over to help her, grabbing a couple of the samples, as well. These held various kinds of tile and the ones Erin carried to the house had pieces of wood attached to them.

"So what did you figure on doing?"

"I want to replace the flooring," she said as he tried to get ahead of her to open the door. But he couldn't keep up, his leg stiff from climbing up and down the scaffolding all day.

He was glad Erin hadn't been around to see his slow progress. It had been disheartening even though he had gotten more done than he figured.

If he didn't have his bad leg he would have been able to take down the scaffolding and accomplish so much more.

So now Erin was holding the door open for him and he had to move awkwardly past her, trying not to wince as he carried the heavy samples into the house.

"Just put them in the kitchen," she said as the door fell shut behind her.

"Where's Caitlin?" he asked as he carefully set the boards down, leaning them against the kitchen cabinets.

"Sleeping in her crib. She's had a busy day. Got passed around at Brooke's beauty salon while I got my hair done."

"I imagine she'd been quite the hit," he said with a grin. "She's such a little muffin."

Erin's expression grew suddenly serious and he wondered if he had overstepped some invisible line as she held his gaze. "I sure think so," she said, her voice quiet.

Dean wasn't sure what she meant by that or what he was supposed to say so he poked his chin toward the wood samples she was laying on the carpet of the living room. "I'm guessing you want to put down hardwood flooring?"

"And tile in the kitchen."

"That's a lot of work."

"I've done it before," she said casually. "In the house I owned in San Francisco."

"All by yourself?"

She chuckled at that as she stood up, walking around the samples as if surveying them from various angles. "No. I had help. Mostly my roommates and I, though Sam helped—" she stopped abruptly there.

Sam.

Dean remembered her saying that same name that morning when she had fallen asleep on the couch. She had sounded panicked when she said it, though.

"Was Sam one of your roommates?" he asked, trying to sound all casual. Like it didn't matter to him who this guy was.

Erin shook her head. "No. Just someone who helped out." Then she turned to him, her chin up, her eyes narrowing as they met his. "Actually, he's more than that. Sam is, no, was, Caitlin's father."

Dean heard the angry edge in her voice, the repressed anger.

"I take it he's not in the picture?" he asked, even though he knew he was edging toward a place he had no right to go.

"You take it correctly," she said, her shoulders lowering as she looked away. "He's not...not part of my little girl's life."

Which made him curiously relieved.

"Did you have any more samples to bring in?" he asked.

She shook her head. "No. But thanks so much for helping me."

"No problem."

He held her gaze a moment longer than necessary, as neither of them looked away. Old feelings blended with new and his breath caught in his chest.

Then Caitlin whimpered and his cell phone rang and they broke the connection, each attending to other obligations.

And as Dean walked away, his phone still ringing, he felt a tiny sliver of hope because of her anger with Caitlin's father.

But even as he went through the usual list of "reasons why he couldn't date Erin," he couldn't discard the moments of connection he had felt around her. And this time around, he had a strong feeling she felt the same.

"Dean here," he said as he stepped out of the house, closing the door behind him.

"Yeah. Just thought I'd let you know that I can't come on Wednesday to help with the windows," Jan was saying. "Sorry about that. I can't come until Friday."

"Can you spare a guy to help me?"

"Not really. Sorry, bud. I'm running crazy here."

The apology puzzled him. "So, did you want me to come work on the Mercy job?"

"You could," he said after a long moment of silence. "I got all the guys I need but if you need to keep busy…" His sentence trailed off and while Dean appreciated the sentiment he also guessed that Jan was desperately thinking of a make-work project for him.

"That's okay," he put in, cutting off Jan's attempt to make him feel useful. "I've got enough here to keep me going for a while."

"You sure?"

"I'm sure. Thanks." He hung up and suppressed a sigh.

He knew that working for Jan was a two-way street. After his accident Dean had taken a couple of months off and Jan had held his job for him. As well, Jan had given him time off for his ongoing physiotherapy. Which he'd been neglecting the past months because he felt so guilty for having been away from the job so much.

Which meant he wasn't seeing the gains the physiotherapist promised.

He fought the usual feelings of uselessness, then pushed them aside. He'd just have to keep himself busy here. He really didn't have much choice.

He heard Erin talking quietly to Caitlin and he felt his own heart foolishly respond, thinking of that moment they'd shared.

He just hoped he'd be able to keep his wits about him around her.

Especially now that she was looking even better than before.

Chapter Seven

"So I thought you could ride Roany," Jodie said as she held the door of the house open for Erin, who carried Caitlin in her arms. They stepped outside and Erin couldn't stop a quiver of anticipation as they walked toward the corrals.

This morning Dean had come just for a short while and then left again. She had hoped to see him. To talk to him, but that chance was gone. She needed a distraction. So she'd called Jodie and asked if she could watch Caitlin. Asked if there was a suitable horse for her to ride. She wanted to go out into the hills she had spent so much time in as a young girl.

Thankfully Jodie had agreed. And she had her distraction.

All the way here her excitement had grown at the thought of going riding again. The sun was shining and the day was surprisingly warm for late September. "I thought you might not want to get too adventurous today so I picked my best-trained horse."

"No. I'd like to come back to Caitlin in one piece,"

Erin said with a chuckle, brushing a light kiss over her daughter's fuzzy head.

Though Erin had been excited about the prospect of spending some time alone, riding through the hills, the thought of leaving Caitlin behind also created a clench of uncertainty.

"You'll be okay, I'm sure of that," Jodie said as if sensing her second thoughts.

As they neared the corrals Erin saw a familiar truck parked there, as well. What was Dean doing here?

"Excellent. My helper has arrived," Jodie said.

"Helper?" Erin asked, puzzled why Jodie needed help with the horses.

"Yes. He's going to help me by going riding with you."

Was this why he had left early this morning?

Erin wasn't sure how to process this. Not sure she wanted to have Dean with her on what she had hoped to be a time of solitude.

And yet the thought held a surprising appeal.

"I wanted to make sure you'd be okay," Jodie said as they walked toward Dean. He was petting Mickey, one of their older horses who was also tied up.

"Hey, Dean," Jodie called out as they came closer. "Thanks for coming."

Dean straightened, but the brim of his cowboy hat shadowed his eyes. By the grim set of his mouth Erin guessed that he wasn't entirely pleased with the unfolding events.

"So, you want me to go riding with Erin?"

He didn't sound happy about it. At all. Did he know what he was in for?

"I need to know that Erin will come back in one piece." Jodie's grin and perky tone showed Erin she wasn't the least bit fazed by Dean's apparent antagonism.

"I can go on my own." Erin wasn't sure she wanted to spend time with someone who clearly didn't want to be doing this.

Or didn't want to be with her.

"I'm sure you can, but you're a mom now and I'm your daughter's aunt and if something were to happen to you I would feel horrible. I'm sure Dean can agree with me there."

Dean didn't reply, instead he busied himself adjusting the saddle, checking the stirrups with jerky movements. To keep himself from looking at either of them, Erin guessed.

"Okay, then, maybe you two should get going," Jodie said, reaching out to take Caitlin from Erin.

Her trepidation returned with a vengeance at the sight of Dean avoiding her.

"I can do this another day," Erin protested.

"Today works best for you and for Dean," Jodie said, seemingly unfazed by the obvious reluctance of the two main participants. She kept her hands out and Erin reluctantly handed over her baby to her sister.

"Okay, then, I'll go," she said knowing that her sister could be more stubborn than her. If she gave in, she and Dean could go for a short ride, placate her sister and come back right away.

She drew in a deep breath, brushed her hands over her jeans, then walked over to Roany and slowly untied the leather reins.

Dean walked around his horse and did the same. She lifted her foot to the stirrup and with one little hop managed to get astride the horse. Roany didn't so much as blink.

"Stirrups okay?" Jodie asked while Erin tested their length, the leather of the saddle creaking as she did so.

She nodded, then glanced over at Dean, wondering why he was waiting. Was he changing his mind about coming along?

But while he stood by his horse, his hand on the pommel, reins gathered in his hands, shoulders rising and falling as he breathed she felt a sudden flash of insight.

How would he get on with his bad leg? She knew he was proud and she guessed that he didn't want them to watch.

"Actually, this one on the left is a bit wonky," she said, turning away from Dean, bending down to inspect a nonexistent problem on the opposite side of her horse.

Jodie looked confused and Erin shot her a warning look, tilting her head ever so slightly in Dean's direction, hoping her outspoken sister would play along.

Jodie seemed to get the hint, because she started to fuss with the stirrup with one hand while she rocked Caitlin in her other arm. "I think it's okay," she said. "Let me have another look."

While they fiddled and adjusted a buckle that was fine, Erin could feel the tension emanating from the man beside her. She shot her sister a meaningful look, hoping Jodie understood what she was telegraphing.

What were you thinking?

But Jodie just bent over enough to look under Erin's

horse, then gave her sister a discreet thumbs-up. She guessed Dean was finally mounted.

"There we go. I guess Mommy's stirrup is all good to go," Jodie said to Caitlin, nuzzling her with the tip of her nose. Then she flashed Erin a grin as she stepped back. "Have fun. Do you have your cell phone?"

Erin nodded, patting the button-down pocket of her shirt just to make sure. "Caitlin should be good for the next couple of hours. I did put a bottle in her diaper bag if she gets fussy." But even as she spoke the words so confidently she felt a tremor of apprehension. What if Caitlin cried too hard? What if something happened to her? Was she being irresponsible by leaving like this? "You're sure you're going to be okay?" she asked again.

"We will be fine," Jodie assured her. "I'm looking forward to some aunty-and-niece time." She stepped away from the horse and tossed off a wave to Dean. "Thanks so much for going with my sister, Dean. I feel better knowing that she's with you."

Erin shot a quick sidelong glance at Dean. She couldn't see his eyes as his hat was pulled down low, but his jaw was clenched, his hands bunched on the reins. He looked like he was in a lot of pain, which puzzled her. Though she had never witnessed it, she knew he climbed up and down ladders and scaffolding at her house.

Maybe this was different for him?

Anger at Jodie flashed through her for pushing Dean to do this. But she kept her comments to herself. They would make this ride quick to keep up appearances. As soon as was reasonable, she would be coming back.

"If you're ready to go, we should leave," Dean said

his voice sounding strained as he kept his gaze firmly on his horse's head.

She pulled gently back on the reins, shifting her weight, signaling to Roany that she wanted to back up. And just like that her horse dropped his head and took a few hesitant steps back then stopped when Erin settled ahead again.

Like riding a bike, she thought, shooting another glance at her baby, tucked now in her sister's arms.

"You'll be okay?" she asked, trying not to sound like a harried mother, but feeling like a string that tied her to Caitlin was slowly being pulled tighter with each move away from her.

"We'll be fine," Jodie assured her.

Then there was nothing left to do but leave.

"Maybe just make a few turns around the yard at first," Dean suggested, pulling his reins to the side, turning his horse away from Jodie. "Just to get the horse used to you and you comfortable with the horse."

Erin simply nodded, doing as he said, putting Roany through a few turns, to the left, then to the right. The gelding easily responded to her lightest touch of the reins on his neck, the faintest nudge of her heels in his sides. "I think I'm good," she said, noticing, with surprise, that Dean did the same thing. Probably just getting used to an unfamiliar horse.

"You sure?"

"You know where to go?"

"I've ridden this ranch many times."

He sounded strained and she could see lines of tension around his mouth.

"Are you sure about going?" she asked. "We can do this another day."

"No. We're here now. May as well do this."

He sounded angry so Erin said nothing more, realizing that pushing the issue too hard would humiliate him. Oh, well. He had to know what he was capable of. So she followed him as he rode around the large red barn where a tractor and baler were parked. Just where her father always had it.

Erin felt the pull of nostalgia and a thread of sorrow at the sight. Her life had been so crazy the past while that she felt as if she hadn't even had time to mourn her father. To miss him. She thought again of the letter she had skimmed, vowing to read it more closely tonight.

Dean seemed to know where he was going so she was content to follow him past the yard and along the rail fence edging the winter pasture for the cows. A trail led from here into the trees and then up the hills toward a lookout point she rode to when she was younger.

Dean sat awkwardly in the saddle and Erin could see he was favoring his injured leg. Though she wanted to ask him if he wanted to quit she knew it would insult his pride. She'd seen a few flashes of that the past few days.

She watched him from behind as he slowly, imperceptibly seemed to relax. To sit back, his shoulders lowered, his hips centered, swaying gently with the horse.

The air was cooler in the shade of the trees, a whispering breeze scattering golden leaves on the path and on them. Soon the trees would be entirely orange and yellow, and the countdown to winter would begin. Erin couldn't help a touch of sentimentality. She and her sisters had never been here through the fall. They'd spent that time back in Knoxville and as soon as they were old enough, they'd stopped coming back to the ranch.

Had their father missed them? They never knew because he never answered any of their letters or returned their phone calls.

How lonely it must have been for him here!

Erin shook off the gloomy thoughts, preferring to focus on this time here and now. To enjoy the silence, and, if she was honest with herself, some time with Dean away from the house.

They rode on, the thud of the horses' hooves the only other sound in the gentle quiet. And as they did, Erin felt peace slowly wash over her. Finally they came to a place where the trail widened out and Dean pulled back for her to catch up to him.

"You doing okay?" he asked, glancing down at her feet as if making sure the stirrups she and Jodie had been fussing with were good.

"I'm just fine," she said, giving him a cautious smile. She wanted to ask him the same, but if he wasn't he wouldn't say, and if he was she didn't need to ask.

But from the tightness around his mouth, she guessed it was a struggle for him.

They rode for a while and finally Erin couldn't stand it any longer. "Look, I'm sorry you got roped into this, if you'll pardon the cowboy reference. I didn't have anything to do with it. I just wanted to go riding, like I used to. I didn't ask if you could come along."

She shot him a concerned sidelong glance, but he kept his face resolutely ahead, as if he didn't want to look at her.

"I'm sure this was Jodie's idea," she continued. "You riding with me."

"Vic's, too," he said. "He called me at your house to tell me that Jodie needed some help. When I came here I found out this was what she wanted help with." He kept his gaze fixed on the trail ahead, his eyes narrowed. She wanted him to look at her so she could read his expression better.

"I'm sorry this took you away from your work," she added. She guessed he was angry or in a lot of pain. What she wished he would do was either get over it or admit it and stop. She preferred not to keep riding if he was going to be all annoyed or if his injury would get worse.

He shrugged, shifting in the saddle again, his jaw clenching.

"Doesn't matter," he replied, his tone terse. "Truth is, I was done and my boss Jan didn't have any work for me on the job in Mercy. So it's not like I'm out anything because of this." He didn't sound pleased. They rode along for a while longer, but Erin was far too aware of the tension in the air. This wasn't how she had envisioned her ride so she pulled her horse to a stop.

"Look, again, I'm sorry you had to do this," she said, struggling to keep the frustration out of her voice at her repeated apologies. "We should just go back or you can go back on your own and I can keep riding."

He pulled up as well, his horse shaking his head at the sudden stop, bridle jangling. Dean just looked ahead, as if ignoring her, then finally he turned to face her.

"I'm sorry," he said finally, his voice sounding rough.

"I know I'm being a jerk. I know I have been a jerk the last few days. It's just…" his voice trailed off and he winced, adjusting his seat and stretching out his one leg. Then he gave her an apologetic look. "This is the first time I've been on a horse since the accident."

Erin could only stare at him, surprise and shock flowing through her. "You mean…you're saying…"

"I'm saying I haven't ridden since I got out of the hospital."

"Because you can't?"

Dean pressed his lips together, looking ahead again. "No. My physiotherapist encouraged me to ride."

"Then why not?"

He said nothing for a moment, which made Erin even more curious.

"I haven't because…" He paused, as if the words were too hard to get out.

But Erin waited, sensing he was on the cusp of something difficult. Something important.

He moved to one side, wincing, then shook his head lightly, as if shaking off an errant thought.

He finally looked directly at her, his hat tipped back so she could see his eyes, the sheen of sweat on his face she hadn't noticed before.

"Because I'm afraid."

Chapter Eight

His words echoed in the silence. He had never dared admit that to anyone before. To say the words aloud, to talk openly about his fear made him feel foolish and weak. But when he looked at Erin the only thing he saw was admiration.

"Are you afraid now?" she asked.

Dean squeezed his hands to stop the trembling and looked ahead again, drawing in a long, slow breath. "Not as much as when I started."

It was pride pure and simple that got him to the ranch. When he'd found out what Jodie had wanted help with, his initial response was to outright refuse. Until she'd said she needed his help with Erin. His ego had taken a beating the past while with her and he couldn't stand for it anymore. When Jan had called to offer him the job in Mercy he knew he was only doing it out of sympathy.

And he was tired of it. Tired of looking like the helpless ex-cowboy. Out of anger and frustration he'd agreed.

Trouble was, he didn't know how hard it was going to be once he faced the horse. But Erin was there and Jodie was watching. It had been pride that got him awkwardly in the saddle and stubbornness that kept him mounted.

Thankfully neither Jodie nor Erin had to witness his ungainly and fearful clamber onto the horse. And even more important, Mickey had stood solid as a rock while his good foot scrabbled to find the stirrup, his heart thudding like a jackhammer in his chest.

He had hoped to do a few more circuits around the yard to ease the pounding in his heart, but Erin seemed to catch on very quickly. So he simply had to push on and hope the fear would die down. That and the pain that was like shards of glass in a leg unaccustomed to this position.

"So you haven't ridden at all before this?"

"No. I tried to mount up a couple of times but just couldn't make that final move."

"Do you want to get off now? Rest for a few minutes? I'd like to check out Pigeon Point."

"Pigeon Point? I've never heard it called that before."

"My dad took us here once. To shoot clay pigeons."

In spite of the pain shooting through his knee and the fear that still hovered, Dean had to smile. "Can't imagine that."

"I have a country side," she returned. "So, you game?"

Dean nodded, but then realized if he got off, he would have to find a way to get back on again. Or run the risk of leading his horse all the way back to the ranch.

He was about to change his mind but Erin had already dismounted and was leading her horse to a nearby tree. So he slowly pulled his foot out of the stirrup, then rolled himself sideways and slid off the saddle, landing on his good leg, flinching when Mickey moved his feet as if impatient.

But nothing happened and his racing heart rate eased down again.

He stretched and tested his weight, thankful the pain was ebbing away. He was pleased it didn't hurt more. Maybe his physiotherapist was right. He needed to ride again.

He led Mickey to a tree close to Roany and quickly tied him off.

Erin had pulled her cell phone out of her pocket and thumbed it on.

"Calling to check in?" he asked, a playful note in his voice.

"Yes, I am," she said sounding somewhat defensive. "This is the first time I've been away from Caitlin and I know Jodie is my sister, but still—"

"I get it," Dean said, flashing her an understanding smile. "I was just teasing you."

Her mouth twitched, but she completed the call anyway. From what she was saying to her sister it sounded like all was well with her daughter. He walked away to give her some privacy.

A worn path led through an opening in the trees. He knew about this lookout point. Had ridden past it many times on his way to the far pasture to check on the cows. He'd never had the time to stop and look, but judging from the easily visible path, other people had.

He pushed through the underbrush and the land

opened up and flowed away from him. The Saddle-bank River spooled out below him a band of silver, flashing in the sun, flanked by clusters of trees that showed hints of the orange and yellow that would soon blaze from this valley.

He heard a rustling behind him and there was Erin, her hands shoved in the back pockets of her jeans, a smile playing over her face as she looked out over the valley.

"I forgot how beautiful it is here," she said, a reverent tone in her voice. Then she eased out a sigh, lowering herself to the ground. "Do you mind if we sit awhile? If we're going to be admitting stuff, my legs are sore, too." She flashed him a smile, her hair bouncing on her shoulders, her eyes fringed with dark lashes drawing him in.

"I don't mind." Spending time with Erin held a bittersweet appeal. But as he clumsily sat down he was reminded again of his own weakness.

She pulled her legs up, wrapping her arms around them, then glanced his way again. "I feel like I have to apologize yet again for my sister's unwelcome intervention. I don't think she realized—"

"That this ex–saddle bronc rider is afraid of horses?" He couldn't keep the bitter tone out of his voice. "Wait until that gets out."

She ducked her head and looked away and once again he felt like a heel for being so abrupt. He wanted to blame the throbbing in his leg, though it was easing away, or the relief he felt now that he'd survived his first time back on a horse. But there was more. A feeling of not knowing who he was anymore.

"I don't think anyone would have guessed that," she

said, her voice quiet. "And I won't say anything if you don't." Then she gave him a careful, sidelong glance and he recognized her gentle peace offering. A way of bridging a gap he had created.

"It's just… I've wanted to be a saddle bronc rider as long as I could ride. I lived for the thrill, the challenge, the pitting of my skills against this out-of-control animal." He leaned back against the tree behind him and stretched out his leg. "Sounds kind of shallow, but it was my life. Who I was."

"I remember watching you that one summer," she said, resting her chin on her knees as she looked out over the valley. "I thought you were good."

Her praise warmed him more than it should.

"I never knew. I always got the impression that what I did was beneath you. That going to rodeos was for rednecks and cowboys."

"You can't live in Saddlebank and not go to the rodeo at least once," she said with a grin. "My sisters convinced me I should go. You were competing that night and, well, I was impressed."

"Really? I impressed you?" he asked.

"If you're fishing for compliments, you already got one bite." She shot him a sideways glance. Added a smile. Tucked her hair behind her ear.

The tilt of her head, the glint in her eye, the half smile made him wonder if she was flirting with him.

"So you must miss it?" she asked, her voice growing more serious.

"I do." The simple statement didn't cover the disappointment twisting his stomach at the idea that he couldn't do the one thing that he thought defined him.

"It was who I was. What I wanted to be. Everything I ever did was with the hope of competing at a higher level."

"And the lifestyle? Do you miss that, too?"

Her question puzzled him. "What do you mean?"

She shrugged. "Sorry. None of my business."

He looked over at her, but her eyes were fixed on the valley below them. Yet something about the question she asked niggled other thoughts. Questions he'd had himself the past half year. Before his injury he'd been on the road more and more. Gone from the ranch. Riding over the weekends. Partying hard with his buddies.

His accident, however, had shifted his point of view. And thinking about his previous life, sitting beside the one person he'd always considered the epitome of goodness and kindness, pushed him even further down the path he'd started in the hospital room. When the doctor told him how long rehabilitation would take.

"Truth to tell, I don't miss the overall lifestyle," he said. "And looking back now, I knew how shallow it was. Lying in a hospital bed for an extended period tends to give a guy some perspective. I had time on my hands. And one of the things I thought about was something you said to me the last time I saw you. That summer you spent here in Saddlebank."

She shot him a look of puzzlement. "What was that?"

"That I was headed down a one-way road to nowhere. That the journey would make me unhappy and unsatisfied." He lifted his knee, resting his forearm on it as he fiddled with a piece of grass. "I think getting injured was a reality check and a chance to reassess my life. My girlfriend had broken up with me and for a while I blamed her. I blamed Vic. I blamed everyone. But then I thought of what you said and I got to look back over my life through your eyes. And I didn't like what I saw."

"Why are you telling me this?" she asked, looking ahead. He wasn't sure how to read her expression.

"Because I know what you thought of me then." Dean knew he was exposing his deeper self. Things he'd hidden all these years under a blanket of swagger and tough talk. But she'd already seen him at his most vulnerable. Had heard about his fear and seen his helplessness. It bugged him and he hated admitting that, but he wanted her to know her opinion had mattered.

"I know I wasn't good enough for you. You weren't the only one who thought that. You were this sweet, caring person who was a strong Christian. I know I poked fun of that part of your life and I'm sorry." He stopped, feeling again the shame that had dogged him the past few months since the time he'd begun reading his Bible again. Returning to the faith he had once mocked. He had his ups and downs and his moments of weakness, but he felt he was taking slow, uncertain steps back to his faith. "In spite of how I acted and how I treated you I think there was always a part of me that wanted to be worthy of you. I never really forgot you."

There. It was out. Poor, lonely Dean. Always keeping a space in his heart for a girl who had never encouraged or shown him that he mattered to her as much as she had mattered to him.

"You should have" was all she said. "You should have put me right out of your head."

She blinked and he was shocked to see a tear trickling down the side of her face. She quickly swiped it away, but it was too late.

"What's wrong?" He moved closer, and gave in to the impulse he had felt previously and gently brushed her hair back from her face. "I'm sorry if something I said bothered you."

She had gone perfectly still and he thought he had gone too far, intruding too closely into her personal space.

But as her eyes met his a feeling of rightness permeated the atmosphere. That everything he had waited for and wanted at one time was right here. His breath quickened and he felt as if the world had narrowed down to this moment, this space. Just the two of them.

He let his finger trail down her cheek, easing away the tears that had drifted down.

"You're so beautiful," he whispered, the words slipping past old barriers that didn't seem as necessary as they once were. "You always were."

"Why...why did you always ask me out?"

Her unexpected question set him back, but he recognized her attempt to bridge the then and now.

Well, he had started this. May as well take the full plunge into humility.

"Like I said, even though I was a jerk, a part of me always appreciated your faith. I know many of the girls I dated weren't the kind of girl I would bring to see my mom. But you were. You had a sweetness that intrigued me. A goodness that, whether I wanted to admit it or not, was something I wanted in my life. I just thought I was too cool to try. But you..." He paused, cupping her face in his hand, his thumb caressing her chin, surprised that she allowed him to do this. "You were special. Pure."

Even as he spoke the words he realized how they might sound to her, given that she had come to Saddlebank with a baby. Yet, he still meant them.

Her eyes locked on his, and her hand came up and gently covered his, pressing his hand against her face.

He stopped breathing for a moment, connected by the warmth of her palm and his hand on her face.

"Erin," he said softly, leaning in, trying to get closer to her.

She didn't look away and all the intervening years fell away as he closed the distance between them. As his lips brushed hers he felt as if he was finally where he should be.

Her breath sighed against his mouth. Then her other hand came up and cupped his cheek, and when he gently pulled away they stayed connected. Hands. Eyes. Hearts.

"You are such an amazing person," he said, holding her gaze, wanting to extend the moment, to build on the connection they had just shared. "I've always admired you. Always appreciated who you were. You made me... made me want to be a better person."

Her expression hardened and the words he thought might encourage her made her pull back.

Then she released a harsh laugh, pulling back from him and breaking the connection.

"You don't know anything about me anymore," she said. "I'm not that same girl now."

"You may not think so, but I know you're the same caring, loving person. The same faithful Christian."

She just looked at him. "I'm a single mother."

He heard the unspoken hurt in the words and guessed how she saw herself. "You have a little girl," he said. "But to me that doesn't change anything."

"I haven't been in church for months."

"I didn't think I belonged there, but church has become a place I feel like my soul can rest when I'm there. I feel like I get support and strength to carry on for the week." He was quiet, realizing the irony of the situation. Him encouraging her to go to church when years ago it would have been the other way around. "Why don't you come on Sunday?"

She looked away from him, her eyes resting on some faraway place across the valley as if looking back over her life. "I don't know. It will be hard."

"I'll be there."

He threw the words out casually hoping they would encourage her.

She gave him a weary look, then shook her head as if pushing the thought aside and quickly got to her feet, ending the conversation. "I think we should go back to the ranch."

Then before he could say anything, she turned and strode away from him, scattering leaves as she plunged into the underbrush.

Dean dragged his hands over his face. This wasn't the first time she'd pushed him away. But it was the first time he'd kissed her.

He rolled onto his good knee and slowly got up, grabbing a nearby tree branch to stabilize himself. He caught his balance, his leg stiff and sore, frustration clawing at him once again. Had he misread her so badly?

For a brief moment after he kissed her, he'd thought things were changing between them. But as he limped to where the horses were tied he realized he faced another dilemma. How to mount the horse with legs that still felt the strain of riding. He paused, watching Erin easily mount up.

Please, Lord, he prayed as he walked over to his horse. *Let me get on the horse in one go.*

After spilling his guts to her and having her push him away—again—he figured he could use a win.

Erin rode back to the ranch, her mind a whirl of emotions.

What had she done? Why had she let Dean kiss her? She didn't have room in her messy life for this. She wished she could put it behind her, but her heart was still trembling from the feel of his mouth on hers.

Even now she was too aware of Dean behind her as they rode back to the ranch. How would she cope with him at her house every day after this?

Roany whinnied as they came closer to the ranch and as they came around the barn she saw Jodie walking toward the house.

What was she doing? Did she leave Caitlin alone in the house?

But as her sister turned, Erin saw her holding her daughter, and her fear eased.

Too vulnerable, she thought as her heart slowed again. Too many things happening too quickly. And the man behind her was part of her fragile and teetering emotions.

Jodie walked toward them, and as she came nearer

Erin caught her frown. "I thought you guys would be gone much longer," Jodie called out.

"I got sore," Erin said. It wasn't entirely untrue, though any stiffness she'd felt after not being in the saddle for so long had eased away by the time they came back to the ranch.

"I figured you were being too ambitious taking on such a long ride."

"Bit off more than I could chew," Erin muttered as she slowly dismounted. She loosened the halter rope off the saddle horn and tied Roany to the hitching rail, dismayed to see her hands still trembling.

"Did you at least have fun?"

Erin chose to ignore the insinuation in her sister's voice, baffled once again at the shift in Jodie's attitude toward Dean.

Which, in turn, only proved to show her how completely the axis of her life had tilted.

"Yeah, it was good" was all she said, keeping any emotion out of her voice.

She caught Jodie's puzzled look but ignored her, slipping the reins over Roany's head and letting him spit out the bit.

"How are you feeling, Dean?" Jodie called out, looking past Erin to where she guessed Dean was slowly dismounting.

Erin tried not to pay attention to him, just as she had back in the clearing when he'd struggled to get back on his horse. Though she hadn't looked directly at him it had been painful to witness what she had. At one time Dean could easily vault on a horse in one smooth movement and had, the few occasions she'd seen him, done so with a flourish and a cocky tip of his hat to her.

But this Dean was awkward and ungainly and she guessed, ashamed of his disability. As a consequence the ride back to the ranch had been quiet. And the entire time Erin had stayed ahead of Dean, struggling with her changing emotions.

They were having such a nice visit until he'd brought up the past. The other Erin.

There was always a part of me that wanted to be worthy of you.

She knew he meant the words as an encouragement and at one time they might have been. But now, after the past year of her life, they felt more like a condemnation. She who had prided herself on her values, her faith, had helped a married man break his promises.

"I'm okay. I'll be stiff this afternoon," Dean said with a grunt as he slipped the saddle off Mickey.

Erin finally got her own saddle off and set it on its edge by the fence. Dean was already leading his horse to the pasture. He favored his good leg more than ever and again Erin looked away, quite sure he didn't want spectators.

Then Caitlin let go a little peep, lifting her head from Jodie's shoulder, then dropping it again.

"Can you take Roany back to the pasture?" Erin asked, handing the reins to her sister. "I'll take Caitlin."

Jodie did as she was asked, shifting Caitlin to Erin's arms and taking the reins.

Erin held her daughter close, brushing a gentle kiss over her head, inhaling the sweet, precious scent of her as she hurried back to the house. She probably should thank Dean for coming with her on the ride, but she wasn't the one who had asked him so she figured Jodie could do the honors.

She just wanted to retreat, to create some space between Dean's words and her present reality. But as she stepped into the house, she realized her mistake.

Memories of her father's letter bombarded her as she walked into the living room. She had sat exactly here while she read the letter that stated the same things Dean had just told her. What a good, sweet girl she was and how sorry he was that he didn't take care of her or appreciate her like he should have.

If she was a more philosophical person she might think her relationship with Sam was a way of dealing with her "daddy" issues. But the reality was simpler. She thought she loved him and he would give her the happily-ever-after she had always envisioned. A husband. A home. And someday, a family.

First comes love, then comes marriage, then comes Erin with a baby carriage.

But she'd got that wrong, too.

She looked down at her daughter, a motherly rush of love washing over her.

"I promise to take care of you," she whispered.

And even as she spoke her errant thoughts drifted back to Dean and the kiss they'd shared. The changing of the relationship she didn't dare indulge in.

She put Caitlin in her bouncy chair, then hurried to wash her hands. But through the window above the sink she could look over the yard.

Jodie and Dean were talking while he brushed down the horses. She saw Jodie's hands fluttering the way they always did when she was fired up about something. Erin wondered what it could be.

She settled on the couch, watching Caitlin, who was batting her tiny hands at the animals suspended above the bouncy chair. She had already grown so much and was becoming more aware of her surroundings. And each change made Erin realize how much her baby depended on her to make a home and a place.

Erin leaned forward to adjust her blanket around her legs and as she did she saw a Bible sitting on the table. Jodie's? Lauren's? Did it matter?

One of her sisters was nourishing her soul.

Erin had moved away from her God the past year. Sam wasn't a Christian and though he had never mocked her faith, he had never encouraged it, either.

And why would he? That would mean coming face-to-face with what he was doing to his family.

She pulled the Bible closer and opened it to one of the bookmarked pages.

Her eyes skimmed over the verses, then stopped at one that was underlined.

"Psalm 146:9. *The Lord watches over the foreigner and sustains the widow and the fatherless.*"

The passage struck a chord deep in her lonely soul.

Her daughter was fatherless and it hurt Erin more than she could say. She had grown up in a broken family and she wanted more than the mess that was her childhood for any child she would have.

Erin put the Bible down and pressed her fingers to her eyes, other memories intruding on her fragile peace. During the last few months of their relationship things hadn't been going well for her and Sam. She had talked about ending it. But Sam had broken down, pleading with her to stay with him. In a moment of weakness and possibly fear of being alone, Erin had given in.

It was that night Caitlin was conceived.

And it was a week later that Sam's wife, Helen, holding their five-year-old daughter, stood on her doorstep, begging her to let Sam go. To stop seeing him.

That was the first she'd known of Sam's marriage and his unfaithfulness to his wife. She'd broken up with him immediately.

Five weeks later she found out she was pregnant.

Erin fought down the memories, wishing she could find some peace from the guilt and shame that haunted her still. She was tired of crying over things she couldn't control and the breakdown of a marriage she knew nothing about.

Yet she felt responsible.

Therefore, there is now no condemnation for those who are in Christ Jesus.

The Bible verse from Romans that she had at one time memorized shimmered on the edges of her mind like a promise. But somehow she couldn't make it real or make it her own.

Then the door opened and her sister swept in, scattering her self-recrimination.

"Has Dean left?" she asked, quickly setting the Bible aside.

"Yes. Did you want him to stay?"

Erin waved off her question. "Just curious, that's all."

"So, did you enjoy yourself?" Jodie asked, lowering herself to the floor beside her niece. She stroked Caitlin's cheek and was rewarded with a lopsided smile. "Look, she's smiling at me."

"It's just gas," Erin returned.

"You say gas, I say smile." Jodie seemed unfazed by Erin's semigrouchy reply as she lifted Caitlin out of the chair. "And you love your Aunty Jodie, don't you," she said, switching to the singsongy tone women everywhere use with babies. "You been giving Aunty Jodie smiles all morning though it was a lot shorter morning than I thought it would be. Mommy says she got stiff and sore, but I think something else was going on, don't you?"

Erin chose to ignore her sister's not-so-subtle subtext. "I should probably head home, too."

"To what?" Jodie gave her a pointed look.

"I need to get some work done before I order flooring. I'm thinking of redoing the kitchen. Putting tile down there and hardwood in the living room."

But Jodie would not be deflected. "Dean seemed in a rush to leave."

Erin guessed her sister was fishing, but Erin wasn't biting.

"Did you have a fight with him?" Jodie pressed. "Did he come on to you again?"

Erin thought of that moment when his hand had cupped her chin. That electric moment when they had kissed.

"He did, didn't he?"

"You wouldn't have sounded so happy about that a few years ago." Erin knew the blush warming her cheeks only affirmed what her sister said, so she didn't bother refuting the comment.

"I know. But people change," Jodie said. "He comes to church now and I know it means something to him."

And didn't that only add to her own burdens? "I've changed a lot the past few years, too."

Jodie looked down at Caitlin, the clear evidence of that change.

"How much different are you from when you were younger. The dear, sweet sister we've always loved?"

"Enough to have a baby."

Jodie snorted. "Seriously, do you think you're the only female in the history of women who ended up in this situation?"

"It's not that simple."

"Actually, it's fairly simple."

Erin wanted to challenge her statement, but if she did, too much would come out. Things she wasn't ready to face herself.

Jodie held her gaze for a few more beats, then nodded, as if acknowledging that this topic was closed.

"So we'll talk about something else. I was wondering if you would be willing to come with me to Bozeman next week. I thought you and Lauren could try on bridesmaid dresses."

"Of course. I have some time between jobs."

"What are you doing now?"

"Book cover mock-ups for a publishing company I hope to get work with and an advertising campaign that isn't due for a month yet."

"You've kept busy with your work?"

"Not as busy as I want to be." She could use some more of it. Like she'd told her sisters, she had a few feelers out, but nothing substantial had come back yet.

From there the conversation slipped to Jodie's job, Lauren working at the flower shop and the plans for Jodie's wedding.

But even as they talked, she couldn't help the tiny flicker of unwelcome jealousy at how settled Jodie's and Lauren's lives had become. Future husbands, a home they would be sharing. She tried not to let panic come over her as she looked at Caitlin, so helpless and so dependent as she lay quiet in Jodie's arms. The fact that she was solely responsible for her daughter's upbringing became more real the more time she spent here.

But you're not on your own.

She looked at her sister and though she knew that was true, she still felt left behind. Alone.

You don't have to be.

And why did those words bring up a picture of Dean? Holding her chin, looking into her eyes as if offering her something.

But did she dare take it?

Chapter Nine

Erin heard the sound of a vehicle and despite knowing it was Saturday and that Dean wasn't coming to work today, either, she hurried to the window to see who it might be. But it was only a truck driving by on the road.

She wondered if she had chased him away the day they went riding. He had tried to be kind and she had overreacted.

Jan had phoned on Wednesday, full of apologies to tell her the windows had been delayed and could they come Monday instead. So Dean hadn't come by, either. Thursday he'd told her he was stopping by to pick up some tools and she had taken extra care with her clothes, putting on one of the new outfits. But then Lauren had called to ask if she could come to town for lunch with her and Jodie. So she'd met her sisters in town, but by the time she'd returned she realized Dean had come and gone while she was away.

He'd also told her he would help her measure the house for new flooring, but either he'd forgotten or was avoiding her. So to keep busy she had measured up the rooms herself and driven into town to order the flooring. She'd told herself repeatedly the past few days that she had done the right thing when they went riding. That her feelings for Dean were changing and she didn't want to encourage something that couldn't happen.

The sound of Caitlin fussing snapped Erin from her thoughts. She walked back to her bedroom. Her little girl had been out of sorts all morning, which was unusual for her. Caitlin lay crying in the crib, her arms waving, her tiny fingers curled into miniature fists, her legs kicking with little jerks.

"Oh, honey," Erin cooed, picking her up and holding her close. Caitlin immediately grew quiet, snuffling against Erin's neck, her tiny hands tangling in her mother's hair.

Erin frowned as she cuddled her. Her baby felt warmer than usual. Erin touched her head. Definitely warmer. The thermometer she had wasn't working properly so she had no way of checking if she was running a fever or not.

Should she take her to the doctor? Would it seem pointless? She wished she knew what to do. Jodie was in Great Falls today, and there was no answer when she called Lauren. She tried her aunt Laura's phone, but there was no response there, either.

Caitlin arched her back, growing more distressed, and Erin's concern grew. She pulled her phone out and did a quick search of fevers in babies, hoping to find something. Everything she read recommended medication and tepid baths.

Caitlin's cries became more frantic.

Should she bring her to the hospital? What if it was nothing?

Erin closed the browser on her phone and went to her contacts. Maybe Vic would know how to get a hold of Lauren. She dialed the number, holding Caitlin close, walking back and forth and growing more anxious with each step.

"Hello, this is Vic's phone, but it's Dean talking."

Erin's heart jumped into her throat. "Um…this is Erin…" She was disappointed how the simple sound of his voice could send her into a tailspin. "I need to talk to Lauren."

"She's not here. She and Vic went out and Vic left his phone behind."

"She's not answering her phone," Erin said, unable to keep the fear out of her voice.

"Are you okay? You sound worried."

"I'm fine. It…it's Caitlin."

"What about her? Is she okay?"

"I don't know. She's running a fever and I don't know how bad it is because the thermometer I bought doesn't register." She sucked in a quick breath realizing how panicky she sounded. "What kind of mother has a mal-functioning thermometer?"

"A mother who just moved and is probably still un-packing," Dean said.

His words made her feel better about herself. Just a little. "But still—"

"Are you at home? Do you want me to bring you to the doctor?"

"I don't know what to do." And for the first time since she had moved into this house located on an isolated corner of the ranch she understood her sisters' concern about her moving here. She should have found a place in town. Closer to the hospital. She was a terrible, selfish mother.

"I could drive myself."

"I'm sure you can, but if I drive you in you won't be distracted. Why don't I come anyway and bring you to the hospital. What do you think of that?"

Erin hesitated. It was a battle between a fear of and a deep yearning for seeing him again.

"I promise I won't try to kiss you," he added.

He sounded like he was teasing her, but his voice held a faint edge and she knew it was a response to her reaction to his kiss.

"I can drive myself," she repeated. But even as she bravely spoke the words she heard the faint tremble in her voice.

And Dean must have heard it, too.

"I'll be right there," he said, then ended the call.

Erin held Caitlin close, a mixture of emotions tumbling through her as she set her own phone down.

Dean was coming, after all.

She wanted to see him.

But at the same time, she didn't.

It's all for your daughter, she admonished herself.

And somehow that made her feel a bit better.

The smell of the hospital brought back too many bad memories for Dean.

He fidgeted in the hard leather chair just outside of Emergency, remembering too well the agonizing pain that had ripped through him the last time he was here.

He had been stabilized and from here it had been a speedy ambulance ride to Bozeman where he spent a month, then back here for the long haul of therapy and the slow recovery he had neglected.

Just as he formulated that thought, Mike Sawchuk, the very physiotherapist he'd been avoiding, strode down the hallway, his rubber shoes squeaking on the shining floor.

"Hey, Dean, what brings you here?" Mike stopped by Dean's chair, his hands shoved in the pockets of his track pants, the overhead lights gleaming off his shaved head. "Do I dare to hope you're here to make an appointment with me?"

Dean shifted uncomfortably under Mike's slightly mocking look. "I know I haven't followed up—"

"For the past couple months," Mike interrupted. He was grinning, but Dean heard the reprimand in his voice. "You know that you need to keep this up. You're going to lose mobility if you don't."

A myriad of excuses jumped forward, but Dean knew Mike would accept none of them.

"How has the leg been?" Mike asked, dropping into a chair across from him as if he had all the time in the world.

"Actually a bit better. I even went riding the other day."

"Really? That's progress."

While Mike would know about the pain riding caused, he had no idea of the fear. No one did.

Except Erin.

But he had gotten through that, as well.

On a plug horse Erin's baby could ride.

He dismissed the critical thought. It was still riding. A small step to be sure, but a step.

"But you still have to be careful to make sure you don't have the wrong muscles overcompensating and causing problems down the road," Mike said. "I know you can feel like you're having some success now, but you need a comprehensive program to work all your muscle groups properly."

"I guess" was all Dean could muster. "I didn't feel like I was getting anywhere. It seemed pointless."

"Baby steps, if you'll pardon the expression." A hint of frustration entered Mike's voice. "Building a strong foundation to work off of. I'd like to see you come more often. Give me a chance to show you what can happen. Even though you rode that horse I'm sure it hurt and I'm sure you're feeling it yet."

Dean shifted awkwardly in his chair, as if in memory of the pain which kept him from working for a couple of days. He had felt pretty good after riding, but the next day he'd been hurting just as Mike had correctly assumed. He hadn't called Erin to tell her why he wasn't coming. He didn't want to recognize that part of it was the discomfort he felt, but a larger part was her reaction to his kiss.

"So, what do you say? Give me a decent chance to help you get more mobile?"

For some reason the sympathetic looks Erin had given him when he'd tried to get on the horse, when he'd had almost fallen in her living room, dropped into his brain. It still stung and he didn't want to see that again.

"Let me check my schedule" was all he was giving Mike for now.

"Taking physical therapy doesn't mean you're weak," Mike said, sounding even firmer than he had before. "It means you're smart."

Dean nodded at that, thinking of how happy Vic would be if he started therapy again. His brother had been nagging him for months to go back. To get riding again.

And if it made a difference?

Again his thoughts drifted to Erin.

"I'll call you next week," he said. "After I talk to my boss."

"Sounds good." Mike slapped his knees and then stood. "I can't fix everything, but I know we can get you walking better than you are now." Mike patted him on the shoulder, then walked away, whistling. Dean sighed as he watched him leave knowing he was in for a lot of work.

But if it helped?

He saw Mike slow down just as he saw Erin coming out of Emergency, holding Caitlin, wrapped in a light blanket, close to her chest. Mike stopped and seemed to be asking her something. Dean couldn't hear what they were saying, but it wasn't hard to miss the appreciative look on Mike's face. The physiotherapist lifted the blanket and smiled down at Caitlin, which bugged him more than he wanted to admit.

Then Erin laughed, which annoyed him further.

Dean slowly got to his feet, the ache in his muscles a reminder of what Mike had been saying and of his own limitations. He watched Mike saunter off, showcasing the obvious the difference between Dean and a healthier man.

The smile on Erin's face when she turned and saw Dean made him feel marginally better. She walked toward him, shifting her purse on her arm.

"What did the doctor say?" he asked, trying not to wince as he straightened out his leg.

"She's not running high fever. The doc figured it was just a cold, from a virus." She looked relieved. "But I should stop at the drugstore and pick up some medication and a new thermometer for her. If that's okay."

He nodded at her but couldn't get the sight of her and Mike out of his brain.

"So how do you know Sawchuk?"

"Michael?" Her soft smile didn't bode well for his own presence of mind. "I remember him from church. He led a Bible study I went to the summers I was here."

Of course he did, Dean thought, stifling a flash of annoyance.

Seriously, how could he be irritated with a guy who led Bible study? How petty was he?

When it came to Erin, he realized he didn't like comparing himself to Mike and being found wanting in so many ways.

"He's a physical therapist in the hospital here," Dean added, trying to be generous.

"I remember him talking about that," Erin said. Caitlin was crying again and Erin shot her daughter a look of concern.

"We should probably get that medicine for her," Dean offered.

"Yeah. I think so." As they walked toward the entrance, Erin slowed her steps to match Dean's—adding another layer to his insecurity—and put her hand on his arm. "Thanks so much for bringing me. I feel a bit foolish, seeing as how it was really nothing important, but I'm much more at ease now that she's seen the doctor."

"Then I'm glad I could help," he said, trying not to read more into her gentle touch than simple gratitude.

But as they walked together back to his truck he knew his feelings for Erin were becoming more difficult to sort out the more time he spent with her.

Chapter Ten

The gathering dusk closing in created a tiny cocoon in the cab of Dean's truck.

The radio played country music, a quiet counterpoint to the hum of the tires on the pavement and the faint snuffling coming from Caitlin tucked in her seat in the back. Dean had kindly waited while Erin opened the baby medicine they had just bought and gave some to Caitlin right away. It seemed to be working because she had stopped fussing about ten minutes ago.

"I think she's settling," Dean was saying, shooting a glance across the darkening cab.

The lights from the dashboard threw his features into interesting hollows and crags, highlighting how good-looking he really was.

Erin felt a curl of appreciation as he looked back to the road again. She had always thought he was attractive, but time had matured him and made him more handsome.

"Thanks again for driving me and for taking me to

the pharmacy," she said, relieved now that they were on their way back home and she knew Caitlin was okay.

"I wasn't that busy anyhow. I was just glad I answered Vic's phone when I did."

"Me, too."

They rode in silence for a few more miles, Erin clutching her purse and the bag from the pharmacy, feeling suddenly tongue-tied and shy.

He'd had the ability to do this to her in the past, but now her reticence was because of her shifting emotions. Bringing her and Caitlin to the hospital meant more to her than she wanted to acknowledge. It was what a friend did and thinking of Dean as a friend was disconcerting.

Dean reached over and turned the music up and it filled the silence hanging between them for the rest of the way to her place.

When they got to the house he turned the truck off and got out. Erin managed to get Caitlin's car seat out of the clips that held it secure and then Dean was beside her.

"Let me take something," he said, indicating her purse and the bags she was trying to juggle. While they were at the pharmacy she'd bought some diapers and a few other baby supplies.

She wanted to protest that she could manage, but it was nice to have help so she handed Dean the bags and she took her purse and the car seat.

Erin couldn't help the twinge of embarrassment she felt when she turned on a light and looked over her house. Her computer sat on the coffee table with a few rough sketches torn out of her sketchpad beside it. A basket of laundry, waiting to be folded, was pushed up against the couch. Dishes sat piled up on the counter in the kitchen and her blender, still rimed with leftover smoothie, sat in the sink.

"Sorry about the mess," she murmured as she carried Caitlin into the living room.

"Looks cozy," Dean said following her, bags rustling as he laid them on the kitchen table. "Lived-in."

Erin set the car seat on the floor and her daughter immediately expressed her displeasure. She quickly undid the buckles, laying the back of her hand against Caitlin's forehead as she slowly settled. Still warm but not as bad as before.

She was about to take her out of the car seat when her cell phone rang.

She glanced at the screen, her heart skipping a beat when she saw the number. It was the client she had been wooing for the past half year. A small publishing company that had just started up and was looking for someone to do marketing materials for them.

Caitlin started complaining just as she connected to take the call.

She answered the phone, fumbling one-handed with the clasp on Caitlin's car seat. "Hello, Erin McCauley here," she said, hoping she didn't sound as breathless as she felt.

"So glad we could finally connect," an unfamiliar voice said on the other end, speaking so loudly Erin had to hold the phone away from her ear. "Do you have some time to talk?"

She didn't really, she thought as Caitlin began crying again, but she wasn't about to tell a prospective client that.

Then Dean was beside her, brushing her hands gently away, motioning for her to take the call somewhere else. Erin shook her head, but he pulled the car seat away, taking the decision out of her hands.

"I'll take care of her," he whispered.

Erin was about to protest, but he shooed her away.

So she went into her bedroom to take the call.

Dean watched as Erin headed toward her bedroom, her phone clamped to her ear. Just before she closed the door behind her she glanced over at him. He gave her a thumbs-up and an encouraging smile.

"So, I guess it's just you and me for now," Dean said looking down at Caitlin, who was staring up at him as if wondering who her mother had left her with now.

She looked tiny in the car seat, held in by straps wider than her arms. Then she waved her hands, sticking out her feet, and her mouth curled up in protest. She whimpered and looked like she was about to cry. He guessed she wanted to come out of the car seat.

So he began the complicated task of figuring out how to unbuckle this little mite from the contraption. He fought with the straps, fighting down his frustration. He knew how to throw a double diamond hitch on a packhorse, rig up a running martingale, saddle up a rangy bronc in a metal bucking chute, but this set of straps and buckles confounded him.

"I don't suppose you can help me out," he muttered as Caitlin let out another squawk. He didn't want to interrupt Erin. She had looked so excited when the call had come through and he guessed it had something to do with the work she did from her home.

He looked at the harness from a few angles, trying not to feel pressured by baby's screwed-up face and flailing arms. He pushed on a button and, yahtzee, there it was. One of the straps came unclipped. Moving quickly now he pulled the other one free and then, finally, lifted a squirming and somewhat upset little girl out of the seat.

She felt so tiny, like she was just a bundle of bones and skin. Other than a puppy, he had never held anything this small.

Not sure what to do, he rocked her slowly, walking over to the couch.

He sat down, swung his legs up and lay back easing out a sigh of relief. He adjusted Caitlin, hoping he didn't hurt her as he shifted her arms and legs. She laid her head in the crook of his neck, her snuffling cries quieting.

"I got the touch," he murmured as he felt her melt against him.

She still felt overly warm, but she didn't appear to be distressed. He wondered if she needed a diaper change but figured mastering the car seat was enough for now.

Caitlin lifted her head and it wobbled as she looked at him, her lips pursed in a perfect cupid's bow. Her eyes crossed and then her head dropped again, her one hand inching upward. Her minuscule fingers latched onto his shirt and as he snuggled her close he felt a melting in his heart.

How could such a tiny person tug so easily on his soul? And so quickly?

He brushed his cheek over the downy fluff that was her hair, surprised at how sweet she smelled.

He'd never held a baby before, but somehow he felt comfortable with her. Maybe he was better at this than he thought.

She moved a bit, then her breathing became more even and in minutes she was asleep.

Her warmth, the amazing feeling of her in his arms created an unforeseen softness in his heart.

I could get used to this.

But no sooner did that thought slip into his mind than his musings shifted to Erin. She hadn't exactly encouraged his kiss, but, as he mulled it over for about the hundredth time since it happened, she hadn't exactly discouraged it, either. And behind that belief crept the vague hope that things were changing between them.

Did he dare allow that?

He looked down at Caitlin now sleeping on his chest, one tiny hand curled up beside her face, her lashes a faint shadow against her round cheek. This little munchkin came with Erin. She was part of the package and an extra responsibility he couldn't treat lightly.

Could he do this? Could he take this on?

Then she sighed lightly, her fingers twitching, and again a surprising wave of affection came over him. And with that, he had another reason to try to get his mobility back.

Chapter Eleven

The client, Gretchen Shorey, was effusive about the samples Erin had sent, and complimented her on her versatility. Erin had sent a couple of mock-ups of some book covers. One was for a nonfiction self-help book, the other a dystopian novel for young adults. Plus some basic ad concepts for marketing connected to the books.

"I'm so glad you like them," Erin said, feeling a rush of pleasure at the praise. She hadn't done much work the past half year and was afraid she had lost her edge and connections.

She'd gotten this opportunity from a fellow graphic artist she was friends with on Facebook, who had turned down a chance to work for them. Her friend had encouraged Erin to send some samples and cold-call, and here she was.

"Love them. Fantastic work. So, what we're looking at is print as well as ebook. Got to cover all the angles these days," Gretchen said with a quick laugh. "We're just starting out and don't have a huge lineup. I can't promise you all the covers but I do have some connections to a tech company which might be looking for ad work as well."

At her words Erin felt a surge of hope for future work. She didn't want to tell her sisters that she had been a bit concerned. It would make her look irresponsible but this affirmation made her relax her unease.

They talked details and compensation and Erin grew even more positive. When she finally ended the call she held onto the phone a moment as if to cement what had just happened.

Thank you, Lord, were the first words that slipped into her mind as she released a long, slow breath, looking around the room. Her eyes fell on the clock first then Caitlin's crib. She realized with a start that in the excitement and the pleasure of talking shop for the past twenty minutes, she had forgotten about her daughter.

She shoved her phone into the back pocket of her blue jeans and yanked open the door of her bedroom.

But she couldn't see either Dean or Caitlin. Heart pounding now she rushed to the front door, passing the couch on her way.

What she saw there made her come to a halt.

Dean lay on the couch, his head on the armrest, his legs stretched out along the length of the couch. Caitlin lay curled like a ball on his chest, his arms curved around her.

Both were asleep.

Erin stood over them, her breath quickening at the picture of her daughter in Dean's arms. The planes of his face had softened, his mouth was relaxed, his head angled toward Caitlin's. He looked like he was protecting her and the sight made Erin's heart hitch.

Dean, a man she had never thought of as fatherly, looked so comfortable and at ease. As if he had done this many times before.

She thought back to Sam, Caitlin's real father, and how faithless he had been to his own child. The child in his wife's arms when she'd come to see Erin.

Don't think about that. You didn't know.

But here was Dean, holding her daughter while he slept.

A quick glance at her watch showed her that it was getting on to 5:00. Supper time. She had pulled out a casserole Lauren had delivered yesterday and had figured on heating it up.

Should she ask Dean to stay?

She shrugged off the question, trying not to let herself read too much into the situation. He had brought her to town—the least she could do was feed him.

As the casserole warmed up in the oven she set the table for two, feeling a hint of intimacy as she laid the plates out across from each other. Was she presuming too much? Would he want to stay? It wasn't like she'd been the most cordial to him.

She pushed the thoughts aside and grabbed cutlery. Just a simple dinner with old friends. Yet even as she told herself that, another part of her mocked that idea. Dean had never been a "friend."

She busied herself in the kitchen, feeling rather domestic. A man holding her sleeping baby on the couch while she made supper. Like a little family.

The thought snuck up on her as she cut up vegetables for the salad and try as she might, she couldn't dislodge it. Because with that thought came the memory of Dean's kiss—something else she hadn't been able to dismiss.

She heard a groan, then a heavy sigh and she guessed Dean was waking up.

"Hey, little girl," she heard him mutter. "Is your mommy still yapping on the phone?"

She smiled at that, unable to take offense at his comment because she could hear the underlying humor in his tone.

Then she heard another groan and wondered if his leg bothered him. She hurried over to the couch just as he sat up, still holding Caitlin. He grimaced as he did so and her suspicions were confirmed.

"Here, let me help you," she said, reaching out to take Caitlin from him.

She was surprised when he didn't protest. But before he handed over her daughter, he brushed his cheek over her head. It was such a small thing and if she hadn't been watching she would have missed it.

But it landed in her heart and stuck there.

She eased Caitlin out of his arms, and holding her close, brought her to her bedroom, gently laying her down in the crib.

As she looked down she felt a pang of vulnerability blended with a fierce protectiveness. Caitlin had only Erin to take care of her. She depended on her fully.

While her feelings for Dean were changing she knew she had to be careful.

Yet, in spite of her self-talk, as she closed the door behind her and saw Dean standing in her living room she felt an eager anticipation.

* * *

"That was delicious," Dean said, wiping his mouth with a napkin. He folded it up and set it on his plate, shooting a cautious smile over at Erin. "Thanks for having me."

When she'd invited him to stay for supper his first reaction was to say no. But the welcoming smile on her face made him change his mind. That and the fact that she said she'd wanted to pay him back for helping her out.

Balancing the scales he understood.

"You're welcome." She fiddled with her knife, moving it to one side of her plate then another. Then she glanced over at him again. "It was nice to have company for dinner, though I can't claim any credit. Lauren made the casserole."

"She's a good sister."

"She and Jodie both are, in their own ways, though they do like to boss me around." Erin fiddled a bit more with her knife.

"She has that ability," Dean said with a grin. "But in the end it worked out good." Then he caught himself, realizing how that sounded. "I mean, for me. For riding," he amended quickly. "I hadn't been on a horse since and I was scared and—"

Erin reached over and put her hand on his arm. "I know what you were saying." But she kept her hand there. "And I appreciate what you told me. About being afraid. That can't have been easy to admit."

"Always been told to cowboy up," he said with a short laugh.

"I never did understand what that meant or where it came from. I mean, why up? Why not down?"

Dean laughed. "Not sure myself. It gets tossed around at rodeos so much no one every really stops to think about it. Anyhow, it took a depressing amount of cowboy upping to get on that old nag Jodie picked out for me."

"I think you showed more courage getting on that old nag, who just so happened to be a horse I used to ride, than getting on any saddle bronc you've ever ridden."

"I don't know about that," he said, standing to clear the table. "But I'll just say thanks."

She smiled and got up, as well.

He brought his plate to the counter and then returned for the rest.

"You don't have to stay to help with the dishes. I'm sure you've got things you need to do," she said, setting the half-full casserole dish on the counter.

He did have to get back to the ranch to help Vic with the tractor that had broken down yesterday when they were loading up bales for Monty Bannister. And his mom wanted him to help her clear out her greenhouse.

But he wanted to prolong this time with Erin. Vic could clean up the clogged fuel line on his own. And the greenhouse could wait.

"Not really. I don't mind to help."

"I don't have a dishwasher," she warned him.

All the better.

"Just another chance for me to cowboy up," he joked.

She chuckled, which made him feel better than it should.

"So did you make up your mind about your flooring?" he said as he scraped the dishes while she took care of the leftovers. "I said I was coming to help you measure..." He let the sentence trail off. He felt bad, but after Tuesday he needed to retreat and lick his wounds.

"That's okay. I figured it out myself. And I got it ordered already."

"Wow, you're efficient."

"I've learned to do things for myself."

Her comment raised another blitz of questions and curiosity about her life before she came back to Saddlebank. "You said that you rehabbed a house?" he asked as he set the plates aside.

"With my roommates, yes. And Sam."

"Is that what he did for a living?" He knew he was pushing his luck, but he felt a need to know more about this shadowy figure who was, hopefully, part of Erin's past.

"No. Nothing like that. He's a doctor. Surgeon in fact."

Dean shoved the stopper in the sink, nodding. Surgeon. Rich, probably.

"And if you're wondering why I left him, well, I got pregnant and he didn't want Caitlin and...there were other reasons."

He turned to her, hearing the understated pain in her voice. And though he wondered what those "other reasons" were, it didn't matter. She sounded sad.

"That must have been hard," he said, turning on the taps to fill the sink.

"I was the one who ended the relationship." Erin set the casserole in the fridge, then closed the door, her back to him. "Things hadn't been great before...

before I got pregnant. But…" Her voice broke and she lowered her head. Dean, unsure of what to do, took a chance and walked over to her. He put his hand on her shoulder to comfort her.

She straightened as if gathering strength from a place he supposed she had drawn from before.

"Sorry," she said, her voice matter-of-fact.

"You don't have to apologize," he said, keeping his voice quiet as if to encourage her to entrust him with what she held back.

She turned to him then, a wry smile on her face. "I have got to stop making a habit of getting all sappy in front of you. I guess it's just with Caitlin and all…"

Her voice trailed away as she looked up at him, her soft blue eyes locked on his. They stood close enough that he could smell the scent of her shampoo, catch the faint smudge of mascara under her lower lashes.

"You're feeling vulnerable," he finished for her.

"That and…other things."

It was the breathy way she spoke those words, the way she kept her eyes on his that raised his hopes and ignited old dreams.

In spite of his promise not to kiss her again, he lowered his head, pausing within inches of her lips as if to give her the opportunity to pull away. Instead, she closed the distance between them.

Their lips met, warm and soft, a connection that shook him to his core. He held her mouth against his for a few more seconds and then she gently drew back.

He rested his forehead against her, her face a delightful blur.

"So, this changes things," he said, his voice quiet as if he didn't want to disturb the moment.

"Yes. It does," she returned. He heard her swallow and then, regretfully, she lowered her hand and drew back, resting against the door of the refrigerator, her hands now at her sides.

He pulled back as well, trying to get a read from her expression. Her lips held a smile and though she looked down he caught a sparkle in her eyes, a crinkle at the corners.

"I know this is a complication for you," he said, preferring to voice her potential objections.

"I do have Caitlin to think of," she said, acknowledging where he was going.

"And her father?" he prompted, needing to get that much out of the way before they moved in the direction he thought they might be headed.

"Like I told you, not in the picture."

"I'm glad to hear that," he said. "I'm not so sure I want to share."

She sucked in a quick breath, her eyes shooting to his.

"Really?"

"Yeah, really."

"Well, it was a bad relationship that was a mistake. The only good thing that came of that mess was Caitlin." Her quiet vehemence made him wonder if there was more to the situation. Right now, however, he didn't want to know. Because talking about Caitlin's father brought him into the present and Dean wanted him planted firmly in Erin's past.

But he did want to fix the regret and bitterness in her voice.

"I know how easy it is to make mistakes," he said. "I've learned a lot about God's grace and how He helps us work through those missteps in life."

She looked up at him, frowning, and he wondered if she was going to, once again, push any talk of God aside.

"You sound so wise."

"You sound so surprised."

Her laughter made him feel good.

"Anything I know now was hard-won," he said, fingering a strand of hair back from her face, tucking it behind her ear. "I learned how valuable life is and not to mess around with it. That and to let go of my pride."

He thought of his chat with Mike and how long it had taken him to admit he needed the man's help. But as he looked down at Erin he knew he had another reason to improve his life.

"We have that in common, then," she said, touching his hand with hers.

"How so?"

She twined her fingers through his in a gesture that spoke of a comfortable familiarity. "I struggled with pride, too. I was ashamed to come back here, a single mother. My sisters and I have always had our roles. Jodie was always the rebel. Lauren was always the responsible one. But me, I was always the good girl. The one that reminded them to go to church, to read their Bible. To stay close to God." She released a short laugh. "So you need to understand how hard it was to come back to them not only a single mother but someone who had strayed from the faith she had encouraged them to follow."

"But you know you can always go back," he said. "And if God accepts a selfish and cocky cowboy like me I know He will take back someone like you. Someone who is so—"

She put her fingers on his lips as if to forestall anything else he might say. "Please, don't say it again."

He didn't, knowing that it would make her upset.

"Come to church" was all he said instead.

"I'll think about it."

He wanted to say more but he gave in to an impulse and kissed her again, cupping her face in his hands.

And when he looked into her eyes he caught a shadow of pain that made him wonder yet again what she wasn't telling him.

Though he wanted to know now he also knew she had to learn to trust him.

He just hoped that what she was holding back wasn't something that could break the tender relationship growing between them.

Chapter Twelve

Erin stood with Caitlin in her arms in the back of the church, firmly in the grip of second thoughts, as she looked over the scattered congregation.

Her sisters weren't here yet. They had promised they would meet her and sit with her, but she didn't see them.

She regretted the impulse she had given in to this morning. It was because of Dean she was here. His gently spoken invitation to come to church was a surprise, but it was also encouraging.

Her aunt Laura was playing the piano, the sounds of the familiar hymn making Erin smile.

She looked down at Caitlin, wondering again if she should have brought her to church. According to the digital thermometer Dean had insisted on buying for her, her fever was down. He had checked her a number of times, apparently fascinated with how the thermometer worked. Erin had, however, drawn the line on Dean pasting a bug-shaped fever patch he had purchased on Caitlin's forehead that would give a readout of her temperature. He'd tossed those in the shopping cart, as well.

She stroked Caitlin's soft cheek, smiling at the memory of her little shopping trip with Dean yesterday. He'd acted like a fussy old grandma as he read every label of every product making sure she bought exactly the right kind.

"Erin. Welcome to the services."

She looked up as Brooke Dillon came up beside her, laying her hand on Erin's shoulder. Behind her slouched George Bamford, the owner of the Grill and Chill. He gave Erin a quick uptick of his chin, which, she guessed, was his version of hello. "Nice hair," Brooke said with a grin.

"Thanks again. I really like it."

Brooke fluffed Erin's hair, then fluttered her hands in an apologetic gesture. "Sorry. Habit. Is Lauren or Jodie here?"

"Not yet, but I'm early."

"You can come and sit with us, if you want."

The offer eased away her misgivings about coming to church today. "Thanks so much, but I think I'll wait."

"And here's your enchanting little girl." Brooke fingered the blanket away from Caitlin's face, smiling that tender smile women reserved for little babies. "We do have a nursery downstairs."

"I know, but I felt too nervous bringing her there. Besides, she hasn't been feeling well so I want to keep her close."

"And she's such a good baby. If she can sleep through all the noise in the beauty shop, I'm sure she'll sleep just fine with your aunt Laura playing." Brooke's mouth fell open, her eyes wide with alarm. "I mean, she'll sleep well. Not that your aunt is a boring player or anything.

Just quieter than the group we usually have. They're pretty loud in comparison, that's all I was trying—"

"She gets it," George interrupted, putting his hand on Brooke's shoulder. He angled Erin a questioning look. "Right?"

"I knew what you meant," she assured Brooke with a smile.

"Let's sit down," George added.

But before he left he paused to look down at Caitlin, who still slept. "Cute kid," he said tersely.

Then he took Brooke's arm and together they walked down the aisle to an empty seat.

Erin grinned as she watched George step aside to let Brooke sit down. As soon as he was settled he draped his arm over Brooke's shoulder. *Guess it's official*, she thought. Sitting in church together showed as much of a commitment as an engagement ring.

When her phone buzzed, Erin jumped, feeling guilty for not turning it off. She finagled it one-handed out of her purse and thumbed the screen to life, frowning as she saw Lauren's name. "Hello," she said walking toward the door, speaking quietly as she sat down on an empty chair just near the door.

"It's Lauren," Erin heard her sister say in a tone of disgust. "And big surprise, we'll be late. Finn's working so we took Jodie's car and it broke down, another big surprise." She heard a laughing comment in the background. Jodie probably. Then Lauren was talking, her own voice muffled. "I don't care. I told you we should have let Vic pick us up."

Erin heard a sassy rejoinder and smiled as her sisters lobbed snide comments back and forth.

"So you're saying I should just go in by myself?" she asked, hoping to catch Lauren's attention.

"I know you wanted us there for you and I'm sorry that we can't be." She sounded so contrite, but edged with that was frustration with their flighty younger sister.

"I'm a big girl."

"I know you are," Lauren said, "But I also know you were hoping we could be there to support you."

"I'll be fine."

They made plans for after church. They were going to have lunch and then work on decorations for Jodie and Finn's wedding, which was coming up in a couple of months. Erin said goodbye, then turned her phone off and dropped it in her oversize purse-slash-diaper bag. She shrugged her purse over her shoulder, adjusting the blanket around her baby.

People walked past her, smiling in greeting. She didn't recognize any of them and she wondered if she should go in.

But it would look silly if she left now.

She smoothed one hand over her skirt, checking it again. She hadn't worn it since she got pregnant. In fact, she was pleased it still fit. The skirt had been an impulse buy when Sam had canceled one of their dates. Again.

Erin looked down at her daughter, feeling a twinge of sorrow at the life she was giving her. Erin had always hoped to have a husband who loved her and respected her. A man she would be faithful to, unlike her own mother. They were going to have three, maybe four kids. Live in a house out in the country so she could have the chickens she always wanted. The outdoor clothesline. Maybe a horse or two for her children.

She pushed down the thoughts, relegating them to the same place she had put other dreams that had died. Her mom and dad back together again and all of them on the ranch that she loved so much.

Caitlin yawned, her tiny mouth opening so wide Erin thought it had to hurt. Then she shifted around and opened her eyes zeroing in on Erin.

I'll take care of you, little bug, she thought, smiling down at her precious daughter. *I promise.*

She was about to walk back to the entrance to the sanctuary when the door behind her opened, bringing with it the cooling air of the approaching fall.

She turned and there was Dean.

He wore a plain white shirt and dark jeans that rode low on his hips, cinched with a leather belt holding a simple buckle. His hair was still damp and his cheeks shone from being freshly shaved. And when he saw her his smile lit up his face.

"Hey, there, you came." He walked over to her in his now-familiar hitching step. He stopped beside her, towering over her, smiling down. "And how's the babe?" Without waiting to hear an update he laid the back of his hand on Caitlin's tiny forehead, dwarfing it. "She feels good, though it's hard to say without a fever bug on her forehead."

He sounded so serious, but when Erin met his gaze she caught a twitch of his lips and a wrinkling at the corner of his eyes.

"That fancy thermometer you bought works great."

she retorted. "I don't need to slap sticky bugs on her head."

"I think a little frog would go perfectly with that blanket," he said, curling it around Caitlin's arm.

His gentle touches, light adjustments of Caitlin's blanket and the way he looked down at her dove almost as deeply into her soul as his kisses had.

Her cheeks warmed at the memory of that gently smiling mouth on hers. She knew she was falling for him. That he was becoming more and more important every day.

She just wished she knew how to proceed.

"By the way, Vic called," Dean continued, looking back at her. "He's on his way to rescue your sisters. So if you want to wait for them we can."

Erin knew the service would start in less than five minutes. She didn't want to disrupt it by coming in late.

"No. Let's go in."

As soon as she spoke the words she felt silly. As if she assumed that Dean would be with her.

But he just nodded and together they found a seat close to the back.

And as they did, Erin felt a surprising peace.

That peace had nothing to do with sitting beside Dean, she tried to tell herself. Or his arm brushing hers. Or that she felt, for the first time in over a year, that her life was falling into a good place.

The words of the songs Aunt Laura was playing were projected on the large screen at the front of the church and a sense of homecoming washed over her.

The song was an old favorite of hers and she wondered if Aunt Laura had chosen it or if it was simply a coincidence.

"My comfort is in You, Lord. As long as life goes on, in life and death, with every breath, I call You the risen Son."

She felt a prickling in her throat as she sang the words in a church she had attended as a young girl and then as a teenager. And now she was here, many years later, holding her child in her arms. The prodigal daughter.

Her voice broke on the second verse that spoke of God's yearning faithfulness and how He calls and waits to *"...wipe away tears and calm deepest fears and erase our every stain."* She thought of how far she had strayed, of promises she had broken and caused to be broken. The stains on her own life.

But this old song with its promises of a faithful, loving God whom she had known in a different time of her life and who, she knew deep in her soul, still loved her as she was at this moment, permeated her lonely, parched soul.

Dean knew he was supposed to keep his attention on the pastor, but it was difficult with Erin sitting right beside him. He knew he took a chance asking her to come sit with him especially with her holding her baby. He knew people would wonder and talk just as they had when he first started attending church. Not just about Erin coming back to Saddlebank as a single mother, but about Erin and Dean sitting together in church.

That was usually reserved for the postengagement part of any relationship. Like Brooke and George.

Always was a rebel, he thought, adjusting his hips to compensate for a growing cramp in his leg.

Tomorrow he was calling Mike to set up a schedule of appointments. He had hesitated, balking at the time it would take him away from work, but he also felt a renewed sense of purpose. And it was all thanks to the beautiful woman sitting beside him.

He glanced over at Erin, who was looking down at Caitlin. Her features possessed a serenity that tugged at his heart. She reminded him of his own mother who was so caring, so loving. Who, he knew, had prayed daily that he would come back to faith.

He smiled just as Erin looked up at him, their eyes holding again. Then she looked away to the pastor.

"Grace is a word that, unlike many other church words like charity or love or faithfulness, has stood the test of time," Pastor Dykstra was saying. "Grace still lingers in our vocabulary as a touchstone for the undeserved. For something received, given freely. The only catch is we have to reach out and take it." Pastor Dykstra paused there as if to give his congregation time to ponder this thought.

Dean knew this as well, but hearing the pastor speak of grace while sitting beside the girl who was, at one time, someone so unreachable made the notion of that same grace all the more real and true.

He didn't deserve Erin. But somehow, in some weird and strange way, they had found each other at this point in their lives.

He knew he didn't deserve her any more than he deserved God's grace. Both were a gift and he knew he was foolish not to take it.

Chapter Thirteen

"She's so adorable. Look at her tiny hands." Ellen Bannister let Caitlin's finger curl around hers as she smiled down at the baby, the light reflecting off her glasses as she sat down beside Erin in the pew.

The service was over and Ellen, who had been sitting across the aisle from her and Dean, had come over as soon as the last song was done, shooing Dean away so she could sit beside Erin.

The wrinkles near her friendly eyes deepened as Ellen smiled at Caitlin. From her memories of the older woman, Erin knew the lines around her mouth came from laughter. "She is such a gift, you know." Erin heard the sincerity in her voice and, slowly, as other women came to them, she felt as if she was cocooned in caring and acceptance and, for lack of a better word, grace.

The minister's words settled in her soul as she looked around the gathered women, all of various ages. All smiling at her. All accepting her.

Why had she been so hesitant to come?

Then she felt a hug from behind and a hand on her shoulder and she turned to see her sisters standing there.

"Sorry we were late. We sat farther back," Jodie said, bending over Erin to look at her niece. "Hey, baby girl, were you good for your mommy?"

"Thank goodness Vic was able to pick us up or we'd never have gotten here," Lauren complained.

"We could have hitchhiked," Jodie murmured, unperturbed by Lauren's annoyance.

"Right. On a Sunday. Like we'd get picked up."

Erin had to smile at her sisters' exchange, remembering other times when their bickering would be irritating. Now it was familiar. It was home.

"Loved your playing this morning," one of the ladies gathered around was saying as Aunt Laura came to join them. Laura just smiled, her attention focused on Caitlin as she sat down on the other side of her niece and gave her a quick hug.

"So good to see you here," she said, her hands lingering on Erin's face as she held her gaze.

"I loved the one song you played."

Aunt Laura just smiled and gave her another hug. "I know you liked it."

So she had chosen it for her.

"And I'm looking forward to you girls joining me for lunch," she said, looking at Jodie and Lauren, as well. "And your young men."

"Finn is working," Jodie said with an exaggerated pout.

"Well, how about Vic and his younger brother, Dean?" She looked back at Erin with a conspiratorial smile and Erin knew that Aunt Laura had seen her sitting with Dean.

"Great idea," Jodie said. "I mean, he's going to practically be family once Lauren and Vic get married."

"Hardly," Lauren put in, still sounding confused. "He's going to be my brother-in-law."

"And you're our sister," Jodie said in a tone that seemed to say that was the end of that.

Half an hour later, the five of them were sitting around a large wooden table tucked in one corner of Aunt Laura's apartment above the flower shop.

"It's just soup and buns," she said with an apologetic tone as she set a large, dented pot on the table.

"Smells good for just soup and buns," Vic said, giving her a charming smile.

Was Aunt Laura simpering? Erin had to chuckle. Not that she blamed her. With his dark slashing brows, deep brown eyes and strong jaw, Vic was one appealing man.

Though Erin found her gaze drifting more to Dean than his brother. She was pleased he had accepted her aunt's invitation to join them for lunch. But while it meant she could spend more time with him, she felt bad for him because it also meant that time was spent under the watchful eyes of her sisters and aunt.

"Did Caitlin settle down okay?" her aunt asked as Jodie set a plate of buns on the table, then sat down to join them.

"She did. And how could she not in such a pretty room." Erin was touched that her aunt had a room set up for her baby. A crib complete with a mobile and a pink bedding set took up one corner and a change table was pushed along a wall. Both were a soft ivory and looked brand-new. One wall was papered in a green-and-white striped paper and pink-and-green balls of tissue hung from the ceiling in one corner of the room.

It gave her a peculiar feeling. The same feeling she'd experienced at church this morning and in Brooke's hair salon. She'd thought she would have to come back to Saddlebank humiliated and ashamed, but it seemed that the people of the town were far more welcoming than she had given them credit for.

Aunt Laura just smiled and shrugged off the compliment, then she looked around the table. "This is so lovely," she said, a hitch in her voice. "I surely didn't think that all my girls would come back home. And settle down here."

This engendered more smiles and a gentle murmuring of assent. Then just before Aunt Laura bowed her head to pray, Erin shot a quick glance across the table at Dean. She was disconcerted to see him looking intently at her.

Just as he had in church.

She couldn't look away, nor did she want to. Feelings uncertain and new arced between them and with that came a sense of anticipation. Of waiting.

And more than ever Erin looked forward to tomorrow when Dean would be helping her in the house. And there wouldn't be anyone else around.

"I'm so glad we took out that carpet on Tuesday," Erin said as she handed Dean another board. "I still can't believe how much gunk there was underneath it."

"You'll be happy once this is done, I'm sure," Dean replied, slowly getting to his feet.

Jan had shown up on Monday with his crew and by the end of the day the new windows were in and the siding patched up. Erin felt as if she were closer to being ready for the winter that was slinking around the corner.

Tuesday they had ripped out the carpet and they started on the flooring on Wednesday. Today was Friday and they were still working on it. It could have been done quicker, but Dean had left every afternoon for physiotherapy.

She had to admit she'd been a touch flattered when Dean's therapist had flirted with her at the hospital.

But he wasn't her type.

She looked at the cowboy across the room, a man who at one time she hadn't considered her type, either. As he laid the last bit of carpet on the pile she saw a grimace creep across his face and guessed that between all the work and the extra physio he was hurting. But she knew Dean wouldn't appreciate it if she said anything.

Erin grabbed a broom and began sweeping up all the dirt that lay on the subfloor. "I'm so glad I never laid Caitlin down on the floor. Who knows what kind of germs and grossness she would have inhaled," she said.

"It's been here a few years," Dean said with a wry look as he stretched. He glanced around the house, his hand in the small of his back. "You put a few more pictures up since yesterday," he said.

She nodded, glancing over at some of the artwork she had done when she took her graphics art course in Nashville. "Just some stuff I've dragged around in my travels."

He walked over to a sketch, in which her father was

kneeling down by a newborn calf, still holding the reins of his horse, who stood obediently and quietly behind him.

"That's a great picture," he said, his hands resting on his hips.

"One of the few tender moments I got to see in my dad," she said.

"Keith was a tough guy." Dean gave her a wry look. "I got to be on the receiving end of a few tongue lashings from him in my heyday. Every time he pulled me over I got the lecture."

"I can imagine."

"I'm sure he told you lots of stories about me."

She heard the faintly defensive tone in his voice and shook her head, slanting him a smile that she hoped showed him it didn't matter anymore. "Dad never said much about the people he dealt with. Though he was a demanding father, he was a principled man."

The closest he ever got to bringing anything home from work was to warn her to be careful who she went out with, glaring at her over his reading glasses, his bushy eyebrows bristling.

"It mustn't have been easy for you girls. Coming back here for a few months every summer and then going back to Knoxville." Dean took the dustpan from her, caught her by the hand and helped her to her feet. Except he didn't let go right away.

Erin looked down at their twined hands, smiling at the sight. It seemed so normal now. The past few days had been a slow movement together in the same direction. The delightful beginnings of a new relationship.

She considered his question as she tightened her grip on his hand. "My sisters didn't enjoy it that much, but

I liked it. I missed the ranch when my mother left my father."

Dean was quiet a moment, then set the dustpan aside, catching her by the other hand. "So why did your mother leave?"

Erin hadn't been there that day when her father had ordered her mother and the girls off the ranch. But she'd heard about it from Jodie. Whispers under bedcovers in their grandmother's house in Knoxville. Quiet conversations away from their mother who grew more withdrawn every day.

"My parents didn't have a happy marriage. Aunt Laura told my sisters that Mom got pregnant with me and Lauren before they were married so Dad stepped up to his responsibilities. He cut short his dream of becoming a marine and became a deputy instead. I guess things just went downhill from there." Erin was disappointed at how her voice faltered, but she pushed on. "In the last years of their marriage Mom was cheating on him and when Dad found out, he told her to leave. Apparently there was even a time when Dad suspected Jodie wasn't his daughter."

"And you girls? Didn't he want you to stay with him?"

"I don't know. My mother never talked about it and she never sent us here. That happened after she died. Our grandmother thought Dad should take responsibility, and sent us here over the summer. I didn't mind as much as my sisters did. I enjoyed being on the ranch." She glanced over at the picture. "I loved going out with Dad to check the cows when they were calving. We'd ride all day, say practically nothing to each other, but it was a time of closeness that Lauren and Jodie never had with him. But he was still a complicated man." She thought of the letter he had written to her full of apologies and regrets.

Dean tipped her chin up with his finger and as she looked into his eyes she saw understanding, which slowly warmed to something else entirely. When he kissed her again, her hands clung to his, as if to anchor herself. Then he drew back and smiled. "I hope I'm not a complicated man."

She heard the underlying tone in his voice. The unspoken question.

He wasn't complicated, but he did create a complication. Working a man into her life wasn't as easy as it once was. She now had Caitlin to think of.

But behind that warning came the memory of Dean holding her baby. How happy he was that Sam wasn't involved in their lives.

This could work, she thought. This could happen.

And it was that thought that made her kiss him again.

Then she heard Caitlin rustling in her crib and Erin drew away.

"I should go..." Her voice trailed off, breathless.

Dean just grinned. "Yeah. You should."

Then he grabbed the dustpan to empty it out.

She watched him go, bemused at how natural this felt. Having Dean in her house as they worked together.

He shot a glance over his shoulder and his smile leaped across the distance between them.

As she walked to the bedroom it was as if she could feel his eyes on her. Hope grew and she allowed herself hesitant glimpses of a future.

And that's when she got the text message.

Chapter Fourteen

"So. That's finally done." Dean set the last nail on the baseboards, then set the hammer and nail set aside. He was sweating and his leg hurt, but the job he and Erin had been working on all week was finished.

Now, instead of dingy carpet, warm wood covered the floor, gleaming in the afternoon light.

"It looks great," Erin said, her hands on her hips as she surveyed the new flooring. "I can't thank you enough."

He heard her thanks but sensed a tension that had been around since he'd arrived this morning. In fact it had started yesterday afternoon. After he kissed her.

He'd gone over that moment again and again. She was so happy then and he'd felt a real connection between them.

But when she went to get Caitlin she'd stayed so long in the bedroom he thought she wasn't coming back and when she did, she seemed tense.

"You're welcome," he said, carefully stretching out his cramped leg. He knew he'd pushed it a bit hard today, but in the last couple of days his movements felt less restricted. A month ago he would have been in agony by now. It was good to know the therapy was helping. "Are you sure it's what you want? You seem, I don't know, disappointed," he hedged, wondering if she would say anything to explain her subdued mood.

"I'm not. Truly." And as if to underline her approval she rushed over and grabbed him in a tight hug.

He wasn't expecting it and he lost his balance and fell backward. Fortunately a wall was right behind him, but he twisted his bad knee, which sent a jolt of pain up his leg, clear into his skull.

He clenched his teeth as he rode out the pain. Erin grabbed him by his shirt, hauling on him.

"I'm sorry," she said. "I didn't think you would fall. I thought you were getting better."

Her words were well meant and to some extent she was right. He had been getting better. In fact, he had had gone riding with Vic last weekend. Sure, approaching the horse he had to fight down his fluttering nerves and dread, and yes, he had to take his time getting on, but once he was mounted, his fears stilled. And once they got going, riding up to check the cows to see if they needed to be moved had given him a glimpse of hope of a future on the ranch.

He glanced over at Erin, who was watching him with guarded sympathy in her expression. Though he knew she was concerned, it still annoyed him. He didn't want sympathy from her. He much preferred the admiration he'd just seen.

"I'm okay," he grunted even as the pain slowly subsided.

"I'm sorry," she said again, reaching out to him and he had to push aside his own wounded pride.

"It's okay. I'm still a little shaky on my feet," he said, trying to ease away her concern with a joke. "Still a cripple."

Her eyes narrowed and she dropped her hands on her hips in a defensive posture. "Don't talk about yourself like that," she said her voice tight. Hard. "I hate it when you do that."

Her eyes were snapping and her mouth was tight and he got a glimpse of an agitation simmering since yesterday. She was always so easygoing, but she'd been kind of edgy all day. When he'd asked her if anything was wrong she'd brushed him off.

He was about to ask her again but she turned away, gathering leftover pieces of baseboard and tossing them into the garbage box.

He collected his tools, the two of them working in a strained silence he didn't know how to break.

A few moments later the tools were back in his truck, the furniture was back in place and it was getting dark. Almost supper time.

Each day he'd worked here she had invited him for supper but today he had other plans.

"So, to celebrate finishing the flooring I thought we could go to the Grill and Chill," he said. "What do you think?" Though it wasn't the most private place, he hoped they could talk and he could find out what was bothering her.

Erin bit her lip as she looked away. "I... I don't think that will work."

"Oh. Sure. Okay." He felt dumb for assuming and

as he saw her apologetic look he couldn't help a feeling of foreboding.

"I appreciate the invite," she said, "But I'm tired and I thought I would just stay home. Make some sandwiches."

He was about to say that he didn't mind, but he got the sense that she wasn't inviting him to share said sandwiches. "Sure. That's fine," he said, wishing he sounded more casual than he felt.

She looked at him then, but her expression was unreadable. For a panicky instant he thought she was going to tell him it was over, but then she laid her hands on his shoulders and stepping into his automatic embrace, she pressed a kiss to his lips, then laid her head on his chest.

Puzzled at her varying emotions, he held her close, laying his head on hers.

"You mean a lot to me, you know," she said.

Her comment should have encouraged him, but the somber tone of her voice created a niggle of unease.

"And you to me," he said, holding her even closer, as if to stop whatever hovered behind her. A shadow. Something he couldn't put his finger on.

She was the first to pull away and he laid his finger under her chin, gently tilting her face up to his. "Is everything okay?"

She nodded, but her eyes skittered away from him and he knew she was hiding something. But he also guessed she wasn't going to tell him.

Then Caitlin started crying and Erin pulled away, hurrying to the bedroom. He heard the baby stop and then Erin's soothing voice as she changed her daughter.

Dean waited until she came back, still uncomfortable with how things were between them but not sure how or what he had to fix.

Erin came out of the bedroom holding Caitlin up against her, the baby's head tucked into her neck. Dean felt his insides melt at the sight and he wanted to take Caitlin from Erin. Hold her himself.

He was surprised at how paternal he felt about the little girl. There was a little curl of panic inside him at the thought that things were off between him and Caitlin's mother.

"I'm going now," he said as Erin looked up at him.

"Will I see you tomorrow? At church?"

"Of course." Her matter-of-fact tone reassured him.

"Good. Do you want me to pick you up?"

"Thanks, but I'd like to take my own car. Just in case Caitlin's not feeling well. But I'll be in church."

Again he felt brushed aside.

"Okay. Well, if I don't see you there, then I'll be back Monday to finish up the siding."

He took a chance and walked to her side, bending over to brush a gentle kiss on her cheek, then on Caitlin's head. "See you both tomorrow," he whispered, touching the baby's soft hair.

He caught Erin's expression then and saw a yearning in her eyes. But as he left he couldn't completely erase his concern.

Caitlin twisted and wriggled as Erin got to her feet to sing the opening songs of the church service. All the way to church this morning Caitlin had been squirming in her car seat as if she didn't want to go.

As if she sensed the stress her mom was dealing with.

"Do you want me to take her?" Dean asked as she tried to settle her daughter.

"It's okay. If she gets really bad I'll take her downstairs."

He held her eyes, his gaze questioning, but Erin looked away, trying to still her disquiet as she followed the singing. Sam's text on Friday afternoon had unnerved her. He was supposed to be out of her life. Supposed to be leaving her alone.

She hadn't responded, but he'd sent a few more on Saturday morning. Then he'd called. She hadn't answered and he'd left a message. She knew she should have ignored the voice mail, but she couldn't. His too-familiar voice told her that he wanted her back in his life and needed to talk to her.

When Dean came yesterday to finish the flooring, she hadn't been able to shed the clawing feelings of trepidation. Consequently she'd been out of sorts with Dean and she guessed he sensed it.

She shot him a quick sidelong glance and was rewarded with a wide smile and the light touch of his hand on her shoulder. But she could see the questions in his eyes. She knew he had picked up on her anxiety.

She forced her attention back to the song, trying to draw strength and encouragement from the words.

"Though the earth beneath me move, though the heavens move mightily, God who holds the stars will never abandon me."

Erin clung to the promise given to her not only in the song but also in the many Bible passages she'd been reading the past while. Though she had turned away from God, she knew He had always been there, waiting for her to come back. And now, as she stood beside Dean, she felt the assurance of that promise.

And yet Sam hovered in the background.

What did he want now? What did he hope would happen?

Caitlin tossed her head back again and let out a little cry. Erin knew she wouldn't be able to concentrate on the sermon if Caitlin got worse.

She tapped Dean on the shoulder to get his attention and he bent his head to catch her words.

"I'm going to bring her to the nursery," she said.

"You want me to come with you?" he asked, touching her shoulder in a gesture that was both assuring and comforting.

"I'll be okay."

She grabbed the diaper bag she had packed that morning and walked down the aisle, catching people's understanding smiles as she left.

Why had she thought she would be met with condemnation, she wondered as she walked down the steps? Since she had come back to Saddlebank as a single mother, the only time she'd felt uncomfortable was when Kelly had made her somewhat snide comment her first day here about how people could change. For the rest, everyone had been unfailingly understanding and caring.

And then there was Dean...

Again she felt a shiver of apprehension as thoughts of Sam shadowed thoughts of Dean. She and Dean were becoming closer and she had allowed herself hazy dreams of a future with him.

But as she walked down the stairs to the nursery, second thoughts dogged every step.

I need to tell him.

And hopefully when she did, Dean would understand.

She followed the signs to the nursery. As she came to the large counter between the hallway and the nursery, a woman with long dark hair and expressive amber eyes saw her and hurried over.

Abby Bannister. Erin remembered that she would be taking the photographs at Jodie and Finn's wedding and that she was married to their distant cousin, Lee Bannister.

"Hey, Erin, did you give up on keeping her in church?" she asked, grabbing a clipboard and a pen and setting them in front of Erin.

"She's been fussy. I can stay with her."

"No need for that. We'll take care of her." Abby grabbed a page of stickers and quickly wrote Caitlin's name on one without asking. Again Erin had that feeling of belonging.

"Any special instructions?" Abby asked as she pasted a sticker on the back of Caitlin's little dress.

"She's been fed and changed. There is a bottle in the bag if she needs it and a second set of clothes." Erin first handed her Caitlin, then the oversize bag that she had spent all morning packing up, unpacking and packing again. "I think everything is in there. If she cries, you'll call me, right?"

Abby's encouraging smile made her feel like she was being overly cautious. "Her number is 28. We'll flash it on the screen if she gets out of control."

Erin nodded, knowing this was for the best. Then, before she could change her mind, she hurried back the way she came. She wanted to be with Dean. To be standing beside him, worshipping. Being connected by their shared faith.

The last notes of the final song resounded through the sanctuary and Dean felt a sense of well-being wash over him. The sermon was encouraging and the songs uplifting.

But almost as important, Erin had sat beside him through the service, her hand twined in his.

It was as if the discomfort of yesterday was eased away in the space of the service. He thought she might be uncomfortable with Caitlin downstairs, but she didn't seem bothered by it.

And it was nice to spend time with her, even if it was in church, just the two of them.

He turned to Erin and was pleased to see her return his smile with a broad one of her own.

"I should get Caitlin," she said as people dispersed.

"Before you do, I'd like to ask you if you'd be willing to come to my mom's place for lunch."

She gave him a peculiar look. Had he pushed things too quickly? Though he'd had lunch last week with her aunt, it still seemed different for her to come to his mother's place. He felt as if it took their relationship to another level. Meeting parents made their situation more permanent and formal.

But then her bright smile melted away his misgivings. "I'd love to," she said, touching his arm with her hand.

He wanted to say more, but just then Keira and Tanner Fortier joined them. Tanner held a baby in the crook of one arm, looking as if he had done this all his life.

Keira caught Erin by the arm, grinning at her. "Hey, cousin, I haven't had a chance to see you since you came."

He saw Erin's face twist and she caught Keira in a hug. "It's been ages," she said, her voice muffled against Keira's neck. Then they pulled back, still holding onto each other's arms, their eyes looking each other over as if taking stock of the changes time had wrought.

Dean knew some of Keira's story. Knew that she and Tanner were once engaged. That Keira had mysteriously called it off and then disappeared for a while. She had come back to Saddlebank to take over her father's saddle-making business. When Tanner had come back to get his own saddle repaired they had gotten back together again. Now they were married.

Even though the circumstances were different, their story gave Dean hope for his own happy-ever-after with Erin.

They were chattering away, intently catching up so Dean tapped Erin lightly on the shoulder. "I'll get Caitlin," he said.

Erin glanced over and looked like she was about to protest.

"I won't drop her," he said with a half smile.

"I wasn't thinking that," she sputtered.

Then he gave her a grin to show her he was teasing. "Just stay. You two look like you need to catch up. I'll be right back."

To his surprise Erin nodded. So he left and while he made his careful way down the stairs he sent up a prayer that he wouldn't fall down. He waited in line to get Caitlin, exchanging smiles with the other mothers and feeling very much a sensitive and caring man. But when it finally came time for him he found out that Caitlin was gone. Jodie had already been there and had taken her. Stifling his annoyance at the missed chance to prove himself capable of helping Erin and capable of doing this small job, he turned to leave.

He slowly worked his way up the stairs, disappointed at the sudden twinge he felt. All part of the process, Mike had told him whenever Dean felt like he was going backward in his therapy.

But his limp was more noticeable as he got to the top of the stairs. He paused, hoping the unexpected pain would ease away. Then he saw Erin and his heart stilled.

She was talking to a man wearing a suit like it was a second skin, his hair cut like he had just stepped off the cover of *GQ*. He didn't look familiar. At all.

But from the way Erin was talking to him and the way he leaned toward her, his hand on her arm, he guessed she knew him well.

He limped over and as he joined them he caught the man's eye's shifting to him, then a frown creased his forehead.

Erin turned to him and he saw fear flicker in her eyes and then relief.

"Dean, I'm glad you're here." She sounded breathless. Had this man created that flush on her cheeks, the glisten in her eyes?

"I think Jodie picked up Caitlin—"

"I'd like you to meet Sam," she said cutting him off

midsentence, gesturing toward the man standing so confidently in front of them.

Sam. The name rang like an alarm in his head.

Sam. The old boyfriend. The father of Erin's child.

"Actually, it's Dr. Sibley," Sam said with a condescending tone.

Which immediately set Dean's hackles up and made him suddenly aware of his own faded jeans, worn boots and shirt that should probably have been ironed before he put it on this morning.

Dean was no judge of clothes, but even he could see that this man's suit wasn't bought off the rack. That he didn't get his hair cut at the local barber.

Dean had never felt more like a hick than now.

"I noticed you were limping when you came here. You hurt yourself?" Sam—correction, Dr. Sibley—asked.

Dean wondered why he cared or why he thought it necessary to point out. "Rodeo injury."

Sam nodded slowly, then looked over at Erin, shifting his body, effectively turning his back to Dean.

"Do you have to be anywhere?" he asked her, putting his arm across Erin's shoulders in a proprietary gesture. "We have lots to talk about. Catch up on. I have important news for you."

Dean couldn't help a shiver of apprehension at the man's smug tone. The way he assumed that Erin would simply go along with him.

Erin shot a panicked look at Dean and he was about to intervene. To tell the guy to buzz off and leave them both alone.

But to his shock and dismay Erin turned back to Sam. "I can spare a little time for you."

"Excellent." Then without even a backward glance at Dean, his arm still draped over Erin's shoulders, Sam escorted her away.

Dismissed, Dean thought, hands curled into fists at his sides as he watched them leave, panic and fear coiling in his gut. He wanted to run after them, to ask Erin what was going on. To ask why she was going with this guy.

Ice slipped through his veins.

Maybe Sam wanted Caitlin and Erin. Maybe, just maybe, he wanted them to be a family. Maybe he wanted to get together again.

He couldn't stay here and witness this.

He spun around and limped back through the sanctuary, heading toward another exit. He didn't want to see Erin with this man.

Caitlin's father.

A doctor. A successful man who had so much more to offer her than he did.

A messed-up, washed-up ex–rodeo cowboy.

Chapter Fifteen

"Why did you come here?" Erin demanded as soon as she and Sam were out of the building.

A chill autumn wind whistled around the church, making her shiver both with apprehension and from the cold.

Though she felt horrible about ditching Dean, she wanted to separate him and Sam as quickly as possible. She didn't want Dean to find out this way the truth about her relationship with her very ex boyfriend.

And she prayed, hard, that Jodie wouldn't come looking for her, carrying the baby Sam had told her to abort.

Sam reached out to touch her and she pulled herself back.

"I came looking for you, babe," he said, looking puzzled at her reaction.

"Why now?" She dared look at him and was pleased that those pale green eyes that could at one time send pleasant shivers down her spine no longer affected her.

"Look, I know I was wrong. I shouldn't have left you in the lurch like that. I got scared. But everything's changed now. I'm divorced. I left Helen. I knew it wasn't right to love you and stay married to her."

Each word falling from his full lips was like a blow. "You're divorced?"

"Yes. Like I said, I love you. I did it for you."

He spoke the words like they were supposed to be a signal for her to fly into his arms. Instead they made her ill to think of his wife and child alone because of her.

When he reached for her again she pulled back. "Don't touch me," she said, her voice full of contempt and anger.

"But babe…"

"And stop calling me that. I'm not a horse."

"What?"

She waved off his puzzled question, her anger and frustration vying with a sick fear of what he had done because of her. "I don't want to have anything to do with you. I would never have gotten involved with you if I had known you were married."

"My marriage to Helen was a mistake."

"You had a child," she ground out, her hands now hard fists at her sides. "You had a child you were responsible for and who depended on you."

"When I met you, I knew how much I had been missing out on," he said, ignoring her accusations. "You were—are—so much more to me than Helen ever was. I've missed you so much. I haven't stopped thinking about you. So beautiful and precious."

Erin could only stare at him, trying to figure out what she ever saw in this man who seemed to think that now that he was supposedly free she would be more than willing to take him back.

She mentally compared him to Dean and in every respect this man fell short.

"Just go away. Stop phoning me and leave me alone." She wanted him gone before Jodie found her. Before Sam found out that she hadn't done as he asked and gotten rid of the baby she was carrying. Before he might decide to exercise his rights as a father. "You were a mistake I never should have made. I don't care for you one iota. You mean nothing to me. Less than nothing," she amended.

"You can't mean that." He took a step closer, reaching out to her again. "We were so good together."

She cringed at the memory and his words and stepped back. "I'm leaving now. Don't contact me ever again. We are done. Over."

And before he could say anything else, she strode back to the church, her heart beating a heavy rhythm, her blood surging. As the door to the outside thudded shut behind her, cutting her off from Sam, she stopped where she was, waiting to make sure he didn't follow her.

But the door didn't open and finally, a few minutes later, she dared to leave.

She went to find Dean and her daughter, hoping she'd find both at the same time.

Jodie stood at the back of the sanctuary, still holding Caitlin, chatting with Aunt Laura. Erin shot another glance behind, but Sam hadn't followed her.

"Have you seen Dean?" she asked as she gently extricated Caitlin from Jodie's arms.

"No. I thought he was with you." Jodie looked puzzled as she handed Erin her daughter's diaper bag.

"He was, but then…" Erin let the sentence fade away as she hooked the heavy bag over her shoulder.

"Goodness, girl, are you okay?" Aunt Laura asked. "You look pale as an Easter lily."

It was that obvious?

"I'm okay," Erin said, waving off her concern. "Just tired." The eternal excuse of any young mother.

"And who was that man you were talking to?" Aunt Laura asked. "He didn't look familiar."

"An acquaintance from back in California." Erin ignored Jodie's questioning look. "Someone I used to know." She looked around, hoping to catch a glimpse of Dean.

But she didn't see him. Which meant she would have to call to see if his invitation to have lunch at his mother's still stood. She knew she shouldn't have walked away from him, but she'd been afraid and had panicked. She didn't want him to find out from Sam that he had been married while they were dating.

You have to tell Dean. He needs to know the truth.

The pernicious voice just wouldn't leave her alone. She knew how he talked about Tiffany and how angry he'd been when he found out that she had dumped him for his brother. That she'd been pining for Vic even while she was dating Dean.

What would he think of her?

And would Sam stick around? He had come all this way; she doubted he would simply leave because she asked him to.

She pulled in a long, slow breath, trying to quiet the roiling questions.

"Can you come for lunch again?" Aunt Laura was asking.

Erin thought of Dean's invitation and shook her head. "Sorry, Aunt Laura, I'm not feeling well. I think I'll just go home." There was no way she could visit and make idle chitchat either with her aunt or Dean's mother. Not when she felt as if she were being sucked into a storm of events she couldn't stop.

Jodie shot her a questioning glance and Erin prayed that her sister would simply take her excuse at face value and not grill her. She couldn't handle any questions right now.

She needed to talk to Dean. Needed to connect with him and explain.

"Poor girl." Aunt Laura patted her shoulder gently, then stroked Caitlin's head. "You be good for your mommy now," she said, smiling down at her great-niece.

Caitlin's mouth twitched and then she seemed to break into a smile.

Erin's heart stuttered at the sight and behind her daughter's first true smile came the words of the song they'd been singing.

"Though the earth beneath me move, though the heavens move mightily, God who holds the stars will never abandon me."

She had to cling to that promise now. To trust that whatever happened, God would be with her and her little girl.

"Sorry, Mom, but there's been a change in plans." Dean grabbed a saddle one-handed from the shed, set it on his hip and walked over to his horse, Duke, while he held his cell phone with the other. A cool wind whistled through the trees edging the corral, scattering orange and gold leaves through the air. Winter was coming. "Erin had other things to do so I thought I would go riding instead."

"Can she come another time?"

Dean heard the disappointment in his mother's voice. She'd been thrilled when he asked if Erin and Caitlin could come for lunch and he knew, in her mind, she was already planning a wedding.

His mom tended to jump ahead like that.

"I don't know. We'll see." Too easily he remembered the sight of the very successful Dr. Sam Sibley. Handsome. Self-assured. Well-off. And the way he talked to Erin, it was as if he was once again laying his claim to her.

What chance did he have? So he left without checking to see if she was still coming, guessing that her plans had changed.

He tucked his phone under his ear as he hefted the saddle up and settled it on Duke.

"You didn't do anything, did you?"

"No, Mom. She just had something else going on." He wanted to sound reassuring, but he had a hard time believing this man wasn't insinuating himself back in Erin's life.

The biggest obstacle to his own plans for Erin was the fact that Dr. Sam was Caitlin's father. When he had asked Erin if Caitlin's father was involved she had been so adamant he wasn't. But what would she do now that he was back? Would she see the necessity of Caitlin having a father?

He remembered a conversation they'd had about her father. How she wanted so badly for any child of hers to have a secure, stable family.

And what could be more secure than to end up with the biological father of her daughter?

"So are you at the Rocking M?"

"No. Just on the yard here."

"Oh." In that single syllable he heard her question. Why didn't he come into the house?

Because he was a coward and didn't want to see first-hand his mother's disappointment. Though his invitation to Erin had simply been for lunch, he'd also never brought any other girl, not even Tiffany, to his home.

So they both knew what this simple visit represented.

"I just thought I would let you know I'm going riding up into the back pasture. Vic was going to check the cows to see if they needed to be moved so I thought I would do it for him."

"Should you do that alone? Shouldn't Vic be helping you? You haven't ridden for a while."

"I'll be fine, Mom." His comment came out more abruptly than he liked, but his frustration with Erin, Sam and his own situation leeched into his voice. He took a breath and then in a softer tone of voice said, "Truly, Mom, I'll be okay. But can you make sure Lucky doesn't follow me? I tied her up but she might pull loose."

"Yes. Of course. I can do that." Again he heard the edge of disappointment that he had tied up their dog but couldn't come into the house. He shrugged it off, ended his phone call with his mother and then turned the ringer off.

Erin had tried to call him a few times but he was

afraid to answer. He didn't want to hear her carefully worded apology. Didn't want to hear her telling him that Caitlin's father was back in her life and that being with him was the right thing to do.

He simply didn't want to face the potential rejection. He'd thought losing Tiffany was difficult, but he had woven more fantasies around Erin and her baby than he ever had around Tiffany.

Erin had always been a part of his dreams. And now, even more than before.

With quick movements he got the saddle on Duke, tightening the cinch, then slipping on the bridle. He took a deep breath as he finished buckling the head-stall. He looped the halter rope around the saddle, gathered the reins and then, quickly, before he chickened out, grabbed the saddle horn and shoved himself off.

To his relief and immense surprise, though he felt a twist of pain, it was nothing like it had been. And as he set his feet in the stirrups and pulled gently to one side on the reins and nudged Duke in the side, he felt a tiny victory.

One good thing Erin had brought to his life. It was because of his pride that he had gotten on a horse for the first time, and it was because he wanted to be better for her that he returned to therapy. Thanks to both those events, he sat on his own horse, riding out on his own for the first time since his accident.

And now, because of that same girl, his heart was shattered and broken.

Despair washed over him and he struggled to shake it off, clinging to the promises he'd heard in the sermon and in the songs they'd sung. That though people may let us down and life may bring its disappointments, God was faithful and that He held us close.

Dean had learned this lesson before, but it seemed to bear repeating.

Forgive me, Lord, for depending on things and people to bring me happiness, he prayed as he led his horse through the trees raining their leaves down on him. *Help me to put my trust in You. And only in You.*

And with that prayer echoing in his mind he straightened his shoulders and allowed himself to enjoy his small accomplishment.

As for Erin?

He knew he would have to find a way to release her. To do what he knew was best for her and for her baby.

Yet a part of him fought that. Was he really ready to just let her go?

He nudged his horse in the side, shifting it from a walk to a trot as if to outrun the question. But soon he felt the first jolt of pain shoot up his leg, so he pulled the horse back.

Baby steps, he reminded himself. But for now he was thankful he could get back on the horse on his own.

As for Erin, he needed to calm his own fears.

Maybe he should take a chance and talk to her face-to-face.

Tomorrow. When he went to work on the house. He would talk to her then.

For the fourth time that morning Erin picked up her phone to call Dean and then put it down again.

Yesterday after church, when she'd heard he was gone, she assumed his invitation to have lunch at his place had been withdrawn. She'd tried a couple of times to connect with him, but her calls had gone directly to voice mail. She hadn't left a message. What could she possibly say? How could she explain what had happened Sunday morning when Sam showed up?

Deep in her heart she'd hoped he would call her back, but that didn't happen, either. *He's coming to work on the house,* she told herself, looking away from her cell phone. *You can talk to him then. Face-to-face.*

She clicked her computer's mouse to open her latest project.

It was for an advertisement for a new line of paper her client was putting out. She'd just got the go-ahead email late Thursday night. A month ago she'd sent them a basic proposal knowing she was competing with dozens of other graphic artists. But thankfully, she'd been chosen and had been thrilled and grateful for the work. She was looking forward to sharing the news with Dean.

But then Sam had sent his first text.

He'd called a number of times this morning as well, but she'd simply let the phone go to voice mail.

The same thing, she suspected, Dean had done to her.

She forced herself to concentrate. She'd been roughing out some ideas for the papers, trying to create the sense of fun and excitement the company wanted. In the years she'd been doing this Erin had learned to look at ordinary objects from a different angle and connect with the ideas the customer hoped to present.

She'd come up with a basic concept. A stop-motion video of the various colors of the company's papers flipping like book pages and each one morphing into butterflies that would then fly up and...

This was where she got stuck. She had thought to render the video so the butterflies would blend and spin to become the company logo, but the logo was bland and uninteresting. So she thought of getting them to change into a catchphrase that encapsulated what the company did.

But she hadn't figured that one out, either.

Usually it wasn't difficult to come up with concepts. But she couldn't concentrate today. The last time this happened was when she'd found out she was pregnant with Caitlin, but she had gotten through that.

However, this time she felt as if more was at stake. When she'd found out about Sam's deceit, anger had been her foremost emotion. Behind that had been shame at what she had participated in.

But now a deeper fear crept around the periphery of her thoughts. What if Dean didn't want her anymore?

Let go. You haven't talked to him yet. You can explain everything when he comes.

But the thought of having to tell him exactly what had happened between her and Sam and the fallout for his wife and child created a spiraling dread in the pit of her stomach.

Caitlin's sudden cries created a thankful distraction.

Her little girl lay in her crib, hands clenched in fists, her fitful cries tugging at Erin's heart. But as soon as she saw Erin, she stopped, her smile sudden and breathtaking.

"Oh, baby girl," Erin cooed, carefully picking her up and cradling her soft warmth in her arms so she could better see her face. "Was that a smile for Mommy? Did you have a smile for me?"

Caitlin's response was an even wider smile and a wiggle of her little body as if she couldn't contain her own happiness.

Erin closed her eyes as she rocked her baby. "I love you so much," she whispered, her heart twisting at the thought of Sam somewhere in the vicinity. What would he say if he stayed and saw her? Would he want to be involved?

Erin pushed the thoughts aside and, as she had all night, sent up another prayer for patience and trust.

Our lives are in Your hands, Lord, she prayed. *Please take care of us.*

A knock on the door broke into the moment and she felt her soul lift. Dean was here.

She wanted to rush to the door, but the vain part of her stopped by her mirror to check the hair she had painstakingly brushed and braided this morning, smooth the yellow sweater she had chosen because Dean had, at one time, mentioned he liked yellow.

She drew in a shaky breath knowing this was the moment of truth.

Please, Lord, let him understand, she prayed as she shifted Caitlin in her arms, tugged on her frilly pink dress and dropped a kiss on her forehead. She set Caitlin in her bouncy chair, hoping she would stay quiet for a few more minutes.

Then she hurried to the door, nerves and fear and anticipation swirling around her.

She stopped at the door just as another knock came. She pulled in a steadying breath and yanked it open.

"Hey, babe, I was wondering if I had the wrong house."

Erin could only stare at Sam, standing on her door-step, his one hand resting on the door frame, the other on his hip. His blue-and-white striped shirt and artfully faded blue jeans made him look much more casual, but the leather loafers and the cologne he wore underlined his success.

"What are you doing here?"

"I found out where you lived. Thought I would talk to you in a more private place."

Erin's heart plunged as he moved closer, his grin making him look as if he had every right to be there.

"I told you to leave me alone," she said, her heart now racing with a combination of fear and nerves.

"I was hoping to talk to you." He lowered his voice, taking her hands in his. "Please. Let me explain."

He could do that so well, she thought, as his eyes softened and his smile tipped his perfectly shaped lips just so, his hands gently caressing hers.

But what would have at one time melted her resistance now just served to make her angry.

She jerked her hands free and took a step back just as he stepped inside the door and closed it behind him.

"I just need to talk to you," he said, touching her.

Fear sliced through her, but she pushed it aside. Sam would never do anything to her.

Then Caitlin squawked and Erin's heart tripled its pace. She hurried over to Caitlin's chair and carefully took her out.

Please, Lord, was all she could pray as she snuggled her close and turned to face an incredulous Sam.

"Is that ours? It that baby ours?" he asked, pointing to Caitlin, his eyes wide, his mouth slipping open in surprise.

Erin fought down her panic and slowly nodded. "She's my daughter."

"I'm the father." He spoke the words in a matter-of-fact tone as he shoved his hand through his perfectly styled hair, rearranging the immaculate waves she knew he had probably spent too much time on.

"Yes. You are."

Her prayers were fragments of fear and concern as she faced him down. His features registered surprise, then slowly shifted.

Into anger.

"I thought I told you to get rid of it."

It. The single word laced with contempt was like an abomination. As if this precious child was no more than an inconvenience. But at the same time his reaction created a glimmer of hope.

"I didn't. I could never do that." Erin looked down at Caitlin's sweet head and brushed a kiss over her hair, holding her even closer as if to protect her from the horrible words that Sam tossed around.

"Don't tell me you expect me to help you out with her."

"Have I asked at all?"

"No."

"Can I see her?"

Erin wanted to say no. To run away and hide her. Once he saw her face and saw how beautiful she was he would want to be involved with her.

But he was her father and so she stifled her trepidation and gently turned her baby to see her father for the first time. Erin kept her eyes on Caitlin, not sure she wanted to see Sam's reaction.

"Oh, babe," he whispered, his voice holding a melancholy edge that frightened her.

He took a step closer, his hand reaching out. Erin's heart thudded harder but all Sam did was lay his hand on Erin's shoulder and squeeze. "Why did you do this?" he asked.

"It was my choice." She looked up at him, fear lancing her at the anger in his expression. "I wanted her. I couldn't do what you asked."

"This wasn't supposed to happen. I told you to get rid of her." He squeezed harder. "I divorced Helen and walked away from her kid so I could be with you. I don't want any kids in my life to complicate things."

Suddenly fearful now, she pulled away from his grasp and he released her, his hand dropping to his side.

"So you don't want any part of Caitlin?" she asked.

He shook his head, his hand slicing the air between them. "I never wanted kids. That's why I fought with Helen. I thought you…you would understand."

She wasn't sure why he assumed that, but she didn't want to get into that discussion now.

"So you aren't going to claim any rights to Caitlin?"

"No. Never. I don't want to have anything to do with her." His expression grew pleading. "I just wanted you to be with me. No one else getting in the way."

She could only stare at him, wondering how he thought she would have ever agreed to this. But even more importantly, wondering what she had ever seen in this self-centered, venal man. The thought made her almost as sick as the words Sam had been saying to her.

"So you just walked away from your other responsibilities thinking I would gladly take up with you?" She couldn't begin to articulate the disgust she felt for him.

"Yeah. I guess so."

"I would never do that. Even if I didn't have Caitlin. Once I found out you were married, it was over between us."

"I told you, I never loved Helen." His anger had shifted and now he was almost begging. "I only loved you. I want us to be together. But now... Now you've got this baby. That changes everything."

"Enough," she snapped, taking control of the situation, her voice growing hard. "You didn't want me to keep Caitlin and you don't want to take responsibility for her, is that right?"

"Yes. Of course it is."

Erin's shoulders sagged with relief but she knew she wasn't done yet. "I want that in writing. In front of a lawyer."

Sam just stared at her, as if he couldn't understand this person she'd become.

Then his features hardened. "Works for me. I don't want any part of any kid." He almost snorted. "And I want to make sure you won't come after me for child support."

"I wouldn't take one penny from you," she said.

Sam looked around her house, his eyes narrowing. "Well, if this is the kind of life you want for your daughter..." He turned back to her, not finishing the sentence, his tone saying everything his words didn't. "And I suppose you're dating that cripple—"

"Don't you even mention him." Her eyes narrowed,

her teeth clenched in rage as she resisted the impulse to slap his face. "Dean is ten times, no, one hundred times the man you are."

Erin grabbed Caitlin's diaper bag, the jacket she had draped over the back of her chair and tucked both over her arm. "Let's go to town," she said. "The sooner we get this done, the happier I'll be."

Sam hesitated and for a heartrending moment she thought he was changing his mind.

"We would have been so good together, babe," he whispered.

"No. We wouldn't have. The only good thing that came out of being with you was my daughter. Now let's finish this."

Chapter Sixteen

Dean turned his truck around and drove down the highway toward home, his hands wrapped around his steering wheel.

Erin had called him numerous times, but she hadn't left a message. He wished he could simply let it go, but he was concerned.

But then he'd arrived at her place in time to see Sam get out of his fancy red sports car and step into Erin's house.

Dean gritted his teeth, fighting down his own fears. This was only right. Erin had grown up in a fractured family. Getting back together with Sam, the father of her child, was the right thing.

So why did it make him feel so hollow inside?

Why did he constantly compare himself to the suave, rich-looking guy who looked as if he could give Erin anything she ever wanted or needed?

He drew in a deep, slow breath and struggled, once again, to give his life over to God. To let go of control.

It had been hard enough when he was laid up in the hospital facing an uncertain future.

But now, even though his leg was better, his future as far as work was concerned was brighter, what he wanted more than anything was out of his reach.

Vic was in the corrals when he got back home, reinforcing fences and getting them ready for when they brought the cows back down from pasture and they would process them.

He lowered his hammer when he saw Dean walking toward him.

"What's up? Aren't you supposed to be working at Erin's place?"

Dean walked through the gate and picked up the fence tightener. "I'm not working there anymore."

Vic frowned as he finagled another staple out of the pail in front of him. "Why not?"

Dean tightened up the wire as Vic pounded the staple in. "Don't feel like being there. Jan can send someone else to finish up."

Vic rested his hammer on the fence post, turning to his brother. "What's going on?"

Dean moved a little further down the fence line and reattached the tightener. Vic stayed where he was, waiting. Dean suspected he wasn't going to leave him alone until he spilled.

"Erin's old boyfriend came back. Caitlin's father."

"When?"

"Yesterday. At church. They were talking privately."

"So that's why Erin and Caitlin didn't come here for lunch?"

"I figured she'd want to spend time with him." Dean

didn't want to admit that seeing Sam all dressed up and looking so successful had sent him scurrying away before he knew exactly what was going on.

"He's there right now," Dean added. "I saw him go into her house."

"So they're getting back together?"

"He's Caitlin's father. So I'm guessing she would want to do the right thing. I mean, she grew up without her dad around a lot. Divorced parents. I know she wants only what's best for Caitlin."

"Did she tell you she was seeing him again?"

"Well, why wouldn't she?"

"So you didn't actually talk to her?"

Dean yanked on the tightener. He should have just gone straight to the house. He didn't need this, though that meant dealing with questions from his mother. He wasn't sure which was worse.

"What's to talk about?" Dean returned finally. "He's Caitlin's father. He can provide a life for her and Erin that I couldn't begin to."

"How do you figure that?"

"He's a doctor, Vic. He drives a car that's worth ten times what my truck is. He's not some…crippled cowboy." Dean didn't want to look up at his brother. Didn't want to see the pity in his expression, but it was as if he couldn't stop himself. And when he snagged his brother's gaze he saw not pity, but exasperation.

"Why do you talk about yourself like that?" Vic ground out, his one hand clenched around the hammer. "Like you're looking for sympathy."

"I'm not—"

"Ever since your accident you've been putting yourself down. Seeing yourself as less than who you really are. Why do you do that? Why are you putting down what God has done in you?"

Dean was shocked at his brother's anger, but Vic's words also created an answering shame.

"It's not that," he protested. "It's just for Erin's sake. I can't do for her what that other guy can."

"If that other guy was so great, don't you think she would have stayed with him?" Vic crossed his arms over his chest, his expression softening. "Don't minimize what you have to give to someone like Erin. You're a great guy. You'd make an amazing father. And I'm sure she cares a lot for you. At least that's what I've been hearing through Lauren. And if anyone should know, her twin sister should."

Dean let his brother's words assure him but at the same time he couldn't rid himself of a niggling feeling that Erin would want to do the right thing. And as far as he could see, that would be staying with Caitlin's father.

"You don't look convinced," Vic said.

Dean sighed, leaning on the fence post, looking out over the yard. The place that had been his home all these years. A place he had never wanted to leave and a place that, for a time, he thought he would settle down with Erin and Caitlin as a family.

"Erin grew up with a part-time father. I know she wants more than that for her daughter. If there's a chance—"

"You don't think you can be that father?" Vic interrupted him.

"I haven't lived the best life. I haven't been the best

person. Erin turned me down all those years ago for a good reason. And now, compared to this guy—"

"Stop it. Stop comparing yourself." Vic walked over to Dean and put his hands on his shoulders and gave him a light shake. "You may not have been the best person at one time in your life, but who of us have? We all have made mistakes. Done things we have had to ask God's forgiveness for. But you never hurt anyone. You never caused anyone sorrow or grief. The mistakes you made were your own. And the one thing you have truly going for you is your faithful love for that girl. Even when you were dating Tiffany I know you mentally compared her to Erin. In many ways, you've probably been the most faithful person in her life."

Dean felt a warm glow at his brother's words. At the comfort he knew Vic was trying to give him.

"I know she cares about you, Dean," Vic continued. "You shouldn't assume that just because this guy is back she wants him in her life. You should probably find this out for yourself."

Dean nodded slowly, recognizing the wisdom in what his brother was saying.

He knew it would be hard. It would mean putting himself at risk of being rejected by Erin McCauley yet again.

Could he do it?

"Let's finish this fence" was all he said to Vic. But as they worked in silence, the thin warmth of the sun slowly waning, Dean couldn't let go of what Vic had told him.

Later that night, alone in his bedroom, the one he'd stayed in since he was a young boy, he took his Bible and flipped through it, looking for the passages that had given him comfort when he was in the hospital, thinking his life was over.

He had made a choice then to let go of himself. To let go of what he thought his life should look like. It hadn't been easy, but he'd been comforted by the passage in front of him.

In repentance and rest is your salvation. In quietness and trust is your strength.

He had always found it interesting that in the middle of woes and prophecies, in the middle of seeming chaos were these two lines that promised so much more.

It was like his own life. The mess, the busyness, the chasing after things that didn't satisfy.

In the middle of all of that had come these words to calm and still him and turn him in the right direction.

And now, as he felt as if his life was turned upside down yet again, he took these verses to heart.

In quietness and trust was his strength.

He had to let go of his pride and tell Erin what he needed to tell her. Not for his sake, but for hers. To give her a choice.

He bowed his head and slowly let God's peace wash over him. No matter what happened, he knew where his strength and peace lay.

Erin lay in bed, the morning light washing over her. She could only stare at the ceiling trying to absorb what had happened the last couple of days. On Sunday, Sam had showed up full of ridiculous hope that they could get back together again.

Then yesterday they had gone to the lawyer. She

was happy that Drake Neubauer could take them in right away and was only too willing to help her draft an agreement. They got it notarized and it was over.

That shadow was removed from her life.

Sam had wanted to give her money, but she refused. She didn't want any connection to him in any way. The only thing she had wanted from him, he had given her reluctantly.

Helen's phone number.

He had looked regretful when he left and had tried to kiss her goodbye, but Erin had turned away. It was over.

She sat up slowly feeling a sense of emptiness in spite of the relief she felt at knowing that Sam was out of her and Caitlin's life. Dean hadn't come yesterday at all. Nor had he returned her calls from Sunday.

She wanted to call him again, but every time she picked up her phone guilt held her back. She knew she had to tell him everything about her relationship with Sam and should have a while ago.

Erin pushed herself out of bed and quickly got dressed. She would shower later. Once Caitlin was bathed and taken care of.

"Hey, baby girl," Erin whispered as she picked up her precious daughter. "It's a new day."

Caitlin cooed softly, then broke into a smile that dove straight into Erin's heart.

As she fed the baby she choked down a light sob at the emptiness that yawned ahead of her.

Why didn't Dean call her?

She shook off the questions and focused on feeding and bathing her daughter. Then dressing her in one of the many outfits her sisters and Aunt Laura kept buying for her. When she was finally done, she put Caitlin in her bouncy chair and sat down with her phone. One big thing needed to be done yet.

She swallowed as she pulled out the piece of paper Sam had given her and stared at the phone number she insisted he write on it.

Help me, Lord.

Then she dialed the number.

Helen answered on the first ring. As if she was anticipating her call.

"Hello, Erin" was her quiet response. She knew who was calling.

Erin swallowed at the reality that Helen could identify her number. Had she seen it on Sam's phone when they were seeing each other?

She fought down the shame once again and pressed on.

"I felt like I needed to call you," Erin said, glancing over at Caitlin, who was clean and fed and now so happy. How could such an adorable child have come from such perfidy?

She shook that thought off. She couldn't think of Caitlin that way. Her baby was a gift from God pure and simple.

"I'm glad you called," Helen said.

Erin felt confused. She hunched over, clinging to the phone, bewildered by Helen's response.

"Why are you glad? I would think you should be angry with me."

"I was. For a while. But you need to know that I forgive you. I know the breakup of our marriage wasn't your fault."

Erin sagged back against the couch, shocked at how easily Helen spoke those words.

"I don't feel like I deserve your forgiveness," she said, her voice quiet with shame.

"You do and you need to know that I should ask your forgiveness, as well. When I came to your place I was afraid. Clinging by the thinnest thread to a marriage that I should have known was over long before you came on the scene."

"What are you saying?"

"You weren't the first one Sam was cheating on me with. I found out that even while he was supposedly with you, he was seeing someone else, as well."

Shame engulfed her but behind that rose an anger with the man who had so brazenly shown up on her doorstep claiming that he loved her. What hubris. What arrogance.

"I'm so sorry" was all Erin could manage.

"Don't worry. You didn't break up our marriage. Sam did. I finally saw the light and divorced his sorry self."

"But he came here to tell me—"

"That he divorced me." Helen released a heavy sigh. "He's such a prideful idiot. I only wished I'd seen it sooner."

Erin was quiet as she grappled with what had just happened. The gentle promise of peace that lingered on the horizon. "Again. I'm sorry. Will you be okay?"

"I hit him financially for all I could," Helen said. "Every month when those withdrawals come out of his bank account he'll remember me. I'll be fine."

Erin didn't know what to say after that.

"Well, I don't suppose we'll be exchanging Christmas cards even though we have quite a bit in common," Helen said. "You take care of yourself. Please don't let what he did to you determine your self-worth. I know I had to struggle with it. I'm just glad I took control of my life. I hope you can do the same."

Erin let her comment settle in her soul. Helen seemed to know exactly what she was feeling.

Then as they said goodbye, she realized that Helen probably, better than anyone, knew what she was dealing with. The shame. The sense of being less than.

She looked around the house that she and Dean had spent time fixing up. The dreams she had woven around this home. Thinking that it would be a home for her and Dean and Caitlin.

She thought of what Helen had said. That she was glad she took control of her life.

Well, maybe it was time she did the same. Maybe it was time she faced down her fears. Realized she had much to give Dean. That Helen had forgiven her. That God had forgiven her. That in God's eyes she was valuable and important.

She needed to talk to Dean. To tell him the truth. To realize that she had made an innocent mistake.

Knowing that Helen had forgiven her made it easier to think that Dean might understand.

She packed up Caitlin's diaper bag and just as she grabbed her car keys off the key ring she heard a knock on the door.

Her heart jumped.

Was Sam back after all?

She hesitated, breathed a quick prayer, then slowly opened the door.

Dean stood there. Hat in hand.

But he wasn't smiling. "Can I come in?"

Erin simply nodded, then stood aside.

Dean looked around the house feeling a sense of pride in how good it looked.

He had been a part of this.

And, Lord willing, he still would.

He laid his hat on the table and turned to Erin, who was looking at him, apprehension in her eyes.

He wasn't sure what she was about to tell him. He didn't want to wait until she said that she and Sam were getting together. He needed to get this off his chest before he changed his mind.

He needed her to know that she had options. If he could be considered one.

"I need to tell you—

"I have something you need to know—"

They both spoke at the same time and at her words Dean's heart sunk. But he shook his head, swallowed his pride and held up his hand.

"I'm going to be rude and ask if I can go first," he said. He drew in a shaky breath and forced himself to look deep into her eyes. "I don't know what's happening in your life right now. I don't know where you're at. But I need to tell you where I am." He paused as memories of Erin's previous rejections skimmed too easily back into his mind.

But he clung to the more recent memories. The kisses they'd shared. The work they had done together. He had to tell himself that what they'd had was real no matter what may happen in Erin's life. And that he too had something to offer her, as Vic had said.

"I want you to know that no matter what happens to you or has happened to you, I have always cared for you," he told her, his heart pounding in his chest now, knowing what was at stake. "You've always been a part of my life. You've always been the one I've used as my standard for any woman I've ever dated. They all fell short."

Her cry of dismay nearly stopped him.

"I love you," he said, pushing on before nerves and fear kept him from what he wanted to say. "I love your daughter. I know that Caitlin's father is back in her life and while I don't know what that means for you, I need you to know that I am willing to go with whatever happens because I only want what's best for you and for Caitlin. I know that you've lived without your father for many years and I know what it means for you to have an intact family. But I want you to know that I love you. I can't let you go without you knowing that."

She wasn't looking at him, but he could see tears running down her cheek. He wanted to grab her, pull her close, but he waited.

"Please say something," he finally asked, tossing his pride away yet one more time. "Tell me to leave. Ask me stay. Something."

"I want you to stay," she whispered.

As her quiet words registered his heart sang. But her tears confused him.

"Why are you so sad?" he said, laying his hands on her shoulders, trying to find his way through this situation. "Is it Sam?"

She shook her head, hard. "No. It's not Sam. He's gone. He's out of my life and Caitlin's."

Was that why she was crying?

"I'm so sorry to hear that," Dean said.

"It's not what you think." Finally she looked up at him, her eyes red-rimmed and brimming with tears. She put her hand on his chest, creating a small connection. "I sent him away. He didn't want to have anything to do with Caitlin and I didn't want to have anything to do with him. He hasn't meant anything to me since I walked away from him after I found out I was pregnant."

Each word she spoke created another surge of hope. He gently brushed a tear from her face, still puzzled. "Then why are you crying?"

She swallowed, holding his gaze, her expression almost pleading. "Because you talk about me like I'm some wonderful person and I'm not."

"Erin, honey, you made a mistake. We all do. It doesn't mean you're a bad person—"

"He was married when I was dating him," Erin said suddenly. "He was committed to someone else."

Dean could only stare, trying to absorb what she was saying.

"He was married."

"Yes."

"Did he tell you?"

"Of course not."

"Then it was hardly your fault."

Erin held his gaze, her features softening. "So that doesn't matter to you?"

"What matters to me is that you're so upset."

Erin pressed her trembling lips together, looking away. "I thought you would be angry. I was so ashamed. Bad enough that I'd been intimate with a man as a single girl, worse that he was married. You always talk about me like I am such a good person, when I did this horrible thing."

"But you said you didn't know so it's not like you did this deliberately. It's his fault for being such a jerk."

She was silent a moment and Dean couldn't hold himself back. He pulled her into his arms, holding her close. "You are an amazing and wonderful and good person," he said, pressing a kiss to her forehead, then curling her head against him. "You really are. Nothing you tell me changes that. I've told you before that you were always an example to me of goodness and kindness and you still are."

Erin drew back, looking up at him, her face still holding shadows of sorrow. But in her eyes he saw a glimmer of hope.

"I love you," he said. "I think I always have."

Her smile brightened her face. "I love you, too. So much."

"I want to be a father to your little girl," he said. "To Caitlin. I want to be in your life."

And then he sealed that promise with a kiss.

Epilogue

The mini lights sparkled in the rafters of Finn's barn. Clusters of Christmas trees full of white lights and red balls were scattered along the hall. The tables covered with thick, white tablecloths held crystal vases filled with red balls. Red napkins tucked under plates carried out the color scheme Jodie had decided on as soon as she and Finn had settled on a winter wedding.

All the plans had come together for a fairy-tale wedding for Finn and Jodie.

Erin looked around the hall, but Dean was still gone.

The past few weeks were a whirlwind of preparations and decorating and last-minute running around. Also, between his therapy and helping Vic get the corrals ready on the Rocking M and her increasing work load, she and Dean hadn't spent much time together.

She had been looking forward to today, but they had only managed to spend some time together between the ceremony and picture taking. The men had been gone the past twenty minutes while Abby Bannister, the photographer, took a number of photos of just the sisters.

"Okay, girls," she was saying now. "One last one of the three of you by the largest Christmas tree."

"Can we just be done?" Jodie groaned as she gathered up the yards of raw silk that made up her wedding dress. "My feet hurt and I heard Santa Claus is coming for a visit."

Christmas wasn't for a couple of weeks yet, but that hadn't stopped Jodie from going all-out with a Christmas-themed wedding.

Or from getting someone to play Santa Claus for the kids that were in attendance.

Lauren just tut-tutted as she arranged one of Jodie's curls, then turned to Erin to help her, as well.

"I'm fine," Erin said, holding up her hand to forestall her sister's attempts at taming her hair. Caitlin had gotten her sticky fingers entangled in the curls Brooke had sprayed to battle-ready stiffness, and they were askew, but she didn't care. "And I'm with Jodie. I'm tired."

She was impatient to get the pictures done, as well. She wanted to find Dean.

But Lauren ignored her and pinned one of her curls back, smoothed out her dress and gave a decisive nod. "You look beautiful. And just relax. You only have to do this one more time. For my wedding."

Erin forced a smile. The thought of doing this all over again wasn't appealing.

"And don't look like I just asked you to help butcher chickens," Lauren admonished her. "You'll be glad to help out again. Just as I will be glad to help out when your time comes."

Her sister's comment was encouraging, but while she and Dean had been dating for a couple of months now he hadn't said much about their future and she wasn't about to bring it up. She was still learning lessons in trust, she realized.

The three girls obediently posed in front of the tree, gathering close, cheek to cheek, bouquets of red roses and white lilies close to their faces as cameras flashed all around them.

Finally Abby was finished, and Jodie and Erin both heaved a sigh of relief.

Erin hurried over to Heather, who was playing with Caitlin and her stepdaughter Adana, her stomach just starting to protrude. It was baby central in Saddlebank these days.

"So, she's adorable," Heather said, smiling up at Erin.

In spite of being dressed up and made up and hair professionally done, Erin felt just a bit dowdy around Heather. The former model was stunning, even pregnant and with a three-year-old toddler leaning against her, holding up a stuffed rabbit for Caitlin, who wasn't paying her any attention.

"I'm glad she's been good."

"She's been a perfect baby. I can only hope mine is as well behaved," Heather said.

"That would depend who she takes after. You or John," Abby joked as she joined them, then crouched down to snap a picture of Caitlin, who was grabbing at her satin shoes, gurgling and drooling all over the red silk dress Jodie had insisted on buying for her.

Erin looked around with a tiny niggle of anxiety. She saw Lee standing by Vic, Finn was now with Jodie, but she couldn't see Dean anywhere.

Then the jingle of bells sounded and Adana's head popped up as she heard a distinctive "Ho, Ho, Ho."

"Ith it Thanta Cwauth?" she lisped, eyes wide, staring past Erin to the entrance to the hall.

Erin and everyone else in the hall turned around in time to see a man dressed up in a Santa Claus suit complete with fake beard, fake belly, and the faintest limp enter the room.

"Merry Christmas," he bellowed, jingling the string of sleigh bells and looking around the room.

Erin just laughed.

Dean. Of course. No wonder he'd been so secretive.

He had a bag in his hand and he made his way to a large chair set aside and decorated for the occasion. The children in attendance crowded around him as he slowly sat down.

"One at a time," he bellowed in true Santa fashion. "One at a time."

Erin just smiled as she watched him with the children, her heart full of warmth and love for this man. He was such a natural. He took the time to talk to each child. To lean close and listen. He had a gift for each one as well and remembered who was who. No small feat considering there were about a dozen youngsters in attendance.

"I hear there's a baby here that needs a present yet," he called out when all the children were finished with him. "Caitlin. You tell your mommy to come and bring you here, too."

Chuckling, Erin took Caitlin from Heather and made her way through the excited children tossing wrapping paper aside as they tore into their gifts.

Out of the corner of her eye she saw Abby approach and her heart sank. More pictures?

She pushed the thought aside as she brought Caitlin to Dean.

He pulled them both onto his knee, his eyes twinkling underneath the fake eyebrows.

"So, have you been a good girl this year?" he asked.

"I tried," she returned.

"And how about this little one," he said, tickling Caitlin under the chin with his forefinger. "I'm sure she's been good," he said with forced heartiness.

"As good as gold."

"Of course she would be with such an amazing mother." Dean shifted his arm, reaching for his bag one-handed.

"So, why don't you tell me what you want for Christmas?"

He had dropped the fake Santa voice, speaking to her normally.

She looked deep into his eyes and said, "All I want for Christmas is you."

"Well, now, I think I can manage that," he said, his eyes twinkling. "But how about I tell you what I want for Christmas?"

"I didn't think Santa Claus had any wishes."

"Well, there's world peace and high cattle prices. And then there's this."

He dug into his bag and pulled out a tiny box.

Erin's heart stuttered in her chest. She hardly dared to believe what might be happening.

Dean flipped the box open and under the glow of

Christmas lights the diamond on the band sparkled with hundreds of lights sending out rays of hope.

"Erin McCauley, will you marry me?"

His words resonated in the silence that had fallen on the gathering.

Erin's throat thickened with a myriad of emotions as she looked at the promise held in Dean's hand and echoed in his eyes.

All she could do was nod her agreement.

A huge cheer went up from the people now gathered around them as Dean slipped the ring, one-handed, onto her finger. Lights flashed as people took pictures. Erin ignored them all, pulled the fake beard down and kissed Dean fully on his lips.

He held her close, returning her kiss. Then he drew back, looking from her to Caitlin nestled between them.

"You know I love you dearly," he said. "I love you both. And I'll spend the rest of my life proving it."

"You don't have to prove anything," she said, as he stood up and pull her along.

He kissed her again and another cheer went up.

"Hey, Santa, what are you doing for an encore?" Vic asked, standing beside him, his arm draped over Lauren's shoulder.

"If I'd known he was giving out engagement rings, I might have stood in line myself," Jodie joked.

"You already have one," Finn growled. "And a wedding ring as well, I might add."

Jodie grinned up at him. "Just teasing."

Erin looked from Jodie and Finn to Lauren and Vic and all the people gathered around them, an accepting loving community who had taken her and Caitlin in.

Her heart overflowed with happiness and joy and an incredible thankfulness.

"I think it will be a wonderful Christmas," Lauren said, with a kiss to her sister, then her niece and finally giving Dean a hug.

"It's going to be amazing," Jodie said, laying her hand on Erin's shoulder. "And in the classic words of Tiny Tim, God bless us, every one."

Erin turned to Dean again. "I love you so much," she whispered.

"I love you, too."

She laid her head on his shoulder, and Dean curled his other arm around Caitlin, closing the circle and completing it.

A promise of the future. A family for both of them.

A gift from God.

* * * * *

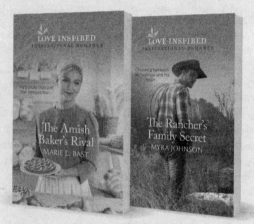

SPECIAL EXCERPT FROM

🌿

LOVE INSPIRED
INSPIRATIONAL ROMANCE

*When a therapy dog trainer must work with her
high school crush, can she focus on her mission
instead of her heart?*

Read on for a sneak preview of
Their Unbreakable Bond *by Deb Kastner.*

"Are you okay?" Stone asked, tightening his hold around
her waist and gripping one of her hands.

"I— Yes." She didn't have time to explain to Stone
why this had nothing to do with her sore ankle, nor why
avalanches were her worst nightmare and that was the
real reason why she'd suddenly swayed in his arms.

Not when there was work to be done. There were
people in Holden Springs who needed help, and she knew
she should be there.

Tugger whined and pressed against her leg as he'd
been taught to do as a therapy dog. He could tell her heart
rate had increased and her pulse was pounding in her ears,
even if she didn't show it in her expression, although
there was probably that, too. The dog was responding to
cues most humans couldn't see, and Felicity reached out
and absently ran a hand between Tugger's ears to steady
her insides.

"Have they set up a temporary disaster shelter yet?"
she asked.

"Yes. At Holden High School," her sister said.
"They're using the cafeteria and the gym, I think. I'd go
myself except I have clients in the middle of service dog

training back at the center. Do you mind taking Tugger and heading out there?"

Felicity did mind. More than anyone would ever know, because she never talked about it, not even to her siblings. But now was not the time to give in to those feelings. She could cry into her pillow later when she was alone and the people of Holden Springs were safe.

"I'll take Tugger." She nodded. "And Dandy, too," she said, referring to a young black Labrador retriever who was part of the therapy dog program.

"I can tag along, if there's anything I can do to assist," Stone said. "That way you'll have an extra person for the dogs."

Felicity was going to decline, but Ruby spoke up first. "Thank you, Stone. They need all the help they can get. From what I hear, there are a lot of families who were suddenly evacuated from their homes."

"It's settled, then," Stone said. "I'm going with you."

Felicity didn't feel settled. The last thing she needed was Stone alongside her. It would distract her from her real work.

She sighed deeply.

A bruised ankle.

Stone's unnerving presence.

And now an avalanche.

Could things get any worse?

Don't miss
Their Unbreakable Bond *by Deb Kastner,*
available January 2022 wherever
Love Inspired books and ebooks are sold.

LoveInspired.com

LOVE INSPIRED

Stories to uplift and inspire

Fall in love with Love Inspired—
inspirational and uplifting stories of faith
and hope. Find strength and comfort in
the bonds of friendship and community.
Revel in the warmth of possibility and the
promise of new beginnings.

Sign up for the Love Inspired newsletter
at **LoveInspired.com** to be the first
to find out about upcoming titles,
special promotions and exclusive content.

CONNECT WITH US AT:

 Facebook.com/LoveInspiredBooks

Twitter.com/LoveInspiredBks

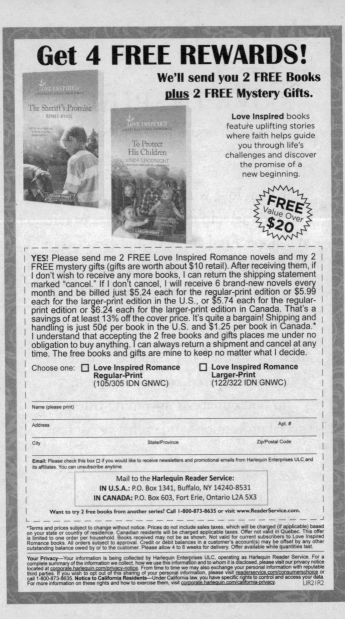

Get 4 FREE REWARDS!

We'll send you 2 FREE Books plus 2 FREE Mystery Gifts.

Love Inspired books feature uplifting stories where faith helps guide you through life's challenges and discover the promise of a new beginning.

FREE Value Over **$20**

YES! Please send me 2 FREE Love Inspired Romance novels and my 2 FREE mystery gifts (gifts are worth about $10 retail). After receiving them, if I don't wish to receive any more books, I can return the shipping statement marked "cancel." If I don't cancel, I will receive 6 brand-new novels every month and be billed just $5.24 each for the regular-print edition or $5.99 each for the larger-print edition in the U.S., or $5.74 each for the regular-print edition or $6.24 each for the larger-print edition in Canada. That's a savings of at least 13% off the cover price. It's quite a bargain! Shipping and handling is just 50¢ per book in the U.S. and $1.25 per book in Canada.* I understand that accepting the 2 free books and gifts places me under no obligation to buy anything. I can always return a shipment and cancel at any time. The free books and gifts are mine to keep no matter what I decide.

Choose one: ☐ **Love Inspired Romance Regular-Print** (105/305 IDN GNWC) ☐ **Love Inspired Romance Larger-Print** (122/322 IDN GNWC)

Name (please print)

Address   Apt. #

City   State/Province   Zip/Postal Code

Email: Please check this box ☐ if you would like to receive newsletters and promotional emails from Harlequin Enterprises ULC and its affiliates. You can unsubscribe anytime.

Mail to the Harlequin Reader Service:
IN U.S.A.: P.O. Box 1341, Buffalo, NY 14240-8531
IN CANADA: P.O. Box 603, Fort Erie, Ontario L2A 5X3

Want to try 2 free books from another series! Call 1-800-873-8635 or visit www.ReaderService.com.

*Terms and prices subject to change without notice. Prices do not include sales taxes, which will be charged (if applicable) based on your state or country of residence. Canadian residents will be charged applicable taxes. Offer not valid in Quebec. This offer is limited to one order per household. Books received may not be as shown. Not valid for current subscribers to Love Inspired Romance books. All orders subject to approval. Credit or debit balances in a customer's account(s) may be offset by any other outstanding balance owed by or to the customer. Please allow 4 to 6 weeks for delivery. Offer available while quantities last.

Your Privacy—Your information is being collected by Harlequin Enterprises ULC, operating as Harlequin Reader Service. For a complete summary of the information we collect, how we use this information and to whom it is disclosed, please visit our privacy notice located at corporate.harlequin.com/privacy-notice. From time to time we may also exchange your personal information with reputable third parties. If you wish to opt out of this sharing of your personal information, please visit readerservice.com/consumerschoice or call 1-800-873-8635. **Notice to California Residents**—Under California law, you have specific rights to control and access your data. For more information on these rights and how to exercise them, visit corporate.harlequin.com/california-privacy.

LIR21R2